Blade
Warriors

K. K. Poole

GWL
PUBLISHING

First Published in 2018
by GWL Publishing
an imprint of Great War Literature Publishing LLP

Produced in United Kingdom

ISBN 978-1-910603-46-8 Paperback Edition

GWL Publishing
Forum House
Stirling Road
Chichester PO19 7DN
www.gwlpublishing.co.uk

K.K. Poole was born in 1969. He is the son of Australian parents and was educated at Magdalen College School and St. John's College, Oxford. For three successive years he rowed in 'The Boat Race' against Cambridge.

After University, he taught science, coached rowing and gained a doctorate in epilepsy epidemiology before qualifying as a general practitioner in 2003. He is married with three sons.

Dedication

For Mike Poole, inspirational surgeon
– Dad

Acknowledgements

My thanks to: Ali my wife, for all of her help, Juliet Solomon, for her encouragement, and GWL publishing. Thanks also to the staff at the Dunhill library (Chichester Medical Education Centre) for providing a warm haven in which to write, and the team at the Forum café for extending the same courtesy.

I would like to acknowledge the skill of the plastic surgeons at East Grinstead, particularly their work on pilots during WW2. The world renowned Queen Victoria Hospital drew my father from Australia to train there in the early 1970s – he would sometimes see the ageing pilots for check-ups.

Acknowledging the bravery of the RAF pilots and SOE agents feels too easy and obvious, and I suspect they would all downplay their role, saying they were 'just doing what needed to be done', but I pay tribute to them nonetheless.

Sometimes when writing about the past, the feeling of stepping into that time becomes especially vivid, with your characters almost whispering across the void: finding the balcony from which a Resistance fighter was hanged was one such occasion, visiting a lonely memorial cairn on the South Downs Way in Sussex was another. The significance of these places will become apparent in the story.

May the whisperers rest in peace.

Disclaimer

Blade Warriors is a work of fiction. However, some of the characters, settings and situations are factual. Small liberties may have been taken with certain elements of these characters' lives, their whereabouts and the timings of events, for the purposes of telling the story.

'Towards thee I roll, thou all destroying but unconquering whale; to the last I grapple with thee; from hell's heart I stab at thee, for hate's sake I spit my last breath at thee.'

Herman Melville, *Moby Dick* 1851

Prologue

Copenhagen had lost none of its former beauty – its medieval buildings had emerged from the war virtually unscathed, unlike the savage destruction that had befallen Germany's cities to the south.

Proud stories were already doing the rounds, of war heroes who would one day be celebrated by statues and memorials. Those who had chosen the losing side were keeping very quiet indeed, hoping their sorry histories would soon be forgotten. Many would get their wish, blending back into society and picking up from where they had left off before the war. For others though, it would not be that easy, because some they had wronged would not forget, remaining so consumed with rage that they would not be at peace until scores had been settled. In other words, for some on the losing side, retribution awaited. As the old line goes, 'For whatsoever a man soweth, that shall he also reap'.

On this summer's day, however, the focus of most inhabitants was on relaxation rather than recent history; families on bicycle outings, amorous couples at cafés sharing *Smorrebrod*, children paddling in the warm waters of the Yderhavnen. The whole population seemed at ease with itself. Across the city, scattered church bells tolled single chimes for the half hour, and the fact they were slightly out of synchrony only served to make the sounds more endearing. The orange tiled roofs and copper spires basked in the mellow sunshine of the late afternoon.

One squat tower jostled for position amongst the more slender spires of the cityscape. The Danes called it the *Rundetaarn* – the 'Round Tower'.

A dusk flying nightjar, perched on a window ledge, suddenly took flight, startled by a movement within the building. A minute later, the echo of fast moving footsteps sounded at ground level and a man could be seen striding away from the tower, disappearing in and out of the sharp shadows cast by the ancient walls of the Latin Quarter. He passed through darkness, then through light, and then through darkness again, the shadows reaching out for him like claws.

He turned a corner and was gone.

Part One

Chapter One

England, March 1936

I remember when I first brought up the subject of medical school; we were sitting around the dinner table and my father was in a bad mood already. Perhaps it was the wrong time to have mentioned it, but I thought it would actually cheer him up, not make things worse.

Evening meals were a special affair in our house. They were always in the large dining room, the table laid with the best cutlery and lit by half a dozen candles. A certain standard of dress was expected too – I would wear my blazer and school tie, my father a smart suit, and mother one of her elegant gowns, like a lady from another century. She made sure there were fresh flowers in a vase, and that a starched linen tablecloth graced the old mahogany table. We didn't have any servants, but that didn't matter because cooking was something my father enjoyed doing anyway. His experience in the war – the hunger, the filth and the danger – had turned him into a man who treated every meal as a blessing from the gods, and he would spend hours in the afternoon sorting out the ingredients and preparing the feast. Most nights, he would open up a bottle of claret, and if it was a really good one, he would say it was 'almost as good' as a Chateau Lafitte he and his commanding officer had drunk in 1917, in the shattered ruins of Ypres.

Just prior to dinner, he had been taking a well-earned break from the cooking to read the newspaper. "Look at this," he had said, showing me the headline and shaking his head. I had only had time to glimpse the words 'GERMAN TROOPS ENTER RHINELAND', before he had screwed up the paper and thrown it onto the floor in disgust. He had been quiet during the meal, and when I mentioned wanting to become a doctor, he just let out a long sigh and said nothing.

In the ensuing silence, my mother and I cleared away the plates, while my father rolled himself a cigarette.

He rarely smoked, and when he did it was because he was brooding on something. As the cigarette took shape in his fingers, he was looking at a framed photograph on the piano – I knew exactly which one because I had been watching him do it for years.

The image was of two young men in strange outfits, smoking together on a bench at the end of a pier. In the far background was a grand building, so wide you couldn't see where it ended.

The men were very similar – obviously related – and neither was smiling. They were sitting there like a couple of outlaws from a Wild West 'wanted' poster.

One was my father, and the other his twin brother, my uncle Freddie. I had never met my uncle and this was the only image I had ever seen of him.

The handwritten caption in the corner of the photograph read: *'MAY 1900, SPIKE ISLAND'*.

I knew the story well enough; how in the Boer War they had both contracted typhoid fever and been shipped back to England to convalesce. The large building in the background – the Royal Victoria Military Hospital at Netley, near Southampton – was where they had been sent to recover; a place the patients called 'Spike Island'.

Propped up next to Uncle Freddie was a pair of crutches. His right trouser was tied in a knot at the knee; the lower leg having been amputated after Spion Kop in January of 1900. He had won a medal for his actions in that battle and, according to my father, Queen Victoria herself had been the one to pin it to his chest. Freddie's adventures were like folklore in our house, right up there with those of Robin Hood, King Arthur and Robinson Crusoe. Sometimes my father would retell his brother's exploits with enthusiasm, his face lighting up like a cinema screen with projected memories. More often than not though, when he had finished telling the anecdotes, a graveyard silence would fall over him and mother and I would stare down at our empty plates, not quite knowing what to do or say. That was when he would roll himself a smoke and stare at the photograph, sitting there until the cigarette was just a stub and a cold pile of ash on his plate.

The plates cleared away, mother and I returned to the table. My father was still smoking and brooding, his forehead creased and his eyes squinting towards some unknown horizon. It was a physical trait I had inherited and, as I waited for some kind of reply, I was sure I was his mirror image, worrying what I had said wrong. For the life of me I couldn't work out what I had said to upset him – I had genuinely assumed he would have been happy to hear I wanted to become a doctor. In the end I had to say something.

"Is everything all right, Father?"

He turned to me. "When fate arrives, the physician becomes a fool."

"John!" my mother said.

He looked at her, a little startled.

"What? It's true."

"Maybe so, but our son doesn't need to hear it."

His darkening expression reminded me of the sky when a thunderstorm is on its way.

"There's going to be another war, Jennifer," he said, raising his voice, "and I don't want him caught up in it."

I spoke again, thinking he must have misheard me:

"I didn't say I wanted to join the army, Father. I said I wanted to study medicine. That's not fighting."

He shook his head and pressed his index finger and thumb onto his temples.

"Sometimes in life, son, things don't happen quite as you'd expect."

"I don't understand."

He shifted forward in his chair.

"In war, people end up in danger, even medics. And a war is coming. I've seen the prelude more than once before. And I've seen the bright look of excitement in men's eyes – the zeal they get when they think they'll be the ones to make a difference. As a medic you'll end up in it, just as I did. And I can guarantee you'll have no control over what happens."

He gestured at his cherished 'Spike Island' photograph.

"My brother died a week after that picture was taken... from pneumonia. His body was weakened from the amputation and the typhoid fever, you see. You think I could do a thing to stop it from happening? Me, the great physician? Not a damn thing. When fate arrives, the physician becomes a fool. You understand now? You think I want to be looking at a photograph of you on the piano one day?"

The wine had loosened his inhibitions and amplified all his worries.

I said nothing.

"Well, do you, Ed?"

"No."

"No indeed."

Mother had heard enough.

"John!" she said again, like a referee telling off a boxer for a low blow. "That is absolutely irrelevant to his wanting to become a doctor. You're being irrational. A war is a war, and his being a doctor makes no difference to that. We can't wrap our son up in cotton wool because of what we saw back then. Think about it for a moment – if war is coming, being a doctor is the safer option, much safer than being a soldier... like your poor brother."

Mother was well qualified to include herself as a witness when alluding to the grim realities of conflict. During the Great War, she had nursed wounded soldiers at a hospital in the south of England and seen all the gory ramifications of shell fragments, bullets and gas.

She softened her voice a fraction. "Freddie was unlucky."

"The wrecking ball doesn't care who it hits, Jennifer," my father said, more quietly now. "It just swings away..."

When I saw my father like this I felt incredibly sorry for him. The pain was still there. Thirty-six years since his brother had died and he was still afraid the 'wrecking ball' might swing in the direction of someone else he loved. Living with that kind of fear must have been exhausting.

My mother leant right over until she was about two inches away from him and their noses were almost touching, so that their entire visual worlds became their faces. As they stared at one another I saw my father's entranced expression. She whispered something, and then kissed him quickly on the lips like a punctuation mark to whatever it was she had said. This action seemed to have the desired effect – when she pulled away, all vestiges of his dark shroud had gone.

"Son," he said to me, forcing a smile, "you do what you want to. That's all that matters. I'll support you. Of course you should become a doctor if you want to be one… I'm sorry."

"You don't have to apologise, Father."

"I do," he said. "What I was saying makes little sense. It was my memories getting in the way, that's all. Of course it wouldn't be the same."

"Well, I'm glad I have your support, Father, because the interviews are the week after next. I've applied to your old college… for a place starting this autumn."

He frowned briefly, and then managed to smile again.

"That's good, Ed. I'm sure you'll do well."

My mother took hold of his hand and caressed it as a reward for his having come back to her. That's what he had to do when he got this way – return from whatever trauma he was revisiting. "Come back to me, John" she would sometimes say, and I would watch him struggling with himself to do just that.

Beautiful mother… the only one he would ever listen to, the only one who could allay his fears. "She's cast a spell over me," he once told me, as if she was a kind of good witch.

It wasn't just losing his brother in 1900 that troubled my father so. He had also been at Passchendaele in 1917.

Even the word 'Passchendaele' was like a trigger in our house; just the mention of it would change the atmosphere in a room. During my childhood I had overheard murmurs of what he had gone through there; snippets of conversation and asides which I collected like stills from a film reel and then spliced together into some kind of coherent narrative. A night trapped in a cemetery, surrounded by the cries of dying men and the silvery light of ghosts. Yes, ghosts. 'Angels of Death' he had called them. Losing the power of speech and ending up in an asylum. His undergoing electrical shock therapy… the narrative was patchy and, in my mind's eye, the film jumped about a bit, but it was the best I could do with what I had garnered.

For these old ordeals I readily forgave my father his cynicism about the workings of the world. His disillusion was entirely understandable. He had seen and experienced horrors in his time, the like of which I could not even begin to imagine, but his negativity still didn't change the sense of duty I felt towards following a medical career.

The family tradition was weighing heavy on my shoulders: not only had my father been a doctor, but his father too – a surgeon in the Crimea. And before him, there had been a Hunston at the Battle of Trafalgar. We had his surgeon's box displayed on our mantelpiece – knives, hooks and bone saws sitting in neat grooves, lined with red velvet.

I could see why my father associated war with medicine and why he had become agitated about my entering into the profession – all my forebears had ended up plying their trade on the battlefield. It wouldn't have surprised me if one of our ancestors had knelt over a fallen warrior at Plataea or Troy, with the same creased worry lines on their forehead wondering 'how on earth do I fix this bloody mess?'.

I ignored my father's misgivings and embraced our ancestral history.

I was still eight months shy of my seventeenth birthday. My parents had cared so much about my education that, as a kind of insurance policy, they made me sit the entrance exam for my school a year early, in case I failed the first time. It was a good school and they were keen I go there. As it was, I managed to get in on the first attempt which meant that throughout my schooldays I was a year younger than my classmates.

At first, it had been fine; easy enough academically as well as on the sports field. Then in the third year everyone started growing and I stayed the same size. Seeing all my friends reach puberty so much earlier than me hadn't been fun. The popularity I had enjoyed dwindled as the other boys noticed how the age gap had become obvious. Perhaps that was why I had chosen tennis, a sport that depended as much on skill as on strength. That was the only realm where I had felt completely secure, where I could 'stand tall'.

And now here I was, grown at last, but still underage for the next step.

Chapter Two

Interviews

I was slowly pacing the large hall of a grand house, wearing that worried Hunston frown. Slow steps, made with trepidation, like a man walking the plank. I didn't want to have to go through this torture twice. Inwardly, I was deciding that this was the one and only time I would be applying here. It had all been to try and make my father proud, to let him see that I was following in his footsteps and he hadn't even been pleased about it. What the hell had I been thinking?

The path my life would follow depended on the next half hour. Right down in the core of my being, I could feel this was a moment of profound significance. I was thinking about something my father had once told me: "Two or three times in your life fate will tap at your shoulder, and if you've got the guts you'll listen to what's being said."

Fate was right here in this hallway, pacing with me and saying in a gentle but firm voice: "This is it, Ed, this is it. This is your destiny. It all hangs on how today goes. TRY NOT TO MESS IT UP."

The intimidating grandeur of the hall, with its glittering chandeliers and life-size oil paintings of distinguished-looking old men, was making me feel way out of my depth. The stone turrets, the old libraries full of old books, the immaculate lawns on the quadrangles – it seemed beyond my reach.

I was an average student really, my grades nothing very special. Even if I performed at my best, I would still need a large dose of luck to get through this.

I had a go at downplaying the situation: "This isn't that important," I said to myself. "It doesn't really matter if I don't get in. I can always apply somewhere else next year."

"You're bloody well joking aren't you?" fate said straight back at me.

I swallowed and tried hard not to feel sick.

A young man walked out into the hall, looking very pleased with himself.

He went over to the coat stand.

Desperate to say something to ease my nerves, I called over to him, "How was it?"

He glanced at me with what could only be described as an expression of bored disdain – the sort of look he had probably practised in the mirror – letting his eyelids lower as if my question had fatigued him somehow. He had a large promethean head, with the sort of cranial capacity easily able to hold the volume of grey matter a person needed for a place like Oxford.

"It was straightforward enough," he said with a smooth confidence. "I expect I'm in."

"They told you that?"

He approached me, holding his coat under one arm.

"Not in so many words, but I think I gave a pretty good account of myself. They saw my strengths and were suitably impressed."

He said it in a monotone loud voice, as if there were a great crowd of people there in the hallway and not just me, two feet away. Even the shape of his mouth had an arrogance to it – the upper lip curled up into a half sneer.

I recognised his tie – that summer our tennis team had visited his school for an away match. The first thing their captain had said to us was: "What does it feel like to go to an inferior school?" Fortunately, a witty team-mate of mine had delivered the sound rejoinder: "I don't know yet, I've only just arrived." The ensuing matches had seen a whole series of bad line calls on their part, and then, when we had won the deciding rubber – their refusal to even shake hands at the net. The lowest of the low.

"Oh, I almost forgot" the candidate said, "I'm supposed to give you this. They'll want to know what it is."

He placed a model of a molecule into my hand, one of those ball and stick models that biochemists used in their laboratories. It consisted of six red balls held together in a hexagonal structure, with a smaller blue ball joined to each of the reds, splaying outwards like a shining sun.

I held it up for a moment, staring. Something sparked in the back of my mind, nothing more than that. I couldn't readily place the molecule though.

"Graphite, of course," he said. "I'll give you that for free."

"Oh, thanks."

He smirked at me in response.

I wasn't sure I agreed with him, but before I could debate the point, the door of the interview room rattled as someone turned the handle from the other side.

Hearing this, the candidate turned quickly and strode away, and as he left by the front door, a man came out into the hall to fetch me.

My first impression was of his sheer size. A giant – easily six foot five. And that was with a stoop. His brown corduroy trousers covered a pair of enormous shanks and his shirt sleeves were rolled up to reveal outsize forearms, like Popeye's, but without the tattoos. When he shook my hand I was aware of being in the grip of someone with enough latent power to crush me if he chose. I couldn't help thinking what an impressive skeleton his bones would make – the sort of exhibit one might see gracing the entrance hall of the Natural History Museum.

"Mishter Hunsh - toon?"

His voice seemed to split into two separate components; as if half of the sound wave went downwards from the larynx and bounced around his cavernous insides for a moment before joining forces with the other half of the wave which had gone straight up to his mouth. The end product was distorted, like listening to two gramophones playing the same song but with a split second's delay, and you had to listen hard to work out what was being said. The voice came with a loud volume, befitting his barrel chest, so that the word *Hunsh - toon* echoed all around the stone hall. If he ever decided to shout, the whole building would fall down.

"Yes, sir. I'm Hunston."

He smiled, and lifted a massive arm to invite me into his den beyond the door.

"I'm Doctor Bob Kynance, Please go in."

The room had tall windows and a high ceiling, but it was smaller than the hallway, and because there was carpet, it didn't echo as I walked in. I took a seat awkwardly on a long couch, trying to keep my hands from fidgeting and remembering to breathe.

It wasn't until Kynance had taken his seat that I noticed another man was in the room. He was sitting stiffly on a wooden chair in one corner, his position completely out of kilter with a normal seating arrangement designed for a three way conversation – facing the opposite perpendicular corner and not diagonally into the room towards my position. Small and ratty looking in comparison to Kynance, I sensed straightaway that this fellow was only there to catch me out.

"That's Doctor Gilligan," I heard Kynance say by way of introduction.

He waved his hand in Gilligan's direction in a way that suggested it wasn't of too much consequence whether we registered one another or not.

Gilligan peered at me. His face was red from age, cigarettes and probably too much port taken at high table.

"Hello," I said.

Instead of replying, he simply smiled the thinnest smile for the briefest of moments and looked at me as if to say: 'I'm not stupid. You'll not be able to bluff your way past me. I'm onto you. I'm watching you. I'll spot any slip up you make. Any slip up at all.'

Unsettled, I switched my attention back to Kynance. I tried to look clever, in anticipation of the highly intellectual and taxing interview question he was undoubtedly about to ask:

"How do you travel to school?"

"Pardon me, sir?"

"Do you walk or catch the omnibus?"

"Er… I take the 'bus, sir."

"Tell me about your journey."

What that had to do with medicine was anyone's guess, but I went on for a few minutes, happy to ramble away on the banalities of my daily commute. Kynance asked the occasional question, and made some one word comments, but for the most part he let me do all the talking. As I spoke, he sat back in his enormous armchair, grunting encouragingly as I described the bearded tramp who always stood at the same place each morning, even on the coldest days.

As my nerves settled I noticed Kynance doing something odd. He kept looking over to an oil painting on the wall – one of a gentleman, perhaps sixty years old, sporting a large grey bushy moustache – and when he commented he would obliquely refer to the man, almost including him in the conversation. "Isn't that interesting?" he would say to the picture, or, "What do you make of that?"

When I had finished talking about my bus ride, I joined him in looking at the picture.

Kynance introduced me by holding out a hand to the painting:

"That's Jonners."

"A colleague, sir?"

"He was… poor fellow passed away… just the other day, in fact. Thought he might have had a few more years in the tank, but it wasn't to be."

"I'm sorry to hear it, sir."

Through his sadness, he seemed pleased I had shown an interest and launched into an account of a trip they had made to a mountain called Pike's Peak as young men. I was becoming ever more confused. It didn't seem to be much of an interview; first the bus journey question and now this recital of Kynance's and Jonners's research breakthroughs into high altitude physiology.

I listened attentively, trying not to let him see that:

1. I had absolutely no idea who this 'Jonners' fellow was;

2. I was in complete ignorance as to where in the world 'Pike's Peak' happened to be;

3. I had no clue about what physiological changes occurred in the human body at high altitude, even though I kept nodding as if I did.

I knew the signs when someone was bereaved, that far-off look they had in their eyes when describing the person who had gone. The sound their voices made – slightly constricted as though something was gripping their throat. It reminded me of my father, with that same sad look of nostalgia. I felt as though I had been brought in here just to listen – to help poor old Kynance get over the loss. Of course he was too nice a fellow to see I was doing anything other than being genuinely interested in what he had to say; he certainly did not appear to realise that I was worrying about points one to three inclusive. But I was fairly sure my vacuum of knowledge was being noticed by the other man in the room.

Gilligan was hovering in my peripheral vision, sitting bolt upright and watching from his corner. I couldn't help feeling that it might be a pre-arranged hunting routine; Kynance there to soften up the prey and Gilligan stalking in the long grass until he had the best position from which to make the kill. Gilligan wasn't just eyeing me with suspicion; he was looking for a soft part of my neck to sink his teeth into.

Finally, Kynance steered the chat to the last book I had read, perhaps hoping it might be something from his specialised field of altitude physiology, and preferably authored by 'Jonners'. I couldn't please him on either front; all I had to offer was Professor Pirbright's seminal book – *The Gene Machine*.

Pirbright was a well-known evolutionary biologist at Oxford, almost as famous as the London-based JBS Haldane. The two of them were often in the newspapers, making pithy quotes on evolutionary matters and much else besides; clever men whose opinions were worth soliciting. Pirbright had become a hero of mine.

"It was *The Gene Machine*."

"Oh?"

Kynance looked over to his painting of Jonners sadly, as if to say, 'I'm afraid this one's an ignoramus, old boy.'

"I have an interest in modern evolutionary theory, sir."

I said it quietly and almost apologetically, crushed I had disappointed him. My medical future was going down the drain.

That was the moment Gilligan decided to pounce.

"Two brothers and eight cousins," he said, his words coming completely out of the blue. It was the first time he had said anything in the interview. The cadence of his sentence was clear, precise and considered, in direct contrast to Kynance's looser conversational style.

"Pardon me, sir?"

"Two brothers and eight cousins," he said again, his death stare piercing into me. "Why don't you tell me what I mean?"

Miraculously, the answer came to me through the panic.

"I believe you're paraphrasing JBS Haldane, sir… one of the other Neo-Darwinists."

I noticed Kynance sit forward with interest when I said this.

Gilligan gave me an acidic smile.

"Go on," he said.

"Well, when asked if he would die to save a drowning brother, Haldane said, 'No, but I would lay down my life for two brothers or eight cousins'."

"Ah, can you explain what he meant by that?"

I swallowed. "Well, sir… on average you share half your genes with a brother and one eighth with a cousin. The number of relatives mentioned is how many are needed to be saved in order to break even."

Gilligan nodded. "Indeed."

Unbelievably I was managing to parry Gilligan's blows.

He continued to stare at me. "And would you?"

"Would I what, sir?"

"Would you give your life to save your two drowning brothers?"

"In an evolutionary sense you mean, sir?"

Gilligan seemed to wince slightly at my question.

"Don't fence with me, Hunston."

I felt my face turn crimson.

"Let me simplify it further for you," he said. "Would you give your life to save just *one* brother?"

The room fell silent.

The oil painting of Jonners looked down on me from the wall. 'Well would you?' he seemed to be saying.

Kynance had his head cocked to one side to hear my answer better.

"Tell the truth," fate was saying. "Don't try and be clever like the evolutionists. Don't bloody *fence* with him!"

It was odd advice, but I decided to follow it.

"I don't know, sir."

Fate rolled its eyes. "You idiot. Not that truth. What your instinct tells you is the right answer."

Now Gilligan sat forward from the shadows, and I saw the long pale scar coming down his forehead – surely a war veteran, perhaps a medic on the Western Front. I could tell something was eating away at him and his question was personal. Maybe in his mind were all the men he had failed to save in that War. Maybe he was carrying the same kind of guilt as my father, who could not forget the soldiers dying under his watch at Passchendaele.

"Can you elaborate on that, Hunston?"

He was throwing me a lifeline. I needed to say something vaguely intelligent… and say it now. I supposed it wouldn't hurt to say what I felt deep down.

"Well sir," I said, hesitant, "I don't have a brother, so it's hard to know what I would do. And even if I did, it's hard to predict how I would act if the situation arose – in the heat of the moment, I might choose to run a mile, or I might decide to sacrifice myself. The truth is, sir, I don't think anyone has the right to answer that question unless they've been in that exact position. Although I can't tell you which of the two impulses I would follow, the strange thing is, I feel that the *right thing* to do is to sacrifice myself. And I'm not sure where this thought comes from – this part of me that says saving the brother is the *right thing* to do. You could call it my conscience, I suppose… though God only knows how that evolved…"

Gilligan looked across the room at his colleague, his stern features breaking into a genuine smile. I suppose what I had said made old Gilligan feel a bit better about what had happened to him in the war.

Kynance looked over at the painting of Jonners once again and then at me.

"What an interesting answer," he said. "And I'm sure that my dear recently departed friend JS Haldane here would have enjoyed hearing your sentiment about his son's work."

I looked at the painting again with new eyes.

The moustachioed man, Kynance's old co-worker – 'Jonners' – was John *Scott* Haldane, a scientist who had been equally as famous as his son, John *Burdon Sanderson* Haldane. No wonder Kynance had sat up to attention – JBS Haldane was the son of his best friend.

I had pleased Gilligan, Kynance and Jonners all in one go, with an answer belonging more to a theology interview than one for medical school. I felt a growing confidence that things were going my way, but tried not to let it show.

"So?" Kynance said.

He was pointing at the molecule in my hand.

"Do you know what it is?"

I had forgotten all about it.

The candidate before me had called it graphite, but that hadn't felt right. For the whole interview a separate part of my brain had been working on the problem, some poor homunculus sifting through all my dusty files looking for the answer. As if in a moment of revelation the answer came to me – the relevant file rushed over to the front of my mind by my breathless and rather sweaty inner librarian.

"Ah yes… well… Benzene. I think, sir."

Kynance raised his eyebrows in surprise.

"Are you sure? Everyone else has said graphite."

"Well, sir, it's a little like graphite, in that there's a hexagonal carbon ring."

He smiled. "Go on."

"But these are hydrogen atoms," I said, pointing to the smaller blue balls radiating from the red ring, "and not other carbon atoms as there would be in graphite." I held the molecule aloft. "Put it this way, sir… You wouldn't want to put this stuff in a pencil."

Kynance laughed, a big booming, discordant eruption of sound.

When I left the room, another candidate was waiting in the hall just as I had been. He was thick-set like a wrestler, with a pug face, his hair ruffled and greasy from continuously dragging his hand through it. Though he can't have been more than eighteen, it already looked as though he had lived a life. I did not recognise the school tie he was wearing – a diagonal red and white stripe on a dark blue background.

I gave him the molecule and he looked down at the model and frowned.

"They'll want to know what it is," I said to him in a whisper.

Terror lit up his eyes. It was obvious he did not know.

"Are you all right?" I said.

"No. What the fuck is it?"

Hearing him swear like that sounded comical and I almost laughed.

I checked to make sure Kynance hadn't come out yet. He hadn't. I wondered if the two old bastards had plotted it this way for a reason – like some kind of psychology experiment.

I had an innate urge to share the answer, and it was no more than that. Plus, I just liked this chap straightaway, the way he wore his heart on his sleeve. No pretence and no arrogant swagger.

"It's benzene."

"Are you sure?"

"Yes. Those are carbon atoms, and those are hydrogen. Everyone before me said graphite, but they've been wrong."

He looked from the model to me, his expression wary, like I had been with the other interviewee. But then he must have seen that my eyes were telling the truth because he nodded in acceptance.

Kynance's heavy footfall sounded from behind the door and I turned to leave.

"Thanks," I heard the candidate say.

He would still need something else to get in, a bit of extra luck, but all you needed was a cornerstone of confidence to build on and now he had it.

I lifted my right hand in acknowledgement, but didn't look around.

When I stepped out into the street I felt a terrific lightness in my body, as if I was about to take off in flight. I started running and laughing.

I was in!

A stoney-faced pedestrian watched me go by.

****

Coincidentally, the benzene molecule featured in one of my father's old stories about Uncle Freddie; he had told it years before over dinner, and I couldn't remember all the details, just that when they were in a two man rowing boat together, the puddles they had created were like the benzene rings they had learned about in school Chemistry lessons. The reason I remembered that part well was because, in his enthusiasm to explain, my father had turned his empty wine glass upside down and imprinted two lines of faint red circles on the white table cloth, much to my mother's consternation: "John, darling! It's a lovely story but that is a brand new tablecloth. Quickly Ed, get the salt before it stains."

I had the fleeting thought that fate – in the guise of my uncle's ghost – might really have been with me that day, standing there in the cold hall and silently agreeing that the 'sacred' benzene knowledge should be available to the deserving, especially those with the humility to admit they didn't know 'what the fuck' it was. From everything my father had told me about Freddie, the unaffected honesty of the scruffy lad would have really appealed to him.

There was a rational explanation of course; one which didn't need any ghosts or fate. The stories were all in my head somewhere, rolling around like marbles in a school yard, and my brain had simply latched onto that one as soon as the molecule was put in my hand, the round wine stains on the tablecloth slowly materialising in my mind's eye. Pirbight's *The Gene Machine* had said we just existed to pass on our genes to the next generation. I suppose that was how the Freddie of long ago lived on, in our shared genes, but also through the stories I had heard about him. As did my father and mother, through their stories, and for that matter all my other ancestors. Isn't that what we are? Just temporary repositories for old stories – with the chance to pass them on one day, if we are lucky enough, perhaps along with our own, before they are all forgotten.

Chapter Three

The 'Lamb and Flag' pub was our nearest drinking hole, crammed as it was between two sections of college buildings facing on to St. Giles.

The roof was sagging dangerously, and the overhanging branches of the oak tree in the lane were reaching out, as if offering to take up some of the strain. It was a futile gesture – gravity had been acting on the building for so long, it appeared to be sinking into its own foundations as each brick lost its structural integrity, like an old man gradually losing height as he aged.

The saloon bar was half full with the early evening crowd; some students, but some ordinary hardworking townspeople too – labourers with calloused hands and tired-looking city clerks. The place had a decent balance of 'town and gown' which made me feel more normal, one step removed from the University 'bubble' of red faced students, drinking champagne and jabbering about nothing.

Here, everyone was hunching over their pints as if they were flasks of hot soup. A feeble fire burned in the grate, providing scant heat to the drinkers.

Underneath my coat I had four layers on – a jersey, a woollen shirt, a cotton undershirt and a vest – and I was still cold.

The winter skies were clear. All week, morning frosts had been covering the roofs with a thin layer of whiteness.

I pulled my collar up high to cover my neck.

"There'll be another frost tomorrow," I said.

Sitting opposite, my roommate and fellow medic Tom Shaw was silent, but he was clearly tense, jiggling his legs up and down and sipping his beer with a worried look on his face.

He was the one I had helped at interview; and right now he was looking just as agitated as he had been then.

Tom had been acting strangely all day: in lectures, away with the fairies – not concentrating at all; back in our digs, uncharacteristically quiet.

"What's got into you?"

Instead of answering me, he just held up the telegram.

Although it had only arrived that morning he had handled it so much, the piece of paper looked like an ancient fragment of papyrus.

It was from his brother and I knew what it said, because Tom had shown me at breakfast:

T. ON LEAVE. L & F TUES, SIX. R.

Tuesday was today.

Tom's older brother Richard had been at our college some years before and that is why he had chosen the Lamb and Flag as our meeting place.

Now it was my turn to frown.

"Spit it out, Tom. What are you trying to say?"

"It's my bloody brother," he said, as if that was all the explanation I needed.

"And? I thought you two were close."

"We are, but the guy's a war hero."

"So?"

"So?" he said, repeating my word. "So? Oh, for fuck's sake…"

Tom was struggling to express himself. His usual way, at least with me, involved a fair degree of swearing.

"What does that mean?"

"I just feel like… I feel a bit…"

I laughed, suddenly understanding.

"Inadequate?" I said, finishing the sentence for him.

He flushed with embarrassment.

"Yes, I suppose I do... a little. Well, quite a lot if you want to know the bloody truth."

He looked into the amber depths of his beer for solace. Tom had never said a bad word about his older brother – he worshipped the ground he walked on. I imagined it must be hard living in Richard Shaw's shadow.

Tom would never be able to escape his brother's glory, because Richard, along with several dozen of his colleagues, had effectively saved the country from tyranny. Back in the summer of 1940, he had been a pilot in the Battle of Britain. Not only that, but he'd been injured in the process – shot down over the English Channel and barely surviving. That made him a complete hero.

My friend didn't talk much about his brother's injuries; all I knew was that Richard had sustained serious burns, and then undergone a series of operations to help repair his face and hands.

I had only ever seen him in a photograph which Tom kept on our mantelpiece in our digs, dating from before the burns. It was of the two of them together, with Richard in his RAF uniform – the picture taken just after he had received his orders from fighter command to move to frontline combat duties.

As well as being older, Richard was slightly taller than Tom. Objectively, one would say he was the handsomer of the two, not that that was too difficult. While Tom had been given the pug face of his father, his brother had inherited the more aquiline features of their mother. In the picture, the brothers' arms were around one another's shoulders.

"Did I ever tell you that my father had a brother?"

Tom glanced up from his beer with surprised interest.

"No, you didn't."

After being together on an almost daily basis since the autumn of 1936, Tom knew pretty much everything there was to know about me, so it was no wonder he was surprised.

"He died a long time ago."

"Oh... Sorry."

"My father never really got over losing him."

He sat back and threw up his arms.

"Christ, Ed! Why the hell are you telling me this now?"

I was thinking of how similar Tom's photo was to the one on our piano at home; images of brothers in their prime with strong, unbending wills, the same looks etched on their faces as they stared ahead into their immortal futures.

"I don't know really. Seeing you waiting here to meet your brother, I suppose. My uncle died young… during the Boer War. He was a headstrong type apparently – always ready to throw himself into the fray at a moment's notice. The daring type… you know… one of those guys who doesn't take shit from anyone – a lot like these pilots."

Tom nodded and held up his pint.

"That sounds like Richard."

I drank with him in a silent toast and we both put our glasses back down on the table.

"I suppose I'm saying that my father would give anything to be able to meet his brother in a pub for a beer."

I paused and tried to formulate my next sentence before opening my mouth.

"What I mean is, you're lucky, Tom… your brother too. Yes, he's burnt up, but at least he's still alive. That makes all the difference in the world."

Tom looked at me for a moment, then picked up his pint glass and took another swig.

"This is a good thing," I said, pointing around at the pub, "so try not to be too nervous."

He shivered.

"I'm bloody freezing" he said.

I shrugged.

"It's a lot colder elsewhere… outside Moscow where the Germans are fighting, it's minus thirty. The batteries in their radios have frozen. Imagine being that cold."

"I hope the bastards all freeze," he said.

I kept quiet. Tom hated the Germans a lot more than I did. It had become personal after what had happened to his brother, whereas for me the war was still what I read about in the papers. Apart from having to put up blackout blinds each evening, I hadn't really felt its impact all that much.

That changed when Richard Shaw walked in to the pub.

As soon as I saw him, I knew we were in a real war.

Underneath his open greatcoat, he was wearing a blue RAF uniform which had a noticeable effect on the other drinkers – it was as if Clark Gable himself had just come in. Fancy red socks, and a smart blue tie. Suddenly, the pub crowd, who a moment before had been cold and morose, were rosy cheeked and star-struck.

At first he didn't see us. In fact, he didn't even bother to search us out; he just went straight up to the bar to get himself a drink.

The usually taciturn barman handed over a frothy pint of ale and waved him away when he tried to pay.

"It's on the house," he said, with a stupid grin.

"Are you sure, old boy?" I heard Richard say.

"No bother at all, sir."

Tom and I were watching all this unnoticed. It was only then that Richard turned around and caught sight of us. He was having difficulty holding his pint even though he was using both hands, and he spilled a little on the way over to our table. After managing to put down the pint without losing any more, he removed his coat and hung it over the back of his chair. When he plonked himself on the chair next to mine, the first thing he did was take off his peaked cap and place it next to his beer.

From ten yards away he had looked fairly normal, but now he was close and without his cap I could see the scars. Portions of his face looked like a jigsaw which didn't quite line up, like some bullish child had tried to ram the wrong pieces into place to make them fit.

"You must be Ed Hunston," he said.

I held out my hand.

"And you're Richard Shaw. It's a great pleasure to meet you at last."

It was like shaking hands with a shop window mannequin and not a normal human with soft, pliable skin. His fingers were withered and hardened with scarring.

He looked at me intensely for a few more seconds, giving me a prolonged close up of his damaged features. I suppose he wanted to get the staring out of the way right now, rather than have to put up with it all evening.

The skin graft around his nose looked slightly bulbous compared to his old nose I had seen in the pre-crash photograph, but it wasn't a disaster. All things considered, he didn't look too bad; more like a roughed up bare-knuckle fighter than some hideous circus freak.

"So," he said, turning away from me and addressing his younger brother, "I gather it's nearly 'Doctor' Tom…"

Tom could not have appeared or sounded more humble if he had tried.

"Nearly, Richard. Just the finals to go – we'll know for sure by June."

Richard smiled broadly, with what looked to be genuine respect.

"Well, I'm bloody impressed. I'll drink to that!"

I watched as he picked up his pint awkwardly with his mangled hands and took a long draught, his Adam's apple moving up and down his throat in a steady rhythm as he swallowed half the pint in one go.

By God, he looked thirsty as he drank.

I had heard about the RAF boys and how they liked to put it away. Booze was an integral part of their lives, and even deaths – when one was killed, the black-humoured expression was: 'He's gone for a Burton', as in Burton Ale.

I found myself wondering how long it would take for Richard to drink a yard of ale; not long, judging by what I had seen. The record here was seven seconds – a small plaque was set into the wall above the place where the yard glass hung. Lewis Sorrin – an unknown legend who had left the college some years before. By all accounts not even a big drinker – he must have been able to pour the stuff straight down into his stomach without even swallowing. No gag reflex was Tom's theory – something wrong with his ninth and tenth cranial nerves, if you wanted to get technical.

"And what will you do when you're qualified?" Richard said to his brother, wiping the froth off his mouth with his sleeve.

Tom looked to me questioningly as if I might have the answer, but I just made a face – I had never thought further than our next exam.

"I don't know," he said. "Maybe join the Royal Army Medical Corps and do my bit."

I frowned.

He had never mentioned that before; either the idea had just popped into his ugly head, or it was a secret he had been holding onto, one dredged up from his pond of truth under the direct questioning of his god-like older brother.

"Good stuff," Richard said loudly. "You'll be able to fix up other poor blighters like me, perhaps."

Tom looked flustered, knowing that his mention of the RAMC had thrown me. He scratched at his scalp as he sometimes did when feeling nervous or embarrassed.

"What about you?" he said to his brother, bouncing the question back.

Richard nearly dropped his pint in surprise.

"What do you mean 'what about me'?"

"Will they let you fly again?"

"You're damn right they will. When I'm better I'll be straight back into it… In the hospital there was another pilot like me with the same burns. He said that for each operation he'd had, he was going to shoot down a bandit."

"And how many is that?" I said.

"How many what, Ed?"

"How many operations…?"

"Oh… I see what you mean. I think it was fifteen."

"How about you?"

"I've had seven on the hands alone, mostly to get rid of scar tissue, but also for grafting too. Luckily all my grafts took first time…though I'll need some more operations in a few years to try and straighten out some of the finger contractures."

"And the face?"

"Well, I had second and third degree burns to the mask area, and needed new skin for all that. That took four ops."

"So you've had eleven operations," I said. "And you really want to fly again? After all that?"

He just stared at me, not even deigning to answer. To him, the question was tantamount to an insult – and his non-response had me kicking myself for even asking. Richard's festering hate for the enemy came off him like a strong aftershave.

From his steely look, I had no doubt he would be getting back in an aircraft and I couldn't help but admire his grit. No wonder Tom was a nervous wreck in his presence.

If it had happened to me – the crash and the burns – I wouldn't have wanted to go anywhere near an aeroplane again.

I felt pleased people like Richard were on our side.

"Do you mind if I ask about what happened?" I said to him, "the day you were injured, I mean."

He frowned at me and I thought I had overstepped the mark again. It must have shown in my expression because Richard clapped my back and laughed.

"It's alright, Ed. I like your honesty. Everyone's been tiptoeing around me for too long. Ask anything you want to. Fire away, old boy…"

"Well… were you in a Spitfire?"

"No. I was actually in a Hurricane, powered by high-octane gasoline. The Hurricane has two 33 gallon tanks in the wings… self-sealing tanks, lined with a special rubber coating to prevent fire, but the bad news is that there's also a 27 gallon header tank which isn't self-sealing, and the header tank sits right in front of my instrument panel. That was the tank which exploded… WHUMPH! Suddenly there's an inferno in the cockpit." He held up his claw hands. "I never wore gloves as it interfered with the joystick control, and I hated wearing my oxygen mask because it made me feel claustrophobic. And that's essentially where the flames got me – the hands and the face – I'm a classic example of what my surgeon called the airman's burn. Thank Christ I was wearing my goggles that day, or my eyelids would have been burnt away too. It was my hooter and my hands that took the brunt of it."

"Crikey…"

In the silence, we all took a swig of our pints.

"So...what was your squadron?"

"The 601... flew out of Tangmere – the 'Millionaires mob'."

"Why's it called that?"

"Because to get in you had to be rich. All the originals were members of Whites... one of the most exclusive gentlemen's clubs in London. If you could drink a large glass of port and still behave yourself, you were in." He pawed at his tie. "A bunch of rebels who are used to doing things their way... the boys in the 601 have always flouted the rules and regulations. Strictly speaking, in the RAF, this tie is supposed to be black, not blue. These red socks, the red silk-lined jacket... it's all non-regulation. Our way of saying to the world, we're different. Half of the squadron turned up to the airfield in flashy sports cars. God only knows what the casual observer must have thought of us. Possibly that we were only playing at it. But make no mistake, Ed, we certainly took the fighting seriously enough."

I looked at him, holding his stare.

When a scarred up pilot tells you he took the fighting seriously, you believe it.

"You're not a millionaire though."

Richard shook his head.

"No. You're right about that... and I'm not even a member of Whites, but the 601 took on sportsmen too you see – and I had done some Alpine skiing in my youth."

The way he said it made him sound like a middle-aged man, even though he was only in his mid-twenties.

Richard was being modest. I had heard all about his sporting exploits – winning the Oxford and Cambridge ski race in 1935 and then representing Great Britain at the 1936 Winter Olympics in Garmisch. Not only that, he had even managed to get a first class degree in 'Greats'. Richard Shaw was good at everything.

"When were you shot down?"

"August 1940. August the 13th – that's the day my life changed. The first day of the Battle of Britain."

Tom and I leant our heads in closer, as Richard's voice became quieter.

"We'd already been at it all morning in the skies above Sussex. Then by twelve-thirty, I was having a scrap with some Messerschmitt 110s even further west, right over by Weymouth. I was just about to add to my tally of kills – was already picturing scratching another swastika onto my fuselage on my return to the aerodrome – when I heard bullets hitting my starboard wing and the gas tank in front of my control panel. BANG, BANG, BANG! Three large bangs. And then the flames... WHUMPH!"

Richard stopped to take another swig of his pint before continuing.

"I remember bailing out and smelling myself burning as I fell towards the Channel. Smelt a lot like roast pork. Funny what goes through your mind in such situations. Could hardly pull the ripcord of my parachute because of my buggered fingers... Remember a Messerschmitt having a go at me with a short burst as I dangled there in the air, but he missed. So there I was, floating in the sea, and nearly drowning in my own bloody parachute because I couldn't twist the release disc... got the bastard off in the end though. Not long after, two merchant seamen rescued me. At first they thought I was a Jerry and were reluctant to pick me up."

"Christ," Tom said, evidently not having heard this story before. "What on earth did you tell them?"

"Well my exact words were, "You stupid pair of fucking bastards. Pull me out!"

Richard's robust response had us snorting into our pint glasses with laughter.

"I was transferred to a lifeboat and given a cigarette to smoke. I vaguely recall an ambulance ride to Portland hospital, and long corridors and a pretty nurse, but then it gets hazy because they dosed me up with morphine."

I took a sip of my beer and waited for him to continue. His voice was very quiet now and we were leaning so far in to hear him better that our heads were almost touching.

"Something strange happened that night, as I lay up in the hospital bed… I became convinced I had foreseen my fate the night before, absolutely convinced of it."

Tom's eyes opened wide.

"What the hell did you see, Richard?"

"Well, on the night of the 12th I'd been lying on the grass in the airfield, right next to my Hurricane, waiting for the call to scramble. I was staring up at the night sky and all these lights shot through – dozens of them."

He paused and craned his head up at the pub ceiling.

"Whoosh… whoosh… whoosh," he said, drawing the trajectories in the air.

"What were they?" Tom said. "German planes?"

"No. They were the Perseids, a meteor shower. Happens on August 12th each year, but I only found that out much later. The next night, in my hospital bed, I started to believe they'd been an omen of some kind – that instead of shooting stars, they were sparks spewing out from my burning Hurricane. It seemed so vivid… really spooked me at the time." He saw our guarded looks. "Don't worry; I know it was the morphine clouding my mind."

As we all drank the remainder of our pints in silence, I stared out of the pub window at the clear night filled with a million stars.

"Twenty men," Richard said, looking sadly into the bottom of his glass. "At the start of the Battle of Britain, the 601 squadron had twenty men. Within a month that number had been cut to nine… the rest killed or injured."

He pulled a tin of tobacco out of his breast pocket, along with a packet of Rizlas and rolled himself a cigarette. He reminded me of my father doing the same, although it made me wince to watch Richard struggling with his claw hands.

I wondered why on earth he didn't just buy himself a packet of cigarettes instead of opting to roll his own. Why go through this palaver every time he wanted a smoke? Then it occurred to me the routine must be comforting for him – something that hadn't changed after the events of August 13th 1940. That made sense.

Tom's eyes filled with tears as he watched his brother's fumbling efforts. It felt wrong for me to be seeing this – too intimate.

I stood up.

"I'll get the next round."

Without taking their focus away from the half constructed cigarette, the brothers nodded their assent and I left the table.

As I waited at the bar for the pints to be pulled I turned round to see Richard light up, take a drag and then pass the cigarette across to his brother. He did it almost without thinking – whatever was his was automatically Tom's too.

I knew Tom pretty well – as well as anyone – but when I saw this I realised I would never be as close to him as Richard was, no matter how much time we spent together. I had thought of Tom as practically a brother – up until this point anyway. Seeing the way they smoked together though, without conversation and in silence, made me see that kin functioned on an entirely different level. At the end of the day, Tom and I weren't blood.

For the second time that evening I thought of Uncle Freddie and my father – and the way they were smoking together in the photograph on the piano at home.

My father had told me that Uncle Freddie kept his tobacco and Rizlas in a converted chocolate tin which the troops had been sent by the queen in the Boer War. He still had the red tin with a portrait of Queen Victoria on the lid in a drawer in his study. It didn't contain tobacco any more – although if you inhaled deeply you could just about detect the faintest whiff. Instead, it held my uncle's old letters – sent to my father from the four corners of the globe during the time Freddie had been away after leaving school.

Tom had received letters from Richard too, from the RAF hospital where he'd had his eleven operations. While my father had let me read all of Uncle Freddie's letters, Tom had kept his brother's missives private.

He would read them silently at breakfast in the College Hall as he waited for the meagre butter ration to melt on his toast.

I would say benign non-specific phrases, such as: "All okay with Richard?" or, "Is he doing well?" and in reply Tom would nod. Then he would fold the page away and we would go on with our breakfast and talk about other things.

I carried the pints back to the table, acutely aware of my hands being dextrous enough to hold the third glass in the middle with my outstretched fingers. I was really appreciating my hands after having seen Richard's.

As I sat down he held out the roll-up to me.

"Thanks," I said, taking it from him.

The gesture made me feel like part of their inner circle, a kind of adopted brother, and I passed it back with a smile on my face.

I reached for my pint.

"To brothers," I said, holding it up to them both.

"Brothers," they said in unison, touching their glasses against mine.

A short while later, Richard said he was feeling tired and so we all walked back to our college lodgings through the crisp cold night.

There were a few glowing embers left in the ash and, with some hearty blowing and the addition of some extra kindling and coals, I managed to re-ignite the fire.

As well as the luxury of a fire, our living room had a large ratty-looking sofa which had probably been there since the turn of the century. When you sat in it, you sank down so low that it was quite a struggle to get up again. Many a night, we had just slept there in front of the fire, even though our digs had a bedroom with twin beds.

Unselfconsciously, Richard removed his jacket and then his shirt. There was a large neat scar extending from his right shoulder across his upper right chest.

"You were injured there too?"

Richard rubbed it gently.

"No, Ed. It's where they grafted skin for my burnt nose. A 'tubed pedicle' they called it. It looked like I had an elephant's trunk attached for a while, running up from my shoulder to my nose. When I asked why they did it that way, the surgeons said it lessened infection rates, and kept a decent blood supply going to the nose. Did its job I would say… look how handsome they made me…"

"*Tubed pedicle*," Tom said, laughing. "Sounds like something from botany, not medicine." He threw Richard a woollen blanket. "I'm turning in. Are you alright with the sofa?"

Richard wrapped himself in the blanket and looked at the piece of furniture.

"It'll be paradise."

"Night then," Tom said, wandering through to the bedroom.

"Goodnight."

"Not too cold?" I said, seeing Richard hunching over. Despite the fire, our foggy breaths were still visible in the air.

"I'm fine."

I knelt down and heaped another few lumps of coal onto the fire anyway. When I picked up the poker I dropped it almost immediately. I hadn't noticed that the handle had been heated by the fire.

"Ouch! Bugger…"

I heard Richard call over at me: "Burn?"

"It's just a small one," I said, blowing on it.

A large blister had already appeared on the skin of my palm. It was smarting but I knew the pain would go away before too long.

"You sure?"

"It's nothing," I said, embarrassed he was giving me sympathy.

"You were asking me earlier about my injuries," he said.

I looked at him. "Yes."

"Well, imagine the pain you're having right now and multiply it by a hundred… all of your hands, all of your face… an unrelenting, throbbing, exquisite pain."

I thought about this for a moment.

"I think I understand now why you want to keep fighting."

Richard burst out laughing as I said this; but it was a harsh sound, like the laugh of a boy killing spiders in the garden. I might have read too much into it, but his laugh seemed to express all the conflicting emotions which he had kept bottled up for the last eighteen months.

After I had turned in, I could still hear Richard chuckling quietly to himself on the sofa. Perhaps it was the sound he made when he had a German fighter in his sights. Not that he would be finding it funny – as Richard Shaw had just taught me, laughing could sometimes be a serious business.

Chapter Four

Oxford, May 1942

Tom poked at the gory mess on the ground, his face creasing up like a bulldog's in disgust, but he still kept poking.

"Jesus, what a stink, let's just bury the bloody thing, Tom."

"Give me your handkerchief, will you?" he said.

"Why?"

"Because I've got blood all over my hands."

He raised his right hand so that it was inches from my face.

"Oh, for Christ's sake, Tom…"

I jerked my head back to avoid the cloying iron smell and tried not to let him see how it made me feel. I hated blood. You would have thought that, coming from a family of medics, I would be impervious to it, but I wasn't.

I pulled out my handkerchief and threw it at him.

He started to clean his hands, but wasn't about to let me off the hook. He held out the now heavily stained handkerchief, sniffed the air and laughed at me.

"My God," he said, "can you smell that? It's rank."

I edged further down the bench we were sitting on.

"Keep it away."

"Some doctor you're going to make."

"That may be so, but that's another handkerchief you owe me."

Blood had featured heavily at medical school – in fact it had been there on day one, dripping out of Tom's nose spontaneously and without warning during our first tutorial with Gilligan.

"What is wrong with your nose, Shaw?" Gilligan had said, as if it was an extremely rare condition.

Tom was the only other medic at the college, the only other candidate who had got the name of the molecular model correct in the interview.

"Sir… I… um… seem to have a nosebleed."

Gilligan had lit a cigarette and grinned, revelling in Tom's embarrassment.

"Well help him out, Hunston," he said eventually, his beady eyes moving from Tom to me. "Give poor Shaw a handkerchief."

So I had handed over my expensive monogrammed handkerchief and Tom had accepted it gratefully, ruining it in seconds. When the bleeding had stopped, Gilligan offered us both a cigarette and a glass of port and proceeded to teach us the embryogenesis of the human gut, using a tea towel to demonstrate the twists and contortions involved. After the tutorial Tom had bought me several pints in a nearby pub as recompense, our friendship firmly establishing itself through another molecule – C2H5OH – better known as 'alcohol'.

That said, the benzene molecule was what bonded us together most strongly – as elemental as the bonds holding the carbon and hydrogen atoms together. Because of my tip, he had got through the admissions interview. I suppose there are times when you owe someone a debt so large, that it cannot be repaid in effusive expressions of gratitude; it has to be paid back in another form. Though I hope he would have grown to like me anyway, Tom had repaid the debt by an unwavering, dogged loyalty right throughout medical school.

The irony was that Tom was by far the cleverer student – the structure of benzene had just happened to be his Achilles heel. He knew more in relation to everything else – anatomy, physiology, biochemistry, pathology – you name it, he knew it.

Perhaps this was how fate worked, shaping events this way in order to ensure I became a doctor. Without Tom helping me along, I think

I would have been sent down near the beginning of the first term for poor aptitude. For the last six years he had been my own personal tutor, single-handedly getting me to understand and remember the important facts. When the war began they had shortened other degrees - like Modern History - from three years to two, but the medical course had stayed the same. Six long years; three 'pre-clinical' followed by three 'clinical', which basically meant three years of humiliation in a class room, and then another three of humiliation in the hospital wards. Only that week I had been called a 'decerebrate monkey' for my stumbling attempts in trying to decipher an electrocardiogram. It had been Tom who had whispered the answer to me: "AF," – meaning 'atrial fibrillation' – and saved my bacon for perhaps the hundredth time.

Whether he had been sent from the heavens by my physician ancestors, my Uncle Freddie, or the very gods themselves, having Tom Shaw as my fellow student seemed providential.

"Come on, slowcoach," I heard Tom saying, dragging me back from my thoughts. "We need to revise this. It may come up in finals… if you mix up the lung with the spleen, they'll laugh you out of the exam halls."

He pointed at a crescent shaped blob on the ground.

"What's that?"

"It's the superior lobe."

"Right or left lung?"

I turned my head to get a better look, as if that would help.

"Right," I said, guessing.

"Good. And this?"

"The oblique fissure?"

He sighed.

"No, if it's the right lung and it's not the oblique fissure then what fissure must it be?"

I frowned.

"Come on, Tom. Let's just bury it."

He shook his head.

"What fissure must it be?"

"I can't remember."

"Hor-iz-on-tal," he said slowly, drawing a line in the air for me with his index finger.

"Damn. Of course, horizontal."

"If you've forgotten the right lung has three lobes, then you're in big trouble."

"Thanks a lot."

If Tom registered my sarcasm he didn't let it show; instead he decided to try again.

"How many lobes in the left?"

"Two. The superior and inferior."

"Good. And why are there only two lobes in the left lung?"

"So there's space for the heart. I'm not completely stupid."

"Alright, clever clogs," he said. "Here's a harder one – what's the anatomical parallel of the middle lobe in the left lung?"

"Ah, I know this… it's the *lingua*… a remnant of the middle lobe, lost through evolution."

Evolution was the only thing that made sense to me.

He looked impressed.

"Nice. You should've done anthropology, you know. Neanderthals and fossils… you're good at that stuff."

I knew he was right. I found it way more interesting too; I understood the principles and the theories without much effort. I should have heeded my father's initial advice and stayed away from medicine, but the pull from my forebears had been too strong, like a receding wave dragging me into the ocean.

"I had to follow the family tradition…"

"It's a sad thing not to follow your own heart."

"Just keep on with the lesson, will you?"

He blinked. "If you say so."

Rather too gleefully, he lifted up a section of bronchus with his bare hand to show me. A dribble of blood ran down his wrist and onto his forearm.

"Here, see how it divides into smaller airways – always the same asymmetric pattern… one branch always long, the other always short. I say, Ed… you've gone completely white."

"Keep that away from me, for God's sake."

The world was becoming muffled and I had to lie flat on the bench.

"Some doctor you're going to make," Tom said for the second time in as many minutes.

His repeating it wasn't really boosting my confidence, though he probably had a fair point.

I continued gazing up at the blue skies, my head slowly clearing.

"Maybe there'll be an air-raid warning," I said, "and then we can leave it here and go back to the library. Learn it from a book like everyone else."

"No. This is best. We won't forget it this way."

Tom liked practical sessions, with me as his unwilling accomplice. In the second year he had taken me down to the dissection room and made me work with him on a brain for a fortnight, dissecting away the grey matter until all the cranial nerves were exposed. In the end it hadn't looked much like a brain at all, more like a ragged old cauliflower with some white strands hanging off its underside. Hours we had spent over that damn brain, like two American hillbillies' whittling on a piece of wood. He was right though, because I remembered the cranial nerves after that and we had both scored well in the neuro-anatomy exams.

Now here we were revising the lung – from a pair of sheep's lungs, or 'lights' as Gilligan had called them. In a tutorial on the respiratory system he had suggested we get our hands dirty with the real thing and so we had gone to *Hayman's* in the covered market – a place with lines of pheasants hanging out on hooks, alongside whole pig carcasses and dozens of rabbits, fresh fish and crabs on ice. You wouldn't think there was a war going on when you walked past Hayman's.

When we had asked for lights, the ruddy faced butcher had gone out into the back through the beaded string curtain and returned a minute later with a package, double wrapped in brown paper bags. "Let me guess," he said, "you're medical students of Mr. Gilligan. You'll be in for an 'art next week, and then a liver…'e always does that in the final term." As he explained, he poked the corresponding anatomical areas on his blue and white striped apron. "I've 'ad lads like you walkin' in 'ere for the last twenty years."

He had refused payment: "Just 'ave 'em – once a year, Mr Gilligan 'as me over to the 'igh table at the college. We drink nice claret and talk about dissection… what knife works best where, the fastest way to gut a fish… 'e says I could've been a surgeon."

That had been two days ago. The reason we were examining them way out here in the University parks was because people on our staircase had started complaining about the smell.

I turned my head to see Tom throwing the piece of lung back down with the rest.

He was studying the pile of gore, looking as disgusted as I had been earlier.

"Jesus," he said, his mind drifting from the subject,"… almost three years of war and still no sign of it ending. It would be nice to play tennis again, instead of pulling up spuds."

It was my mention of an air raid warning that had made him reflect on the war.

The previous day he and I, along with a reluctant band of fellow students, had been roped in to harvest a crop of potatoes from ground which had once been the college tennis courts. 'War tasks' they called it. Before the war had begun, Tom and I had played on the courts most days, each of us trying to be as stylish as Fred Perry but never quite succeeding.

The crunch of footsteps on the stony path alerted us to someone's approach.

A man was hurrying home, walking with his head down and carrying a sheaf of papers under one arm.

Despite the fact that Tom and I had brought the package to the far edge of the parks, and were examining its contents on a secluded riverside path, it seemed we had not come far enough.

It wasn't until he was right on us that I recognised the man as Professor Pirbright. His photograph adorned the dust jacket photograph of his book *The Gene Machine*, a copy of which still had pride of place on my bookshelf. Seeing him threw me right back into my interview and the 'two brothers, eight cousins' conundrum.

Pirbright stopped and looked first at the contents of the paper bag and then up at us.

"What on earth are you two doing?"

His accusing look made me feel like we were a couple of murderers caught red-handed with body parts.

I had never heard him speak before – his voice was hard and clipped. When I had read his brilliantly written book, I had imagined his speech to be grandfatherly and kind, at least that's how I had heard it in my head.

"We're medical students," I said, "studying the lung."

I stood up, ready to introduce myself properly and explain what a formative influence he had been on me, but before I had the chance, he spoke again, abruptly and with surprising bitterness.

"Well, I hope your venture fails."

With that, he pushed past me and strode away.

I looked at Tom.

"I hope your venture fails?" I said repeating the line. "Christ Almighty! Was it something I said?"

Tom didn't seem too bothered. He was looking at the blood on his hands again.

"Just some duffer," he said.

"You don't know who that was?"

"No. Why don't you bloody enlighten me?"

I laughed. Tom's ignorance made me feel a lot better.

"So?" he said. "Who the hell was he?"

"Never mind… It's not important."

He shrugged and looked over in the direction of Pirbright who was scurrying along a hundred yards away.

"Whoever he is" he said. "The bastard's probably off to tell the progs…"

The 'progs' were the University Proctors – a sort of unofficial police force, there to keep students in line.

"Let's dump this rancid mess," I said. "We've learnt enough now."

We dug a shallow grave with sticks, buried the lungs and started back across the Parks towards the Lamb and Flag.

As we marched along, I knew that in future I would always associate the lung with Pirbright's sneer. It was a hard lesson in the risks of hero-worship. In a single moment, my enthusiasm for the theory of evolution and my all anthropological leanings had been jaded. For every academic or don in Oxford who was alright, like Kynance or Gilligan, there was one who was just plain nasty. After one dire pharmacology paper in pre-clinical, I had been called into the office of the lecturer – Dr Greenley – and he had said straight out: "Were your parents getting divorced when you wrote this?" He'd said it with a vindictive half smirk, thinking he was funny, though it wasn't at all, not if you thought about it. All he needed to have said was that my paper had been terrible and that I had better try harder, and I would have listened. In fact I wouldn't have minded all that much if he had called me an idiot or a dunce, because it was the truth when it came to me and pharmacology. But to bring my parents into it – well, that had really thrown me. It was just a downright spiteful thing to have said. I imagined him saying it to some other poor blighter whose parents *really were* getting divorced, and how that would have made them feel. The irony of it was that this kind of cruel wit got you places, the esteemed Pirbright being a prime example. In recent times, Greenley had been dishing out his wisdom in the newspapers and on the radio, telling everyone how the chemicals in the brain worked, but also commenting on other subjects in which he was far less qualified to express his opinion. They had even made him a professor. That was the problem with some really clever people – it sometimes went to their heads.

"You know how I got into this place?" Tom said to me, once we had sat down in the pub with our pints.

"What, Oxford you mean?"

"Yes."

He had never talked about this before. Maybe he could see how much Pirbright had got to me, because I had been quiet on the walk over.

"Sure," I said, grinning at him, "I told you the name of the molecule, you great dunce."

"Yes you did. I will always remember that."

His face had stayed serious.

"You're thanking me now? After all this time?"

"I suppose I am."

He drank some of his pint.

I laughed and shook my head and drank mine too.

"It was the one thing I knew," I said eventually. "It was only luck that I knew it. Or fate, I don't know which. Either way, I was glad to help you."

Tom put down his beer.

"It wasn't quite as simple as that."

"Oh?"

He was frowning in deep thought.

"Well, when I told them it was benzene, they both seemed very interested in my answer. First, Kynance asked why I didn't think it was graphite."

"Ha! They asked me the same thing. What did you tell them?"

"I just told him I was certain it was benzene – because the blue balls coming off the ring represented hydrogen and not carbon. And that was when Gilligan asked if you had given me the answer."

Now he had my attention.

"Jesus... What did you say?"

"I told him the truth – I said when you had given me the molecule I had been terrified because I didn't know what it was. So I had asked you and you had told me the answer."

"My God, Tom!"

I stopped talking for a moment, shocked.

"And they liked that?" I said.

"They seemed to. Said honesty went a long way in their book. It didn't matter I hadn't known the molecule, you see, it mattered more I hadn't lied."

I was shaking my head in disbelief.

"Bloody hell..."

"You know what Gilligan said to me then?"

"What?"

"He asked why I had trusted you."

"That's actually quite a good question. Shrewd old bastard."

"I agree."

"So what did you say?"

"I said it was just my hunch you had told the truth. It wasn't enough for him. He wanted to know more… kept delving. You know the way he is? So I said I wanted the world to be a good place, where you didn't have to assume the worst in people, but the best instead. It made me feel better to assume you had told the truth. He seemed to like that… it even made the old goat smile."

"Blimey, Tom…"

I kept drinking, not knowing what else to say.

I was actually feeling humbled.

I thought of the lad who had been so sure that the molecule was graphite. Now I could see how he had tried to help me; in his own, slightly arrogant manner, granted, but he had still tried to help. Maybe I should have assumed the best in him, and not the worst, just because I didn't like his face and his school tennis team. He hadn't lied – he could have said it was gelignite just to scupper my chances – all he had done was pass on what he thought was the correct answer, and even though he had been wrong, at least his motives were genuine. Maybe I should revise my opinions of people, and not be so judgmental.

Tom was right.

I tried to look at things from his perspective. I should try and forgive the 'divorce' barb from Greenley the pharmacologist and put it down to him having had a bad day. Tom had cheered me up considerably. In fact, I was in such a good and forgiving mood, that I even decided to try and think better of Pirbright and turn the episode to my advantage.

Over the following days and weeks of revision, Pirbright's rebuff made me commit myself to being a medic – and to move away from relying on Tom to walk me through the learning like a child. It was time to do something worthwhile instead of musing on evolutionary theory and how things may or may not have been at some stage in prehistory. Studying the ancient skulls of the first hominids was only useful up to a point – it didn't really make a difference and wasn't very practical. Scientists could put forth any number of theories on cousins and genes and 'survival of the fittest', but did it actually help mankind?

Look where the concept 'survival of the fittest' had got us: I had read about the German concentration camps, heard the rumours of what they were doing there – to those they considered 'unfit'. Forget sacrificing yourself for two brothers or eight cousins in the interests of preserving your genes, the Nazis were deliberately eliminating whole genetic lineages.

My new outlook – that of forgiveness and assuming the best in people – could only get me so far, because whichever way you looked at it, what was going on over there was unforgivable.

Chapter Five

I woke up, brushed off the flakes of grass from my dark suit and made my way back to college. It was six in the morning.

At this hour the streets were deserted, but it was light and I felt like the last person in the world. I walked right down the middle of the wide road of St. Giles.

In a few hours, cars, buses and bicycles would be thronging this thoroughfare, but for now it was only the sycamore trees with their dappled trunks, bordering both sides of the street which saw me pass. My mind was wandering. Without people, the greenery would one day reclaim all of this. How long would it take? One hundred years? I tried to picture Oxford as forest, having reverted to its prehistoric state – with all its man-made glory gone and the fallen pale-stoned buildings hidden amongst the undergrowth and the groping roots of soaring trees.

The porters had just opened the front gate at the lodge and they didn't seem to mind when I strolled through, merely glancing up from their newspapers, before going back to the headlines and reaching for their mugs of tea. There were always two of them in the lodge, like a pair of tag team wrestlers. I could see something of Tom and me in their co-dependence, or that other word that biologists liked to use – symbiosis.

They were usually fairly strict about unauthorised absences from college, and going by the rules I should have filled out an 'exeat' form. So when the porters ignored my presence, the thought occurred to me that maybe they just didn't care anymore, because my time here was nearly over.

To the sound of my own footsteps, amplified by the enclosed stone walls, I walked the path which ran around the edge of the quadrangle. A loose paving slab made a loud satisfying clunk as I deliberately trod on it, my habit through all the years of medical school. There was a solidity to the sound that made me feel secure. It was dependable, always answering my weighted step with that same welcome thud. Since the incident with Pirbright, my obsessive habit had morphed into a superstition – I had started to believe that for my day to turn out well I had to step on the slab, like some kind of curious sacrifice to please the gods. That is the other thing Pirbright had done to me – turned me against his religion of science. Up until he had said, "I hope your venture fails," my world view had been one of ideas founded on solid logic. Afterwards, a troubling feeling had crept up on me; if science's greatest spokesperson had his faults, then perhaps the science itself had shortcomings too. Maybe things were not the way I had always assumed them to be. Pirbright's truculence had been like a peal of thunder in the mountains, and it had made my previously unshakable belief in science start to slip, like the start of an avalanche. To my surprise, the exposed rock underneath had been this primitive superstitious belief in gods and other unseen powers – powerful enough to make me step on the stone slab in the quadrangle out of fear that if I didn't, the gods would be displeased.

It wasn't only Pirbright though.

The years of dissecting cadavers, smelling blood, conducting pharmacological experiments and studying physiology had also turned me away from certainty. The clinical medicine, the actual dealing with patients, had completed the transformation. Through encountering sick people I had seen life was not like it said it was in the textbooks; there were rarely simple categories of illness with 'cures'. Knowing nicotine made the heart rate rise counted for naught. People were complex and unpredictable. The human condition was like a deep pond and we doctors were only insects skipping over the surface, like water boatmen, with no real idea of what lay beneath. Knowing some anatomy and a bit of physiology and pathology, for instance, didn't amount to much in the face of a terminally ill patient. My father had said, "When fate arrives, the physician becomes a fool," and I was starting to see his point.

I climbed the staircase to our shared digs and pushed open the door. The blackout boards were still up, casting a twilight hue over the shapes in the living room. I went through to the bedroom where Tom was sleeping. His torso barely moved as he breathed.

The room smelt strongly of alcohol – an empty bottle lay on the floor next to his bed.

"Wakey, Wakey."

I gave his mattress a firm kick and then sat down on the edge of my bed a few feet away, putting my head in my hands and massaging the rims of my eyes – the zygomatic arches if you wanted to be anatomical about it.

Tom stirred.

"Hey," he said, his voice a low growl. "What the hell happened to you? One minute you were with me and the next you were gone."

"I'm not sure. I woke up by the hospital fountain."

In front of the Radcliffe Infirmary – the hospital where we had done all our clinical medicine, including the final exams – was a fountain statue of the sea god Triton, surrounded by a circular grass lawn. I could not remember how I had ended up there.

Tom sat up and moaned as the balance mechanism in his hung-over head tried to adjust to this new upright position.

"Jesus. I'm still drunk. What the hell did we end up drinking?"

"Whisky," I said, pointing at the bottle on the carpet.

We had been in a pub called the Royal Oak, celebrating the end of our exams. Not a place we went very often, but close to the hospital and the first pub we had come to.

Tom looked over at me and smiled stupidly.

"You're still in your bloody subfusc…"

"Look who's talking."

He hadn't even pulled over the covers before falling asleep, just collapsed onto his bed fully clothed.

I examined myself.

It was true – I was dressed in a white shirt, white bow tie, black suit and my commoner's gown, rucked and dirty with some of the grass cuttings still glued to the material by the morning dew. Incredibly, it was the required dress code for the clinical exam, complete with the square mortar boards on our heads. God only knew what the patients must have thought of us.

In one case, I had been asked to examine some old boy with a pituitary tumour who couldn't see anything at the outer edges of his vision. This was because the tumour was pressing on a certain section of his optic nerves – at the point where they crossed over right above the pituitary gland, the so-called optic chiasm. I could remember the exact location from the brain Tom and I had dissected and turned into a cauliflower. Of course the patient was not allowed to tell me what was wrong with him – I had to work it out by doing a cranial nerve exam – checking his visual fields by waggling my finger in various positions and asking him if he could see it.

The surgeons would be taking the tumour out at some stage, getting access either through the top of his mouth – a 'trans-sphenoidal hypophysectomy' – or just through the head itself – the 'transcranial approach'. I got some extra marks for telling the examiners that. Medicine was all about knowing which long words to use, words that could make you sound cleverer than you actually were. You didn't say 'skin cream', you said 'topological dermatological agent'.

"Where's your mortar board?"

"On Triton's head," I said, remembering the first thing I had seen on opening my eyes that morning. "I left it there. It suited him."

Tom laughed and winced as the sound he made aggravated his hangover.

"Well, you won't need it again in a hurry. We're doctors now. Do you realise? Bloody doctors! It's white coats all the way from now on."

"We haven't heard for sure yet."

"Come on, Ed. Everyone passes. Do you think they've taken us through six years just to fail us now? In the middle of a war, when they need medics the most?"

I leant forward and picked up the empty whisky bottle.

'Gilbey's Spey-Royal' it said on the label. Perhaps that was the real reason I had been so reflective this morning, the peaty remnants in my system making me wonder about the trees colonising the city and the sound of the stone slab as it rocked under my foot in the quadrangle.

"I suppose you're right," I said.

"Of course I'm right."

I looked into the opening of the bottle and held it up to my eye like a telescope. I could see Tom, liquid-looking and distorted, through the bottom of the bottle.

"Fancy a brew?" I said.

It was too early for the college dining hall to be serving, so we went straight to the St Giles' café – the 'caf' – without changing. We retraced my steps around the quad and then left through the porter's lodge. The college rowing team were gathered there, about to set off down to the river for an early morning outing. They stared at us in our disheveled state, and what was behind those stares was hard to say.

"Perfect physical specimens," Tom said, after we had passed by.

"Thinking of trying out for the team, Tom?"

"See how tall they were? All of them six foot or more."

"And?"

"They would all qualify to get into the Waffen SS."

"Really? You have to be a certain height?"

"You do, apparently. Five foot ten minimum."

"How do you know this?"

"Richard told me. No tooth cavities, no spectacles. Physically free of problems – no acne even. He said that was the type of person he was trying to prevent from ruling the world. Had the entry requirements stuck on the instrument panel of his Hurricane."

"Blimey."

Tom mimicked a German accent:

"Ja Hunston. Ze so-called 'Leaflet for enlistment in the SS-Special Purpose Troops and Death's Head Units', published in 1936."

"Why did he have it there?"

"He said it helped him press the firing button with no qualms whatsoever."

"But pilots aren't Waffen SS."

"No, but Richard lumps them all into one category – says they've all 'pinned their colours to the same mast'."

"Fair enough."

As we crossed the road to the caf, I thought about the entry criteria. I had grown in the end, despite the head start all my contemporaries had taken at school. I was six foot tall now. I would have qualified on height for the SS, but apparently not in other respects.

"Tom… I wear glasses for reading," I said.

He chuckled. I guessed he had been thinking the same thing as me.

"And I've got a gold filling" he said.

"Some 'master race' we'd make. They wouldn't let us through the front door, would they?"

"Oh, I forgot to mention, you also need to provide evidence of racial purity dating back to 1800."

I made a whistle. "Crikey" I said. "That far back? That's stricter than my father's golf club."

Tom snorted.

"And the leaflet said they have to be free of any criminal record. That's a joke. I would've thought for the SS it should be the other way round. Richard told me about SS atrocities during the British retreat to Dunkirk in 1940 – how they shot surrendering soldiers. Now the bastards are halfway to the Urals. God only knows what they're doing out East right now."

"Nothing good."

"Can you imagine it, Ed?" Tom said. "A world full of tall people with good eyesight and perfect teeth?"

"As opposed to one with us – with our hangovers and our fillings and spectacles – I suppose that, when you look at it from a 'survival of the fittest' standpoint, we're way more degenerate, just evolutionary cul-de-sacs – well at least you are… you ugly ape."

We both laughed.

"But you've forgotten the one major difference between them and us" he said.

"Oh?"

"They're a bunch of fucking fuckers and we're not."

"I like your logic Tom, and very eloquently put. Fucking fuckers – who can argue with that? You should pen a note to Himmler suggesting they be re-named the FF instead of the SS – it's got a certain ring to it."

The bell on the door to the caf rattled in its familiar way when we pushed it open.

Even at the start of the day, the place smelt of rancid fat, and the cook had a sheen to his skin, as if he lathered up in the left-over grease instead of scraping it into the dustbin.

I ordered the usual – mug of tea x2, eggs and toast x2 – and put the correct change on the counter.

The cook poured the teas there and then and I carried the mugs to the table Tom had selected by the front window, furthest away from the serving counter. The room was long and narrow, like a train carriage, with the galley kitchen and counter at one end and the glass fronted door and window at the other. A set of narrow booths ran down both sides, each table having a dirty tin ashtray and a grimy pair of glass salt and pepper shakers, almost opaque with people's greasy fingerprints. Before the war, there had been ketchup and sugar pots, but they had been cleared away when rationing began.

Despite having no sugar to add to my mug of tea, I still stirred it with the stained teaspoon, hoping that just by making the action I might fool myself into believing there was something sweet in it. The clinking sounds were soothing. Soon the scalding tea would be restoring me to an acceptable functioning state. This was one of the good things in life. I brought the rim to my lips and took a sip.

"How's your head?" Tom said.

"Fragile. But I'll be better in a minute."

He was stirring his brew and grinning at the liquid in his mug with real affection.

"Tea," he said. "It's a bloody lifesaver."

"Food!"

I turned around. The cook had put the breakfasts on the counter and was standing there waiting for someone to go up and collect them.

"While it's hot," he said, with a little more volume than was necessary.

I got the hint and stood up with a sigh.

On each plate was one measly egg, floating in a lake of yellow-tinged cooking oil. Four triangles of thinly buttered toast were beached like landing craft around the rims of the plates. The cook knew our usual order was four eggs each.

"Where are all the eggs?" I said.

He shrugged.

"The Ministry of Food says only one egg per meal now… new rule."

I looked down at the paltry meals and then back at him.

"At least it's cheaper," he said, handing back some of my money.

He must have caught my expression, because he held up his hands defensively. "Don't blame me, blame the Germans."

Resigned to the situation, I nodded at him and carried the food back to the table.

"Hey!" Shaw said. "What's happened to my eggs?"

"New rules."

His face fell. "Bloody hell," he said. "*Rationing* in the caf – things *must* be bad."

Wordlessly, we started to eat, not stopping until our plates were scraped clean.

"How many eggs do you think we've eaten in this place?" Tom said, putting his knife and fork down.

"I don't know, Tom. A few hundred at least."

Established in 1937, the caf was an institution – as important to Tom and I as the department of anatomy or pathology were in our University education. Actually, more so. We came here several times a week, spent more time here than in the library, even more than in the Lamb and Flag. The sign above the door – 'LUNCHES, TEAS, SNACKS' – suggested a wide variety of choice, though in the caf, it basically meant 'eggs and toast'. That had now become '*egg* and toast'.

Tom looked down at his empty plate and ran his index finger around the rim to scoop up the leftover runny yolk.

"There won't be many more," he said, licking his finger. "Soon everything will change and we'll be gone."

"Don't say that, you're depressing me."

"How come?"

"It makes me think about my father giving me shoulder-back rides when I was a boy. He must have given me hundreds. And there must have been a last one, not that either of us had known it at the time. But it was the last ever, just as I was getting too big to be carried. Sometimes I think about that last ride, with neither of us knowing it. Makes me sad, the same way I'm feeling sad now, that these could well be our last eggs in the caf."

"Jesus, Ed," Tom said. "Now you're the one depressing me."

"Sorry, I think it's the whisky. Made me all maudlin."

We sat silently and drank our tea.

In the background I could hear the cook pottering around in his small kitchen. He had the radio on, but it wasn't loud enough for me to be able to hear the words properly. It was probably an update on how far the Nazis had progressed into Russia. Apparently they were almost at the Don River now. I had looked it up on an atlas the other day – to the North East of the Black Sea. They were giving the Russians a right hammering. Our boys were getting it too in North Africa, surrounded at Tobruk – 35,000 of them.

Outside, traffic was starting to rattle down the road, though there still weren't many people about. It was only six-thirty in the morning.

Tobruk, Rostov on Don – faraway places. I felt helpless in the face of the German machine – just a lad with a hangover in an Oxford café, a clueless student irritated at only being allowed to eat one egg with his breakfast. For the first time in the war I had a pang of guilt that I wasn't doing something more to help. What if the fucking fuckers *did* win? Joking aside, the scenario was a frightening one.

An old man pushed his face against the caf window, saw us, then opened the front door and strode up to the counter.

He bought a cup of coffee and came back down to the table near the front, next to ours.

It was only then that I recognised him. He had been one of the external examiners from the clinical vivas the day before, one of the unknown faces brought in from other hospitals to scare us witless.

His most memorable feature were his eyebrows, which had retained their darkness despite the white wisps growing from the sides of his balding head and the grey moustache. Beneath the half-moon spectacles, his eyes reminded me of Gilligan's, in the way that they silently warned: 'I do not suffer fools'. And like Gilligan, there was a gentleness in his look as well, a hint of wisdom, if you wanted to call it that.

My slowly recalibrating mind recalled the events of the previous day.

I had walked into a windowless room to find the examiner in a white coat standing beside a muscular man dressed only in his underpants. It had been quite disconcerting, and perhaps that had been the intended effect, there to disorient the nervy finalist a notch further, to try and put him off his game.

The examiner had pointed to the man, and then turned to me and said, "How many lobes are there in this man's right lung?"

I could hardly believe my good fortune.

"Three."

"And his left?"

"Two."

Thank you Pirbright, you bastard, I was thinking. My answers had come out automatically, as if I had been studying nothing but the lung for the last six years.

"What muscle is it that gives him his triangular torso?"

"Latissimus dorsi, sir."

"Insertion?"

"The floor of the bicipital groove."

"Any other muscle insertions in that groove?"

"Yes, sir. The insertions of Teres major and Pectoralis major."

I only remembered this because of a dirty mnemonic Gilligan had taught us: 'The Lady lies between the two Majors'. The lucky hand of fate again.

"Which side is which?"

"The insertion of Teres major is on the medial lip of the bicipital groove, sir. Pec Major inserts into the lateral lip."

The examiner brought out a pen and ticked a list on a clipboard he was holding. I had the feeling that he wanted to be somewhere else and not wasting his time asking students simpleton questions on anatomy.

"Tell me something interesting about Pec Major."

"Interesting, sir?"

"Yes, something interesting about the chest… anything you want to. This is for bonus marks…"

He prodded the skin overlying the man's upper pectoral with his index finger.

"Well?"

What came to mind was Richard Shaw's scar.

"Well, I know plastic surgeons use the skin there for grafting onto the burnt faces of pilots."

"Oh?"

The examiner looked up with mild surprise – for the first time, he seemed interested in my answer.

"Tubed pedicles, sir."

"Go on."

I had read up on these since seeing Richard Shaw's scars.

"Well, sir – the way I understand it, when a skin flap is raised from the chest, it has a natural tendency to curl. Back in the Great War, surgeons had the idea to stitch the curled edges into a tube, and then attach one end to the damaged area on the face. It was essentially a cylinder of living tissue, with a preserved longitudinal blood supply even though the cross-vessels had been cut in making the flap. Because it's a closed system, infection rates are reduced."

The examiner raised his eyebrows.

"You know how it's done?"

"I know the basics, sir. It's quite complicated."

"Try me," he said, with a crocodile smile.

Because I had seen the results close-up on Richard, what I had read had stuck in my mind.

"The process is done in stages. The first operation involves raising an acromio-thoracic tubed pedicle approximately 9 inches long, like a suitcase handle, running from the shoulder to the upper chest. Some three weeks later, once the blood supply has been established, the distal end is freed from the chest, swung up and sewn into position on the injured part of the face, the nose for example. So now the patient has a tubed pedicle running from his shoulder up to his nose. A disconcerting sight."

"And then?"

"Another three weeks is given to allow the blood supply to mature, and then the pedicle is detached near its nasal extremity and used to form the nose. The remaining portion of the pedicle is returned to the shoulder. Later the surgeons can operate again to shape and thin out the nose if necessary."

"What's the medical term for shaping the nose?"

"Um… a rhinoplasty, sir."

"Have you any idea why they often use skin from the upper chest?"

Richard hadn't told us why that was, and neither had the surgical papers I had read. I would have to make an educated guess.

"I suppose it's similar to the skin on the face."

"In what way?"

"Well, the skin there blushes. When my mother is angry her face and her upper chest turn red, so I suppose the vascularity there is similar to that of the face."

The examiner laughed, though I couldn't tell if he was impressed or just shocked at my ignorance.

"So?"

I was thinking on the spot now, just speculating, with no idea if what I saying was complete tripe or not.

"Well, it matches better, sir. Why would a patient want a white patch on their nose if they had the option of one which blended into background?"

"You're saying it would be more aesthetically pleasing?"

"I suppose I am, sir."

"Would you want a pink nose, or a white nose?" the examiner said to the man.

"Pink, Doctor."

The examiner nodded and made another mark on the page next to what I presumed was my name.

"You can go. Send in the next one."

It was this same doctor who had come into the caf and who was now sitting down at the next table.

Tom had noticed too. We both looked across and nodded at him in recognition, but didn't say anything.

He took a sip of his coffee and then locked his serious stare onto Tom.

"You two did well yesterday."

"You remember us, sir?" Tom said.

The man put down his cup, crossed his fingers and smiled so that his stern gaze became suddenly kind.

"Yes I do," he said, looking at me too now. "You were the two who talked about tubed pedicles. When I checked on the list of names I saw you were both at the same college. I wondered what had got you two interested in that side of medicine, in plastic surgery. The fact you both mentioned it piqued my interest."

Tom glanced at me and I nodded at him to tell Richard's fateful story.

As he did, the man was evidently touched, nodding with what seemed to be profound sympathy as Tom spoke.

"I presume he was at East Grinstead."

"That's right, sir. He's out now... The mad bugger has gone back to flying, if you can believe that. Said it was 'his place' to fight on."

The man kept staring at Tom.

"Either fight or die."

"Pardon me, sir?"

"Either fight or die – *Aut pugna aut morere* – it's the motto of my oldest son's squadron. He flew Spits."

"Flew?" Tom said, his voice quiet.

Now the man looked grim.

"Shot down by a Messerschmitt in 1940. He survived, but he's a POW in a place called Stalag Luft 3, in a part of Germany called Lower Silesia."

The café fell almost silent. Even the cook at the back had stopped clattering about. Just the radio droned on at low volume.

"Actually, you two remind me more of my youngest lad," he said, changing the subject. "He's a medical student too. Likes bugs… into malaria and mosquitos."

I was only half listening to him; my mind still on his other son, the one stuck in some hut in the middle of a forest in a place called 'Lower Silesia'. I wondered if he wanted to fight on, like Richard Shaw, or whether he was pleased just to be alive, without half his face burnt away, sitting out the rest of the war in confinement.

"Anyway," the man said, "you two seem like a good team."

I picked up on this.

"We've gone all the way through med school together, sir."

He started rummaging around in his coat pocket for something.

"Surgery relies on teamwork," he said, pulling out his pipe and packet of tobacco.

"You were a surgeon, sir?"

He smiled.

"Still am."

"Can I ask you why you came here to invigilate? Are you an Oxford man yourself, sir? Originally, I mean?"

He shook his head.

"No. I went to the other place. I get asked to examine all over."

Without mentioning the name, he was telling us he had been at Cambridge.

"Cambridge eh, sir?" I said, "Well… not everyone's perfect."

He seemed to take this in good humour, smiling and continuing to stuff his pipe with tobacco.

"Yes, well, I seem to remember beating your lot in the Boat Race."

This was news. My father had rowed in the Boat Race himself; three times, from 1896 to 98.

"You're a rowing blue, sir?"

He did not look at me but kept concentrating instead on lighting his pipe.

"I am," he said, puffing away to get the pipe going. "1904. Sat in the seven seat."

"You're not very big," Tom said.

I kicked him under the table.

"What I mean is, sir, the oarsmen of today seem a lot taller."

The man was laughing.

"You're right. I was the lightest man in the boat. But like I said, teamwork wins the day."

He puffed on his pipe again happily.

"I have a proposition for you both," he said, pausing briefly to get our full attention. "You're intelligent lads. How do you fancy working down there, helping out with the war effort by treating the pilots?"

"Down where?" I said.

"Down in East Grinstead. The Queen Victoria Hospital. My cousin runs the place."

He pulled put a card from his coat pocket and handed it over.

"You show him this and you'll get a job."

Tom held it up so that I could see it too.

'Sir Harold Gillies' the writing on the card said. Sir Harold Gillies was probably the greatest plastic surgeon in the world.

"My God," I said. "I'm sorry, sir, I didn't recognise you."

"Why should you? It's my fault entirely. I should have introduced myself."

The exam from the day before began to make sense now.

"You pioneered the plastic surgery the airmen have now, didn't you, sir?"

He rocked his head from side to side, in a magnanimous way.

"Well, I was one of the first to perform a tubed pedicle – operated on a chap called Able-Seaman Vicarage in October 1917. He'd sustained terrible facial burns from a cordite explosion on HMS

Malaya at the Battle of Jutland in 1916…Extensive scarring, just like the airmen of this war. Anyhow, the outcome was a half-decent reconstruction – he had his nose back. I did a few more at Sidcup during the war and afterwards."

"A few, sir?"

He nodded. "Well… I suppose more than a few… thousands."

I couldn't conceive of doing a thousand of anything, not even eating a thousand eggs in the caf. I tried to imagine a thousand mangled faces.

Gillies drained his coffee, and then stood up.

"My cousin's name is Archie McIndoe. He's looking for extra help – I'm sure he would appreciate a couple of new recruits. You both seem bright enough, but like I say, teamwork is what gets you through in the end, and that's the reason I think you'll cope."

"McIndoe was the man who operated on my brother," Tom said. Gillies nodded.

"That would make sense – he's the head surgeon down there. Can I take it you're both keen?"

Tom and I looked at one another and in that split second we both decided.

"We should just call him up?" Tom said. "And quote your name, sir?"

Rummaging around again, Gillies pulled out a folded letter and put it down on our table.

"It's Ed Hunston and Tom Shaw, correct?"

"Yes, sir," we said in unison, surprised at the fact he knew our names.

"Good. This is your letter of recommendation gentlemen, to accompany my card. I wish you both all the best."

"How did you know we'd be here, sir?" I said.

"Your porters are omnipotent."

We laughed as he shook both of our hands.

After he had left, we slowly unfolded the letter. It was handwritten and dated that day.

Together, we read the missive which would change our lives:

Re. Ed Hunston & Tom Shaw
19/6/42

Archie,

I had the chance to examine the finals students at Oxford yesterday and these two young men showed potential – their anatomical grounding was sound and they even showed a grasp of some of the basic principles of plastic surgery.

They both attend the same college and by way of references I spoke to their tutors to ensure my conclusions were not unfounded.

Mr Gilligan – a neurosurgeon before becoming the full time anatomy tutor – won an MC in 1915. Gilligan vouches for his two charges. Knowing his surgical pedigree explains their strong anatomical knowledge. The other tutor, Dr Kynance, is a physiologist – an amiable chap, whose poor hearing didn't make for the easiest of conversations. He worked with JS Haldane on altitude physiology before the Great War and then became one of the foremost experts into the physiology of gas warfare.

Kynance had no complaint either. One insight he shared was that Hunston and Shaw work best as a team and in his opinion they should be kept together. Said he and Haldane had their biggest breakthroughs as a team and he recognised the same dynamism with these two.

Therefore cousin, I write this letter recommending you take the lads on as a pair – presumably in the capacity of Resident Medical Officers. I know you were on the lookout for some.

I aim to discuss the proposition with them this morning and will only arm them with this letter and my card if they are in agreement with my suggestion that they work under your wing.

Yours,
Harold.

Chapter Six

Queen Victoria Hospital, East Grinstead, Sussex
February 1943

It was 3am.

A covered walkway – open to the elements from both sides – linked our room to Ward Three. In wet weather you had to walk right in the middle of the path to avoid getting soaked. Tonight, it wasn't raining – just very cold, with a frost on the grass. My breath was fogging in front of me, and I was shivering too, but I was so tired I wasn't registering the temperature anymore. In fact I felt like a detached observer, experiencing it all from another place entirely; I was in a strange limbo where events drifted by, like inanimate objects on a conveyor belt. Things were happening sure enough, but they were not really happening to the entity that was *me*. I knew why I was in this altered state – complete exhaustion. When you are spent – be it mentally or physically, or both – a part of you retreats right into a hidden place where nothing can touch you anymore; some inner chamber deep in your mind… a kind of sanctuary for your soul, a realm existing outside of normal time. From there you can relax, put up your metaphorical feet and watch life happening as if on a small cinema screen on the wall of your consciousness. That's how tired this bloody job was making me.

I watched Tom shuffling along a yard or so ahead, his bare feet in a pair of white clogs just as mine were. We were hardly even bothering to lift our feet off the ground, just dragging them over it so that we clunked and scuffed our way down the exposed corridor.

"Whose bloody idea was it to come and work here?" he was saying. "Yours or mine?"

"It was a joint decision."

"Lesson number one" he said. "Never make a big decision on a hangover."

I didn't have the energy or inclination to make a witty response.

We took turns to be on-call every other night – a 'one in two' rota – though in terms of sleep it didn't matter, since our digs were in the same room, just like they had been at College, and when the phone rang it woke us both up anyway.

As it happened both of us were needed tonight – our destination, the bathroom near the entrance to Ward Three.

We shoved open the rubber swing doors and a blast of warm air greeted us in the atrium. It was a beautiful feeling, that warmth. I ventured back out of that inner place. For the first time since having been rudely woken ten minutes before, I felt able to deal with what they were about to throw at us. It was astounding, the change – how rotten you could feel one minute, to a feeling of being able to face anything the next. As far as I could see, that was essentially what being a junior house surgeon entailed. You didn't need to be very clever, you certainly didn't need top marks in exams, you just had to do what you were told and have the ability to drag yourself out of bed when every cell in your body was screaming 'leave me alone!'.

They kept the whole of Ward Three well heated with paraffin burners, even in the summer, because the Boss reckoned the warmth helped the patients recover more quickly. It was a perpetually sultry place, with huge aspidistras thriving on the table near the central nurses' station and two dozen sweaty patients with stinking bandages that needed constant changing.

Once inside the bathroom, Tom and I put on clean white aprons and 'gloved up' in a sleepy silence. We were already wearing surgical 'scrubs' – our green uniform of a short sleeved shirt and baggy trousers, which served just as well as pyjamas. Unless we happened to be leaving the hospital grounds to go to the pub in town, this was all we ever wore. Well, that and our white clogs, with our initials written on in large red letters: EH and TS. Surgeons were on the whole quite protective about their named clogs, though there was one sloppy registrar who always seemed to be wearing someone else's and sometimes those from two different people. Once I had seen him wearing one of Tom's clogs and one of mine, but hadn't dared challenge him because the registrars could make your lives a living hell if they wanted. At school, there had always been someone like that, some blighter with no respect for other people's gear. They would borrow your books and never return them – you would later see your book happily sitting on their shelf and you still felt guilty to be asking for it back. One boy, drenched and mud spattered after a cross country run, had picked up my clean towel in the changing rooms and wiped himself down with it – every filthy crack and crevice – and then put it back by my things before taking his own clean towel with him into the showers. I had been there, seeing it all in the mirror at the sinks. The way he did it almost seemed to be absent minded, as if he was doing it by mistake. But he wasn't. They never were. Those bastards always knew exactly what they were doing.

The windows had misted up in the bathroom and condensation was dripping down the white tiled wall. In the warm steamy atmosphere, we could have been Roman slaves working in a *thermae*, except that our clientele were very different.

Hoping Tom wouldn't notice, I unhooked the hose nozzle from the wall. The rubber hose was connected up to copper pipes which ran from a large brine tank hidden in the ceiling. The salt water was maintained at a comfortable 105 degrees Fahrenheit – a little warmer than blood temperature.

"No, no, no. It's your turn," he said, snatching the hose with his right hand and holding out a pair of steel tweezers in his left.

Sulkily, I kept my gloved hands together, fingers entwined, refusing to accept the gleaming instrument which he continued to wave in front of me.

"Come on, you bastard… take these. It's your bloody turn."

When we were tired we both tended to swear like troopers.

"Piss off, Tom… it's yours."

He smiled.

"Nice try."

He wasn't conning me. It was my turn.

Dread welled up from deep inside me. I hated the tweezer job – all the blood and pus and gore.

A trainee surgeon who hated blood and gore – it was farcical really. Gillies' compliments in the caf had been the bait luring me in and my own vanity had done the rest. I was here for all the wrong reasons. I had made a bad decision, my thoughts dulled by a night of whisky drinking.

Another time, I might have argued more, but tonight I was too tired, so I just gave in and took the tweezers from him.

"Thank... You," he said slowly and sarcastically. Almost as an afterthought, he said, "MP has removed most of the tan under anaesthesia. Pretty badly burnt pilot they said on the telephone. We're to clean him up and get the rest of it off."

"Oh, for Christ's sake," I said, realising exactly what the next hour was going to entail.

Pulling off the remnant black crust caused the patient a lot of pain – that's why most of it had to be done under a general anaesthetic. In the salt bath the tweezer man had to peel away all the loose bits of skin and any Tannafax crusts the surgeon had missed, a process incurring the patient's wrath, since they were conscious now. They would complain in a cacophony of the most colourful language you are ever likely to hear, Shakespearian in its inventiveness. The hosing job was definitely the easier task; you just stood there, keeping your distance, like a gardener watering the lawn.

Our burnt airman had been 'tanned' in his previous hospital – that is to say another medical team had covered his burns in tannic acid. To be applying tannic acid in 1943 was just plain ignorant, because at the close of 1940 the Ministry of Health had told all civilian hospitals to stop using it.

At the war's onset, tannic acid jelly – or 'Tannafax' as its manufacturers called it – had been the standard burns treatment. It came in a tan coloured tube and you simply squeezed the gel straight onto the burn, whereupon it dried to form a protective 'coagulum' – a thick black crust, like dry lava from an old volcanic eruption.

For mild first degree burns, Tannafax worked quite well, but for the more serious airman's burns it had proved a disaster. The coagulum had a tendency to shrink as it dried and the unforgiving crust cut off the circulation in the fingers, causing them to 'necrose' – a medical word for tissue death – and leading to the useless spindle-shaped appendages like those on Richard Shaw's hands. In the worst cases, the airmen had lost their fingers altogether.

When used on faces, it caused the eyelids to stiffen, contract and even turn inside out. Not only was this a grizzly deformity, but the unprotected eyeballs became prone to corneal ulceration which could damage the sight permanently. Tannafax caused a hideous retraction of the lips too – exposing the teeth and making the patient look like a grinning Halloween monster. If that wasn't enough, the 'tanned' airmen nearly always developed infections; there was nothing worse than seeing and smelling the pus as it seeped out through cracks in the casing.

"Evil stuff," McIndoe – the Boss – would say, "made by the Devil himself, and anyone who still advises its continued use is a total bloody ignoramus."

In November 1940, the Boss had presented a photographic record of pilots treated with tannic acid to the Royal Society of Medicine. It had been more like a horror slide-show, the images of Richard Shaw's hands being among the worst. Soon afterwards, the Ministry of Health had issued their decree against its use, but despite this there had still been resistance in some quarters – eminent doctors included – men too proud and arrogant to take advice from an upstart New Zealand plastic surgeon. These were the same sort of men who, in antiquity, would have continued thinking the world flat, in the face of all the mathematics proving otherwise.

McIndoe's nemesis in this regard was a surgeon called Burges who worked at the Royal Masonic Hospital in London. Burges was one of the 'total bloody ignoramuses' to whom the Boss was referring in his condemnation, one of the dinosaurs. The burns subcommittee had forced Burges to abandon publishing a paper entitled *The Burnt Hand* in which he had criticised the Boss's photographic evidence, a climb-down leading to an angry exchange of correspondence between the two surgeons.

Burges' basic premise was that the hand contractures occurred at the moment of a 'flash burn' – medusa like – a result of the already gripped position of the pilot's hand around the joystick and other cockpit instruments.

I had seen some of the letters in the Boss's office, pinned onto the corkboard.

Intriguingly, he had placed Burges' letter directly next to an advert for 'Tannafax', the implication being that Burges was in the thrall of the drug company. The advert was a pictorial sequence promoting the treatment: the first image a severely blistered hand – 'burns on the hand and wrist', the second a painted hand – 'Tannafax applied – black coagulum formed' – and the third a normal hand – 'Coagulum removed – healthy new skin revealed.'

'This is complete nonsense' the Boss had written in reply to Burges' flash burn theory, *'...and he cannot have questioned any pilot who has had this experience. A petrol flame burn is not an instantaneous flash and the vast majority of pilots whom I have questioned most carefully have an extremely vivid memory, not only of what happened, but exactly what they did.'*

Burges' response had been to deny having treated any hands in his practice and that was when the Boss had got personal:

'... he claims he has never treated a single hand burn. There he is wrong, for in fact he did treat one and that with a rigid tannic casing. Later he quoted this patient's clinical history to me entirely wrongly, not knowing that I had him under my care at the time, and was aware of what had happened. The man's hands are among the worst of this whole doleful series.'

Tom and I suspected this last sentence was a reference to Richard, since he had been transferred to the Royal Masonic soon after being shot down.

Inevitably, the passage of time had proved the Boss, and his evidence, to be right. In July 1942 the Middle Eastern Forces at the 62 General Hospital in Tobruk had looked at a series of one hundred cases of bilateral limb burns in soldiers: one limb treated with tanning, the other with sulphonamide antibiotics and tulle-gras dressing. The contrast between the two had been so striking that tanning on the front line had ceased immediately.

Now, the first aid kits of RAF bomber crews were being stocked with 'Number 9 cream' - a thick antiseptic and not a coagulant. And the Americans were changing their stocks too.

The outer double doors of Ward Three burst open and two tired-looking porters wheeled the new admission into the bathroom.

"Bloody hell," Tom said under his breath, "that was quick, even for MP."

Sister Meally and MP followed on behind the porters.

MP was McIndoe's younger colleague. He had arrived from Australia the year before to further learn his trade under the master, and already he was the fastest operator in East Grinstead, the Boss included. The first time I had assisted him in theatre I could barely keep up. "Hold the retractor in this position," was all he had said, and when I hadn't done it to his satisfaction he had done it himself, setting my hands firmly in the position he wanted. I had once overheard one of the anaesthetists talking to a colleague about MP in the hospital mess: "Doesn't say much. Makes it look damn easy though." He was tall and imposing with a moustache that at first glance made you think he might be one of those raffish sorts. MP was anything but. As the anaesthetist had remarked, he was indeed a man of few words – everything was in his actions; Tom and I were in awe of what he could do with a scalpel in his hands.

Usually, the orderlies did the baths, but they were off with the flu. It had been the worst winter in living memory and half of the hospital staff was laid up at home with hot water bottles and hankies. Tom and I had been too bloody busy to catch flu – in the last fortnight, as well as our normal ward duties and assisting in theatre, we had carried out half a dozen 'baths'. It was a two man job, so when one of us was called to give an airman his post-operative bath, the other had to assist.

The salt bath was one of the Boss's great innovations in burns treatment – though it was fairly specialised stuff, with only three in the whole country. Made of white enamelled ebonite to prevent salt corrosion, the baths featured sophisticated electronics and plumbing which kept the temperature constant at 105 degrees and the salinity at two per cent. Due to the highly conductive properties of the saline, the baths also had to be earthed.

It was actually an old method, used with mustard gas victims in the Great War and then forgotten. But during the evacuation from Dunkirk in 1940, medics had observed that the burnt soldiers immersed in seawater suffered less infection than would otherwise have been expected.

In the same meeting he had damned tannic acid treatment, the Boss told the Royal Society about the good outcomes he was getting with warm saline baths. The technique had been backed by the RAF medical chiefs, and so here we were, Tom and I, about to subject another poor airman to the process. Easy enough for the big-wigs to give it the okay, as they smoked their cigars and sat around their big mahogany tables making their decrees. A different matter altogether to carry out the bathing yourself, in the middle of the night with the accompanying smells, sounds and expletives.

I had to force myself not to step back in revulsion when I saw the pilot. His face and hands were a mess, featuring large red raw patches, with a few flecks of black tannic crust in places.

"Clean him up," MP said to us as he pulled off his surgical cap and mask at the doorway. "There are some small bits that need to come off, but once they're wet it should be easy."

He ran his hand through his dark hair and looked at us in turn. You never quite knew what was going on in MP's mind – he was all business, never anything else. There had to be a human in there somewhere, but so far neither of us had seen it. The man seemed to be without emotion – when he was at work anyway.

We just nodded at him from behind our masks, knowing he didn't expect a reply. In fact, the instruction had been fairly verbose for MP and I think we were both slightly surprised by it.

"Look after them, Sister Meally," he said with the faintest trace of humour, as he turned and walked away.

To help make things go as smoothly as possible during the gruelling process, Tom and I had developed our own routine:

First we checked the patient's name on the accompanying notes, which MP had left on the side. This fellow was Josef Siska, a Czech pilot, brought in that evening from London. The Boss had picked him up on one of his 'rounds' of the country's major hospitals. We saw quite a few Czechs because of the RAF's all-Czech 311 bomber squadron.

As the sister and I carefully removed the airman's white gown, Tom lit a cigarette in anticipation of what was to come and held it in his free hand as he pulled his face mask back up.

As Siska was lowered into the bath, he groaned.

"Arrrgghh... *Kurva!*"

He looked at Sister Meally.

"Sorry to use bad language, nurse. Even if it is in Czech."

She gave a little forgiving nod of her head and stood back, not shocked in the slightest.

"I've heard a lot worse," she said, her eyes creasing into what might have been a smile under her mask.

"What would you prefer to be called?" I heard Tom say, "Flight Officer Siska or Josef?"

The Czech pilot looked up at Tom in mild surprise at this un-British lack of reserve.

It was a symptom of the egalitarian atmosphere the Boss had fostered in the hospital. Being a New Zealander it was something that came naturally to him – and he fought the system without fear.

First he had turned down the offer from the Air Ministry to accept a commission within the RAF, opting to remain a civilian surgeon. Then he had fought the old surgical guard on tannic acid use. Perhaps his biggest act of rebellion had been to go against the King's Regulations, and ban the wearing of the 'hospital blues' for non-commissioned ranks. This was the same uniform my father and Uncle Freddie had once worn during their convalescence from the Boer War; a blue suit, white shirt and red tie. My father had told me that the patients at Spike Island had called it the 'Hospital undress' and that it made him feel like a prisoner. In that era, all patients had apparently worn the hospital undress, but now officers could wear their service uniform, whereas others couldn't. The Boss hadn't liked that, so he had ordered the whole of East Grinstead's batch of blues to be burnt in the incinerator, and told all the men to wear their RAF uniforms if they wanted.

It was beyond doubt that the Boss cared about his patients. I had heard that at Sidcup, where Gillies had worked after the Great War, disfigured soldiers had been allocated special park benches, painted blue to warn the locals that they might see something shocking. In East Grinstead, the Boss had worked for integration rather than separation; the Whitehall complex in town included a cinema, dancehall and art deco restaurant – and the patients from Ward Three were warmly welcomed there by the manager and waitressing staff. Cinema seats were always held on reserve, there were standing invitations to the dances and you could always find a couple of recuperating pilots in the bar, sporting tubed pedicles and downing pints of ale. One time, as Tom and I were heading in for a drink, I overheard a man say to his wife: "Don't you bat an eyelid when you go in, not an eyelid." East Grinstead had become known as 'the town that didn't stare.'

All this striving for equality, and yet everyone still knew who 'the Boss' was; and that his word was law in this hospital.

"Call me Josef," the burnt pilot said.

While I held the tweezers, Tom leant forward and kept up the chatter.

"Right-ho, Josef. You've got the 'A team' tonight. My name is Dr Tom Shaw and the man with the tweezers is Dr Ed Hunston. We're here to clean you up a bit. He'll need to peel away some dead skin and it will hurt I'm afraid. Don't stand on ceremony… you can call him anything you want, but all we ask is that you don't grab the instrument. If you want him to stop, just say so and we can take a small break. Okay?"

Siska nodded.

"Smoke?" Tom said, not waiting for the answer and simply placing the cigarette between Siska's lips.

You didn't have to ask – everyone smoked – but the asking made them feel as though they were part of the process and not just an object.

Tom took it back after the pilot had taken two puffs.

"I'll mind it for you… stop it getting wet. Right then, Josef, I'm going to hose you down gently. Ready?"

Siska made another, grimmer nod.

Tom pointed the nozzle onto Siska's back and I watched on as the water hit and the pilot winced.

"Jesus Christ!"

He even made the sign of the cross as he said it.

Slowly, Tom worked his way up to the head, moving the hose from side to side, and then he held it directly over Siska's head so that he was thoroughly soaked. Siska was sitting up in the bath, around two thirds full now. He was holding his hands above the water like a magician about to perform a trick.

"Not too bad when you're used to it," Tom said.

"Warm. It's okay."

"All yours, Ed."

"Put your hands under the water, Josef," I said, addressing him for the first time. "Move them around a bit. Try and make fists. It will help them."

Slowly, Siska lowered his hands into the salt bath and sighed as he did so. It wasn't immediately obvious if it was a sigh of relief or pain. He started to make fists and then stretch out his hands.

"It hurts a lot," he said to me, his look full of four-letter words, even if his speech wasn't.

A few minutes later I told him to lift them out and I started in on the edges of the peeling skin while Tom continued the banter as a diversion to the pain. He was the friendly hose-man in this process. I was the silent punisher. It was the old Kynance/Gilligan interview routine.

"What hospital were you in when they painted on the tannic acid?"

Siska was staying very still as I tugged gently with the tweezers.

"You mean black paint?"

"Yes."

"Royal Masonic. An older doctor… tells me be still and take it like a man. I swear… call him 'man who fucks horses' – all in Czech – but he keep going. That's where Mr McIndoe finds me. He shouts at surgeon in front of all the staff – calls him idiot."

I glanced over at Tom.

"That'll be Burges," he said, meeting my eye. "The arrogant bastard."

His voice had a bitter edge – you had to remember Burges was the same man who had worsened the damage in his brother's hands back in 1940.

I kept working on Siska with the tweezers.

"A man who fucks horses," I said under my breath, with a smile.

Tom snorted and even Siska smiled through his pain.

"Can you imagine?" Tom said, a dreamy sound to his voice. "It sounds like a real heavy weight bout, doesn't it? I would've paid more to see that than Louis fight Schmeling… I can almost hear Burges whining about it later at his club: 'Some damn upstart Antipodean; telling *me* what to do? It's a *damn disgrace*!'"

We both laughed and I had to pull away with the forceps so as not to jab poor Siska.

It was easy to imagine the Boss laying into Burges. I had been on the receiving end of his rollickings a few times, for minor things mainly – a messy hand bandaging when I had first started, lax hand washing technique when scrubbing up once. By God, you soon learnt; you didn't make the same mistake twice with the Boss. Anyone but Burges would have avoided using Tannafax in the future.

I had finished cleaning up Siska's hands now. As red and raw as before, but at least clean and salted and ready for skin grafts if needed; the correct medical terminology was 'good granulation tissue'.

Now I had to move to the face.

"Get some more water on there, will you Tom," I said, pointing the tweezers at Siska's cheeks.

Tom started up the conversation again, helping Siska focus on something else as he gave him another soaking.

"You're from a bomb squadron aren't you, Josef? Is that what you were flying – a bomber?"

Siska nodded. "Wellington. We return from bombing run on U-boats at Wilhelmshaven docks. Take some flack… The plane catch fire and we ditch in North Sea."

Finally, Tom turned off the hose and hung it up. He placed the cigarette between Siska's lips again and the Czech pilot puffed away as I worked as fast as I could on the flaking dead skin over his cheeks.

Then Tom took the cigarette back and Siska continued his story.

"After two days in dinghy, English lifeboat find us."

I pulled away a small segment of Tannafax crust hidden in the hair line which had gone unseen by MP in the operation.

"*Korva!*"

"Sorry Josef," I said.

Siska looked at me.

"Pain make me remember Legion in Algeria. One time they bury us up to our necks as a punishment. Sunburn a lot like this."

"The French Foreign Legion?"

"Yes. When Germans invade Czechoslovakia March '39, I leave and join Legion. Then France enter war and I fly for French… I bomb Panzer divisions. But France fall and I escape to England. Join 311 Squadron…"

The talking was a good distraction for Siska and I managed to clean off the rest of the crud from his face without him really noticing. The granulation tissue on the face looked receptive for grafts too. After a few ops the scarring would be minimal. I was pleased for him because his eyelids had been preserved – he must have been wearing goggles when the fire had engulfed his cockpit, just like Richard Shaw.

The surgeons would decide on what operations they would need to do on the next morning's round.

Tom stubbed out the last of the cigarette into the kidney dish Sister Meally was holding. It had three cigarette butts inside as well as the dead skin flakes and tiny pieces of sopping tannic acid crust.

"You speak good English," I said to Siska, as I straightened up and put the forceps down onto the instrument tray.

He looked at Sister Meally when he answered and smiled at her.

"Two reason," he said. "English girlfriends and Frank Sinatra records."

Tom and I laughed at that one and so did Sister Meally; her blushing just visible above her mask. A naked man in the bath flirting with the prettiest ward sister in the hospital – Siska had some pluck.

"Right," Tom said, "you're almost done, Josef. Sink yourself right under there. It's good for the burns… helps stop infection."

We watched as he held his breath and submerged his head completely for several seconds.

"Better than North Sea," he said on re-surfacing.

We slowly helped him climb out of the bath, stood him in a pair of clean slippers and led him stark naked straight across the corridor to the dressing room. He lay on a sterile sheet as I dusted him with sulphonamides, blowing the antibiotic powder onto the burns with a straw. We covered him with tulle-gras dressings – an open mesh material impregnated with special antiseptic Vaseline. Porous saline packs went on top to keep everything moist. In the day, this would be sprinkled with warm water, while at night they were bound firmly with a crepe bandage and this is what we did now.

From there he was wheeled into the warm ward and given a bed.

"See you on the morning rounds, Josef," I said.

"Thank you."

He closed his eyes. Sister Meally stayed there, adjusting the linen sheets to her satisfaction. It was all linen on the ward – woollen blankets had been shown to harbour infection.

All the time she was speaking softly to the airman and the way she was doing it almost made me want to be in the bed instead of Siska.

When Tom and I left to go back to our digs, the shock of the cold air after the warm fug of Ward Three made me think again of the patient beds in the semi-tropical heat, and the fantasy of being whispered to by a pretty nurse before dropping off to sleep. Our room was freezing in February with ice crystals forming on the inside of the panes, and I wasn't particularly looking forward to getting back there. Unlike college, there was no cosy fire to keep warm by.

"Damn," Tom said, stopping when we were halfway along the outside corridor.

Hunching and shivering, I turned to him. "What is it now?"

"We haven't disinfected the bloody bath."

Full aseptic protocol was strictly enforced by the Boss and the bath had to be cleaned with 1:20 lysol after each patient.

"We? You were the hose man, remember? It's your job."

He sighed in defeat, knowing full well those were the rules.

"Just have a brew ready for when I get back, will you?"

I nodded wearily.

"Damn it," he said to himself, stomping his way back, pushing open the swish doors and disappearing into the entrance area of the ward.

I lingered there in the passageway for a few moments, my teeth still chattering but now choosing to embrace the cold night rather than resenting it. After what I had just seen and carried out, being tired from an on-call was not a problem at all.

I topped up the kettle, using water from the small sink in the corner, brought it to the boil on our primus stove and then re-filled the pot, which contained tea leaves from earlier that day. When Tom arrived back, I poured the weak brew through the strainer, added a dash of milk and handed him a mugful.

"Cheers" he said.

He kicked off his white clogs and sank down into the other chair in the room, positioned at the end of his bed. We had these battered old brown leather armchairs the Boss had bought at discount rates in a flea-market; much more comfortable than the wooden ones which had come with the room.

That sort of thing was typical of the Boss. Just as with his patients' welfare, no one could argue he didn't care for his house staff.

Tom took a sip of his tea and pulled a face at the taste. "Jesus! This is gnat's piss."

"At least it's *hot* gnat's piss," I said to him.

He sat back against the headrest and looked up at the ceiling.

"Hosing that pilot down tonight," he said, forgetting about the tea, "you know it cheered me up in a strange way."

"How's that?"

"Well… Even through all the shit and trauma he's suffered, he still made us laugh. And he's the one with half his face hanging off. It made me feel good about humanity in general."

I held up my mug.

"I'll drink to that."

Tom raised his too.

"And to Burges… the man who fucks horses," he said. "Whose wonderful out-of-date treatment had us dragged from our beds at this ungodly hour."

"To humanity and the man who fucks horses then…"

We drank the rest of our steaming tea in silence and a short while later fell asleep in our chairs, twitching from extreme fatigue and huddled under the scratchy woollen blankets which had been discarded from the ward.

Chapter Seven

Though the surgical registrars were only a notch more senior than us on the rung, from the way they behaved, you could be forgiven for thinking they were already seated at the right hand of the Almighty.

Boreman and Whitehead would do just about anything to get theatre time, so they could make another entry into their beloved surgical log books. All day long they would gently badger the seniors, angling for some 'knife time': "Want some help with that case, MP?" or "Happy to jump in if you need me, Boss…" and sometimes the Boss or MP let them do the easier operations, much to their sycophantic delight. They practically ran at the patients with their scalpels in hand, so eager were they to prove themselves.

The registrars were fond of ordering Tom and I around – that was the way the system worked and how I expected things to be. What grated was *the way* they did it, treating us like the 'untermensch' of the Nazi regimen, with that supercilious scorn designed to let you know just what they thought you were worth. Constant niggling put-downs, completely unwarranted and unnecessary, presumably said to make Tom and I feel worse about ourselves and the registrars a little better about themselves. Allowing us any tasks of consequence, such as helping them out in theatre, was a rare treat. Ambition was fine, but the registrars could just as easily have been ambitious without being arses the whole time.

Our academic credentials from Oxford bothered them a lot and the Boss liked to feed the flames – often remarking on what a good

University Tom and I had been to. The registrars would have to smile and nod because he was the Boss and controlled their destinies, not because they shared his opinion. On rounds, if there was a difficult case and no-one knew what to do, the Boss would sometimes turn to Tom and I with the ghost of a smile on his lips and say: "Maybe one of you Oxford men knows the answer?"

Seeing the registrars squirm would make our day.

Of course it was a complete myth we were cleverer than anyone else, but it was surprising how people acted towards you when they found out you had been to a certain University. When Tom and I were treated in this way I liked to picture Gilligan's reptilian face beaming with pride at his two young protégés forging their way in the world and being grossly over-estimated at the same time.

Boreman was already well on his way to becoming a top knife man, and that was fine with me. I even admired his skill. He was tall and thin with close cropped curly dark hair and wore metal tips on the heels of his brogue shoes which made him sound like a horse when he walked down the hospital corridors. You heard him coming before you saw him. It was a ridiculous sound which smacked of conceited snobbery and for this Tom and I called him 'Trot on'. Of the two registrars, Boreman was the one who treated us most like inferior beings and the one who thought himself extremely witty whilst doing so.

On a round together once, he had said to me: "Pass the Guessing tubes."

"Guessing tubes?" I had said with a blank look, thinking it must be an obscure piece of surgical apparatus developed by a man called 'Guessing' in the last century.

But then he had pointed at my stethoscope and shouted: "The guessing tubes, you moron!"

Burning with embarrassment I had thought to myself: *Who the hell calls them guessing tubes?* Surgeons who don't know what they are hearing, that's who.

Another time, we had been scrubbing in together to help the Boss in a particularly complicated operation for which two assistants were needed. In the middle of washing his hands Boreman had said: "You know what, Hunston? I think you'll make a good country general practitioner. I can really see you doing that. Nice and easy. Not too taxing. But necessary." He had said it with what appeared to be a genuine enough smile, but I knew it wasn't a compliment. He viewed anyone who wasn't a surgeon with complete condescension; it hadn't been a smile at all – it had been a sneer.

Whitehead was equally tall, but plump and with straight dark hair. He dressed more shabbily than Boreman and his personal care was more slip shod too – in the mornings he always had a shaving cut with a tiny piece of tissue paper stuck to his chin. On the outside he was friendlier than his colleague –more garrulous and confiding, but on the inside he was just as competitive as Boreman, maybe more so. At least Boreman didn't hide his naked ambition. Whitehead allowed you a false sense of security; he was your best pal, laughing and joking with you when it suited him, while at other times he would brush you aside like dirt. There were occasions when he would walk right past you and not even acknowledge your presence. I didn't trust him at all.

He was always trying to explain the reasons for being a surgeon, as opposed to being a physician: "Are you a doer, or a thinker?" he would say, grinning inanely at his genius-like analysis of the two specialisms.

Whitehead panicked in tricky situations. Near the beginning of my time, I had assisted him in an operation – a relatively simple procedure which the Boss had allowed him to do unsupervised. Whitehead had nicked an artery by mistake and jets of blood had sprayed from the tiny incision. His friendly persona had vanished in seconds as he fought to stem the bleeder, but not before slicing through my glove with his wayward scalpel. He hadn't been sorry either, just amused: "You've turned pale, Hunston," he said, his swagger back. "Don't be such a fusspot." I hadn't complained, so I'm not sure why he felt the need to call me 'fusspot'. I managed to laugh it off while at the same time hoping never to operate with 'Wildman' Whitehead again, in case the next time he amputated my whole bloody finger.

He was the clog thief too – the careless lout who stuffed his fat feet into whatever pair happened to be lying around in the changing room. Interestingly, he never wore the Boss's clogs or MP's, so perhaps he wasn't quite *that* careless. Just like the boys I had known in school, Whitehead knew exactly what he was doing. He was like an animal marking his territory, reminding the lesser members of the pack – 'his juniors' – of the true pecking order.

So these were our two registrars whom Tom and I, in addition to their individual nicknames of 'Trot on' and 'Wildman', collectively called 'the Bastards'. Not quite 'fucking fuckers', but not far off.

When we walked onto the ward at eight o'clock on the morning after Siska's bath, Boreman and Whitehead were already there, looking well rested and smug.

The Boss and MP followed us in, the two of them deep in conversation. Also in attendance was Sister Meally, looking as bright and cheery as ever, despite having been up most of the night. She was arranging all the patient notes in the trolley, making sure everything was in order for the round.

Tom nudged me.

Freya Nielsen, the photographer, had just walked into the ward, camera in hand and light meter slung around her neck. She was there to take 'before' and 'after' shots of the patients – partly for McIndoe's surgical papers, but also because he knew the surgery on these pilots was a part of history, and keeping a photographic series was going to be just as important for future battle historians as it was for future surgeons. Nielsen was compiling a visual record of the unit's reconstructive surgery and was regarded as an integral member of the team. She was a Danish bombshell – a tall and curvy blonde. What she was doing here in East Grinstead was anyone's guess – she could have been in Hollywood if she had wanted to be, on her looks alone. Tom thought she looked like Lana Turner, I thought Rita Hayworth. We had argued about it for hours in our digs.

The first time I had seen her, she had been walking down the covered walkway and I had briefly met her eye. I had almost gone up to her and prodded her to check she was real. I wanted to say: "You're so beautiful. How can you be here in this mundane place?" That feeling had never really changed in the months I had worked in East Grinstead. The way she walked, talked, moved her head, smiled, breathed even. All of it was hypnotic. The woman was a goddess. Just being around her would nullify all the fatigue from the interminable on-calls. Most nights I would dream about Nielsen – strange dreams where we would be on a ward round together and she would suddenly start dancing with me in time to the gramophone record playing in the background, with the patients and the doctors all clapping in time. Sometimes I would be speaking fluent Danish with her and have no clue what I was saying. Tom dreamt about her too – I knew that because we would compare notes and try to decide which one of us she liked more from our subconscious dream scenarios.

She must have known Tom and I were hopelessly infatuated with her. It was fairly obvious that every man in the building felt the same way, but she seemed immune to the adoring looks, the close attention and the flirtatious chat, and acted as if she had no idea of the effect she had on the men around her.

Nielsen wasn't stuck-up or stand-offish, the way very attractive women sometimes are; she treated everyone with the same degree of friendly attention. That was the problem. For those precious moments when her focus was on you, you felt like the luckiest man on the planet, but then she would be somewhere else, and some other lucky blighter would be basking in the light – the laugh, the fluttering of the eyelids, the hand on the arm. Miss Freya Nielsen was a walking, talking bloody heartbreaker.

Tom had been swatting up on photography so he might come under her searchlight gaze for more than ten seconds at a time.

"Is... is... that a Leica camera, Miss Nielsen?" he said as she came over to join our group at the centre of the ward. MP and the Boss were still in their hushed huddle to one side and we were all waiting for the round to begin.

Poor Tom was flushed and stuttering with nervousness and was moving in a jerky way. She did that to you. You literally seized up in her presence, like the tin man in the Wizard of Oz without his oil can.

Nielsen glanced down at her camera, then looked at Tom and smiled.

"Why, yes it is, Doctor Shaw – a series three. My father gave it to me a few years ago on my twenty-first birthday."

I could almost hear his great clanking machine of a brain doing the simple maths: twenty-three at the most, roughly the same age as us.

Boreman leant forward and smiled obsequiously.

"Ah… the same make as Robert Capa's."

She turned to him.

"Oh, Mr Boreman… you're familiar with Capa's work?"

Having passed his surgical fellowship exams, Boreman was a 'Mister' as opposed to a 'Doctor'.

Tom continued to smile grimly and then hung his head.

"Of course," Boreman said, stepping in front of Tom. "Who can forget his photograph of the falling soldier in the Spanish Civil War?"

Her eyes widened in admiration.

"Oh yes, it's iconic… hard to get out of your head."

Can't you see he's a fraud? I was thinking. *You're really falling for that? Wake up for Christ's sake, Nielsen!*

I caught Tom's eye for a millisecond and you could have written a whole book about that look. Even though I adored her just as much as he did, I felt really sorry for Tom in that moment. At least my friend was being honest with his feelings – I am sure she knew he didn't have the first clue about cameras, but she would have seen he had tried to make a connection. However awkward, he was genuine in his adoration. In comparison, Boreman was a smooth fake, but he was the one who was on a roll now:

"They should have used the image on the cover of Hemingway's *For Whom The Bell Tolls*, don't you think?"

"Oh, you like Hemingway too?" Nielsen said, her interest deepening.

Helplessly, Tom and I watched as Boreman and Nielsen chatted amiably about which Ernest Hemingway novel was their favourite, fluttering around one another like a pair of courting butterflies.

I made a mental note to read some Hemingway.

I had to say something to put a stop to this.

"Fake," I said.

That stopped them both in their tracks; in fact my comment had derailed Boreman completely.

Nielsen frowned.

"What's fake?" she said.

I wanted to say Boreman was.

"The Capa photograph. I think it's a fake… a set-up. I mean, it looks too good, too perfect to have been really caught in the moment."

For a few seconds she considered my view seriously.

"You think?"

I had succeeded. Her attention was off Boreman. *Trot on, you bastard.* But otherwise it wasn't going well – I had obviously upset her by alleging her pet photographer might have staged his most famous work. For the first time I saw a flicker of consternation in Nielsen's eyes. My outburst was backfiring.

"That's just me," I said, trying to dig myself out of it. "I tend to see the worst in people, glass half empty and all that."

I smiled but she didn't smile back.

"How about you, Tom?" I said, passing the baton to him.

Nielsen willingly looked to Tom to cheer her up and, to his credit, he had read the situation well. He didn't fluff his lines.

"I'm more a glass half full man," he said. "I like to think it was a genuine piece of photojournalism."

He was being true to himself by saying that, because he always wanted to assume the best in people, not the worst. It's exactly what he had told Gilligan in his interview when his neck had been on the line. I had set him up nicely. He bloody owed me for that.

Nielsen moved closer to Tom with an intimacy that crackled around the ward like static.

"Me too," I heard her say quietly, looking at my friend with a new-found respect.

The bugger, I thought. Tom probably had no idea what the photograph even looked like. But better him winning her heart than Boreman.

Just then MP and the Boss appeared at the edge of our group.

"Right," the Boss said, looking at Tom and me, "why don't we start with the man you two bathed last night. MP's just been filling me in on the op."

We all trooped over to Siska's bed. One of the nurses had timed her changing of his bandages to coincide with the round and his wounds were on display. They looked clean.

MP approached the bed, nodded at Siska and bent down to take a closer look. He didn't say anything, just straightened back up after a few moments and nodded to the Boss, a look which was presumably saying it was good for grafting.

The burnt area was healthy, with rapidly in-growing skin edges and fresh-looking granulations.

"Bacteriology?"

It wasn't really a question. The Boss was asking if someone had remembered to check.

"Swabbed him in theatre last night," MP said.

The results would take a few days to come through, but if there were no streptococci, then Siska's wounds could be skin grafted.

"Excellent," the Boss said.

He made eye contact with the pilot.

"You okay?"

"Your boys did good job last night," Siska said, "but I feel sore."

"Yes… well, you've certainly had your bark knocked off. But we're pleased with things. If your swabs are negative, we'll begin grafting in a few days. Any that don't take, we'll do again. You're going to need several operations, and it may take a few months until the grafts have fully healed, but we'll get you looking something like the way you were before."

Siska managed a smile.

The Boss smiled back at him and then turned around.

"A shot if you please, Miss Nielsen."

He needn't have asked – she had already checked her light meter and was looking through her viewfinder. A few clicks followed.

"Done," she said.

The Boss looked at me.

"Afebrile?"

I checked the chart.

"No fever."

"Good."

The Boss seemed to be almost cavalier in the way he went about his rounds – listening to the precise, scientific details and then coming out with loose one liners of encouragement.

He looked over at Siska again and said, "It's all good."

Then he moved onto the next patient with us all trailing behind, like small boats in a ship's wake.

Things moved fast with the Boss and MP – the work they got through was prodigious, partly because small talk was kept to a minimum.

The healing was set in motion in the operating theatre, but out here in the muggy paraffin burner warmth of Ward Three, it was nature and luck that determined the final outcome. Infections could start at any time and ruin a graft within hours. It was like a game of snakes and ladders – before you knew it, the wounds would be breaking down and the surgeons would be in theatre again, cursing under their breaths and re-grafting. Siska's fate was in the laps of the gods and we – the house staff – could only steer things in the right direction.

Boreman and Whitehead gave the histories on the round, presenting updates at the level of complexity the Boss needed. The simple things – temperatures, blood pressures and pulses – were left to Tom and I to confirm, if asked. Our rounds reminded me of a Shakespeare play at the Globe; the patients were the actors on the stage, Tom and I were the peasants standing in the pit, out in the open in the rain, while the surgeons occupied the upper balconies.

I watched as Nielsen took more pictures. I'm not quite sure where she fitted into my Globe scenario; perhaps an angel floating over the stage in a dream sequence of the play, held up by ropes and pulleys.

This morning I had lost a bit of ground to my friend in our tug of war over her affections. Funny, I had envisaged our whole future together – the children, a house in the mountains somewhere – her taking photos of it all, showering me with wanton looks, holding my hand all the time and throwing her head back and laughing at everything I said, as if I was the most engaging and wittiest man in the world. It wasn't so bad knowing she might end up being Tom's girl, but I still felt a painful ache in my heart at the thought of my hopes being dashed. If she did choose Tom, I would just have to live with it.

"What do you think, Hunston?" the Boss was saying.

I threw off my cloak of daydreams and flushed. I had no idea what he was talking about.

"Beg your pardon, sir?"

He was sitting on the bed of a patient with claw hands, a lot like Richard Shaw's. The pilot had bandaging around his face. His sisters, who visited most days, would feed him grapes through the mouth-hole in the wrappings. The Boss took off his horn-rimmed spectacles and started to clean the lenses.

"This chap" he said, breathing onto a lens and rubbing it with his tie, "... he was a decent cricketer before the war; you think he'll be playing sport again?"

The question was a loaded one. The Boss's confidence filtered into his patients – and in the months I had been here, I was sure that half the cure was in the way his attitude rubbed off on them. Once, he had said to Tom and me, "If you boys remember one thing about medicine, remember what Galen said nearly two thousand years ago: 'Confidence and hope do more than physic'."

"He's going to play again," I said with conviction. "Perhaps not quite as well as before, but he'll certainly play."

"There you go," the Boss said to the patient. "You'll be hitting like Bradman in a year or so."

He pointed up at me. "Dr Hunston here should know. He studied at Oxford. He's one of the clever ones."

Boreman and Whitehead laughed loudly along with the Boss, hating me hugely. It was good to see them trying their hardest to be magnanimous.

Best of all was the fact that Nielsen was smiling at me now, obviously pleased I had taken a leaf out of Tom's book and was seeing things in a 'glass half-full' kind of way. There was still hope for our mountain-top retreat and the future I had planned.

Such was the daily round; the Boss being up-beat, MP being silent, the Bastards being...well, bastards, and Nielsen making you believe she was in and out of love with you at least once an hour. In the small games Tom and I were playing for her affection, it had been a draw this morning. Who stood at the top of the league table was anyone's guess.

Chapter Eight

South Downs, Sussex
May 1943

"Ed, you've got the bloody map – are we nearly there yet?"

Tom had begun to flag. Every minute or so he was complaining and now had stopped to rest again, hands on knees, his face shining with sweat.

"Hang on a moment and let me check."

I pulled the map from my pocket and unfolded it.

"I didn't know it would be this hard," he was saying.

"Well, Treyford Hill is a hill, Tom…"

The day was a warm one and I was sweating too, but it wasn't just because of the weather – it was because I wasn't exactly sure where we were.

It had been a long time since I had walked this path – not since my childhood on one of my father's interminable treks. We would go for miles at a time, him feeding me dried apricots whenever he saw me flagging, and if I was flagging badly, chunks of chocolate.

I didn't have any treats for Tom, just my tin drinking canteen filled with water. There was a bit of history to that canteen – you could tell it was army issue because of the rope webbing wound around the rim. An Australian veteran from the Boer War had given it to my father on New Year's Day 1901. He in turn had been given it by a Swede who had fought on the side of the Boers and been a POW. I liked this about certain objects, how they could be imbued with quirky stories and provenance, almost like people.

Tom yanked the Boer canteen from my rucksack, uncorked it and took a long swig while I scoured the route with a sense of unease.

As well as old objects, I had inherited my poor map-reading skills from my father; he was totally inept at anything requiring a sense of direction. He used to tell a story of how he had got his medical team lost in the trench system before the Battle of Messines and nearly missed the start. But then he would add: "I did find my way right across the Western Australian desert once, alone for most of it, and on a bicycle… but then again, all I had to do was follow the telegraph poles."

Tom handed the water can to his brother, who gripped it awkwardly but managed to take several large mouthfuls before Tom interrupted him.

"Hey," Tom said in consternation, "don't drink all of it…"

Richard handed it over to me sheepishly.

"Sorry Ed, there's not much left."

"It's alright, Richard."

It was a fair punishment for my having got us lost.

I drank the dregs and put it back into my rucksack.

"Selfish pig," Tom said to his brother.

Half-playfully, half-seriously, he punched Richard on the arm, who returned the favour with enough force to start them arguing.

"I didn't hit you *that* hard."

"What? I barely touched you."

Tom was rubbing his shoulder. "That bloody hurt, Richard."

"How can these damaged mitts hurt anyone?"

While the brothers argued, I checked the map again and then looked to the west. *They must be around here somewhere,* I told myself.

For nearly two hours we had been trudging the path and there was still no sign of our destination. We were on the South Downs, the grassy chalk ridge which rose up from the coastal plain and ran parallel to the coast of Hampshire and Sussex for eighty miles or so.

Our goal was an ancient row of Bronze Age tumuli known locally as 'The Devil's Jumps'.

Richard had shot down a Junkers 88 right above them early on the morning of 13th August 1940, the very same day he was downed himself.

He had confessed to Tom and I that he needed to see the place, not out of some bizarre desire to gloat at his old kill, but to find some kind of resolution; the phrase he had used was 'make the circle complete'. Richard had admitted to suffering recurrent nightmares about that day; ironically, not about his own downing into the Channel and the burns, but his earlier action with the Junkers. He had come to the conclusion that shooting down the German bomber had in some way jinxed him, because now it was haunting him in his dreams.

In the nightmare he was sitting on one of the tumuli and the dead German pilot was sitting on another, nearby, watching him and smoking, and shaking his head sorrowfully. Finally, the German would stub out the cigarette on the sole of his boot and shout over accusingly:

"Ich war glücklich sie wissen, und sie ruiniert..."

The pilot's face would redden with anger and then turn into a skull, still in uniform.

When we asked what the words meant, Richard had looked full of dread.

"I had to look it up because my German is minimal. It means: I was happy you know, and you spoilt it..."

The excursion had been planned for two weeks – Tom and I had persuaded the Boss to give us the time off after Saturday morning rounds, and he had agreed, provided we were back in time to be on-call for the night shift.

We had met Richard at Chichester station at noon and taken the branch line out to Cocking, a small village nestling on the lee side of the Downs. From there we had walked up onto the ridge, aiming for the jumps five miles to the west.

Richard had been allowed a day's leave from his air-base on the condition that he too, was back by nightfall. Although his injuries meant he couldn't return to his old fighter squadron, he had been granted permission to join a non-combat squadron, which by chance was based at Tangmere, the same airfield from which he had flown with the 601 three years before. When asked what type of flying it was, Richard had tapped the side of his nose and said, "Special duties," without elaborating further.

Once we were done, the aim was to drop down into the village of Harting, catch a bus back to Chichester and then get the train back to East Grinstead. Richard would be able to get back to RAF Tangmere easily enough, since it was just east of Chichester.

"They should be around here somewhere," I said, pointing at the map, which bore the markings of five small hills in a line with the word 'tumuli' typed next to them. In a strange touch of synchronicity, I noted the mapmakers had printed the word in a gothic type-script.

"We need to keep walking west," I said, trying to sound authoritative. "Just another five minutes. Agreed?"

Tom looked doubtfully in the direction I had indicated, and then back at me.

"Do we have any choice?"

"Not really."

Richard was looking over my shoulder at the map.

"Hang on a minute, that pint mug sign means a pub. That's not far…"

"Yes, Richard, but it's in the wrong direction to Harting. We would have to go down the hill and then walk back up again afterwards."

"But there's beer there," he said, looking at me as if I was an idiot.

"Yes, there's beer there," Tom said in agreement.

I folded the map back up.

"All right – we'll go there after we've found the crash site. Agreed?"

They both nodded.

I pointed west.

"That forest is Phyllis Wood," I said. "The jumps are in there somewhere."

We started off again along the track towards the wood, the three of us in a line, one behind the other.

I listened to their chatter.

"What was the weather like," Tom said to his brother, "the morning you shot the Junkers down?"

"Low cloud base and raining," Richard said. "Luftwaffe command thought it would be clear, but the high pressure from the Azores had dispersed and it was overcast that morning. It did eventually clear though – by the time I was shot down in the early afternoon it was a fine day."

"And radar picked up the approaching bombers?"

"It did. Just after six that morning – a formation coming in over the coast between Hastings and Bognor. Minutes later, I was leading 'A' flight – heading east towards the enemy. And it was then I saw the formation of Ju-88s on our port side."

We all continued to walk on in silence for a few moments.

"Port is left Tom," Richard said.

"I knew that!"

Richard laughed before continuing, "So I ordered my flight to attack. And as I made my run, I spotted Bf110s at a higher altitude. They started diving."

Tom put up his hand like a schoolboy.

"Bf110s?"

"Messerschmitts."

"Oh, I see. That's not good."

"Not good at all. At the right moment I executed a climbing right turn into them so that I was almost head on…"

As Richard was saying this, he was moving his hands to demonstrate the turns he had made in the dogfight. I had seen the hands before of course, in the pub when we had first met, but out here in the broad daylight, it struck me again just how malformed they were. In my mind I had the brutal contrast between the Hurricane's sleek lines, and then these sorry excuses for anatomy – the end result of his eventual crash. With anatomical form, just as in aeronautic design, there was supposed to be an elegant evolutionary efficiency. In medical school they had talked all about the beauty of the pentadactyl limb and the dexterity of the human hand. But there was nothing efficient or beautiful or dexterous about Richard's anymore – they were just ugly scarified appendages, sinister looking, like those of an old witch.

"… I fire at one and see part of its roof and fuselage break away."

Richard was back in the battle now, talking in the present tense, leaning and moving his shoulders and holding out his hand on an invisible joystick.

"Then I swing around in a tight turn and I see a Ju88 below and dive after it. I fire a five second burst…datatatatatatatatatatatatatatatatatat!"

It sounded like an awfully long time, Richard's five seconds of yelling 'datatat'.

"And then it bursts into flames."

Richard stopped telling his tale. Instead, he looked up at the sky and then drew a line in the air with his hand, retracing the descent of the mortally wounded Junkers bomber.

"It went down and exploded over there," he said, looking over at the forest.

He started to walk in that direction again.

Once in the trees, the sunlight disappeared, and with it went the light-hearted atmosphere of the open downland. The shadows seemed to take hold of our mood, as if the reason we had come out here had suddenly hit home.

From somewhere in the forest, a lone woodpecker made a hollow 'rat-tat-tat' noise against one of the trees.

Otherwise it was eerily quiet.

"Let's fan out," Richard said, stepping away in one direction.

Next to me, I saw Tom screw up his eyes as he searched the depths of the twilight wood, a frown of concern etched on his brow.

"So where are these Devil's Jumps? I can't see anything… Here, give me that map, will you, Ed?"

I passed it over to him and walked off to the north.

Forty yards further on, the first burial mound appeared out of the gloom, grassy and silent.

"Over here," I said loudly.

The others ran over and together we mounted the barrow, only a few steps up the slope to the top. The area was clear of trees and now the rest of the Bronze Age bell barrows – five in all, if you included the one we were standing on – came into view, lining up North West to South East. Each was about ten feet high and spaced apart by a dozen yards or so. It was said that on midsummer's eve, the barrows lined up perfectly with the sunset.

It was Tom who spoke first.

"Why are they called the Devil's jumps?"

"Thor used to sit on this hill to rest," I said.

He looked at me in doubt.

"Thor? What's he got to do with the Devil?"

"I don't know, but that's how the folktale goes… One day the Devil came along and started to jump from one hump to the other for fun, making such a racket that Thor got cross and told him to go away. Then the Devil taunted Thor, saying he was too old to do the jumping himself, so Thor threw a huge stone which hit the Devil in the midriff while he was midair. The Devil yelled out in pain and ran away, and never came back again. That's it."

I also knew that, in the last century, archaeologists had discovered old bones in two of the barrows, the bones of God only knew who – people who had died between three and four thousand years ago.

Despite the warm day, I shivered.

Tom was staring at me.

"How do you know all this?"

"I grew up around here."

The reason I knew was because of my father, who would research all the places we went walking and save up the stories for when I became tired. When he started talking about ghosts, Thor, the Devil and other strange legends, the miles would begin to go by unnoticed, and I would be so enthralled that the end of the walk would suddenly appear out of nowhere.

"Didn't your father ever tell you scary bed-time stories?" I said.

Tom shook his head.

"No. I just fought with Richard."

"I saw these barrows from my Hurricane," Richard said, his tone sober. "His bomber came down and exploded right by here. Before that happened, some of the crew bailed out with parachutes."

"It shouldn't be too hard to find some debris then" Tom said. "Let's spread out again and keep looking."

Together they started back down the side of the barrow and disappeared off into the surrounding trees.

I hung back.

Already it felt like a cemetery and we hadn't even found the crash site.

Ghosts were in this place, the ghost of the German pilot and those of the ancient people in the burial mounds. I wouldn't want to be around here after dark. We were just interlopers, allowed to roam in the daylight undisturbed, but not at night. I could feel it, the way you instinctively speak in low tones in a church, even when it's empty.

I picked my way through the undergrowth, searching for pieces of plane. The Devil's Jumps seemed to be watching me as I walked in the neighbouring wood. I remembered how my father used to scare the living daylights out of me with his stories about the Devil. That the places were really there in the landscape only made the stories seem more real; the Devil's Dyke, the Devil's Ditch, the Devil's Punchbowl… you could visit them all.

Not far away, I knew there were a set of similar burial mounds on another hilltop – the Devil's Humps – supposedly containing the bones of Viking chieftains defeated in a battle with the local Saxons. According to legend, if you ran around them seven times on Midsummer's Eve, the Devil would appear and offer you a bowl of soup. "You must never drink it, or else the Devil owns your soul," my father had told me one December day as we had sat on one of the humps looking out at the view. I was five years old and that story had given me nightmares in the long winter months that followed.

And it wasn't just Thor who battled with the Devil. There was the one about St Dunstan forging horse-shoes in his smithy at Mayfield in East Sussex, and how the Devil came to him disguised as a beautiful woman, making advances and edging ever closer. Aware of who the temptress really was, Dunstan kept working quietly at the forge, ignoring her. Then when she was within reach, he snatched tongs from the fire and clamped them around her nose, not letting go. The Devil turned into a hideous monster, continuing to change shape into something more and more frightening. Still, Dunstan held on. At last, defeated, the Devil turned into his own form and Dunstan released him.

The Devil flew off to Tunbridge Wells to cool his nose in the waters there, and they say that is why the waters have had a reddish colour and an odd taste ever since.

I remembered lying in my bed, wide-eyed with fear and not sleepy at all, with my father standing at the doorway and leaving me with a rhyme from Charles Dickens's *A Christmas Carol*:

'St Dunstan, as the story goes,
Once pull'd the Devil by the nose
With red hot tongs, which made him roar,
That he was heard three miles or more.'

You didn't eat blackberries after October 10th because that night the Devil supposedly pissed on all the bushes and eating berries after this date was bad luck. My father said the date was actually 29th September, because the English calendar had been adjusted by eleven days in 1752. September 29th, he explained, was Michaelmas day, a feast celebrating the archangel Michael throwing the Devil out of heaven. An actual date seemed to give the folklore some veracity, and in our family we never ate them after Michaelmas day. "Why tempt fate?" my father would say.

For a medic, my father was quite a superstitious man, I think partly because of what he had seen at Passchendaele in 1917; grey ghosts keeping a silent vigil over dying soldiers in a graveyard within the battlefield.

Soon, we started to come across bits and pieces of silvery aluminium and other debris, strewn across the forest floor. Our calls rang out around the trees: "I've found something," and, "Here's another piece."

Richard told us the Junkers carried bombs weighing 250kg – and that these had exploded during the crash, which was why there was nothing left much bigger than a fist.

I found a metallic rotor and asked Richard what it was.

"Oil gear" he said.

He told us to leave everything where it lay, because it would be bad luck to take souvenirs, though I knew for a fact that the boys from the local village would have scavenged anything worth taking long ago. Then we found a large scar in the dirt where the main impact must have been. The fuselage had been taken away, and leaves and twigs were starting to fill in the impact crater. We stood around it awkwardly for a few moments.

I caught Richard's eye.

"How many baled out?"

"Three. I saw their parachutes."

"And how many altogether in a Junkers 88?"

"Four."

"Maybe he made it; maybe you just didn't see his parachute."

He shook his head.

"No, he must be dead – why else would he be haunting me?"

Tom knelt down and fingered some old ash from the pit.

"I don't think we'll ever find him. Chances are, the impact and the fire would have been so intense that no traces will ever be found…"

"Let's just get to that pub," Richard said, turning and marching away.

"What's the matter with him?" I said to Tom, under my breath.

He looked over to his retreating brother, wounded and crippled and burdened down with nightmares.

"I don't think he's found the redemption he was looking for."

"It's a bit early to say that… we've only just found the place. What was he expecting? The dead pilot to materialise out of the ground and forgive him?"

Tom shrugged his shoulders.

"Maybe he was."

We emerged from the trees onto a path, our collective mood subdued, despite having found what we had come for.

Richard had left the forest ahead us, and fifty yards on had stopped to look at something on the path's eastern verge, dropping to one knee and peering intently at whatever it was.

As Tom and I caught him up, we looked down to see what he had hit upon.

It wasn't another piece of the aeroplane; it was a small memorial – a wooden cross, two feet high with a bronze plaque attached:

IN MEMORIAM
HAUPTMANN
SEBASTIAN FUHRMANN
PILOT KG54 STAB-1
1915 - 1940

"German Luftwaffe Pilot," Richard said, stating the obvious.

There was a single bluebell at the base of the cross, freshly picked from the hundreds growing all around and deliberately placed there.

Tom knelt down and joined his brother in studying the inscription.

"What does Hauptmann mean?"

"Captain."

Tom pointed at the strange letters and numbers.

"What about all this stuff?"

"KG54," Richard said. "It's the name of his unit. He was in the Kampfgeschwader 54 bomber unit. Stab 1 is short for Stabschwarm 1, which means Staff flight 1. The KG bomber unit is sometimes known as the 'Totenkopf'."

I crouched down to join the brothers.

"Totenkopf?"

"Death's head," Richard said. "They have a skull and crossbones painted onto the side of their aircraft; near the cockpit. I was so close I could see it when I shot him down."

Tom turned to his brother.

"Maybe that explains why he turns into a skull in your dream."

Richard didn't answer; he just kept staring.

"Twenty five years old," he said eventually. "The same age I am now."

Tom touched the flower gently.

"I must say… the locals are respectful."

Richard was frowning now, not listening to his brother's efforts to keep him from becoming too morose.

"This is the man I shot down," he said. "There were a few Junkers shot down that day. They were all attacking RAF Farnborough. It was Adler Tag after all…"

When Richard saw that Tom and I were none the wiser, he explained.

"Eagle day," he said. "The first day of the Battle of Britain. Like I told you before, 601 squadron was busy that morning. Junkers 88s came down all around here – Isle of Wight, Arundel, you name it. The sky was one big criss-cross pattern of vapour trails and smoke."

Richard put his hand on the cross and bowed his head.

Tom patted my shoulder and, without making a sound, we got up and left him there alone.

Half an hour later we were all at the pub.

We had walked down off the hill into a hollow at the bottom of the valley – the map had the place labelled as Hooksway.

People were sitting outside at pub tables in the sun and immediately Tom said to me in a wary and defeated tone, "You're never going to bloody guess who's here."

I spotted them just after he had said it, and my heart sank.

There, on the far table was Boreman, with Freya Nielsen.

"What the hell are they doing here?" Tom said in jealous frustration. "And more to the point, what is she doing with him? Is she completely mad?"

Of course we had to join them and pretend to be civil, and to pass the time with inane chit chat: "What a nice surprise,"… "How nice to see you both,"… "What fine weather," etcetera etcetera.

It turned out Boreman had driven her out here in his new Morgan sports car.

"Freya asked me to take her for a spin," he said. "Wanted to see how fast my new toy is…"

Tom glumly drank from his pint, seemingly resigned to the fact that he would never be winning Nielsen's heart.

Richard knew Boreman from his days as a patient at East Grinstead.

"So, Doc," he said in a friendly manner, not reading the wary looks on my and his brother's faces, "what brings you both out to this part of the world?"

"It was Freya's idea actually," Boreman said, smiling like a cat who had got the cream. "She said she wanted to see the Bronze Age Earthworks up on the hill. How could I refuse? *Ha ha ha!*"

"How indeed," Richard said, smiling at Nielsen.

"Sorry, I've forgotten my manners. Freya, This is Richard Shaw, Tom's brother. Richard, may I introduce Miss Freya Nielsen."

"You're a pilot?" she said, touching her cheek in sympathy at Richard's scarred face.

"Yes."

Tom looked at me over the top of his pint.

Freya, he was saying with his eyes, *Boreman is calling her by her first name.*

Luckily for us, if the body language was anything to go by, Tom and I still stood a chance. She was sitting at a distance from her date and seemed much more interested in what Richard had to say.

"They're called the Devil's Jumps," Richard said, "We've just been up there ourselves. Ed here told us the old legend about the Devil and Thor…"

As he proceeded to tell the tale to a rapt Nielsen, Boreman tried to look interested, but I could tell he was sour that the RAF hero had gained her full attention. He sipped from his pint with a care and precision that I found particularly annoying, but I was savouring his constipated expression – that of playing second fiddle to Richard Shaw.

"You'll never guess what else we found up there," Boreman said, trying to take back the floor. "A Kraut grave. Some pilot shot down in 1940…"

"Is that so?" Richard said, turning to look at Tom and I. "We didn't see anything, did we, lads?"

We read his look, glanced at one another and shook our heads. He obviously wanted to keep it a secret between us.

Boreman put his hand on Nielsen's shoulder, an action which caused Tom to visibly shudder.

"Freya even left a flower there," he said. "She's got a kinder heart than me, I'm afraid. As far as I'm concerned the bastard deserved it."

His ungracious remark was met with an unexpected silence from everyone at the table.

Finally, Richard spoke and, coming from someone with ruined hands and a half ruined face, the words seemed to come straight from the oracle.

"I think the dead should be allowed to rest in peace," he said. "Before the war I imagine the pilot was a happy man. Someone ruined that for him. And now his happiness has gone forever. I think what Miss Nielsen did was a fine gesture."

Tom and I knew he was referring to his dream, almost quoting the German pilot verbatim. Maybe his sentiment was another small step on his road to redemption.

Spontaneously, Nielsen reached across the table and touched one of Richard's claw hands tenderly.

"Thank you," she said. "That's very perceptive of you. It's nice to know that someone appreciates what that pilot lost."

A few seconds went by as they stared at one another, reducing the rest of us to mere bystanders.

Seeing the silent exchange made my heart sink. It made Tom almost fall off the bench and it made Boreman get to his feet quickly.

"Well gents, I've got to be getting this lovely young lady back home. I would offer you a ride, but I'm afraid it's only a two seater."

Nielsen smiled sadly at us all and stood up, looking as though she was sorry to be leaving.

"It's no problem whatsoever," Richard said. "We've got some more beers to drink here anyway. It was nice seeing you again, Doc and very nice to meet you too, Miss Nielsen. Perhaps we'll meet again."

"I hope so, Richard," she said. "Goodbye."

She kissed his cheek and then came over and kissed Tom and me too, though only out of politeness, I felt. Nevertheless, Tom flushed scarlet and was rendered speechless.

The kiss made me feel guilty for judging her on our arrival, when I had seen her with Boreman. Maybe she really was one of those pure open-hearted kind souls who just loved everyone.

We watched as Boreman smarmily opened the passenger door for her and then strolled round to the driver's side.

"Trot on, you bastard," Tom said under his breath, smiling and waving at the same time.

Soon, the powerful car engine sprang into life and Boreman screeched away with one arm waving out of the window.

"We are literally eating his dust," Tom said.

"Your brother and I have both been in love with her since we first arrived at East Grinstead," I said, explaining to Richard.

"I could see that," Richard said, grinning. "And so am I now. What does she do there?"

"Photographer."

"She wasn't there when I was a patient. It was some old cow who smelt of onions. I wish to hell she had been though…"

"Oh God," Tom said, moaning. "If you're throwing your hat into the ring, I'll never stand a chance… Ed and Boreman are enough competition already."

This made Richard roar with laughter.

"I'm getting this round," he said, "so you can drown your sorrows."

When Richard had gone, I looked towards the still settling dust cloud left by Boreman's new car.

"What the hell is she doing with him?" I said out loud.

It didn't make sense to me. The body language had been way off.

"Christ," Tom said. "With a car like that, *I'd* even consider going out with the bastard."

This time it was my turn to bellow with laughter, and despite his being unlucky in love, Tom forced himself to join me.

Chapter Nine

Queen Victoria Hospital, East Grinstead
9th July 1943

It was raining when I woke up.

There was a muffled pitter patter sound on the thin, felt roof of our digs; comforting or irritating, depending on your mood, and this morning it was really bothering me.

Despite being on-call, the phone had been quiet, but even so, I had woken early and couldn't get back to sleep. It might have been the rain, or it might have been the strange absence of the phone ringing, combined with the fearful knowledge that it could go off at any time.

I shaved at the sink as quietly as possible while Tom slept on.

By the time I was finished, there was still another hour to go before the round, so I wandered over to the hospital mess in the main building, keeping to the middle of the walkway so as not to get wet.

MP was in one corner of the mess, sitting on his own and drinking coffee.

I carried my plate of toast over to his table and hovered there expectantly.

He briefly made eye contact and waved his hand in the vague direction of the spare chair.

"You're up," he said.

I pulled out the chair and sat down.

"The rain woke me."

He nodded as if the same thing had happened to him but didn't say anything else.

I could have asked, but thought it best not to crowd MP with too much conversation. Instead I took a bite of toast and looked out of the window.

Two little boys were playing out there in the rain. Their makeshift playground was an iron handrail – painted white – on the sloped concrete entrance to the mess. They were getting soaking wet, but didn't seem to be minding that at all. The larger boy couldn't have been more than four years old, the smaller perhaps only two.

The older one was trying to teach the other how to grip onto the rail and move along it while hanging by the arms, by lifting one hand over the other. The little one didn't have the strength; after letting go, he would jump up again, hold on for a second and drop back down. To help, the older boy crouched down and held him up by the waist so he could do it.

"Little monkeys," I said.

MP was watching them too.

He looked at me momentarily before turning his attention to them again. I suddenly realised they must be his sons and that he was in the mess child-minding.

I had never seen the boys before.

MP lived out of the hospital grounds somewhere in town and it hadn't ever occurred to me he might have a family.

With his brother's help, the small one had managed to complete his traverse of the bar and was now running around in celebration – the happiest boy in the entire world, all because he had held onto the rail the whole way, like his big brother. Then he slipped over in the rain and grazed his knee. A thin trickle of blood ran down his shin and became a smear as the rain joined in with the flow on his skin.

He looked down and there was a short delay before he started to cry.

When he did start to wail, the oldest looked over to us in the mess, then ran up to the window and knocked on it.

Slowly, MP stood up, went over to the exit and pushed open the door.

I saw him go over to the crying toddler and crouch down low to examine the bleeding knee.

While this was happening the older boy stood next to MP watching on, his small hand resting on the surgeon's back.

MP pulled a roll of gauze from his pocket and started wrapping it around the knee.

Spellbound now, the boy had stopped crying.

I heard the older one say, "He's like a mummy from Egypt," a comment prompting the small boy to try and repeat his brother's words:

"Mummy from Eejip," he said, eyes wide in fascination.

For the briefest of moments, MP laughed and then started singing a song. It was a song about body parts – I suppose quite apt for a surgeon – and as he sang he poked each part of the boy with his index finger:

'Head of bubba,
Neck of bubba,
Chest of bubba,
Arm of bubba,
Dada will eat the bubba up, and have him all for breakfast!'

The small one squealed in delight as MP scooped him up and pretended to eat him.

Once the song was over, MP bundled the boys into the back of his car – a battered old Austin parked nearby.

Just before he got into the car he turned to me and waved.

I waved back and watched him drive off.

Alone in the mess now, with just the rain pouring down on the car park and the hand-rail wet and abandoned, the scene I had just witnessed seemed like ancient history. To have seen MP's human side was a rare privilege; he had only said two words to me: "You're up," – but afterwards I had been allowed to share in an intensely personal moment.

All the other sentences he had ever said to me had been strictly clinical in nature: either commands in an operation, or sentences dictated on rounds for me to transcribe into the patient notes. His saying, "You're up," and then his song and the wave over at me, made me feel like his closest friend.

I checked my watch – there was still half an hour until rounds began so I left the mess and trailed aimlessly through the corridors. The main brick building of the Queen Victoria Hospital was really quite small; just two hospital wings branching off a central apex. A few weeks before Tom and I had arrived there, the word 'cottage' had been removed from the name, the institution no longer considered a backwater. Thanks to the Boss it had become a centre of excellence for burns care.

Behind the main entrance was a round tower – some fifty feet high – with a tapering green copper roof, topped with a twenty foot high rod of Asclepius, a snake winding around a staff, the ubiquitous symbol of healing and medicine.

The tower had a winding staircase, and I stood near the foot of the stairs looking out of the large bay windows to the lawns at the rear. The rain was coming down in sheets now, battering the windows, but I could also make out another tapping sound, metallic in nature and distinct from the softer noise of the rain. It was coming from above me, somewhere high up in the tower.

There was a rhythm to it and, my curiosity aroused, I started climbing the stairs to investigate.

"Hello?" I said, half-way up.

No answer, just the incessant, insistent tapping.

I called out again, louder this time: "Hello?"

As I neared the top of the stairs, the sound stopped.

I looked out of the window from the top of the spiral staircase. There wasn't much to see – the rain was blotting out the view and the skies were low and grey. The tapping started up again.

"You can see all the way to the South Downs on a good day," a voice said, from behind me.

I turned round to see a narrow door, slightly ajar, and beyond that, in a tiny office, the agreeable form of Freya Nielsen sitting at a table.

"Hello, Dr Hunston."

I took a few steps forward. She was holding a coin in one hand and her camera in the other.

"Miss Nielsen – what are you doing up here?"

She smiled easily.

"I'm trying to fix the silly shutter mechanism on my Leica. It's been sticking."

Then she held up the coin so I could see the King's head.

"But I don't think a shilling is so good for the job. All I seem to have done is scratch the steel casing."

"Oh… right. That explains it. I heard the tapping from downstairs."

Hunching over the camera, she tapped it loudly with the coin two more times and then held it up.

"Right" she said, pointing it at me. "Cross your fingers."

I heard a satisfying click of the shutter release button.

"Ah" she said. "It's working again. You've brought me luck."

"That's good to hear."

She was so relaxed sitting there, so informal and friendly. I had never been alone with her before. I wanted to run away with her right then and there and start our lives in our mountain cabin. She was tilting her head and looking at me quizzically.

Like an idiot I waited politely on the landing.

'Run away with me Freya' was the message I was trying to telepathically transmit as I stared back at her.

"Come and have a look at my cubbyhole" she said, putting down the camera and the coin and breaking into another smile. She stood up and motioned for me to step inside.

The room was built into the side of the tower, and its outer wall was curved. No bigger than a broom cupboard really, the only furniture a small desk and chair. On the desk was her Leica camera, along with a pile of photographic portraits of wounded patients. A pair of old binoculars rested on the stack.

She picked them up.

"I like to look out at the view with these – it's amazing what you can see from here on a good day."

It occurred to me that she had already talked about the view. I wondered if she was perhaps a little nervous that I was up there, alone with her; nervous in a good way, because she liked me.

"I'll bet."

A battered looking attaché brief case was on the floor.

"Going somewhere?"

She followed the direction of my gaze.

"Oh," she said, flushing. "No. I'm not going anywhere. That just holds my equipment – flashbulbs, films, light meter, spare camera…"

She put down the binoculars and stepped forward a little way.

It felt quite intimate, being in this small space with her – our bodies were practically touching.

"My dark room is in another part of the hospital. This is where I sort out the photographs and keep my gear. I like to keep the door open or it gets claustrophobic."

"It's certainly very cosy. I never knew you had an office here."

"Not many people do. It's my haven of peace and quiet, a place where I can sit and think without being bothered."

I took a step back.

"If I've disturbed you, Miss Nielsen, I'm very sorry…"

She smiled.

"No, no… I didn't mean it like that. You must call me Freya." She winked at me. "In the tower you can call me Freya."

"Just like Boreman," I said, without thinking.

She shook her head and laughed.

"There's nothing between us. In fact, since the day you saw us, we haven't been out again."

This was great news.

"Oh! In that case, call me Ed."

She flushed slightly and touched my arm.

"All right, Ed – for the tower alone."

Then she took off her jacket and threw it onto the case on the ground. My heartbeat quickened. It was hard not to notice her figure – the way she was holding herself made her chest strain against the tight blouse she was wearing. I may have been completely misreading things, but it was as if she was making a conscious effort to make me notice. She was edging herself even nearer to me. And I could have sworn she was pouting slightly. The sexual signals I was receiving were unmistakable and yet I still doubted them because she had never shown any real interest in me before.

I looked away; convinced I must be wrong. It seemed too good to be true.

There was a large photograph on the wall of the room, of a spiral ramp within some kind of building. The bricks on the floor were unusual, much narrower than modern English bricks.

She noticed what I was looking at.

"It's the inside of the Rundetaarn – the round tower… my favourite building back in Copenhagen… my favourite place in the whole world. The walkway spirals around seven times, all the way from the base to the top. Sometimes they race bicycles up and down it. Someone even drove a car up it once. There's an old observatory at the top."

She moved over to the picture.

"Two thirds of the way up is a bench set into a recess in the wall. It's called the 'kysseboenken' – the kissing bench – I used to go there before the war…" Her sentence trailed off. "When I was younger," she said quietly.

"Well, he was a very lucky chap."

She seemed to take my compliment seriously because she didn't smile.

I was thinking I might have overstepped the mark when she moved closer to me again.

My head was spinning. Maybe I hadn't eaten enough toast for breakfast.

"You could be lucky," she said straight out.

I had to repeat her words in my head to double check it was indeed what she had said.

YOU COULD BE LUCKY.

"Me? I um… I ahhh… I had no idea, Freya. No idea at all."

"I try not to show my real feelings… how do you English say? On my sleeve."

She put both her palms on my chest when she said this and a bolt of electricity surged through my body, as though she was a live wire.

"Do you like me, Ed?"

"Of course I like you."

"Then perhaps you should do something about it."

She didn't need to ask twice. I curled my arm around her waist, pulling her close until she bumped up against me and we kissed.

This was unbelievable. The part of me that retreated into the inner recesses of my mind when things were tough had also gone there now. So it could also happen when things were too good and not just very bad. 'Unbelievable,' I was saying in that room in my head. I had come out of my on-call room for a stroll and was now in a tower kissing Freya Nielsen, just like in a fairy tale.

Tom would turn green with envy when I told him about this. I almost felt sorry for him, but not so sorry I wasn't going to take my chance.

She tilted her head back gently from our clinch and smiled. Close up, she had some freckles on her nose. The warmth of her breath on my face felt even more intimate than the kiss itself.

"Will you take me to the cinema this afternoon? There's a Veronica Lake film I want to see."

"Yes," I said, transfixed and disorientated. "I'm sure I can ask someone to cover for me."

Tom could step in, I thought.

From somewhere I heard a church bell ring.

"That's eight o'clock," she said.

I had never resented a ward round more than right now.

"Damn," I said, pulling away and going out onto the landing.

"I'd better get over there, or Boreman and Whitehead will have my guts for garters."

I started down and she watched me from the top of the stairwell, elbows leaning on the bannister. Already, it felt as though she was my girlfriend.

"Guts for garters?"

"I'll explain later."

She smiled.

"I'll see you in the cinema café at five o'clock," she said.

"Five! It's a date."

"Not so loud, Ed," I heard her call down. "I don't want the whole hospital to know."

Boreman, Whitehead and Tom were waiting for me on the ward; in fact they were already onto the first patient.

On Friday mornings, the registrars took the round themselves. It was MP's morning off – ironic he'd ended up in the hospital anyway, even if it was to just sit in the mess and watch his boys play. The Boss used the time to trawl other hospitals around the country for burns cases to take on. It was the one day in the week our two immediate seniors had us to themselves, without any of the fatherly protection the Boss or MP afforded us. Freya only had to attend when the Boss was doing rounds. Ah, she was Freya now. As I had sprinted to Ward Three, I was imagining how our mountain hut would be laid out after we were married. How it would have all her camera things set out on tables and her picture of the Round Tower in Copenhagen on the wall, to remind her of home. I would need to install our own special kissing bench, where we could kiss one another all day long. I wondered what might have happened if the eight o'clock bell hadn't disturbed us.

I joined the others at Siska's bed, out of breath from the run over, my mind a myriad of feelings – exhilaration from what had just happened, but also unease at being late.

Sure enough, it hadn't gone unnoticed.

"Nice of you to join us," Boreman said, before I had the chance to say anything.

"I'm very sorry."

There was no point in giving some elaborate excuse. It didn't matter to them why I was late.

I was trying not to look too happy. I wanted to dance and sing a song, but instead made sure I kept a solemn face to match my apology.

"He's sorry," Boreman said to Whitehead. "That's nice."

Whitehead didn't say anything.

I noticed he had cut himself shaving again. It was fairly evident my tardiness was of no consequence to him.

Boreman, on the other hand, wasn't going to let this one go.

"Bring us up to date on Flight Officer Siska, if it's not too much trouble, Hunston."

Since being admitted in February Siska had undergone four operations, three for an acromio-thoracic tubed pedicle to repair his face, and the latest on his hands, to free up contractures caused by scarring. Tom had dealt with Siska the day before and was holding the notes.

"I'll need to check the notes. It's been a while since I've seen him."

"I'm happy to do it," Tom said, covering for me, "I'm more familiar with the case."

Boreman snapped at Tom, "Is your name Hunston?"

Everyone was taken aback by his aggression. Even Siska in the bed looked surprised.

"No," Tom said.

Boreman turned to me.

"Is *your* name Hunston?"

I nodded at him sullenly.

"I'm sorry," he said. "I didn't quite hear that."

"YES IT IS," I said, getting fed up with his childishness and saying it louder than was necessary.

Boreman just couldn't let it go.

He took a pair of forceps from his white coat pocket and held them up. They were L shaped at the ends – a little like feet sticking out at the end of a pair of legs – two serrated jaws to grasp pieces of crusted tannic acid stuck to dead tissue. Angling the point of the forceps allowed a clearer view whilst doing so. There were all sorts of instruments used here – 'McIndoe's breast knives', 'Waston grafting knives', 'the Padgett dermatome', which the Boss had modified and improved. The surgeons were like old sailors naming islands and countries after themselves as they explored the world.

The name of this particular pair of forceps had slipped my mind.

"You did the original de-sloughing on this patient didn't you?"

"You mean in the salt bath? When he first arrived?"

Boreman just stood there not answering my question.

"Yes I did," I said, answering it for him.

"And what did you use to de-slough Flight Officer Siska's wounds?"

"Forceps," I said. "Like those."

Boreman rolled his eyes.

"Yes, I know that… but what kind of forceps?"

Tom leant towards me and tried to whisper something.

"Did I ask you?" Boreman said to Tom.

"No."

"Then don't try and help him…"

Boreman turned his attention back to me.

"So? What type of forceps did you use?"

"I don't know the name."

At this, Boreman looked at Whitehead as if seeking out someone to validate his incredulity. To his credit, Whitehead just shrugged his shoulders. It didn't really have much to do with his progression up the ladder and therefore he wasn't that interested in using humiliation tactics on me to get ahead. Not today anyway.

"You've been here for nearly a year and you do not know…"

He shook his head.

"These are Russell Davies de-sloughing forceps, you cretin."

I blanched.

Five minutes before I had been deliriously happy and now I felt like dirt.

My embarrassment quickly turned to anger and my hands clenched into fists.

Don't do it, my conventional self was saying, but for the moment no-one was listening. I had reached breaking point with Boreman.

When I spoke I didn't recognise my voice because it was husky with rage.

"Say that again, if you dare," I said, stepping forward into Boreman's personal space. I was so close I could smell his breath: stale coffee and marmalade.

He hadn't said it again yet, but it was obvious he wasn't going to back down either. I prepared myself for God knew what… Fisticuffs on Ward Three? Surely not?

"Whoah there," Whitehead said, stepping in between us.

I had never seen Whitehead move so fast. He was facing away from me and pushing his colleague back gently. A red faced Boreman was trying to push forward to get at me, but Whitehead's corpulent bulk was weighty enough to hold him in place.

"I knew you were a coward," I said, laughing at him. "I thought just as much."

That really drove Boreman mad. He struggled and wrestled with Whitehead, but couldn't get around him. He was almost screaming now.

"What did you say to me?"

"Coward," I said again. "I'm right here…"

Tom yanked me away.

"Ed," he said in a harsh voice, "don't do this. You'll regret it. He's not worth it."

I tried to escape his grip.

"He needs a smack in the head," I said with a snarl.

Then Tom roughly pushed me out of the ward and into the foyer, shoving me up against the wall.

"Listen, Ed," he said, wide eyed and fraught. "We'll get out of this place. But let's do it right. I'd love to give Boreman a bloody nose, but you decking the idiot in the middle of the ward would not be the right way."

My ire was abating fast now.

"You mean it?" I said. "We'll go?"

"Yes. We can't work with these two anymore, can we? The time has come to move on. We'll go… I promise. We'll resign today. Just don't ruin it all by hitting him. What references will we get then? We won't be able to work anywhere."

My next words popped out without any thought. I just had to tell him.

"She kissed me this morning, Tom…"

He pulled a face at my sudden change in topic.

"Who did?"

"Who do you think?"

"What? You mean Freya Nielsen?"

I nodded.

His shoulders sagged. "Bastard," he said, smiling and shaking his head. "You fucking bastard."

"I'm sorry, Tom. It just happened. I didn't expect it at all."

He looked at me and gripped both my shoulders hard.

"Christ Almighty, man… What do you take me for? I'm your best friend. Massively envious for sure… but I'm still pleased for you."

"We kissed, Tom, we bloody well kissed, for about ten seconds."

He released his grip and scratched his head.

"You don't have to go on about it. I'm not that bloody happy…"

Then he started laughing.

"By God, you move fast, don't you? All this happened this morning?"

"It was literally out of nowhere. I bumped into her and things just spiralled…"

Whitehead came out of the ward.

"Hey, you two… are we going to do this round or not?"

Tom looked over at Whitehead.

"He's calmed down?"

Whitehead nodded.

"I've spoken to him. This can all be sorted out later. But not now. We've got a job to do."

"Fair enough," Tom said.

He looked at me.

I nodded and we both followed Whitehead back into the ward.

Boreman was waiting, quiet now. Not trying to attack me anymore.

Perhaps Whitehead had given him a similar speech to the one Tom had just given me – about not throwing away your career prospects with one stupid act.

Neither Boreman nor I spoke during the round.

We stood on either side of Whitehead and Tom, as far apart from one another as possible. The other two conducted the round – doing all the talking; Whitehead made the decisions and Tom gave the updates and took down notes.

Boreman and I were reduced to spectators, like two errant schoolboys.

The wounded pilots, who had seen the whole episode from their hospital beds, acted as though nothing had happened. There were a few stern looks from the nurses – the small melodrama had certainly woken them up – but the patients just kept reading their novels, eating from their bunches of grapes, and writing letters home.

I suppose that on their list of problems, our little spat didn't rank very highly:

1. My face and hands have been burnt off;
2. Most of my friends from the squadron are dead;
3. I'm in constant pain;
4. If this graft gets infected I'll have to have another operation;
5. Will I ever play cricket again?
6. Will a woman ever want to look at me again?

'The idiot doctors looking after me are fighting like children,' was way, way down the list.

I felt embarrassed when I caught their eye. They listened to what Whitehead had to say and answered his questions politely. They let the nurses do their dressings. Underneath, the granulation tissue and grafts were slowly improving. Ever so slowly healing.

Chapter Ten

I never went to the film and I never met Freya, because at half past four the Boss summoned me to his office 'stat' – medical slang for immediately. He sounded more blunt than usual over the phone and I didn't dare tell him I had made other plans.

When I put the receiver down I knew that it meant the end of my date before it had even begun.

"Dammit!"

Tom was lying on his bed looking up at the ceiling with his hands crossed behind his head.

For most of the afternoon we had been debating what we were going to do, where we would go. Joining the Royal Army Medical Corps seemed the most realistic option. My father had served with them in the Boer War, and he had been in the NZ Medical Corps in the Great War, so for me there was a family tradition to uphold – that might swing things in our favour if we went ahead and applied.

"What is it?" Tom said, not really empathising with my distress.

"The Boss is hauling me in."

"You must have expected that."

"Yes, but not now... I'm going to miss Freya at the cinema."

I looked at my watch and groaned.

"What the hell was I thinking this morning?"

"You mean when you kissed her?"

"No, you fool! In picking a fight with Boreman."

Tom thought about this for a few moments. He yawned and scratched at his chest.

"You weren't thinking… that's the whole problem. Sticks and stones will break my bones, but words will never hurt me…"

"You're not helping, Tom."

I looked at my watch again, even more agitated this time.

"Shit!"

Tom still didn't look too concerned.

I couldn't blame him really. He was a bit raw from what had happened between Freya and me; his romantic hopes finally dashed. It would take a while for him to get used to it, despite what he had said earlier. If things had been the other way around, I'm sure I would have felt the same way.

"Tom," I said, hesitantly, "do you want to…"

I stopped mid-sentence, seeing where my thoughts were headed.

He sprang up off the bed.

"What? Go in your stead?"

"No… No… It's a stupid idea. You don't need to be doing that. I'll just call the cinema. She'll be waiting in the balcony café; someone from the box office can go and tell her."

But as I picked up the telephone, Tom was already throwing off his surgical greens and picking up smarter clothes.

"Don't worry," he said, energised all of a sudden, "I'll go."

I put down the receiver and watched him hop into a pair of trousers. Then he put a shirt on, and over that an overcoat – my overcoat, I noticed. It was Dunhill tweed and a lot smarter than his. He was dressing to impress.

I was worried now, wondering if I would be demoted in Freya's eyes and Tom would take on the role of beau which I had just been forced to abdicate. Maybe it would be him canoodling with her on the kissing bench in Copenhagen's Round Tower after the war, and not me, and all because I had squared up to Boreman like a macho idiot instead of keeping my damn mouth shut.

"I don't know if this is such a good idea."

Tom laughed.

He was combing his hair in front of the small mirror above the sink, having wet it under the tap first – one of his so-called 'Italian showers'.

"Don't worry," he said. "I won't be muscling in – I'll just keep her company… promise. Christ, Ed – What kind of friend do you take me for?"

Of course, really, I wasn't worried about Tom. That morning's meeting with Freya had felt so special I hardly dared think about it. It felt like the real thing, not that I would know.

Smiling at my own insecurities, I held my hands up and went over to where he was standing.

"You're a good friend, Tom."

He patted my shoulder. "Yeah, yeah, you too," he said. "A really good pal."

The sarcasm made me laugh.

He bent down to put his shoes on. "Are you going to tell the Boss?" he said as he tied his laces.

"About what?"

"What we've been discussing all afternoon… our future."

"Oh, I see. You want me to tell him now?"

"Might as well."

"So, it's the RAMC then? That's agreed?"

He nodded. "We'll sign up next week."

Shoes tied, he stood up. "Hey… is my tie straight?"

"Yes."

"Wish me luck then," he said with a large grin.

"Hey… Luck with what? Hey, come back here, you bastard!"

But he was already out of the door and all I could hear was his laughter sounding under the covered walkway. It was still raining; the perfect weather for a trip to the cinema, the perfect weather to cuddle up with a beautiful woman in the back row and not watch the movie at all.

As I walked over to the main building, I pictured her waiting for me. There was an art deco style café there on the first floor with a circular balcony and a view down into the foyer. You could sit at a table right by the rail and see who was coming in through the front doors.

She would be there, looking like a goddess, with all the men in the café wondering which lucky young hot shot was going to be joining her.

Boreman was sitting outside the Boss's office in the corridor, and I had the feeling we had both been summoned by the headmaster.

I slowed my pace, not knowing what to say.

He stood up.

"He wants to see you," Boreman said in a way that was without malice but also without any friendliness.

"Yes I know."

"Listen, Hunston…"

I tried to ignore him and was about to knock on the door when I stopped myself and turned around.

"Yes?"

"I'm sorry I was an arse this morning."

I still hadn't forgiven him.

"What got into you?" I said.

"I was just tired and hungry…"

He held out his hand in peace offering.

Boreman was being way too nice. The Boss must have ordered him to apologise. It was a flimsy excuse and he didn't look like he really meant it but I thought it would be churlish not to accept his offer, so I briefly shook his hand.

"I don't like being called a cretin," I said.

"Yes, yes, I realise that."

I pulled back my hand.

"I'm sorry I called you a coward… you're not."

He absorbed this without emotion.

I forced a smile. "Well, I suppose I'll never forget they're called Russell Davies de-sloughing forceps."

He smiled back.

"No, I expect not."

I was feeling awkward now, because this was by far the longest conversation I had ever conducted with Boreman of a personal nature. There was a lot of that going on that day, what with MP in the mess earlier, and the encounter with Freya and then the afternoon's soul searching with Tom.

"You're right, you know," I said.

"Oh?"

"About my being better off as a country GP than a surgeon. You've probably worked out by now that I'm not much of a surgeon. Tom and I are leaving."

Boreman looked at me with mild surprise, and in that moment, I glimpsed a side to him that was human and open, without his spiky coat of protection to keep him from being hurt. Up until now I felt he hadn't been sincere in his apology, but the atmosphere had suddenly changed.

"All right," he said, understanding quickly. "I wish you luck."

We shook hands for a second time.

"Thanks… you too."

I noticed he was looking over my shoulder.

The Boss was at his open doorway watching us. How long he had been there I don't know.

"Ah," he said, "you two have made up. That's good."

He stepped to one side.

"Come in, Hunston."

"Yes, sir."

Without looking back at Boreman, I went into the office.

The Boss followed me in, closed the door behind him, and went over to his desk.

"Sit," he said, pointing to the chair opposite. It was made of black leather and was very comfortable.

I sat awkwardly and glanced at the books on the shelves – all surgical tomes: 'Treatise on otolaryngology', 'Maxillo-facial reconstruction' and the like. There was a framed photograph propped up with the inscription: 'Guinea Pig club' – a small gathering of the first pilots who had received burns treatment under the Boss, seven men outside Ward Three, all smiling at the camera. Richard Shaw was there wearing a chequered shirt; open at the collar, like an American. His hands were in bandages I could see his tubed pedicle coming out from his nose and disappearing under his shirt towards his upper chest, like a flying buttress made of skin. The Boss was in the picture too, smoking a cigarette and grinning – an honorary member, no doubt. Any surgeon who installed a piano and a barrel of beer on the ward was going to be popular with his patients, that was for sure. The club was a tight unit – with their own annual dinners and smart burgundy ties, complete with winged guinea pig motifs. When I turned back to look over at the Boss I saw he was wearing one.

"He apologised?"

I nodded.

"Good," he said. "I heard from Whitehead he laid into you for no real reason. I told him if he didn't say sorry he could look for a new job."

While part of me was pleased Whitehead had fought my corner, another part of me thought what a bastard he was for shopping in his own colleague. I would find it hard to deal with if Tom had done that to me. In my book loyalty was friendship. Evidently Boreman and Whitehead shared neither.

"I appreciate that, sir. We've patched it up. I'm sorry it happened on the ward, in front of all the patients and the nursing staff."

"All right," he said to me, his features neutral. "All water under the bridge…"

Nervously I cleared my throat.

"Shaw and I have decided to leave, sir."

He looked at me from over the rim of his spectacles.

"Had enough?"

"Of Whitehead and Boreman, I'm afraid so sir. They're good surgeons, don't get me wrong, but I just feel I don't fit in here. I'm not sure I want to be a surgeon after all. Neither is Shaw. He said I could speak for him."

"Did he indeed? You're as thick as thieves, you two."

"Been together since the beginning, sir."

He gave a single nod.

"Yes, well… I suppose I had fair warning from Sir Harold's letter of introduction. Being a strong team was what got you two the jobs in the first place."

I glanced at the clock on his wall. Five past five. Tom would be just arriving.

"So what will you both do?"

"Well sir, we're thinking about joining the RAMC – get ourselves a bit nearer to the fighting."

The Boss sat back in his chair and stared at me, serious now, much sterner looking than when I had first arrived.

He removed his glasses and put them on the desk.

"Your father was in the RAMC, wasn't he?"

"That's right sir, once upon a time. How do you know that?"

"I hear things," he said.

He waited for me to go on.

"I only know the basics," I said. "Back in 1900 he was in South Africa. Unfortunately he caught typhoid fever and had to come back."

The Boss looked thoughtful.

"I also heard he served in the NZMC in the Great War. That's where I'm from originally. How come he was with the New Zealanders?"

"Well sir, after the Boer War, he went out to work on the Western Australian goldfields. From there he went to New Zealand… I'm not sure why exactly, although I do know he had a good friend there who had also been in Australia with him, a Wesleyan Minister. Later on, during the Great War, they both joined up, my father as a medic, the minister as a Padre."

"Your father was on the front," the Boss said – a statement and not a question.

"Yes… at Messines and at Passchendaele. He doesn't talk about it all that much."

"Did you know your old man won a Military Cross for his actions at the battle of Bellevue Spur?"

"No, sir, I never knew that."

"Yes, well, I suppose it's not the sort of thing he would want to talk about, not when you know what happened at Bellevue Spur."

I was stunned the Boss knew so much.

"May I ask how you know all of this, sir?"

"One of my old professors at Dunedin was his commanding officer… a surgeon by the name of McKenzie. I saw him recently at a conference. Must be in his seventies, but still working hard. We got chatting and when I told him I had a Hunston on my staff, he immediately recognised the name, said it was one he could never forget. It didn't take long for us to work out you were his son. A doctor son of a doctor father – it's not an uncommon thing. McKenzie knew your father had stayed in England after the war."

"So what happened at Bellevue Spur, sir? For my father to win a medal, I mean…"

"All Kiwis know the date," he said. "The twelfth of October 1917… the blackest day in our history. In just a few waves of attack, over eight hundred New Zealanders were mown down by German machine gun fire. That night, McKenzie ordered your father out into no-man's land to give dying soldiers morphine – because all they could hear were their screams of agony. With a bagful of morphine injections, your father went out into the mud and didn't return. For nearly a year, McKenzie thought your father dead. It turns out he was in an asylum here in England. Something on the spur that night caused him to lose the power of speech. The British had picked him up at Passchendaele and sent him back to England with other shell-shocked soldiers. His medal had been awarded posthumously until he finally started talking again and McKenzie discovered where he was. McKenzie said he never found out what had happened that night on the spur… what your father had seen to take away his voice for a year."

Ghosts, I thought. *He saw ghosts.* But I didn't say anything to the boss. That was strictly private.

I looked at the clock again – a quarter past five. I wondered if they had gone in to watch the film yet.

Just then an air raid siren sounded and, a moment later, an aeroplane flew low over the hospital grounds, speeding towards the town.

The plane was German, with black and white crosses emblazoned on the underside of its wings and on the rear of the fuselage.

What I saw next was hard to process; dark objects leaving the undercarriage, and following curved trajectories towards the ground.

Seconds went by, and then a sound like distant cracks of thunder rattled the windows – a succession of them, almost simultaneous. Over the centre of East Grinstead, a large black cloud was expanding into the grey rainy skies.

The Boss was on his feet and at the window.

He turned to me with a frown and I shook my head at him with the same look – one of disbelief.

We watched on helpless as the plane came back around. A stream of tracer bullets lit up the sky as the pilot strafed the area below with his machine guns.

"Jesus Christ," he said in a whisper. "That's right around the High Street by the looks of it."

It hadn't occurred to me to consider where the bombs might have landed, and if Tom and Freya had been hurt. But now it did. The Whitehall cinema was on the High Street.

"Tom's gone to the cinema," I said, heading for the door, "I've got to get over there."

The Boss's voice came through sharp and authoritative: "No, Hunston. They'll be bringing the injured here. I'm going to need every man I've got. Get yourself to the admissions ward."

I didn't think twice about obeying his order.

"Yes, sir."

As I made my way over to the casualty entrance, I could already hear the ambulance sirens wailing in the distance.

Boreman, Whitehead and I set to work on triaging the first arrivals.

I was functioning on automatic, being the most efficient I could be. To their credit, the two registrars rose to the occasion, assessing each injured patient with a sure deftness and giving clear commands to me and the attending nurses.

Some of the patients had a large 'M' written on their foreheads in blue crayon – meaning they had been given morphine at the first aid post in town. They were all covered in dust. Mixed with the blood, it made for a filthy mess and the pristine white-tiled admissions ward was soon sullied by the influx of the wounded. It looked like we had taken in a group of injured chimney sweeps.

The Boss and MP went straight to theatre and began to operate.

As the evening wore on, I picked up snippets of what had happened from talking to the ambulance crews and civil defence workers who had been digging people out of the wreckage. A convoy of army trucks in the centre of town had been the bomber's target.

My earlier fears were confirmed; there had been a direct hit on the cinema and the building had collapsed in on itself, leaving only the art deco façade standing alone, like a prop in a Hollywood movie set. When the air raid siren sounded, everyone had stayed in their seats because it was a common enough occurrence and the town had never been attacked before. Two bombs had smashed through the ceiling of the cinema. There was a short delay before detonation, during which time only a few had managed to escape. When I heard this news I felt wooden and numb. This was rapidly progressing from the best day in my life to the worst.

Dozens of off-duty Canadian soldiers had been killed or injured. A large contingent was stationed near the town – both medics and soldiers.

Appallingly, most of the patients being brought in were children – the 'B' feature had been a western, *Hopalong Cassidy*, and they had gone straight to the cinema after school, filling up the cheap seats at the front. That's where the bombs had fallen.

One Canadian soldier came into the casualty with a bleeding child in his arms. "There were dozens of dead children in the rubble," he said. "They looked like dolls."

I kept a look out for Tom, expecting he would come straight to the ward to help, caked in dust and saying, "I don't care how bloody beautiful she is, that's the last time I sub for you on a date."

As I worked I went through our reunion conversation in my mind: "The Boss and I saw the pilot strafing the town from his office… the bastard."

Tom would be looking around the casualty: "Looks like you've been busy."

"I wanted to come and look for you, you know, but the Boss had other ideas…"

"I can see that," he would say. "Anyway, what can I do to help?" Together we would work on the new arrivals, inserting cannulas and hanging up bags of fluids.

I kept this dialogue going in my mind until long past midnight, but Tom never arrived.

In the early hours, the Boss came onto the 'shop floor', red eyed – as though he had been crying, though I suspected it was fatigue.

He gathered us around: Boreman, Whitehead, and I.

As a team we had never gelled better than on this tragic evening. Vainly, I thought he might be about to congratulate us on our efforts.

Something wasn't right though. The more I looked at him, the more obvious it was that he had something bad to tell us.

"Chaps," he said, his voice grave, "I've got some terrible news… Tom Shaw was found an hour ago. He's dead."

The Boss hung his head, almost as if trying to lead us in prayer.

For a long time there was complete silence.

We had all turned to stone. No-one moved.

But he's been with me most of the night, I wanted to say.

Only the rattling sound of a trolley being wheeled along a corridor could be heard. It is hard to describe what I felt during that surreal minute, as the implications of a world without Tom Shaw pushed up against my disbelief. 'Terrible' was exactly the right word for the Boss to have chosen.

Then the truth came over me like a wave – I had sent him to his death. It had all been because of my stupid aggression with Boreman that morning.

An awful feeling started to flow through me – like having received a transfusion of black oily guilt to replace my blood. The black liquid trickled into every recess of my soul.

It was my fault.

I continued to stand locked in position, filling up with this new poison.

It should have been me who was dead, not Tom.

The Boss was still staring at the floor when he started to speak again.

"I'm afraid there's more," he said, his voice starting to crack now. "MP's wife and two sons were in the cinema at the time. His youngest son was killed too…"

Amongst our group, there was a collective intake of breath at this news.

"My God," Whitehead said.

Boreman squatted down like a wicket keeper and started shaking his head in horror.

All I could think about was the scene from earlier in the day, with the two boys playing outside in the rain. The small one struggling and then grazing his knee, MP singing a song to him. And then, only a few hours later, being pulled out of the twisted wreckage – 'looking like a doll'.

The Boss summoned the strength to keep talking.

"We've just been to the makeshift morgue in the garage in town. I was with MP. That was where I identified Shaw."

He had to break off because a strange involuntary sound was forcing its way out of his mouth – a choking kind of cry.

No-one said anything.

He may as well have gathered us round and wielded a sledgehammer above his head, swinging it in great destructive arcs and smashing the iron against our skulls, and changing our worlds, because that's what I felt had happened. Instead, he had done it with just a few quiet words.

"Get some sleep," I heard him say through the mist. "The Canadian medics are taking over for the rest of the night. Do the morning round – you've still got a duty to the patients. MP won't be there as I'm sure you'll understand, and I can't make it either – some government people want to see me about today's events."

Back in our room, I sat looking over at Tom's armchair.

The last thing I had said to him was the word 'bastard'.

I laughed out loud in the empty room.

In the bizarre hours that followed I replayed all our time together – even chuckling to myself at some of the situations – the look on his face when he had said, 'what the fuck is it?' with the benzene molecule at interview, his hands draped in the blood of sheep's lights in the parks, his inferiority complex as we had waited to meet his brother in the pub. I remembered the time he had called the SS a bunch of fucking fuckers. Already, I was consigning Tom to history, but making sure my memory banks were fully charged, so that I wouldn't forget him.

This was the strangest time of all, when the shock had knocked me so far off kilter that instead of being bereft and tearful, I was in fact almost the opposite, laughing out loud and smiling at memories. If a psychiatrist had come into the room that night, I am sure they would have certified me insane.

By first light, the hysteria was receding like a tide, and the black rocks and shingle that had been covered up by the strange mad champagne of an ocean were showing up stark and bleak in my mindscape. The new world at low tide was awful.

"Tom is gone," my inner self was saying. "Not for a few days, not for a month… He's gone forever and there's nothing you can do about it. All you have are your memories. That's your only solace.'

Memories weren't enough though. They were just a cine-scope of the real thing – a lousy make-do. The real thing was irreplaceable.

Tom's possessions were scattered around the room – he had been a messy blighter.

His book was lying on the floor by his chair. *Moby Dick*. He had been reading it on and off the previous day, as we had lolled around the room, killing time and talking about the future.

I picked it up and read from a page he had folded over at the corner, near to the end:

'... *Towards thee I roll, thou all destroying but unconquering whale, to the last I grapple with thee; from Hell's heart I stab at thee; for hate's sake I spit my last breath at thee.*'

It was only then I finally considered Freya Nielsen's fate. Though the Boss hadn't mentioned her, I assumed she would have been in the movie house with Tom, or possibly still in the foyer. Perhaps they hadn't dug her out of the rubble yet. It was too much to think about, what with Tom and MP's son, so I blocked out the worst outcome from my mind. Maybe she had managed to get out unhurt and would be knocking on my door at any minute.

Six o'clock in the morning. There was no point in trying to sleep, so I went to the mess to get some coffee.

Loud voices echoed around the corridors from the admissions wards and the engines of vehicles could be heard from outside. The mess though, was quiet.

At first I thought it was empty because no lights were on, but as my eyes adjusted to the gloom, I saw a figure sitting in the same place MP had been the day before. As I got closer I saw it was him.

He had a scalpel in his hand and the table-top was a mass of criss-cross cuts he had been making for God knows how long.

"Christ, I'm sorry, MP."

He looked up at me. He was still in the same crazy zone I had been in during the night. His eyes were open but they were a complete blank. I registered no emotion in them whatsoever. It didn't even look as though he had cried yet.

He was still in his surgical greens – hadn't yet changed from the night's operating – and a large stain of dried blood covered the front of his top. I wondered if it was from holding his dead son in the morgue.

"Sit with me, Ed," he said.

MP had never called me by my first name.

I imagined it was his way of comforting me – without saying it, he was telling me how sorry he was that Tom Shaw had died too.

He pointed to the same chair he had offered the day before.

I sat down and together we looked out at the place where his children had played twenty four hours previously.

"It doesn't seem real," I said.

He nodded vaguely, not really hearing me.

"Your wife and older son are okay?"

"Asleep."

We sat there for perhaps half a minute in complete silence. I was just about to say something else – to ask MP what his younger son's name was, when he spoke instead.

"This is a good blade," he said, holding up his scalpel and examining the steel. "It's very sharp."

I was suddenly worried about his state of mind. He looked frightening, with the blade only inches away from his face. I think he had ventured even further out into the hysterical champagne ocean than I had. He was right out there, treading water in its depths, possibly about to drown in them.

"MP?"

I almost asked if he was all right, but managed to stop myself.

"Know how cave men made their knives, Ed?"

He was still staring at the blade, unsettlingly.

"No."

"They would chip away from a flint block for hours… like this…"

MP put down the scalpel and mimicked the actions with invisible pieces of stone and flint, his movements violent and intense.

I shifted in my chair.

"I saw a flint knapper demonstrating it once in a museum. It's called the Levallois technique. Eventually a rounded core would take shape. In the trade they call it a tortoise core because it looks like a tortoise shell. Right at the end there is a crucial step – a single precision blow at one end of the flint."

MP imitated the strike by slamming his open hand down hard on the table.

BANG!

It was so sudden and loud that I jumped half out of my chair.

He had the enthusiastic look of a madman.

"One blow!"

I nodded at him, to show I was listening, if not entirely understanding.

"If it was done right, a well-shaped shard would split off – the knife the caveman had been wanting all along… the perfect tool, with a sharp edge all around its perimeter. It could cut up meat quickly from a carcass, or be used as a scraper to clean hides… the ideal blade. Palaeolithic man survived for thousands of years in the ice age wilderness because of those Levallois blades."

He picked up the scalpel again.

"That crucial step I mentioned… the single blow. It could be messed up you know. Strike it wrongly and the whole thing just shatters into tiny pieces… ruined."

I stared out at the handrail and, for a while, we were quiet again.

I was struggling to see what it had to do with the death of his son – the poor man was plainly out of his wits with grief. It was understandable he would ramble, the shock hadn't even hit him properly yet.

MP turned to face me. "One instant decides it all, Ed – and the result is either what you had hoped for, or everything is completely fucked."

Then he brought down the scalpel into the wooden top of the table, stabbing it in so hard that it kinked at the handle by 45 degrees.

Staring at the warped knife, the first abstract thought entering my mind was that this new instrument should be named, like a new piece in the surgical range, 'the MP blade of devastation'.

Chapter Eleven

July 10th 1943

I was still on the ward doing jobs when the call came through; another summons to the Boss's office.

Boreman, Whitehead and I had done the round, saying only what needed to be said and doing only what needed to be done. We were civil enough – there was no animosity or one-upmanship anymore; we were a real team now. The previous day's trauma and our night of triaging had forged a spirit of camaraderie. It was a shame it had taken a Luftwaffe bombing raid and the death of Tom to make it happen.

I arrived at the office and could hear the Boss speaking to someone inside, so I sat down on one of the chairs in the corridor and closed my eyes. I was so exhausted I felt I could sleep right there while waiting. Immediately, Tom was there sitting next to me.

He looked pale.

"Tom," I said without actually speaking, "are you okay?"

His expression was one of complete shock.

"I'll see you back at our digs," was all he said.

I jerked awake and rubbed my eyes, shaking my head to make the ghosts inside go away. It was the lack of sleep that had done it – I was seeing things which weren't really there.

Rather than sitting around all day waiting, I decided to knock on the door.

"Come in," I heard the Boss say.

Still distracted by my mind's trickery, I was only vaguely aware of the two men in dark suits as I walked in.

They were seated in front of the Boss's desk and made no move to introduce themselves.

"Ed – these chaps are from Military Intelligence," the Boss said. "They want to have a chat with you, if that's alright."

I scanned the men. Military Intelligence – if there had been an ounce of emotional energy left in my being I might have been surprised. Then I remembered the Boss mentioning something the night before, about Government people coming to speak to him.

"That's fine," I said.

The Boss left the room and shut the door.

I felt suddenly guilty, although I hadn't done anything wrong. Maybe they had come to punish me for sending my best friend to his death.

The two men were fairly young, late twenties at a guess. Both were tall, I could see that even though they weren't standing. One thinner, one bulkier – with an air of menace about them.

"Ed Hunston," I said, holding out my hand tentatively to the slimmer one.

He didn't smile but reached over and briefly shook my hand, squeezing so hard it hurt.

"I'm Mr Farr-Jones," he said. "And this is my colleague, Mr Fox."

Fox just stayed where he was and made no move at all to greet me. He didn't say anything either.

Farr-Jones pointed to the Boss's chair.

"Please Doctor Hunston, take a seat."

As I did so, the silent one – Fox – took a notebook and pen from his pocket.

Farr-Jones moved his chair forward so his elbows were leaning on the table. The fingers of his hands were interlocked.

"I'm sorry about your friend," he said, trying to be kind, though it looked as though empathy wasn't his strong suit.

"Is this about Tom Shaw?"

"No. We're here to talk about Miss Nielsen."

My shoulders slumped.

From the serious look on his face, I guessed they had found her.

"Is she…?"

I hardly dared say it.

"Dead?" Farr-Jones said, answering for me. "No, she isn't actually."

"Oh. Thank God. She's all right then? Not injured? Where is she?"

Farr-Jones's response to my barrage of questions was to turn to his colleague and give him a guarded look, as though I had disappointed him in some way. I was just about to ask where she was again, when he barked out a question:

"When did you last see her?"

Perhaps I hesitated for longer than was appropriate because Farr-Jones scowled.

He reached into the inside pocket of his jacket and for a moment I thought he was going to pull out a weapon.

It was a photograph. Of me, standing on the landing of the hospital tower outside Freya Nielsen's office. In the picture I had a stupid smile on my face.

"What the hell" I said, confused now. "She took that yesterday… how on earth have you got it?

"Just tell us the truth," he said, "Right now, Doctor Hunston."

These men from Military Intelligence were all business and no sentimentality. I suppose it shouldn't have been a surprise, but their manner still shook me.

I had heard talk of the security services, but only that. These two certainly fitted the stereotypes I had imagined. A secret war was being fought, and hard, merciless men were there to make sure England got the desired result. Losing was not an option – they would do anything it took to avoid that outcome. I actually felt relief that these two were on our side, just like I'd felt with Richard Shaw.

"It was yesterday morning…"

"Tell us exactly what happened," he said.

I thought back to twenty four hours ago, a time when the world had been very different; a high tide world without all the shit out on display.

"I got up early, spent some time with one of the senior surgeons in the mess, then went for a wander and ended up at the foot of the hospital tower."

Fox was writing in his notebook.

"When were you at the foot of the tower?" he said, speaking for the first time.

"Between half past seven and twenty to eight."

He wrote this down.

Farr-Jones took over the reins again.

"And you went up the stairs?"

"Yes. How do you know that? Did Freya tell you?"

"Just answer the bloody questions. Had you ever climbed them before?"

They had dropped the polite front now. I had the impression that Farr-Jones wanted to reach over and throttle me.

"I'll repeat," he said. "Had you ever climbed them before?"

"No… no, I hadn't, not all the way to the top."

"Why not?"

"I don't know… the thought had never occurred to me, I suppose. I had always assumed it was out of bounds."

"So what was different about yesterday?"

"There was a noise," I said, remembering. "I could hear it over the sound of the rain."

"What kind of noise?"

"A tapping."

"Rhythmical?"

"Yes, a little…"

"Tap it out on the table."

I tapped out the rhythm I had heard.

"Quick taps like that," I said.

They looked at one another again and Fox wrote something else in his book.

Farr-Jones met my eye.

"What did you think it was?"

"I had no idea – I called out as I climbed the stairs and it stopped. By the time I was at the top it had started again. That was when Miss Nielsen spoke to me from her room – she was trying to fix her camera with a coin… the shutter mechanism had jammed."

Farr-Jones was nodding to himself.

"Have you ever heard what Morse code sounds like when it's being tapped out?"

I felt the blood draining from my face.

"No… well… at the cinema, perhaps."

Farr jones tapped out a rhythm on the table, one that I presumed must have been Morse.

"Could it have been that?" he said.

I cast my mind back to what I had heard.

"I suppose it could have been."

"Were you suspicious?"

"No."

"Why not?"

"Because Morse code is the last thing in the world I was expecting to hear."

He seemed to accept this and sat back.

"Christ," I said, realising the implications. "She was transmitting a message? Is that what you're telling me?"

"Our colleagues from a nearby listening station picked up some unusual radio traffic at that exact time," Farr-Jones said.

A new sledgehammer swung through my already shattered mind, breaking off the last shards of my old world.

"You're saying… Nielsen… is a spy?"

His expression was deadpan. Farr-Jones didn't seem interested in my questions and my stumbling conclusions.

"Did you see anything else unusual?" he said.

His tone was impatient again, as though he was struggling against that urge to do me damage. Yesterday's bombing had everyone on edge.

"Come on, Hunston," he said. "Did you see anything strange?"

"Well… There was a pair of binoculars on the desk. She said she used them to look out at the view. Otherwise it was just her camera and her photographs of the patients."

"Anything else? Think!"

I remembered the bag.

"There was a case for her photographic equipment… on the floor."

"How did you know it was for photographic equipment?"

"Because that's what she told me."

They exchanged looks again, both obviously thinking I was the biggest sap they had met in their entire careers. I had to agree with them.

From near his feet, Farr-Jones lifted up a battered tan coloured briefcase with metal edging, and placed it onto the desk.

"Did it look like this?"

"Yes… that's it."

He flipped open the lid to reveal an array of radio equipment – dials, wires and nobs, and a set of headphones.

I suddenly felt lightheaded.

"Jesus!"

"You know what this is?"

"It looks like a radio."

"That's right. It's called an Afu in the trade – an 'Agenten funk'. That's 'agent radio' in English. It's the standard transmitter-receiver of the Abwehr – our German counterparts."

I was feeling slightly nauseous.

"She was radioing Germany with information yesterday morning?"

Farr-Jones shut the lid of the case and put it back on the floor.

"Yes. We believe so."

"What was she telling them?"

He rubbed his chin.

"We can't tell you that."

"Could she have called in the bomber?"

Farr-Jones kept his poker face and didn't reply.

"Last night," I said, piecing it together for myself, "last night rescue workers said a military convoy was hit in the High Street. Maybe she spotted them from the tower, heading into town… maybe…"

My speculation ran out of steam and was replaced by guilt and shame.

"I should've seen it coming… Maybe I could have averted it if I'd been more aware. Those bombs killed more than a hundred people. My colleague's son was killed. My best friend died. She was right in front of me with that machine and I didn't bloody realise…"

I looked over at the agents in turn, too shocked to carry on. Tears were in my eyes and blurring my vision.

For the first time, there was some softening in their expressions.

"You couldn't have done anything," Farr-Jones said. "She's too clever… and I'm not saying you're particularly stupid, Doctor. She fooled everyone."

I hid my face in my hands, trying to make everything go away, like a child.

"Let me guess," he said, "she came onto you strongly, didn't she?"

I looked up and blinked my tears away.

"Yes. We kissed. I thought it was my lucky day. She's beautiful."

He nodded in agreement, and so did Fox, as if they had seen her themselves and knew exactly what I was talking about.

"Think about it from her point of view," Farr-Jones said. "You come up the staircase as she's sending a coded message. Her best ploy to make you less suspicious is to seduce you. That's tradecraft. The art of distraction – you're only human. It worked too. She made you forget all about what you saw and heard. Didn't she?"

"Yes," I said. "That kiss was like a spell. It was all I thought about yesterday; at least until I saw the bombs drop… Tom and I had been pursuing her for months. I thought she'd finally decided I was the one. It felt real. She asked me if I would take her on a date – to the cinema at five o'clock."

"So you were supposed to go and meet her there?"

"Yes."

Fox leafed back a few pages and showed Farr-Jones something by holding up the notebook.

Farr-Jones grunted and came back to me.

"But you got into an argument with one of the other doctors on the round. Your supervisor told us what happened."

"Yes, that's right. Boreman."

"And you were called in for a disciplinary meeting later that day?"

"Yes, in here with the Boss."

"Which meant you were going to be late?"

"Yes."

"So you sent Shaw along in your stead…"

I wanted to tell them how he had jumped at the chance, but I just nodded instead, not wanting to say out loud how I had sent my best friend to his death.

Farr-Jones placed his hands palm down on the edge of the table.

"You know why she told you to go to the cinema for five?"

The brutal truth hit me.

"She knew the area was going to be bombed," I said. "She wanted me out of the way. She wanted me dead."

Farr-Jones nodded.

"You catch on fast," he said. "After what you'd seen and heard, Miss Nielsen knew she was compromised. Even if her amorous advances had put you off temporarily, it was probably only a matter of time before you got suspicious."

"You're over-estimating me… I don't think I would ever have suspected her."

"Actually, Doctor, you'd be surprised how events slowly percolate through the mind and later result in a sudden moment of revelation."

"I'm a complete fool," I said, my voice full of bitter self-recrimination.

"Look," he said. "She's beautiful. And everyone we've talked to this morning has said what an intoxicating manner she has, how every man she met was spellbound. Why do you think the Abwehr recruited her? They're not stupid."

"But she said she was Danish."

"Yes. We believe that to be true. She must have had strong reasons to join. For the women, it's often because of love. Perhaps she was married to a German soldier killed by the British. That's about the biggest motivator you can have for revenge. Anyway, we'll find out soon enough."

"What do you mean?"

"We have her in custody."

"So you do have her?"

Farr-Jones looked at me with no emotion.

"She was picked up at Newhaven last night. She made a mistake – was seen by a fisherman pulling a boat down the beach. I think she was going to try and row across the channel, or at least make a rendezvous with a seaplane. Her camera was confiscated, along with the Afu."

"Where is she now?"

Farr-Jones raised an eyebrow.

"She's somewhere secure."

"So she'll be hanged?"

He shrugged.

"Possibly, once we've found out all she knows. She hasn't said a single word yet, but we found papers on her person with her photographic accreditation at this institution."

I was shaking my head.

"So the photography job was all a ruse?"

Farr-Jones looked up at me.

"But she was an excellent photographer," I said, almost pleading her case.

"Of course she could take decent photographs," he said. "It was part of her bloody mission."

Farr-Jones brought out more photographs from his inside pocket and placed them onto the table one by one.

"Before your ugly mug appeared on the film, this is what she had photographed."

There were a couple of patients taken on rounds, but then other shots – a few of the countryside, one of what appeared to be a large ditch, with several cube-shaped concrete tank traps in the picture. One taken of a gun emplacement on a hill alongside a windmill: I recognised the place. It was near Chichester. Another had been taken outside an aerodrome through a barbed wire fence. A row of military planes were parked on the runway in the distance.

My leg had begun to shake involuntarily at this slew of incriminating evidence.

"My God," I said.

Farr-Jones kept placing down the pictures in reverse order, going backwards in time.

I recognised another hill near Chichester; a summit called the Trundle, an ancient Iron Age earthwork with commanding views of the coastal plain. One of a beach – fortified with steel tank traps and barbed wire. A few more of a seaside town – Portsmouth by the looks of it – each one displaying anti-aircraft guns and navy frigates moored in the harbour. There was a photograph of a large group of soldiers all smiling at the camera, all of them clearly in love with Freya Nielsen.

"It's quite something, isn't it?" he said. "We believe she's been travelling around the south coast in her spare time, scouting for targets, monitoring troop build-ups and coastal defences."

There were a few from the summit of a place called Kingley Vale – I knew it from my childhood walks. It was where the Devil's Humps were, the burial mounds of the Viking Chiefs. The photographs were of views out to sea – it had been a clear sunny day and whole ten mile sections of coast were visible in the shots, both to the east towards Worthing and westwards towards Portsmouth.

The last photograph Farr Jones put down – the first of the roll – was the cross of the German pilot in Phyllis Wood, the enemy pilot from Richard Shaw's nightmares. Sebastian Fuhrmann. Nielsen was in the picture, kneeling down on the ground. I presume she had asked Boreman to take it. She wasn't looking at the camera lens; she was staring at the cross and there was a bluebell in her hand, the one *she* had placed there.

"The pilot's memorial" I said.

Farr-Jones nodded.

"We found out your senior took that one."

"Boreman you mean?"

"That's right. We questioned him thoroughly and it seems he was duped too. Took her everywhere she wanted that day in an effort to get into her knickers. His words not mine."

Judging by the sequence of the photographs I had just seen, Boreman must have driven her to Kingley Vale after leaving the pub.

"He didn't get anywhere, by the way – if it makes you feel any better."

I pushed the photos back to Farr-Jones and he piled and stacked them neatly, like a set of playing cards.

"But... I don't understand. How could she be a hospital photographer?"

"We checked her application and asked around. We think she arrived here just over a year ago – landed by sea plane and paddled to shore by dinghy – complete with her Afu and a bicycle. The whole thing was planned to perfection. The previous photographer died suddenly and unexpectedly – we're going to exhume the body to find out for sure, but our theory is that Nielsen drugged her and made it look like a heart attack. Then she conveniently showed up a week later and applied for the job. She had perfectly forged papers stating that she'd been in the country since the outbreak of war. She had proof showing she had done a student photographic internship at one of the most reputable newspapers in Denmark: *Politiken* – forged obviously. There's no doubt she was trained in photography, it was just by the Abwehr and not by *Politiken*."

I felt numb.

"Nielsen *assassinated* the previous photographer?"

"She was good... very good. At the start of the war the Abwehr spies were usually bumbling idiots – thinking us all characters out of a PG Wodehouse novel. They would wear brand new tweeds, plus fours and old school ties and then wonder why they stood out when they landed in a remote coastal village. They would cycle down the wrong side of the road, walk into a pub and ask the Test match score... in a war and in November. Some, with their wallets full of British banknotes, would lay down one hundred pounds for a train ticket. Your girlfriend was different – cunning. She acted natural, made everyone love her. Most

148

importantly, she had no fear whatsoever. Make no bones about it Hunston, she's a killer."

The way he had called her my girlfriend made me sound partly to blame.

Farr-Jones pulled something out of his breast pocket.

"Maybe this will help you believe."

He was holding a coin.

"We found this on the floor of her room in the tower. It seems she left in a hurry after your little meeting yesterday."

"That's the coin she was using to fix her camera…"

"Take a closer look."

He dropped it into my palm.

Attached to one side of the coin – hidden by Farr-Jones's thumb and forefinger when he had held it before – was a swivel blade. I carefully pulled the blade out from the coin. It looked like a bird's beak.

"Careful, Doctor," he said, "it's very sharp."

"You're saying she would have killed me?"

He nodded.

"She was thinking about taking you out right there and then. All it would take with a blade like that would be a flick on your neck over the carotid artery and you'd have bled out in less than a minute. It's a good job you didn't put two and two together…"

I handed it back.

"They train for months," he said, returning the coin to his pocket. "It would have been quick."

"That's comforting," I said, trying to muster some sarcasm, though my voice sounded flat.

Fox had stopped writing now and was looking thoroughly bored.

"So her name wasn't Freya Nielsen," I said.

Farr-Jones shook his head.

"We don't know her real name yet. All we know is she signed off her radio messages 'Mrs Carter'."

He stood up and stretched out his arms.

"Anyway… Thank you for talking to us, Doctor."

"I'm free to go?"

He smiled.

"Shouldn't you be?"

"It's just that… I feel terrible… I wish I could do something to make it right."

Farr-Jones looked at Fox, who had also stood up. Fox seemed to give the slightest nod and closed his eyes for a moment.

Farr-Jones pulled out a card.

"Here… it's my number."

I took the card. All it had on it was a telephone number, no names, nothing else at all.

"I've told you everything."

He planted both hands firmly in his pockets

"Keep it anyway… Call if you ever want to talk."

His cryptic comment was confusing.

"Talk about what?"

"Oh, I don't know, Doctor. Anything you want… vengeance for one thing."

I frowned. Was he offering me a job?

"Oh, and by the way, don't talk to anybody else about what we've spoken about in here today. Or there'll be trouble. Understand?"

"I understand."

Dazed, I went back to the on-call room, sat back in the chair and closed my eyes. My hands were shaking and my throat felt dry. I tried to count backwards from ten to calm down, thinking only of the number sequence.

Then Tom walked in and sat down opposite me.

I told him about my interview and, for a long time afterwards, we just sat there not saying anything.

"She played us all," I said in a bitter conclusion.

Tom stared into space and nodded in agreement.

I held my thumb and forefinger an inch apart.

"You know I was this close to having my neck slit yesterday."

He made the same shape with his fingers.

"And I was this close to not being blown up by the airstrike she called in."

"I'm bloody sorry I sent you, Tom."

"I'm bloody sorry I went."

We were silent again.

"They think she may have become an agent because her husband was killed in the war" I said.

Now Tom was staring up at the ceiling, only half paying attention, as if he already knew all of this and was waiting for me to catch up.

"That's the only thing that makes sense," he said. "If she was happy once and then lost it all… had it all… ruined."

"Like the German pilot in your brother's dream you mean?"

He looked at me. "EXACTLY like that. In fact how's your German?"

"What do you mean how's *my* German? Yours is non-existent."

"Ah, well… you're right – my German *was* non-existent, but now I just seem to know it. There are some perks to being dead."

I frowned.

"Go on then," I said. "What are you getting at?"

"Well… there's something very interesting here…"

"How so, Tom? Spit it out."

"What was that pilot's name? You remember – on the cross?"

"Sebastian Fuhrmann."

"Yes, that's it… Fuhrmann. I bet you didn't know that the English equivalent of Fuhrmann is Carter…"

"Her codename – Mrs Carter – you think she's linked to the pilot?"

"That's EXACTLY what I think."

"That she was married to the pilot?"

Tom started whistling a tune, as he waited for me to catch up.

"Wait… wait," I said, "that would mean your brother killed her husband."

"Well, Fuhrmann must be as common a name in Germany as Carter is here," Tom said. "But yes, I suppose it is possible."

I could tell he already knew all this; I could tell by the way he was talking. It was the same as when he had helped me with our studies – when he knew the answer and I didn't.

Suddenly, I sat forward, as it all slotted into place.

"She laid a fresh flower at the cross" I said. "And wasn't it her idea to drag old Boreman out there? He was just an unknowing stooge – to make it seem less suspicious. She must have found out where her husband's plane had gone down. Maybe she even made the cross and the inscription. If it's true, it means she met her husband's killer that day, and didn't even know it."

"She liked him too," Tom said, smiling. "Remember how she reached across the table and held his hand."

The image of her touching Richard's scarred hand came back to me.

"Maybe she forgave him at that moment. Right there in the pub garden she forgave a British pilot because he was expressing compassion at her husband's demise, even if she didn't know he was the one who had actually fired the shots. That part almost doesn't matter… she forgave…"

"Maybe," Tom said. "But for what she did yesterday, there's no forgiveness. I'm afraid the gallows are what awaits Frau fucking Fuhrmann."

After five minutes of sitting together in a brooding silence, Tom made the suggestion that would change my life completely: "Forget joining the RAMC. You want vengeance now, don't you?"

He'd used exactly the same word as Farr-Jones – *vengeance*.

"Yes, I do," I said, my guilt turning to anger.

"Then why don't you ask those two spooks for a job?"

When I woke up in my chair it was late in the afternoon and the sun was coming in through the window.

I remembered the vivid dream and my chat with Tom, with the revelation about Freya Nielsen – aka Mrs Carter.

On the arm of my chair was his book, like a small tent, upturned and open on the page where I had left it earlier. I picked it up and re-read the line:

'Towards thee I roll, thou all destroying but unconquering whale; to the last I grapple with thee; from hell's heart I stab at thee, for hate's sake I spit my last breath at thee.'

At that moment all I wanted to do was fight the Nazis. I didn't understand their evil, just as Ahab hadn't understood the whale. All I wanted to do now was destroy them. Not just as a soldier or a pilot, firing from a distance, but on my own, up close and personal, right in their face so that they could taste the spit from my last breath if it came down to that. To stab at them from hell's heart.

I would join Military Intelligence just as Tom had suggested in my dream; that way I would get to do the damage in the most vicious and underhand way possible.

I would do it right now

I picked up the phone and rang the number on the card. A woman answered.

"Hello?"

"Can I speak to Mr Farr-Jones?"

"He's not here at the moment; may I ask who is calling?"

"My name's Dr Hunston."

"Is there a message?"

"No, can you just tell him I called."

I put down the phone.

"Satisfied?" I said to the empty chair in front of me.

Chapter Twelve

The bizarre experiences straight after the bombing – my trauma-induced dreams and hypnogogic hallucinations of Tom, the sight of MP playing with the scalpel blade in the pre-dawn light, the questioning by Military Intelligence – all soon felt as if they had happened a long time ago.

The Boss accepted my resignation with good grace: "Go and get your head right," were his parting words of advice.

He undoubtedly meant well, though 'getting my head right' would not prove an easy task.

The ten days straight after Tom's death, leading up to his funeral, were very strange indeed. I would stare at simple things, a pencil for instance, and think to myself: 'this is a pencil in a world *without* Tom Shaw. Last week it was a pencil in a world with Tom Shaw in it.' I had never imagined that even everyday objects could be included in grief. The world had suddenly become a different place because of his absence, a twilight version of the real thing.

I went back to my parents' house, walked into my bedroom, shut the door behind me and didn't come out. I didn't want to talk to anyone. My movements were slow and I was unable to engage in even the simplest conversations. Everything – even brushing my teeth – felt like a terrific effort in those first days. My initial burst of decisive energy and hate for the Nazis had been replaced by an apathy which sucked me down. It felt as if I was moving in grief treacle. Time itself seemed to slow to a crawl, and for portions of the day I would gaze at the second hand on my bedside clock, wondering why each movement was taking so long.

I didn't dream about Tom again, or see him in my mind's eye, not like I had in that first twenty four hours. Instead I slept dreamless sleeps, finally catching up on all the broken nights from our months of on-call.

At meal-times my mother came to my door, knocked lightly, and left a tray of food on the floor before leaving. I ate it because I knew I should and didn't want to worry her any further.

I lay on my bed and stared at the white walls, trying in vain to understand the workings of the universe and why things happened the way they did. I wondered where God was in all this. Needless to say, the white walls provided no answers.

I stopped shaving.

The one exception to my self-imposed exile was that every day, late in the afternoon, my father would drag me out for a walk in the fields around our home.

He didn't say much and neither did I – we just walked together, slow and in step. On our first walk I said to him, "You know how this feels – any advice?"

"No," he said. "There's nothing I can say to make you feel any better right now. All I can do is keep you company."

This is how things were for a while – basic existing – eating, sleeping, some physical activity. Occasionally I would find my face wet with tears, not quite knowing when they had come.

On one walk, I told my father I wanted revenge for what the Germans had done to Tom.

He didn't reply right away, and we walked on for a good quarter of a mile before he eventually said, "I can understand you wanting revenge, Ed. For a long time I was angry about losing my brother too. Who should I take it out on? The list seemed endless – the Boer soldier who fired the shot causing him to lose the leg? Or the person in the War Office who had banned mandatory inoculations for soldiers? Or should I blame the typhoid bacterium itself, or the other bacteria which caused his final pneumonia in his weakened state? But how does one take out revenge on a bacterium? I soon realised I might go mad trying to find the culprit. I screamed at God the night after he died, and I wasn't even a religious man. I was on the edge of my sanity for several months. Of course I heard no answer at the time. Only now can I see how my subsequent life has provided me with an answer. I left England because of what happened and met your mother while living in New Zealand. I almost lost her, you know. I had let her go – she was engaged to another man for a while. One day, when still in New Zealand, I went for a walk to see a place my brother had once lived, near a town I hardly ever visited, and I happened to meet your mother again there that evening. Coincidence? Perhaps. But to me it felt like fate. We both knew immediately we needed to give our relationship a second chance. Do you see, Ed? All that stemmed from what happened to my brother – all of it. One great big mad set of coincidences packaged up as fate. You wouldn't even exist if my brother hadn't died. I might have a son by another woman, but he wouldn't be you. And I wouldn't change having you for the world, not even if it meant having my brother back, and I don't say that lightly. Do you see, Ed? Despite it all, I've managed to find peace... even happiness. That, I think, may be the answer to my scream of 'why?'. There are other things too..."

My father stopped talking.

"What things?"

He shook his head. "No – it's probably not the right time."

We kept walking. I knew he wanted to talk about ghosts, but had stopped himself because he realised no amount of sugar coating was going to help at the current time. "Listen Ed," he said eventually. "I believe that one day you will look back on all this and be able to see a strange, illogical yet undeniably beautiful reason for why your friend died. And the reason will involve how it affected the trajectory of your life. You are on a different course now. At the moment it feels like a terrible course, but I urge you to keep an open mind and have faith. Answers will reveal themselves in the course of time and in the end you will have an understanding of sorts. It gets better in the end, son. I promise."

There were of course some events I couldn't avoid – namely Tom's funeral, which was held at our college chapel in Oxford.

Richard Shaw came up from Tangmere and we sat in the caf together before the service.

Having seen dozens of his fellow pilots killed in action – 'going for their Burtons' – he was a lot more used to violent death than me, but this time it was his own brother and he was clearly deeply affected; for one thing he was a lot thinner, and though he was in his uniform, the RAF swagger was completely gone.

I had made the effort to shave out of respect for Tom, but my appearance was still sufficiently different for Richard to do a double take when he saw me.

We spent most of our time in silence, staring into our mugs of tea. We were going to see Tom's body before the service, and speaking for myself, even the thought of the viewing had thrown me into a state of abject dread.

Finally, we crossed the road, walked through the porter's lodge and went into the chapel.

Tom and I had been there only once while at University, during a drunken Burns Night. Fuelled with whisky, as I recall, he had fallen asleep on one of the pews, face down on the hard wood. I had made myself a bed on the stone floor with half a dozen of the kneeling cushions. At six the next morning the chaplain had thrown us out in disgust, just like Jesus clearing the temple.

As soon as I saw Tom in his coffin I regretted having come. The sight would stay with me for a long time.

There were a few black smudges on his cheeks, like an artist had absentmindedly touched his face with charcoal while sketching. Otherwise he didn't look too scratched up – almost too good to have died in a bombing.

For a mad moment, I thought it might all be some ghoulish prank, or that they had got it wrong and he was still alive, but when I touched Tom's face, the skin felt cold and hard.

Someone – the mortician I presume – had dressed him up in a dark suit which he had never worn in his life. The last time I had seen him he had borrowed my best tweed jacket. It must have been torn to pieces in the explosions.

I left Richard alone with his brother and walked out of the college to the Lamb and Flag.

By the time Richard came in to join me I was already on my second pint. He didn't go to the bar – but came straight over and sat at my table.

"Is that one for me?"

He was looking at an extra pint I had bought, perched on the table and untouched. Sentimentally, I had bought it for Tom, and had been staring at it morosely, in the futile hope that a free pint might lure him back from the dead.

I didn't tell Richard this.

"Yes, it's for you," I said, pushing it across to his side of the table.

He picked it up with his withered hands and drained it all in one go.

Following his example, I did the same.

"Another?"

He shook his head.

"Better not – my parents are arriving in half an hour. Don't want to be drunk for the funeral."

The room was beginning to spin a little from the two swift pints on an empty stomach.

"I suppose I should stop too."

A bus thundered by on the road outside and made the pub windows rattle.

I shivered, despite the warm day.

In my alcohol-numbed state, I felt Tom had finally decided to come and join us – perhaps the lure of beer had worked, and even though Richard had downed the lot, he had still come. It made me want to talk things over with Richard.

"Can you believe *she* was an agent?"

Richard put his hands on his face – scars on scars – and tried to massage the top of his eyebrows with his pointed fingertips.

"There's something I want to tell you, Ed," he said, his expression foreboding. He looked even worse than earlier – more strain written into his features now than when seeing his dead brother's body.

"Oh?"

"I told the men from Military Intelligence when they came to see me, and I think you should know too."

"They came to see *you*?"

"Yes, to my base at Tangmere. Came to talk about Tom, but also wanted to know what I knew about her."

He took a deep breath and moaned, as if he was having an attack of nausea.

"What? What the hell are you trying to say Richard?"

"I saw her again."

"What do you mean you saw her again?"

I wasn't quite with him – the beers had slowed my thought processes. Richard had to spell it out for me.

"Freya Nielsen," he said. "After that day at the Hooksway pub with you and Tom... I saw her again."

"You saw her again... *romantically* you mean?"

I was catching on at last.

"Just the one time. You see, in that pub garden I fell for her hook, line and sinker. So I did something about it."

"Bloody hell."

Richard was staring over at the empty chair at our table, as if Tom really was there. "I know you both liked her," he said.

"We sure did," I said, staring at him in disbelief.

"Listen, Ed, I didn't think I was doing anything wrong by Tom, or you for that matter. Let's face it, if she was ever going to be with either of you boys, something would have happened by then."

That was true.

The image of her reaching across the table and holding Richard's hands came back to me.

Tears were coming from his scarred eyes now and his jigsaw face was more of a mess than usual, blotchy with emotion.

"Christ!" he said. "Trying to reconcile the woman I thought I loved – did love – with someone who caused my own brother's death... well, it's... it's been eating me up inside."

I let out a long breath.

"Don't torture yourself, Richard. No-one knew." I remembered what Farr-Jones had said. "She fooled us all."

Richard leant towards me, as if to try and convince me of the truth as he saw it.

"I know all that. But it felt real when I was with her. It had to have been real. If not… then…"

He broke off, unable to continue.

I put my hand on his shoulder for a brief moment in empathy.

The kiss she had given me had felt real too, the one problem was her debating whether or not to slit my throat as she did it.

"When did you meet?"

I was asking questions on behalf of Tom now, things he would want to know; all the details, so that he could go away and ruminate and come to terms with it later.

"Not long after we found the memorial to the downed pilot. I rang her at the hospital and asked her out. She caught the train down to Chichester and we spent the day together – there's a hill behind the city called the Trundle – an old Iron Age hill fort."

"I know it."

From the top you could see for miles around – Tangmere airfield to the south east, a broad swathe of the English Channel, the Isle of Wight to the south west and to the west, Portsmouth, with its naval buildings on the cliffs. It was a good place for a spy to visit, to 'scout for targets' as Farr-Jones would say. Then I remembered the photographs from her roll of film and the one of the Trundle among them. She had taken a bloody picture during their date.

I thought it best not to make Richard feel any worse by saying this, so I kept quiet.

"Well, we visited that," he said, "and then after the trundle we went for a walk up another nearby hill with a windmill."

I knew that place too, but didn't reply, just nodded.

It was near a village called Halnaker. The windmill was an old hollowed out ruin. That was also in the series of photographs Farr-Jones had shown me. Like the Trundle, the coastal views were good ones. There were gun emplacements up there which covered the roads and valleys snaking through the Downs, to try and stop any German invasion.

Jesus, I had already seen the whole record of Richard's date with Nielsen.

"… And later on we had dinner in a pub. I asked her why she liked me, with my scars and injuries, and she said a strange thing… she said it was *because* of the scars, and that at Hooksway she had immediately felt some kind of bond with me – a strong one."

I remembered my dream on the night of Tom's death, when he had helped me to see the connection between Nielsen and the Luftwaffe pilot.

"I have a theory," I said, "and I don't want you to think I'm crazy, but hear me out. The Military Intelligence men told me her code name was Carter. Carter is Fuhrmann in German. I think she was married to that pilot you shot down on Eagle Day – Sebastian Fuhrmann – the one from your nightmares."

I wasn't about to tell him that his brother had told me everything in a dream. "Think about it, Richard. She put a flower at his grave at the crash site. It all fits."

He sat back in his chair and put his hands on his head, as if surrendering.

"My God," he said, giving my hypothesis serious consideration. "Do you remember what I said at the pub?"

"Which part?"

"How before the war, the pilot was probably a happy man and how someone had ruined that for him. I repeated the pilot's sentiments from my own nightmare. If what you're saying is the truth, then I defended her dead husband in front of Boreman without realising the full weight of what I was saying. That's why there was a bond. It has to be… Why else would she fall for a scarred up so-and-so like me?" He smiled sadly, his face slightly lopsided. "Your way makes a lot of sense, Ed. I thought she loved me."

"Maybe she did," I said, trying to buoy him up a little. "For those few hours you were alone together, maybe she did."

I thought of the moment when it seemed she had fallen for me, and of how in those seconds, it felt like our cabin in the mountains had become real.

"Maybe," he said.

He knocked his finger-tips gently against the side of his beer glass.

"When we parted that day, she said she couldn't see me again and I couldn't believe it. Not after what we had done. We had... well, you know... in the windmill..."

"Oh! Right... I see. Yes...indeed..."

"She started crying and wouldn't say why. Now I think it's because she felt guilty at having been with another man. On that day I did love her, Ed. Can you understand that? I can't change the fact. I bloody well loved her. Then she helped to kill Tom and all those others and now I hate her for what she did and who she is."

"We all loved her, Richard; we all did. Tom included."

He laughed, but not in a happy way – it was the same cruel laugh I had once heard when he told me about wanting to kill more German pilots in revenge for his injuries.

"I can never see her again," he said. "She's dead to me now."

His head was in his hands.

I could understand the sentiment. In a way, she was more dead than alive – for all I knew, they had finished their interrogation and hanged her already.

Again, I tried to think of something positive.

"There was some good in her, Richard... I think she had genuine empathy for you as a pilot – you must have reminded her of her late husband. If he had survived his crash, he might have looked like you – scarred but alive. She could see him in you. That was the catalyst for whatever happened between you and her, the connection which Tom and I were never going to forge with our schoolboy infatuations."

Richard pulled his hands away and contorted his face into a snarl, like a beast.

"Death is too good for her," he said, his voice filled with hatred. "Her punishment should be knowing I killed the love of her life... I'll write to her at whatever prison she's in and tell her what I did to Sebastian

Fuhrmann on Eagle Day – describe it all in great detail... how I watched the flames come out of his plane and how it exploded on the hillside. How his own bombs turned him into atoms. I'll even tell her how he screamed at me in my dreams...screams of frustration at his life cut short. When I do that, she'll hate herself for what she did on the day we spent together. She'll want to kill herself."

He had got up a real head of steam.

"Don't, Richard."

"Why the hell not? Give me one good reason."

"It's ugly. You don't need it... Keep the day you had special. It sounds as if she loved you openly and of her own volition. That day she hadn't caused Tom's death. You had prayed for her husband's soul at his memorial and tried to clear away the nightmares. For some unknown reason, at that moment in time – on that day alone – the gods decreed that you and she would spend those hours together. If you really feel it was genuine, then I think it's alright to keep that time as sacrosanct, despite everything that happened afterwards. She's got enough problems without you rubbing salt into the wound by telling her what you did. Besides..."

I paused.

"What is it Ed?"

"If you cause her further anguish, maybe Sebastian Fuhrmann will come back into your dreams and start haunting you again."

A fleeting look of horror crossed his face.

"You're right. I should put it behind me. What's done is done..." he seemed to hesitate for a moment.

"Ed?"

"Yes?"

"There's something else."

"Bloody hell! What now?"

"I'm not sure quite how to say it."

"Just say it, Richard."

"All right then. The day Tom was killed I *saw him*."

"That's impossible" I said. "Unless you were in East Grinstead."

"I know, I know. But I saw him. It was sometime after five o'clock. I wasn't in East Grinstead, I was in the map room at Tangmere on my own, preparing a flight path. Suddenly I was aware that Tom had come into the room and I hadn't heard a damn thing. He was standing right by me, his jacket and shirt all torn up and covered in dust, as if he'd been crawling through an attic. I even spoke to him: "Tom?" I said, "what the hell are you doing here?""

My blood had run cold and I was sober now.

"Did he say anything?" I said.

Richard shook his head. "No. He just looked at me and then, right in front of my eyes, he faded away. Anyway, when the police came later, I already knew Tom was gone."

Gilligan and Kynance were at the service, and the team from East Grinstead – the Boss, Boreman and Whitehead, even MP.

I was surprised MP had stayed in his job; I assumed he would have gone back to Australia – travelled out to some remote post in the outback with what remained of his family, somewhere far from other people. But the more I thought about it, the more his staying made sense. The sanitary world of the operation theatre, where concentration was everything, was his own 'outback', the only place where he was able to shove the pain from his mind. His face was an unreadable mask – God only knew what was going on in there. Losing a child… Christ, it doesn't get worse than that.

When Tom's parents arrived at the chapel, the atmosphere instantly changed, as if an extra curtain of sadness had been pulled across proceedings – they clung to each other as Richard ushered them over to their seats.

Richard's affair with Nielsen was still spinning around my mind like a fast carousel – Nielsen, his brother's killer, and him, her husband's killer – a perverse combination, though at the heart of it, some kind of eerie symmetry. And then Richard's encounter with Tom in the map room. He must have fallen asleep and dreamt the scene, just like I had done on the night of Tom's death. Pilots, flying long missions overnight, they probably fell asleep in the map room all the time.

The college chaplain arrived late looking embarrassed and flustered. He was the classic man of God type, with his head in the clouds and seemingly only half paying attention to what was going outside the Kingdom of Heaven. To his credit though, he managed to give a decent enough speech, quoting the story of Tom's Oxford interview; how he had told the truth when it came to naming the molecule and how the tutors had been struck by his honesty. He must have done some background research by talking to our old tutors. There was the usual smattering of bible speak – how Tom's soul was being rendered unto the Lord and things like that – which all sounded appropriate enough and well-meant, though whether anyone standing at the graveside actually believed any of it was another matter.

Tom was buried in a graveyard at the north end of town.

Staring into a hole in the ground at my best friend's coffin, I felt the anger coming back and replacing my empty lethargy, like a pint glass being re-filled with beer. It kept coming, flowing over the top and spilling everywhere; enough anger to make me feel like running across a battlefield in the direction of the entire German Army. That's what I imagined, something from the Dark Ages and not a modern war; in some big field under a brooding sky, with me sprinting at their swastika flagged lines, waving some broadsword around my head and screaming like a madman.

As soon as the burial was over I left the grave and walked out of the cemetery gates, my walk soon turning into a run, and then a sprint at full pace.

Running like this, as fast as I could, was all I could do at that moment to stay sane. It felt as if I would explode if I didn't get rid of the anger somehow. Though I couldn't avenge Tom by going for Nielsen, I could still take on the enemy – after all, she and the Nazis were one and the same. My father had opened his heart and tried to help, telling me that in time an answer would come, but his way would take too long. I wanted revenge as soon as possible.

Watching Tom's coffin being lowered into the hole in the ground was like being given the green light to act. I couldn't shut myself away forever. As I ran, I felt ashamed for having hidden away as long as I had.

Five minutes later, as I was walking down the long road towards the city, out of breath from my sudden burst of energy, a car pulled up in front of me and a man got out.

To my surprise it was Farr-Jones. Fox was at the wheel.

"You…?" was all I could say, still breathing hard.

Farr-Jones had put his hands in his trouser pockets and was gazing off down the road, avoiding my eyes.

"I'm sorry to disturb you at such a difficult time," he said.

He didn't look sorry at all.

"You were at the funeral?" I said. "I didn't see you."

He glanced back at me and nodded. "We kept in the background."

"Why did you come?"

"To speak to you, Doctor, in actual fact. I was hoping to catch you afterwards for a quick word, but then you took off… so we jumped in the car and came after you." He looked off down the road again – it was largely empty of cars. "I suppose this is as good a place as any to talk," he said.

"What do you want?"

Farr-Jones threw my question back at me. "What do *you* want? You're the one who left the message."

My blood was still up from the sprint of rage.

"I want to fight," I said. "I want to do some fucking damage. Kill some of those fuckers."

He nodded as if he had been expecting I would say that. Leaning to one side, he opened the rear door of the car.

"Get in then."

"What? Now?"

"What's wrong with now?"

I thought about that.

"Nothing, I suppose."

"Alright then," he said, motioning with his free hand for me to get in.

Once Fox had pulled away, I spoke for the first and last time on the entire journey.

"Where are we going?"

Farr-Jones didn't turn around.

"London. We're taking you to HQ for an interview. I can't promise you anything – it depends on what they think you're made of."

Part Two

Chapter Thirteen

London, 23rd July 1943

Through my clouded mind, the sights of the capital came at me in staccato bursts.

Marble Arch: a cinema showing *Watch on the Rhine* with Bette Davis – men in uniform streaming into the entrance with their sweethearts.

Oxford Street: the bombed out ruins of the John Lewis Department Store and a 25 pounder gun on the pavement.

Euston station: A newspaper vendor on the corner shouting: 'PATTON'S SEVENTH ARMY ENTERS PALERMO!'

Soon after passing Euston, Fox and Farr Jones dropped me off outside a mansion block and pulled away.

A young woman opened the front door before I even had a chance to knock.

"Dr Hunston?"

The fact she was ready with my name told me they had been planning this all along – for today – knowing they would collect me from the funeral, and rightly assuming I would be angry enough to come. They thought ahead, these people; dotted the 'i's and crossed the 't's… left nothing to chance.

A team of people had been analysing me from afar, knowing that at the funeral I would be most susceptible, the time when the desire for vengeance would finally spill over.

"Yes, I am," I said, before allowing her to usher me inside.

I was immediately aware that I had stepped into another world. Here, there was a sense of purpose and of efficiency. People were walking up and down a wide staircase carrying manila files. In a room down the hall, I could see two women operating a telephone switchboard with formidable efficiency. A young lad scurried down the corridor with a telegram in his hand.

I was taken to a lift which rose up rapidly to the third floor and led down a long carpeted corridor with numbered rooms on either side.

"Is this a hotel?"

"Yes... well, it was. The Northumberland – it has been commandeered."

She stopped at a room numbered 321 and turned to me.

"Would you like a cup of tea?"

"No, thank you."

She smiled and pointed to a wooden chair in the hallway.

"Do take a seat then. I'll let them know you're here."

I did as instructed. She went inside and shut the door firmly behind her. From the glimpse I had of the interior, the room was bare and dimly lit.

Maybe I should have accepted the offer; my mouth was dry – my last drink had been with Richard in the pub about four hours earlier. But this was all too strange for me to think about drinking tea.

It occurred to me I had missed the wake – they were having it in a Chinese restaurant in Oxford. I would have to write to Richard and apologise.

I looked about to distract myself.

On the wall of the corridor was one of those Ministry of Information propaganda posters. It was of a beautiful, voluptuous woman in a white evening dress, reclining on a sofa and looking seductively out at the viewer. Three officers chatted around her, obviously hoping to impress. The caption was: 'Keep mum, she's not so dumb'. I felt the artist had modelled the poster on Freya Nielsen, and the fawning men were the Shaw brothers and me. It was just as if we had been posing for the drawing these last months, clueless as to who she really was.

Next to the poster was a single piece of paper, pinned onto the wall. There was writing on it, but the print was so small I had to go closer to read it. Someone had typed the following:

NEVER GIVE IN, NEVER GIVE IN - NEVER, NEVER, NEVER - IN NOTHING, GREAT OR SMALL, LARGE OR PETTY - NEVER GIVE IN EXCEPT TO CONVICTIONS OF HONOUR AND GOOD SENSE. NEVER YIELD TO FORCE; NEVER YIELD TO THE APPARENTLY OVERWHELMING MIGHT OF THE ENEMY.
W.C.

The door opened and the woman stood to one side to let me pass. "Dr Hunston," she said. "They're ready to see you now."

I entered the room and heard the door being shut behind me.

In the shadows, two men were sitting at a makeshift trestle table. There was a spare chair – one of those cheap foldaway jobs that people used in their gardens. *What a shithole.* I could smell coffee, though there were no cups in sight.

It took a few seconds for my eyes to adjust before I recognised one of the men as Pirbright.

A bloody spymaster!

Seeing him made me smile. I had a sudden sense that Tom was helping orchestrate all this from his ghostly realm and really enjoying himself as he did so. Here I was, about to face the man whose ideas had helped get me into University, but whose hero status had been lost for me that day in the University parks, the man who was now responsible for my future settling of scores. Tom must have thought it hilarious to stage things this way, watching it all pan out.

I decided to throw all caution to the wind. I was still in a dangerous mood from the funeral and somewhat harassed by my virtual kidnap by Fox and Farr-Jones. I felt I had absolutely nothing to lose.

Without being asked I took the available seat opposite the men.

Pirbright was studying me closely, bemused at my smile.

"May I ask what you find so amusing?"

I wasn't going to tell him the real answer.

"I know your books."

He beamed back at me in a self-satisfied way. He obviously had no idea he had ever seen me before. Right now felt as good a time as any to start getting my own back on anyone who had ever slighted me – it was time to lash out.

"Ah... and?"

"It was a sardonic smile," I said. "As far as I can tell, the Nazis have lifted half of your theories for their own warped ends."

My remark didn't seem to rattle Pirbright in the way I had hoped it would. Instead, his expression turned to one of deep thought.

"Let me tell you a story, Hunston," he said, his voice quiet, "and perhaps by the end of it, you'll think better of me. Before the war, in 1938, I was in Germany attending a science conference. One morning, I saw a poster in the street, published by their so-called 'Racial Policy' office. It was an advertisement for a magazine called *Neues Volk*, or 'New People'. In it, a handsome white-coated doctor stands over a seated shaven-headed patient – with the caption: 'This hereditary defective costs the Volk community 60,000 Reichsmarks over his lifetime... German Comrade that is your money.' And you know what Hunston? You're right, the ideas could have come straight out of *The Gene Machine*. I realised that although the concept 'survival of the fittest' might sound clever in a book, in a social setting you have to be careful, because it easily becomes something ugly and immoral..."

"Is there a point to the story?"

"Yes there is. I was just getting to it. My own son has a crippling disease you see. However, he is not a 'ballast existence', as the *Neues Volk* would have you believe – he is a loving individual who in turn is deeply loved. Seeing the poster made me want to fight the Nazis, or at least use my intellect to protect my son and others who can't defend themselves. So I joined the Intelligence Services.'

I shifted in my chair, now regretting I had laid into him.

"Professor... I'm sorry if I offended you."

He waved his hand at me.

"Not at all, not at all. Actually, I think I'm the one who offended you."

"Oh?"

"Yes, if I remember rightly... in the parks that day... you were with your friend, weren't you? Studying from a pair of lungs if I'm not mistaken..."

"That's right," I said, astonished.

"There's a reason they took me on here, Hunston. I have a rather prodigious memory. Anyhow, I believe I was rather short with you – and that's why I want to apologise. My son was unwell in hospital yet again, you see. Cystic fibrosis… which, as you know, attacks the lungs. I was frustrated at the world. And then I saw your putrid lung specimen taunting me from the path. You just happened to be there… I just wanted to take it out on someone; you understand that?"

"Yes…" I said, humbled in an instant by seeing the whole episode from his perspective. "Completely."

"He's very honest at least," Pirbright said, turning his attention to his colleague. "Not afraid to call a spade a spade."

The other man looked at me, his face expressionless. I hadn't really taken any notice of him until now; just been aware of him staring, like Gilligan in my Oxford interview. He was balding and rotund, but it was the kind of bulkiness you would expect to see in an ex-sportsman who had softened up a bit in his middle age. Perhaps he had been a very fine rugby player. Though that was hard to believe from his current physical state I had learnt over the years that these old sporty types were not to be underestimated – although the body might be shot, the killer instinct within was not. He wore a pair of round spectacles and was fidgeting, as if nervous. Reaching into his breast pocket, he pulled out a small tin and opened the lid. It contained white lozenges of some kind, and I watched on as he popped one into his mouth with a shaking hand.

"My name's Stringer," he said, his voice tremulous with apparent nerves but his eyes telling me the exact opposite. "You know what we do?"

"Run some kind of spy school?"

"Not far off. We're called the Special Operations Executive, formed by Churchill at the beginning of the war to 'set Europe ablaze'. His words. Privately, he likes to call us 'The Ministry of Ungentlemanly Warfare'. We put people into occupied territories where they foster relationships with the local Resistance groups. We run F section. F stands for France. You speak French?"

"Passably," I said. "Studied it at school and used to go on holidays there in my childhood."

"Why did you go to France?"

"Why not? The places we went were beautiful; we used to head down to the Alps, or the French Riviera, stay in nice hotels and go for long walks and swim in the warm ocean. My father served in the hell of the Great War – I suppose he wanted to enjoy the good things in life afterwards."

The Intelligence men smiled at this. "That's good," Stringer said. "There are classes you can take to polish it up. Do you know the French word for a clog?"

"Sabot."

"Exactly so. A century ago, when French factory workers were unhappy with conditions, they would throw their clogs in the machinery and make everything grind to a halt."

"Sabotage," I said, working out what he was trying to say.

"That's it precisely. That's how we help the French. Except it isn't with clogs – it's with weapons, explosives, communications, expertise…"

"I don't know anything about those things."

"Yes, but you can learn. As long as you have some common sense, you can get a long way in this world. A good dose of common sense, combined with a good dose of grit. Do you think you could lie low for weeks… possibly months… and then spring into action?"

"It sounds like one of my on-calls in the hospital – but stretched out."

Stringer laughed.

"Can you stay in role? Can you eat like a Frenchman, drink like a Frenchman…can you fuck like a Frenchman?"

I couldn't work out if he was trying to shock me or whether it was just the way he was.

"Peut-être," I said.

He laughed again, but almost immediately afterwards, the laugh dissolved.

"Even the best can mess up, you know… let slip a loose word in English without thinking… or lose it in extreme moments of stress – make simple mistakes that shouldn't happen. Do that and… well…"

He made the hand action of a knife in front of his throat.

I looked down at the small scar on my hand. His comment about stress made me think of 'wild man' Whitehead cutting me in the operation.

"You've probably not heard of Commando order?" I heard Stringer say.

"No."

"Hitler brought it into effect at the end of last year. Any captured Special Forces soldier – and that includes an agent or saboteur – is to be shot."

"Aren't there rules of war?"

"You mean the Geneva convention? Yes, but the Nazis aren't playing by those rules when it comes to commandos."

"So you're saying don't get captured."

"No, well, not alive anyway."

My initial bluster was gone now. This was getting serious.

Like a mind-reader, Stringer seemed to pick up on this. He sat forward, resting his pudgy elbows on the table.

"Still interested?"

My mouth was dry and it was hard to swallow.

"Yes," I said, my voice carrying less conviction than my earlier remarks.

He leafed through some papers in front of him.

"Your tutors gave you reasonable references," he said, his head down and reading. "And the chief surgeon in East Grinstead said you're a hard worker. Farr-Jones and Fox seem to think you have some innate intelligence." He peeped up at me over the top of his spectacles. "But no-one has said you're *special*. What do you bring to the table? Why don't you just keep on doctoring?"

"Because I want to kill as many of them as I can," I said.

The room stayed silent at this dramatic statement of intent: no 'ooohs' or 'aaaahs' from the two men sitting across from me.

Stringer in particular didn't look very impressed by my tough man act.

"Why?"

"You know why. It must be on your papers there."

"Yes, but I want you to tell me all the same."

"My best friend was killed in a bombing raid, and that bombing was radioed in by an Abwehr agent."

"Ah yes," he said, checking one of the papers, and then holding it out with a shaking hand. "Freya Nielsen... alias Mrs Carter."

"That's right."

He put the page down and sat back in his chair. Everything about Stringer was there to give you a false sense of security – his cuddly teddy bear exterior and his nervous sounding voice, but it was the eyes behind the spectacles which told you otherwise, well, that and the directness of his comments. You immediately felt you were in the presence of someone extremely intelligent and dangerous, a cross between a KC barrister and an assassin.

"You knew her?" he said.

"Yes. We all did at the hospital. I'm sure Farr-Jones and Fox have explained all this in their report."

The tone in my reply was tinged with anger and impatience.

Stringer pushed his chair backwards, stood up and came around the table to my side. He perched himself on the edge so that he loomed right beside me, heavy and swarthy.

"Think you could kill her?"

"What?"

"Could you kill her? Pull the trigger, if you had the chance?"

His face was deadly serious.

"Yes," I said. "But I can't get to her. So, for me, the Nazis are the next best thing."

At that, Stringer stood up and went over to the door by which I had entered. I noticed his shirt was hanging out at the back, his flabby flanks bulging where his braces were doing their best to hold up his trousers.

He opened it and leant out into the corridor.

"We're ready."

There was the sound of footsteps and then Farr-Jones and Fox brought Nielsen into the room. They stood to either side of her, each holding an arm.

Her face was pale, but just as beautiful as ever and, without meaning to, I found myself thinking about the time we had kissed. That was the last time I had seen her.

She said nothing and didn't acknowledge me. It was as if I were a stranger.

Slowly, I stood up, my thoughts blurry and my legs heavy.

Stringer walked over to a briefcase near his chair, pulled something out, and then came over to me. He placed a gun into my hand.

"Go on then," he said. "Here's your chance. She's to be hanged anyway. We could fudge the papers. Go on. Do it if you think you're so tough. Put one in her heart. Actions speak louder than words."

The gun felt weightier than it looked.

I looked at Stringer.

"I mean it" he said, "Do it now!"

Trembling, I raised my arm and aimed at her chest.

She stared at me resolutely; still certain she had done the right thing, ready to die for her cause. I thought of Tom and MP's son and all the other people she was responsible for killing and then pulled the trigger, with no real outward sign of hesitation.

It clicked harmlessly and I was surprised to see a look of disappointment register in her eyes.

Stringer took the weapon back and nodded at Farr Jones and Fox, who led her away without saying a word.

They must have had her ready for me all day. It was a test – perhaps my most important – because if I hadn't squeezed the trigger I am sure Stringer would have told me to get out of his sight.

"Impressive," he said, returning to his seat and looking to Pirbright. "I had thought it all bravado, didn't you?"

"Actually, no," Pirbright said. "He seems to be a very angry young man. Needs to be taught how to control the rage – channel it – but once he's been trained, he should make a decent enough agent."

I was too shaken to make any witty remark.

It wasn't because I had pulled the trigger. No, what had shaken me was the expression in her eyes. The image had seared itself into my brain – the disappointment. But disappointment at what exactly? Not being reunited with her dead husband? Knowing she had turned me into a killer? The realisation that I was now willing to kill her, or any of the enemy, without hesitation? Seeing what she had created?

"So be it," Stringer said. "Get yourself through the training, and you can go to France and have the chance to wreak all the havoc you want. We'll call you with the details. You'll be at your parents' house, I presume?"

I hadn't even thought about what I was going to do next, but I had nowhere else to go.

"Yes, sir."

"Don't mention this meeting to anybody, not even them."

He wrote something down and closed the file.

What had he written?

Prepared to kill?

Has demonstrated the required attitude for a posting?

Is a complete cold-hearted bastard?

He lit a cigarette and didn't offer me one. There was another knock and the woman who had shown me in earlier popped her head around the door.

She looked at Stringer in a way which said he was needed elsewhere.

"I'm sorry, sir…"

He gathered all the papers up from the tabletop and put them back into his briefcase. "Good luck," he said, before walking out.

Pirbright came around the table and shook my hand. My old hero from my schooldays – shaking *my* hand! Maybe he could sign my copy of *The Gene Machine* too.

"Get yourself through selection," he said, "and then we'll send you hunting."

Chapter Fourteen

I stood there watching our instructor, a man we simply called 'the Captain'. He was holding a knife with a double edged blade, some seven inches long and gripping a squealing pig between his legs.

We were a mile away from camp on the shore of Loch nan Uamh and a cold breeze was coming in off the water, chilling me to the bone.

I could understand the knife, the freezing cold, my discomfort – the part I couldn't understand was why we had been made to strip down to our underwear. Even the two females in our twenty strong group. The Captain himself was just in his training shorts, stripped to waist and barefoot like the rest of us. Our battle fatigues and boots lay all in a pile a few yards away on the shingle.

"In silent killing," he was saying, "there's nothing deadlier than the knife."

He started to toss the blade back and forth between his hands, an action so practised that he didn't need to look down at what he was doing – he kept his attention firmly fixed on us.

Yes, yes, but why aren't we wearing any clothes?

He held the blade up and moved it along the eye-line of the group.

"It's essential for the knife to have a good stabbing point and sharp cutting edges… an artery torn through roughly – as opposed to a clean cut – tends to contract and stop the bleeding. If, on the other hand, a main artery is cleanly severed, the wounded man will quickly lose consciousness and die.'

This was the 'close-quarters combat' section of the course, though the Captain preferred his term, 'silent killing'. He looked well qualified to be giving the lessons – the skin on his torso and arms looked like an old butcher's block, criss-crossed with dozens of scars, presumably from knife fights. He was surprisingly old, around sixty I would guess, and he wore a pair of spectacles, similar to Stringer's, which made him look more like a vicar than a killer. The rumour among our group, gleaned I know not how, was that the Captain had once been with the Shanghai Police Force. I had the distinct feeling he had finished off as many men's lives as he had eaten hot breakfasts.

"Gather round closer," he said.

We crowded around in a tight semi-circle, our bare feet treading cautiously on the shingle.

In one swift movement he reached down and slit the pig's throat, and then lifted up the animal so that the severed artery sprayed us all.

"Carotid artery," he said. "Loss of consciousness in approximately 5 seconds, death in 12…"

Without thinking I took a step backwards to avoid the squirting red jet.

"What the fuck are you doing, Ahab?" he said to me. "Don't move. I want you to get used to this."

Ahab was my codename – no real names had been used since the beginning of selection.

The Captain always seemed to pick on me, though always with a humorous glint in his eye. I think he sensed I could take whatever he chose to dish out – maybe he could see the dangerous urge to kill lurking within me, making him recognise a kindred spirit. Or maybe he could see I was well used to being humiliated and that I could ride it out without taking offence. Some of the medical lecturers back at Oxford had based their entire teaching strategy on ritual humiliation. And then I had experienced Boreman for the best part of a year. This stuff with the Captain was fairly mild in comparison.

"Sorry, sir," I said, standing stock still as he held the dying pig up to my face.

"Taste it, Ahab. What's it like?"

I licked my lips.

"It's warm, sir!"

The blood was everywhere. Christ, it was like being stuck in an operation with 'Wild man' Whitehead.

"Good, Ahab – we'll make a killer of you yet…"

He sprayed all the students and, when we were all doused red, he blooded himself before slinging the dead pig on the ground. All this had happened in the last twelve seconds of the pig's existence.

"Strictly speaking, I've made an error," he said. "Quicker still would have been the knife to the heart – loss of consciousness instantaneous, death occurring within 3 seconds…"

I glanced around at my fellow students – a surreal sight against the backdrop of the Loch and the mountains.

"Now I know some of you bourgeois liberals may be shocked that human beings in the middle of the twentieth century would need to embrace the savagery of the Stone Age… but you have to understand we are dealing with a merciless and brutal enemy – an enemy who wants to wipe this nation from the face of the earth. Do you follow me?"

"Yes, sir!" we said as one.

He held up the blood-stained knife.

"So, there must be no quibbling about the methods we have to use in stopping him from achieving his goals… no quibbling at all. Agreed?"

"Yes, sir!"

"We want to do him the utmost damage. YES?"

"YES, SIR!"

There was a short silence.

"Excuse me, sir? What about the pig?"

It was 'Stella', one of the female recruits.

The Captain looked baffled.

"What about it, Stella?"

"Well, isn't it a bit of a waste, sir?"

"Not at all."

He kicked the carcass over to her feet.

"Sir?" she said, confused.

"Well, what did you think we were going to eat tonight, Stella?"

She remained silent.

"What?" he said laughing crazily and waving his knife around at the bleak landscape, "did you all think we were going to have a three course dinner out here?"

He pointed the knife at us in accusation.

"Oh? You think I'm your servant – here to wipe your arses and cook your meals? Is that what you think?"

"No, sir!" the whole group said.

He grinned.

"Glad to hear it. Gather what dry wood you can, light a fire and set about roasting our recently departed friend, Mr Piggy, here. Oh, and I almost forgot, I've bought us a present."

He reached into the pocket of his shorts and pulled out a bag of salt.

"Don't say I don't care… Mr Piggy will taste good tonight. Now get dressed and get going!"

Later that night, as we all huddled around the campfire eating the mouth-watering pieces of salted fatty stringy pork pulled from the roasted carcass, I allowed myself to reflect on what I had achieved so far.

It was our last night of close combat and we had all passed – the 'blooding' earlier had been his hunter's way of initiating us all into his Silent Killing club. As the pig's blood dried under my clothes I felt my skin being pulled taut. A silent killer baptised in blood… *'to the last I grapple with thee; from hell's heart I stab at thee…'*

Most of the time, I had pushed Tom Shaw right to the back of my mind – we weren't allowed to talk about our outside lives so it was best to not even think about them either, especially if they were painful thoughts. But sometimes, without my being able to help it, he would rise to the forefront of my consciousness.

I remembered the start of selection, the code name I had chosen and why.

I had decided on Ahab after the book he had been reading at the time of his death. I thought it would serve as a motivator and I hadn't been wrong. Being called Ahab constantly reminded me why I was doing this. It gave me the will to stand fast while a lunatic knife fighter spray-painted me with pig's blood on a windswept Scottish beach.

First off, I had been made a second lieutenant in the army. Selection had started with the 'Student Assessment Board' at STS 7 – a Manor house in Surrey. STS stood for 'special training school'. The course was designed to assess character, to weed out those applicants who would never be suited to undercover work.

There was a psychological interview and initially I was defensive and cagey with my answers, not comfortable with the probing, unwilling to open up. From their body language – especially the frowns – I knew it wasn't going very well, until it dawned on me that all they were trying to find out was how much I was willing to sacrifice. That was fine with me. I was ready to sacrifice *everything*. Once I got the gist, I started faring better, speaking more freely. Things turned on one question in particular:

"How do you feel about pain?"

"How do you mean?"

"If you broke your ribs in training, for example, what would you do?"

"Strap up my chest and take a painkiller."

"Would you tell the instructor?"

I hesitated, before opting to be honest.

"No, I would hide it."

On hearing this, the interviewer was quiet for a few moments, and he even put down his clipboard. It was obviously the first time he had been given that answer.

"Why?"

"So I wouldn't get kicked off the course."

I could tell he liked that.

"Let's say you did get kicked off the course, what would you do then?"

"Re-apply."

"And say you were kicked off five times, what then?"

"I would re-apply again."

"Name a single good quality you would say you had, if you had failed five times before?"

"Tenacity."

After the interviews, we were given group exercises; as a team of six we had to move a heavy log over high obstacles in a set time, or find a way of somehow getting ourselves over an electrified barbed wire barrier six feet thick, using only a rope and two planks of wood. The tasks were not realistic; they were just a way for the instructors to see which candidates would be a liability later on in the training.

I surrendered my cool autonomy and bonded as best I could with the others to carry out the challenges. Much of medicine had been the same, pharmacology, histology, biochemistry – of little use in the real world, but a necessity in training.

Some of the students became self-appointed leaders, shouting and bossing us all around and getting everyone's backs up straight away. The tone in their voices made you resent them and pull back rather than press forward. When we questioned their orders or ignored them altogether, they became even more dictatorial. These types were used to getting their own way, but you only had to picture them dealing with seasoned, proud French Resistance fighters to see how impossible the relationships would become. They soon got asked to leave – the instructors coming over and whispering in their ears discretely.

There were others who took the lead too, but quietly and without apparent effort. They encouraged the team to go with them – their manner inspiring, not antagonistic. These types stayed on, as did their cheerful, successful teams.

By the end of four days, the forty eight original students had become twenty four.

The paramilitary course was at another Manor house – STS 21 – this time in the wild, unpopulated Highlands of Scotland; a place of dark Lochs, wet heather and grey skies. A real feeling of brotherhood started to develop within the team; sisterhood too, since the two remaining women – 'Stella' and 'Nancy' – were just as tough as the men.

There were six physical training sessions per week, in the form of early morning runs, and we soon became leaner and harder, like the French peasants we were aiming to mimic. Too much muscle bulk would be a giveaway, so our rations were kept tight.

I remembered the distant, aloof way the rowing team at college had stared at Tom and me when we had staggered past them at the same early hour, on our way to the caf. Now the role was reversed – I was the athlete, looking at the person I had once been, and barely recognising myself.

My anger was useful in training because it provided me with an inexhaustible supply of free energy and resolve. There were other trainees who were fitter and cleverer than me, but none were blessed with my abundance of anger. The anger made me stubborn – I was never going to give up, even if it killed me. I really did not care anymore. Grit was the trait Stringer had mentioned in the interview and I could see why. To get through this, you needed grit to an extreme degree. As far as I could make out, not giving up was the only requirement. I was willing to die, and I don't think most of the others were. It was that simple.

One morning, during a particularly cold, wet and miserable session, one of the ablest male students suddenly stopped running, turned round and started walking back to base. He had been one of the effective leaders on the initial assessment, one of the stars so far. Part of me wanted to say to him, 'Hang on, you can get through this, just hang on a bit longer,' but I'll admit most of me was elated to have outlasted him.

It didn't seem to matter if you weren't brilliant, but you couldn't be completely useless; the occasional C or D grade was fine, as long as you didn't get an E in anything. As the course progressed, a few were pulled out for consistently low standards with no improvement – dead last in every run, complete mal-coordination in the close combat drills, a danger to themselves, let alone others, when holding a weapon. They were sent to 'the cooler' – another facility in Scotland, where they had to stay until the military authorities were sure they wouldn't go blabbing about silent killing to their friends as soon as they were let out.

After a time, during those long morning treks into the hills, my body reached a certain level of pain beyond which it held steady. That's what the strong man who dropped out hadn't realised – there was a point beyond which things got no worse. Admittedly, it was an absolutely miserable place to be, not far short of unconsciousness, but the line on the pain graph plateaued. In his head, the star student had extrapolated the situation – thinking it was going to get worse and worse. It was his own imagination that had stopped him, not the pain itself.

I found I could function at the far edge of this pain limit and cope. The longer the course went on, the more familiar I became with this realm. "Hold fast", I would say to myself, "That's all I have to do."

In silent killing we first practiced on straw dummies – attacking them in a set of moves taught by the Captain; edge of the hand blows, chin jabs, side-kicks, bronco kicks, knee blows. Then there were the 'releases'; ways of breaking free of wrist holds, strangle-holds, bear hugs and hair holds. We learnt the 'restraints': thumb-holds, sentry-holds, the Japanese hold, the handcuff-hold, the bent arm hold, the head hold. And then we studied the 'throws' – hip throw, wrist throw, and 'the back-break'. There was even a category the Captain called 'miscellaneous': the match-box attack, smacking the ears, the art of getting up from the ground, attack with a small stick or cane.

"It's not how hard you hit, Ahab, it's *where* you hit," the Captain had said to me on the first day, as I had swung away at the straw torso with loopy, roundhouse punches. With a small chopping motion using the edge of his hand on the side of my neck he dropped me like a sack of potatoes. I came to a few seconds later, on the ground and groggy, and feeling like I was going to be sick.

"Listen to me," I heard him telling the watching students. "Fancy blows like that only go so far and in a real fight situation all of these techniques may desert you in the panic. If there's only one thing you remember when faced with an adversary, it is to kick the bastard in the bollocks as hard as you can. If any of you think that doing such a thing simply isn't cricket, just remember that Herr Hitler doesn't play the game."

We were issued with our own commando daggers.

On the black handle were the letters 'F-S', the initials of the blade's designers, Fairbairn and Sykes. Someone in the group said that the Captain was Sykes but we never found out for sure. I could believe it though – the more I watched him at work, the more I felt sorry for the gang members of the Shanghai waterfront who had once been on the receiving end.

He taught us where the arteries were, which as a medic I already knew, though the way he taught it seemed counter-intuitive, because back in East Grinstead the aim had been to avoid the arteries in surgical operations, not to actively seek them out.

"The upwards thrust is the most effective," he would say, skewering the dummy. We smeared our F-S daggers with lipstick to see how accurate our feigned attacks were – first on the dummy and then on each other. After classes our necks had red lipstick lines all around the carotids.

We practised so much I started having knife fights in my sleep. I wondered if I would ever be able to walk into a pub again without thinking of the various ways in which I could kill the man standing at the bar.

Sometimes, as I went through my moves in front of the mirror, MP would come to mind, specifically his deranged manner in the mess that morning when he had played with the scalpel of devastation – he would have been very good at this part of the course.

I liked the knife. Perhaps this was because I hadn't been allowed to wield the scalpel during operations at East Grinstead – my job there had been only to hold the retractors steady as the seniors did their thing. Now though, I got to play with a big blade for hours and hours – indeed it was encouraged. I seemed to have a knack with the weapon.

"Christ almighty, Ahab," the Captain had said one day, impressed at where my lipstick lines had ended up on my partner's neck, "you're over the carotid each time. If this was Moby Dick, the whale would be stone dead by now!"

The more I practised, the more I found myself wanting to meet a German SS soldier, armed only with my F-S dagger. A sacrificial blood-letting straight out of the Old Testament would avenge Tom – it felt like the only way I would be able to make things right. I wanted to watch the life drain out of the eyes of the enemy – stare into his pupils as they dilated for the last time.

On the weapons course, the Captain stood out on the lawn, a pistol stuffed into his belt and a life size cardboard cut-out of a German soldier propped up beside him.

"Forget marksmanship," he said. "This isn't the Olympics. In most shooting affrays, the distance at which firing takes place is no more than four yards, often less than that. That's why I'm standing right here next to Jerry. Sometimes the only warning of what is about to happen is a suspicious movement of an opponent's hand. Not only that, but he may be on the move. You may be on the move. It may be that a bullet whizzes past you..." The Captain made a sound: *'pfffft!'* accompanied by an arm motion imitating a pretend bullet passing over his head. "I can guarantee that a bullet missing your noggin by inches will throw you into a state you've never experienced before, not even in training. You may piss or shit your pants, you may just freeze, but either way the chances are you'll be dead within a few seconds. It is therefore imperative that you get off the first shot. There's no time to get into a special stance or aim your eye along the sights... forget all that tripe. You've got a fraction of a second to do it."

He whipped out the pistol.

"Hip level with a bent arm... Remember, if you shoot first, even if you miss, you'll have an advantage of as much as two seconds over an opponent, since they'll be the ones pissing their pants or frozen in position trying to recover their wits."

The Captain suddenly shot from the hip at the target.

BANG! BANG!

We all jumped at the sudden noise. Two holes had appeared in the chest of the cardboard German.

"It is literally a matter of the quick and the dead," he said, staying crouched after he had fired, both legs bent at the knee, one in front of the other and his body leaning forward.

"Notice my stance… I'm automatically in a crouching position. Instinctively you'll want to make yourselves as small as possible. Two shots – always do a double tap – double the damage… one shot may not be enough to stop someone fuelled by adrenaline. Some bastards are like wounded elephants. Firing two shots raises the odds of bringing them down."

He straightened up for a moment before ducking down and loosing off another two rounds: BANG! BANG!

"Again," he said, "notice my crouch. Shanghai, 1927… a fifteen man police raiding party moving at night in a very dangerous area. The only approach to the target house was down a narrow alley, we were expecting trouble at any moment and made our way along the alley with our weapons drawn, ready to fire. The mission was accomplished and all targets were neutralised. That's not the interesting point though… The day after the raid, I went back and noticed a series of wires stretched across the alley at face height – lines for hanging washing. Not one man out of the fifteen had touched those wires the night before; we'd all been crouched down low, without even knowing it."

The Captain held up the firearm.

"You will use an automatic pistol, not a revolver. Automatics are quicker to load, they can be fired at greater speed and they are easier to shoot. End of story. We will not use safety catches – these cause unnecessary accidents. Just assume the weapon is always unsafe."

Like a magician, he pulled back the sheet on a nearby table to reveal an array of guns.

"Come and get your weapons. Boys take the Colt 45s, girls take the Colt 32s."

Shooting was fairly straightforward, the Captain seemed happy as long as we had more than a fifty per cent hit rate on the targets. He took us to log cabins and taught us how to shoot four people in a room, by first dropping to the ground by the door lintel to make ourselves smaller targets. In a forest, we fired at cut-outs which suddenly appeared from behind trees, the Captain and other instructors using string pulleys to swing them into position.

We got to know the larger firearms too; the Bren and the Sten sub-machine guns, and the Lee-Enfield Mark 4 rifle.

The first time I fired a Sten, my shots all sprayed way high of the target and then it jammed. The bloody thing seemed to have a mind of its own. One student let go in surprise when shooting and the Sten proceeded to dance around on the ground dementedly; firing on its own until the whole magazine was spent. Amazingly no-one got hurt.

The Captain must have been in a forgiving mood, because he didn't send the student to the cooler. Instead he said it was a lesson well-learned and that many French Resistance fighters had died in exactly this way.

"When firing the Sten, aim low," he said. "Fire from the shoulder in single shots to keep control of the weapon."

He was right – when I started my shooting with the muzzle pointed at the ground, the shots rose up nicely and struck the target fifty yards away.

The Bren was better. It took the same size ammunition as the Lee-Enfield – .303 calibre – but came with a thirty round magazine compared with the Lee Enfield's measly five rounds. It was a lot more accurate than the Sten. The Captain told us the French Resistance loved the Bren and that we would be seeing a lot more of these in the field.

Though I fared 'average' in weapons training, I was less interested in the pistols and machine guns than in the close combat – they were too technical and not as personal. The silent killing made more sense to me.

Things became even more impersonal when we were taught in the use of plastic explosives and hand grenades. We learnt to toss the grenades using a rigid overarm throw, not unlike bowling a cricket ball

– simple enough. The 'gammon' grenade was an improvised device in which an explosive charge was wrapped in fabric and sewn to an impact fuse which detonated on sharp contact. We all sat in a trench for a drill, leaping out one at a time, throwing a grenade and then jumping back into the trench. One idiot – the same one who had dropped the Sten – mucked up his throw and the grenade ended up back in our trench. There had been boys like this at school – lads with no hand-eye co-ordination but plenty of heart. When the grenade landed in the trench, the entire group had leapt out in a heartbeat – at a speed which would have impressed any Great War commander blowing the whistle to go over the top.

The Captain was incandescent with rage.

"That's two huge fuck-ups you've made… You're more dangerous than the bloody enemy."

This time, nothing could save the poor chap from being sent to the cooler, not even his pluck and determination.

'Demolitions' lasted two days. It felt as though we were children playing with modelling clay, until we blew up a stone bridge with the charges we had made. There were all sorts of ingenious ways in which plastic explosives could be hidden in innocent objects – blocks of coal or the carcasses of dead rats, for example – to be left out on railway engine footplates with the idea that a train driver might throw them into the locomotive's boiler and 'do damage'.

I managed the assault course easily enough; crawling on my belly under barbed wire, jumping across large gaps, scaling walls and shimmying like a monkey along ropes strung up between trees. One student was unable to pull himself up and over the wall, despite being given four chances, and that was it for him. Up in the trees was a 'dizzy platform' some seventy feet up, from which you had to leap and catch a rope six feet away to slide down to the ground. Two students froze on this platform and were sent to the cooler.

By the end of the paramilitary course, twenty four had been whittled down to twelve. On our last full day, the Captain divided the twelve into six teams of two and sent us all on a particularly arduous twenty four hour exercise, just to make sure we weren't getting over confident.

A very strange thing happened on that last exercise.

It had rained virtually the whole time and the only food my teammate and I ate was a raw salmon, caught with a makeshift net.

As I squelched through a peat bog under the brilliant stars, the pain humming at a certain pitch in my muscles, and my body in a state where it wasn't possible to be more tired or more hungry, I suddenly 'felt' Tom walking next me. Not like my usual imaginings which had been in my sleep – this time I could sense him as clearly as the man who was actually with me. And I was awake. We were in the remotest part of the route, a place where the wind was driving sideways and I was so cold my teeth were chattering like a set of wind-up dentures from a joke shop. Tom didn't say anything and I wouldn't say I could exactly 'see' him either – it was just that I knew he was there.

The experience lasted an hour or so before I felt him leave. It was at first light and I could see our camp a few miles away down in the Glen.

This wasn't the oddest part though. As my partner and I staggered down the mountainside towards STS 21, he said something that sent a chill down my spine:

"It's the weirdest thing… and you'll probably think I'm losing my mind, but last night it felt like there were three of us out there on that damn mountain, not two."

I had never before considered the possibility of an afterlife or ghosts, or whatever you choose to call this kind of thing. Once, after dinner, my father had alluded to an event out in the Australian desert, in which his brother had appeared to him like a ghost – talking and encouraging him out of danger. Apparently, my father hadn't actually *seen* his brother, more *sensed* his presence. This was when I had been a rational scientist of course, and as soon as my father had noticed my incredulous expression he had cut the story short by saying, "Of course I was dehydrated and hallucinating, but it felt real enough."

After recent events – my vivid dreams on the night Tom had died, Richard's tale of Tom turning up at his aerodrome, and now the experience out on the mountain – I imagined that if my father ever decided to tell me the story again, he would see the change in me and go into more detail. He might even elaborate on what exactly he had seen in the cemetery at Passchendaele during that October night in 1917.

The really interesting thing was that my team-mate on the exercise had sensed it too; startling evidence it hadn't just been a figment of my imagination or a hallucination. Something had happened out there, I don't know what, how or why – but to use my father's understated words: 'it felt real enough'.

Chapter Fifteen

After combat training I was sent straight to the Beaulieu estate in the South of England, to what the agents called 'finishing school'. Unlike the rest, I never went on the parachute course, and it wasn't because I was scared of heights. My training was being fast-tracked and I was soon to find out why.

At Beaulieu, I was ushered into a grand room in the main house, a log fire burning in a great stone hearth.

"You look leaner," was the first thing Pirbright said, standing with his back to the blaze.

"Well, we trained hard."

Stringer was there too, in a red velvet wing-backed chair, leafing through papers. He didn't look up when he spoke.

"The Captain thinks you did alright," he said. "Says you can handle yourself.'

"I liked the silent killing."

He was concentrating on one sheet, pushing his reading glasses back up his nose and peering down, with his face six inches from the page.

"Yes," he said. "The Captain said you had a real knack for it, with the knife particularly."

"Yes, sir. It felt… comfortable."

Finally, he looked up at me and smiled.

"Did it? Did it? Good, that's good…"

"I'm ready for whatever you want me to do."

"Hmm, perhaps not quite yet… but you're getting there. We can see that…"

I was still standing to attention.

"For God's sake, come and sit down, Ahab," Stringer said, indicating the chair opposite. "We've got something we want to discuss with you."

He handed over a photograph of a young man – dark hair, thin moustache and a pair of octagonal silver rimmed spectacles.

"What strikes you about this man?"

"Well… on first impression, he looks a lot like me," I said. It was true – despite the moustache, his facial shape was very similar. The spectacles were different to my reading glasses, but if I was to wear the same pair as his, we would be a close match.

My answer was obviously what Stringer had been hoping for, because he looked at Pirbright and smiled as if to say: 'you see?'.

"Yes he does, doesn't he? That's precisely what we thought."

"Who is he, sir?"

"His name is Xavier Bonnet, a young village doctor from a hamlet in the Dordogne… works alongside his father, Jacques, also a doctor. Jacques has a sister who left France many years ago, before the Great War in fact, and who ended up in living in New York. The reason I mention it is because when France fell in 1940, he wrote to her asking how he might help in the war effort. The letters were passed on to the American secret service, and they passed them on to us. The Yanks thought we might be able to think of a way of using this when the invasion happens."

"And I presume you have?"

Stringer nodded.

"Yes."

He looked to Pirbright to take over.

"A swap," Pirbright said on cue.

"With Xavier?"

"Precisely. You take this young man's place. On the outside you will be the village doctor, continuing to work with your father, conducting your surgeries in the clinic he runs from his house. But on the inside you will be a liaison with the local Resistance. A radio will be installed in your doctor's bag."

"So I'm to learn Morse – you want me to be a radio operator?"

My heart was sinking. In signals training we had played around on a Morse key for a morning, tapping in messages, and I had been one of the slowest.

"No," Pirbright said. "Your Morse skills were mediocre at best. What you excelled in was fitness and silent killing – ideal for a courier. One of our female agents will be your radio operator – in training she was keying twenty two words a minute and is currently refining her technique at STS 52 in Oxfordshire. When they are satisfied, she'll join us here before you both leave for France. It's agent Stella, whom I believe you already know."

"Yes, sir. She's sound."

Her astonished face covered in pig blood, came to mind.

"You'll accompany her for transmissions and then you'll take the set away with you. The set is yours to look after, not hers. Too many radio-operators are getting caught. This is a new strategy to keep the two separate – operator and radio. It will make it safer for Stella…"

There was a nice logic to the plan, a doctor on his rounds with his bag, looking ordinary and natural while doing unnatural and extraordinary things.

"My French will have to be better… and my medicine too… I was only a junior doctor."

Stringer was the one to comment.

"You'll be receiving intensive classes here on both language and rural general practice."

I picked up the photograph. "And I'm to look like him?"

"That's right."

I studied the photograph more closely – a thin scar ran from under the man's left eye, straight down the cheek, all the way to the moustache.

"With a scar like that?"

Stringer shuffled uncomfortably in his chair, as though the padded upholstery had suddenly filled up with rocks.

"Um, yes that's right. We were just coming to that part."

"You're going to put it there with make-up, right?"

He pulled a face of doubt.

"Well, we could. There's a type of wax they can use called Culloden, but we're aiming to have you in the field for months. We need it to be authentic. If you're ever taken into custody by the Germans, having a real scar could save you."

I swallowed.

"So how am I going to get a scar like that?"

"Oh, that's simple enough," Stringer said with a smile.

"I'm to have surgery?"

"I'm afraid so, Ahab."

A short silence ensued as I stared at the photograph. God, the scar was at least two inches long.

"Still good to go?"

"Yes… yes, of course. Anything… just getting used to the fact."

"Excellent – I knew we could count on you."

"Who will do it? A proper surgeon, I hope?"

"Ah," he said, smiling again. "I believe you know him actually – he has recently offered his services to us – an Australian plastic surgeon from East Grinstead."

MP… of course. Why wouldn't he want to do something to help, after what the Germans had done to his boy?

"Actually, Ahab, the surgery is a matter of priority, because the scar must have aged enough by the time you get dropped in France – the inflammation must be all gone. You're to have the procedure today, as a matter of fact…"

"Today?"

Stringer checked his watch.

"You're scheduled for pre-op in half an hour."

I looked at the man in photograph again, stunned.

"His nose is a little narrower than mine."

Stringer nodded. "Yes, that's right… While you're under, the surgeon will be doing a few extra touches – we hope you don't mind. Usually it's agents on their second mission who have plastic surgery – ones the Gestapo have already encountered. Having an operation before your first mission makes you rather unique."

I tilted my head back and looked up at the vaulted ceiling for a moment, before bringing my gaze back down to the two spymasters sitting opposite.

"Unique?" I said. "I suppose I should treat it as a compliment."

My sarcasm didn't seem to register.

Just behind the main house, two large linked Nissen huts housed a clinic and operating theatre. It was odd to say the least, walking out of the ornate surroundings of tapestries and armour, and straight into the pre-fabricated world of hospital beds and bright lights, separated by only fifty yards of immaculate lawn. As I crossed the grass I turned back once, to see the Cotswold stone of the gothic manor standing out pale against the darker wintry skies. What astounded me about these places was that in peacetime the only people who lived here were a few aristocrats, while in the cities the masses lived like sardines, squashed into the poorest housing. The worlds of the haves and the have-nots. The thought struck me that part of the reason we were fighting was to perpetuate this inequity, sold by the newspapers as 'our way of life'.

MP came out of a room and nodded at me, the briefest of smiles accompanying a fleeting look of recognition and welcome in his eyes. "Ahab," he said.

I thought it best not to say his name, since names were a 'no no', so I simply stood up and nodded back at him.

He gestured that I should go inside his consultation room and take the chair. He followed me in and sat down on the edge of the desk, looming over me.

On the table were two large portrait photographs of the French doctor – one taken from the front on, and one from the side – presumably obtained by other agents and smuggled back to England.

MP held my chin in his hand and tilted my head in a few directions, the same way my father used to do when giving me a haircut.

"There are a few procedures I need to do," he said. "The scar obviously, a rhinoplasty, and I'll need to pin back your ears a bit – yours stick out more than his."

I swallowed nervously and nodded my consent.

"Fine. Do what needs to be done."

I was crossing the line now. The war was the most real it had ever been, and I would always be reminded of this, every time I looked in the mirror for the rest of my life.

Finally I dared myself to break protocol.

"MP?"

He looked at me, eyebrows raised questioningly.

"I'm glad you're the one doing it."

He grunted. "Well, I'm glad you've chosen to fight."

As the anaesthetist was putting me under, I counted backwards from five and was gone by the time I had reached two.

I came round later in a bed in the recovery room.

The first thing I did was reach for my face. It was heavily bandaged.

Pirbright was sitting in a chair holding a thin file.

He placed it on my chest.

"Agent Ahab – I want to introduce you to Dr Xavier Bonnet. The new you. Good luck with the French lessons and General Practice training. I'll see you again in eight weeks."

Xavier Bonnet was a year older than me – born in 1918 – which made him twenty five. A bachelor, he had been working in Bordeaux for the last year as a junior doctor, the same stage I had been in East Grinstead. His father Jacques was sixty two years old and still working.

Like my family, the Bonnets were from a line of doctors. Jacques Bonnet's father – André – had been the village doctor too. Both André and his wife had died of old age a few years before the war. There had been two children – a daughter Bernadette, and later a son, Jacques, both of whom had helped in the family business, Bernadette as a nurse and Jacques as a doctor. In the late 1890s, she had left to join a Holy Order in Paris, and the order had sent her to the Australian goldfields to work with a group of nurses called the 'Sisters of the St John of God'. Out there she had fallen in love with an American doctor, left her

Order, and eventually settled in New York. She was the one to whom Jacques had written – a brother asking his sister how he could help.

The reason Jacques wanted to do something 'active' was because his wife – Estelle – had been killed earlier in the war. While visiting a relative in Dunkirk, she had been caught up in the chaos and bombing of the retreating British Expeditionary Force, sharing the fate of a thousand other civilians.

Xavier must have seen the disruption to his life as a small price to pay for what had happened to his mother. Maybe I had found a man who hated the Nazis as much as I did.

The report said the Bonnet family was well respected and well established in the local community. To my relief, the file also stated Xavier to be a shy man, who seldom said much. I might just get away with it. Besides, who notices much about their family doctor? I was sure the patients wouldn't suspect anything – sick people just want to be helped. Their powers of observation are dimmed. I said this to reassure myself, because if I thought about it too much, the whole idea seemed preposterous.

They put me in a house on the estate – officially STS 31 – though everyone called it 'The House in the Wood' because it was in the middle of a pine forest. A French native speaker, known to us only as 'Madame' ran a class with five other agents and all morning we would sit together, chatting in conversational French. After lunch she did one-on-one sessions with me – tweaking my accent so that it fitted with the area where Xavier Bonnet lived. Since he was an educated man, it didn't have to be too parochial, but it couldn't be 'English schoolboy French' either. After two weeks the words started to osmose into my brain and I even started dreaming in French, just like I had dreamt of silent killing up in Scotland. Madame said that was a good sign.

The lessons taught us small details about life in occupied France; how you would never ask for a 'café noir' – a black coffee – because it implied white coffee was an option, which it wasn't. With milk strictly rationed, black coffee was the only available choice, so you simply said you wanted a 'café'. Women weren't allowed cigarette rations either, so Stella would have to go without.

In the afternoons I received tutorials from a country doctor, covering the most common scenarios I might encounter 'in the field'. He was one of those middle-aged ex-military types, with bundles of energy and a 'can do' attitude to everything, the sort of man who made you understand why Great Britain had once ruled an Empire covering most of the globe. He had a bow-legged gait, and a limp which affected his right leg – probably an injury from the Great War, though he never said so. His dress was always a tweed jacket, brown moleskin trousers and highly polished brogues. I had to call him 'BD' and straight from the off we worked well together, his enthusiasm for medicine infectious. His favourite expression was, 'Absolutely'. If I answered a question correctly, or made a comment he agreed with, he would practically jump off the chair in excitement and the word would explode from his mouth, usually accompanied with a hearty chortle, as if I had said something highly amusing. This eccentric positivity, the polar opposite to Boreman and Whitehead's way of teaching, fostered an atmosphere which inspired me to give everything I had to the process. Without BD's input I was certain I would have been found wanting in my undercover role. He was the best teacher I had ever had.

He liked to work from head to toe – dealing with infections first – eye, respiratory tract, urinary tract, skin – and then musculoskeletal problems – jaw pains, frozen shoulder, low back pain, arthritic hips and knees. Madame sat in and taught me the corresponding French words and we conducted three way consultations with Madame acting as the patient and my tutor giving me a running commentary of the relevant symptoms and diagnostic pointers. I found it easy enough, and the lingo continued to sink in; 'a jeun' – on an empty stomach, 'mal à la tête' – headache, 'la grippe' – the flu, 'essouflé' – breathless, 'une douleur lancinant' – a shooting pain, 'sang dans les celles' – blood in the stool. The phrases filled up my grey matter and pushed the English equivalents right back to the perimeter.

As the weeks passed, I slowly metamorphosed into Xavier Bonnet.

MP had done good work; my scar was an exact copy of the one in the photograph and it paled nicely. I actually quite liked my new streamlined nose and pinned back ears. I had grown the same thin moustache and had taken to wearing a pair of octagonal silver rimmed spectacles. I kept my comments brief, to mimic the reserved character the report had portrayed. It was strange becoming someone else. I wondered how he ate – was it slowly or fast? How did he hold his cutlery? Did he smile much? Madame told me the French tended to linger over their food, unlike the British who wolfed everything down double quick. "Lay your knife and fork parallel to each other on the right side of the plate when you have finished eating"… "Both hands on the table, never under the table."

"You begin eating once I say 'Bon appetit'."

"So I don't have to wait for others to start?"

Madame had waved her hand in the air dismissively: "Only Americans wait".

So, as Stringer had advised in my original interview, I started to eat like a Frenchman. To help me think like one Madame gave me a French novel to read – ironically about two friends, one of whom has an infatuation with a seemingly unattainable woman. At one point he writes to his friend, telling him of his 'great distress', a sentiment reminding me very much of Tom Shaw and his angst over Nielsen. I could almost feel him reading it with me and sympathising with the character's plight: "Distress. I know all about how that bloody feels. She had us all wrapped around her little finger. You know Ed, we should never have got tangled up with Freya Nielsen – all she ever caused us was distress. We should have ignored her and concentrated on Sister Meally instead."

Anyway, that was the eating and the thinking taken care of. Stringer had also said I should 'fuck like a Frenchman' too, but there were limits to my training, and I decided he had just said that part to shock me. I did have one very embarrassing dream in which we were back in our on-call room in East Grinstead and Tom was arguing the point about my trying it on with Madame:

"She's a damn good looking woman," he said. "Dresses elegantly, classy…"

"Tom, are you blind? You dirty old bastard, she's sixty if she's a day."

"What do a few years matter, here or there?"

In the dream we were both laughing about it; the scenario of me and the Madame in a sexual relationship, and for days after in our classes I couldn't look her properly in the eye. The dream had lifted my spirits though, because I felt I really had been laughing in the company of my friend.

For Christmas, our class ate a roast dinner with Madame, in the dining room of the house in the wood; French conversation only. She said 'bon appetit' and we tucked in, remembering to keep our hands on the table when we weren't eating.

On New Year's Eve, I walked a few miles down the road to the shore line at Hythe, to where the Test and Itchen rivers merged to become the Solent. On the shingle beach there, I was able to escape from Xavier Bonnet for an hour or so.

To the south beyond the trees, on my side of the water, was a large oil refinery. On the far shore at Netley stood the hospital where my father and his brother had convalesced after the Boer War, the setting for the photograph on our piano. I could see the pier clearly, leading far out into the water. Perhaps that was why I had a feeling of familiarity and peace; in a sense it was our family sanctuary. My Uncle Freddie was buried in the military cemetery there.

I allowed myself to step outside the bounds of my mind, thinking about my real father's experiences in that place and the trauma he had gone through.

Netley was also the hospital where he had been locked away in the Great War, mute in its asylum. I tried to imagine the treatment he had undergone to help bring his voice back – the electrical shocks that sounded more like torture than therapy. In a physiology lesson at medical school, we had attached electrodes to the leg of a dead frog – the bright red muscle exposed – and made it move by turning on the power. Whenever I contemplated my father's shock therapy the twitching frog's leg was what came to mind.

My poor parents would have been in a state of shock if they had known the truth about my SOE training. I had not seen them for some months already. Letters were strictly monitored; I couldn't tell them what I was really up to – on the telephone I had to lie and say I was doing research into exercise physiology with my old tutor Kynance, to help try and improve army training methods.

Thinking about my real parents naturally led me into thoughts of Xavier's father, Jacques, and whether or not we would get along. I wondered what it would be like working with him. BD said that if I had any clinical issues, Jacques would be able to help, just as he would help the real Xavier when he was unsure about a case.

One day in January I was shown a map of Bournemouth with the simple instruction: "Make contact with a female 'cut out' at this location. She'll be wearing a red hat. Make sure you're not followed."

A 'cut out' in spy parlance was a mutually trusted intermediary – a person, in other words, who helped in the exchange of information between agents.

It was a training exercise, but a serious one – to be treated as 'real', the way we had treated the firearms in training as always 'live'. I was told to assume that an enemy would have been furnished with certain pieces of information, and that they would 'almost certainly' be onto me from the start.

I employed the techniques taught in the 'clandestine living' classes to make sure I wasn't being followed: I stood in front of shop windows and used the reflection to observe people behind me, hopped onto a bus and then hopped off again at the last moment. I even went into a department store and did a series of dodges. Eventually, I arrived at the set meeting point only to find two Special Branch Officers waiting for me and holding a young lady in a red hat in handcuffs.

"Here's the slippery bastard," one said, as I approached them.

His frustrated manner confirmed they had been tasked to tail me and that I had managed to lose them. As a last resort, they had headed straight to my end point, supplied by our SOE trainers, to challenge me there. It was obvious they had only been given a brief description of me, and not a photograph, or they would have arrested me on the spot.

I had a letter in my pocket which I had been told to use if questioned or arrested by the authorities – my 'get out of jail' card, so to speak. But I didn't want to use it, not just yet.

"I say old chap" I said, feigning innocence. "What's got into you?"

He squared up to me.

"You're here to meet this woman?"

"Not this woman. I'm meeting my wife. You must be mistaking me for someone else. Now if you gentlemen will excuse me – I'm already late and she hates waiting… I'm sure you understand."

He blocked my way.

"We've been tracking you," he said. "Six foot, dark – wears spectacles, skinny. That fits with the man we were told to look out for. You were trying to lose us."

I took a step forward, summoning some mild outrage at this accusation. "Excuse me! But I'm afraid I've no idea what you are talking about. You describe half the male population of this town. I've been shopping for a present for my wife. I'm meeting her here and then we're off to a show. And you sir, are making me later than I already am."

"Show us the present," the other one said.

Dutifully I reached into my pocket.

"Hold it right there!"

Both men drew their weapons, rather slowly and clumsily I thought. If I had been armed I could have got off the first shot easily. Two shots – a double tap, or even dropped them both with an edge of the hand chop on their necks. Even now, unarmed, I knew the exact moves to disarm them and take their weapons before they would know what was going on. I pictured how I would do it – a series of rapid hand offs and grabs. The Captain would have been proud of me.

Rather than react, I obeyed.

"It's just a present… My God… don't shoot!"

One came forward and held open my jacket pocket. I *had* bought a present – I wasn't a complete imbecile.

It was a small silver necklace with cut three glass jewels in the shape of teardrops – one green, one red and one clear, like a diamond.

The officer held it up, stupefied. I could see the cogs going round in his head as he doubted himself, wondering if he and his colleague had got the wrong man.

I kept sowing more confusion:

"This morning my wife arranged to meet me here; for an afternoon show down at the pier. I was on the bus to go home when I remembered…set me in a right two and eight, I can tell you. I knew I would be late but thought if got her a nice present she would forgive me."

The faces of the men were softening. I knew that I had them. One was even nodding at my story, perhaps thinking of his wife forgiving similar misdemeanours.

"So I jumped off the bus and ran around the store trying to find something nice… It's very pretty isn't it? She'll like it, I think. Do you mind if I have it back?"

The man handed the necklace over and I gratefully popped it back into my jacket.

I looked across the park. One hundred yards distant, a woman was walking away at a decent clip.

"Ah… There she goes now!" I said, as flustered as I could be. "Darling! DARLING!"

I called out with just enough volume to sound as if I was trying to get her attention, but also not quite loud enough for her to actually hear me and turn around.

"Oh, goodness. She's given up on me. I know that fast walk of hers – it means she's not happy. Not happy at all."

I started to edge away.

They were looking around, trying to see if the real SOE agent was about to arrive. As luck would have it, a young man was ambling along towards us; tall, thin and wearing spectacles.

My 'wife' was almost out of eye shot now.

I pointed over at her.

"Do you mind awfully if I get along, chaps? Before I ruin her entire day."

"Let him go," the one holding the cut out said. "Here's our man."

The officer I had been conversing with looked embarrassed.

"We're very sorry, sir. A case of mistaken identity."

"Apology accepted," I said, my tone curt. "I just hope she'll forgive me."

I turned away and sped off in her direction.

I kept running, all the way back to the train station.

Later, back at Beaulieu I was called into a room to report back.

I gave my report to the head of Department A, the man who taught 'clandestine living'. He was smiling the whole time.

"Ahab, you've done me proud. Every other student on the task produced their get out of jail card at the first sign of trouble. You really fooled those two and they're no slouches. Remember; if you're ever caught, feed them horse shit for two days. It's all we ask. Your mock interrogation is soon. Only when you see me will you know it's over... got that?"

I didn't have time to rest on my laurels because that very night, two men dressed as Nazis dragged me out of bed and took me to a cell in the basement of the house. A sign on the door said 'CONFERENCE ROOM'.

I was stripped – completely naked – and had my hands tied behind me to the back of a sturdy wooden chair.

It was only then that I noticed they were the same two officers I had fooled earlier that day.

They looked a lot more frightening in SS uniforms than in suits. On the collars of the uniforms were silver 'death's head' badges of a skull and crossbones.

They were definitely out for revenge.

One started the interrogation by throwing a bucket of ice cold water over me.

They both laughed for a while, pointing at me and making jokes about my genitals.

I was frightened and furious at the same time, but I suppose that was what they wanted me to feel. In finishing school classes, the instructors had said one torture resistance technique was to count slowly in your head and try to ignore everything going on around you. I tried it but kept losing count and coming back into the torture room. I started to shiver uncontrollably and had a sudden panic that, any moment soon, I would start screaming and ask to be let out. If I did that I would be pulled off the course and it would have all been for nothing. The counting technique wasn't going to be enough; if I was to get through this I needed to imagine something more powerful than numbers.

The answer came to me out of the blue – I decided I was a burnt pilot in the salt bath having my skin peeled off with forceps. Yes, there was pain, but at least I was in the warm water. I soon stopped shivering. I thought about Tom placing a cigarette in my mouth and my taking long, comforting drags. I imagined the chemical nicotine working on the parts of my brain which controlled pleasure. Instead of two Nazi henchmen shouting at me, I pictured the old double act Tom and I used to do when bathing the pilots. It wasn't so bad any more – I slipped into a more comfortable place, back in the bathroom of Ward Three and not the 'Conference Room' at Beaulieu. Right from the start I knew this strategy was going to work.

One of the men was shouting in a high pitched scream.

"Wer bist du?"

He looked to be really enjoying his Nazi role.

"Je ne comprends pas," I said, my voice sounding frightened, but my mind calm.

"Who are you?" he said in accented English.

"Je ne comprends pas."

"Qui êtes-vous?" the other one said.

"Je suis le docteur… Docteur Bonnet."

"C'est un mesonge!"

It's a lie.

Another bucket of water thrown over me. It was Tom hosing me down with the pleasantly warm saline.

"Je m'appelle Xavier Bonnet."

Thinking himself quite the film-star, he pulled up a chair, lit a cigarette and leant forward.

"Tu veux fumer?" he said gently, now using the familiar 'tu', trying to get personal and friendly.

"Oui…"

He placed the cigarette onto my lips and I sucked in the smoke. The nicotine rush made me feel lightheaded and tingly. Unknowingly, in thinking he was being some kind of hard-hitting guy from a Hollywood motion picture, the interrogator was only helping fulfil my alternate world fantasy. In my head I was Flying Officer Siska, being bathed by house doctors, while at the same time being given puffs on a cigarette. I almost started laughing at the irony of it.

"Merci," I said.

"Où habites tu?"

"Un petit village dans le forêt, près de la ville de Terrasson, en Dordogne…"

"Ah oui?"

He smiled and looked at his colleague who had another bucket ready.

I probably shouldn't say this, but I was actually, deep down, quite happy. The mind is a powerful thing. I had managed to convince myself I was a lot better off than Siska had been in the salt bath. Yes, I was cold, but at least these two weren't actually peeling the skin off my face without anaesthetic. I wouldn't say I was enjoying the interrogation, but it wasn't *that bad*. I could keep myself warm on the inside with my hate thermostat; it was fairly easy.

I told them the life history of Xavier Bonnet perhaps a dozen times; how he had been scarred on his cheek from a childhood accident, how he would hunt for wild boar in the forests around his home, how from an early age he had felt the call of duty to help his father in the family practice. The lies came easily as I scoured my imagination.

I knew they couldn't kill me, but they certainly gave a good impression of wanting to: one even put a towel over my head and poured water over it so I felt like I was drowning. At the last minute they pulled off the towel and I gasped for air. They were being authentic enough, I had to give them that. To fight the fear, I pictured being submerged in the salt bath, putting my head right under and holding it there.

Reports had filtered back about the Gestapo 'enhanced interrogation' techniques – or 'Verscharfte Vernehmung' – usually involving baths and cold water. The infamous chamber in Paris where they conducted their interrogations was known by the British SOE agents simply as 'Le bain' – the bath, though I preferred what the Belgian Resistance called it: 'The Paris technique'.

The hours passed in a blur – and I continued to talk in French the entire time. I spoke of medical school in Bordeaux, focusing on easily interchangeable scenarios I had experienced in Oxford. I told them about my fellow student, 'Thomas' who had suffered a nose bleed during our first tutorial, how we had studied the lung together from a pair of sheep's lights in a Bordeaux park. On and on I went. I enjoyed talking about my imaginary French Tom; I particularly liked telling them how we used to go to 'Le café' and eat 'œufs et pain grillé' and how it was all we ever had. It brought back some good memories and, while I wasn't exactly cheerful, bearing in mind the circumstances, I felt a lot better than I had done in recent months.

Towards the end of the forty eight hours, the two interrogators were looking a lot worse than I was feeling. They had shadows under their eyes and their breath stank. Thanks to the buckets of water, I was as clean as a whistle and well hydrated.

Then at last, the head of Department A walked in and my hands were untied.

"It's over," he said.

He had a large mug of hot sugary tea and put it in my hands.

Someone draped a blanket over my shoulders and I sat there in silence for a while, slowly coming to terms with the fact that it had ended. I wanted to reach out and hug the head for having saved me, but too much emotion would have been a bad thing so I just held the warm mug near to my lips and kept sipping.

My interrogators were given tea too. They loosened the buttons of their SS tunics and I could see their white vests underneath – a touch of humanity after forty eight hours.

The head of the department stood watching us all.

"So," he said, finally, "how was it?"

I looked up and saw that he was addressing the others, not me.

"He's the hardest bastard I've ever questioned," one said, grudgingly.

The other interrogator looked at me.

"Respect," he said, holding out his mug.

The next big test was the 'honey-trap'.

For having done so well in my interrogation, Pirbright took me into Southampton for a celebratory meal – on the drive he was really going overboard, saying how I was the talk of all the instructors at the finishing school. Then in the hotel lobby we bumped into one of the girls on the staff at Beaulieu; she was one of the nurses on the recovery ward where I had undergone my surgery – extremely pretty with dark chestnut hair tied back in a plait. So striking, in fact that I still remembered her name – Nurse Winter. In looks, an English equivalent of Freya Nielsen. Pirbright asked Winter if she would like to join us at our table and, pleasingly, she did. I felt the chemistry when Winter came over; the body language subtly directed towards me and not Pirbright.

We all started with champagne, keeping the talk bland – the weather, the local news – when the waiter came over to our table.

"Excuse me sir," he said to Pirbright, "but there's an urgent call for you."

Pirbright threw up his hands and shook his head.

"They never leave me alone."

He went away and came back a minute later.

"I'm afraid something's come up. I'm terribly sorry but I'm going to have to leave you. Please charge it all to my account – enjoy yourselves."

After Pirbright had marched off, Winter moved her chair closer and held up her champagne glass.

"Cheers."

Her blouse was just loose enough to give me tantalising glimpses of the delights that lay beneath.

"Cheers," I said back to her, blushing.

"I'm glad he's gone," Winter said. "Now I've got you all to myself."

I think that was the moment I knew it was too good to be true, and the reason I did was because it was exactly how I had felt when Nielsen had come on to me that day in the tower. My heart sank a little as this hit home; that Winter didn't *really* like me and that it was all an act to catch me out.

The perfect ruse; I could see it clearly now. Place a pretty girl as if by chance with the student, ply them both with alcohol to loosen inhibitions – a touch of vanity on the student's part and he would soon be telling all about his new role as a 'secret agent'. A year ago it would have worked, but not now – not after what had happened with Freya Nielsen.

We finished the bottle together before she started to go to work on me.

"So what do you do?" Winter said, laughing as if I was the most entertaining man in the world. All I had done was to confuse which pieces of cutlery I would use on the main course.

"Oh, I'm afraid it's all rather quite dull – I study exercise physiology at Oxford. I just sit in a laboratory watching chaps from the athletic team run on special treadmills, and then take their blood for lactic acid levels and measure their lung capacities."

I could see it in her eyes – the look of disappointment as she realised her beauty and guile had not been enough and how I had seen through her like a new pane of glass.

And that was all Winter got out of me – just my cover story – the same one I had fed my parents.

The next day, Pirbright called me in to the lower drawing room at Beaulieu House.

"I suppose I should've known you wouldn't fall for it," he said, smiling and holding his hands up.

"Once bitten, twice shy, Professor."

"Indeed! You'd be surprised how many we've lost at this last hurdle… after all that training. Winter has caught eight in the last year – she's one of our best."

"I had a good steak… and it was a pleasant enough evening. What did she say about me?"

"Said you were the perfect gent and that, despite talking all night, you didn't say a thing. She enjoyed it though – said it was clear you knew she knew, and that she knew you knew and an entertaining joust ensued."

Stringer came in.

"All good, Ahab?"

"A bit tired. It's been a harder week than usual."

"Yes well, we're pleased with your progress – it's been your best week yet. The instructors are really impressed, Ahab. Stella arrives in a few days and then you'll start to work as a team."

I sat there looking over at both of my senior handlers. Pirbright was lounging in the chair opposite. Stringer was sat behind the large desk. I caught his eye.

"Apart from looking after the radio, sir, what's the actual mission?"

He smiled and nodded to himself.

"Of course" he said, "You deserve to know."

A few seconds went by, as if Stringer wanted to hold onto this secret for just a little while longer, like a boy not wanting to share his sweets.

"So sir?"

"Work with the local Resistance fighters," he said. "Prepare for the big day… Hitler isn't completely stupid; he knows there's going to be an Allied invasion. Needless to say, the invasion won't be easy. They've assigned Rommel to defend the French coast. We'll need every possible advantage – all sorts of distractions for the German divisions… and that's why we need you in place, with a mob of angry armed Frenchmen, ready to act when the time comes."

I wondered if we could really make all that much of a difference. I sat back and stared up at the ceiling, thinking perhaps that joining the SOE had been a waste of time.

"Listen," he said, perhaps detecting my disillusion. "You've done well, Ahab. Madame is very pleased with your French and the doc says you would make a reasonable country doctor here, let alone in rural France. You've proved yourself canny and resilient. We feel confident that as Xavier Bonnet, trusted local doctor, you will be virtually invisible to the Germans. And Stella will be safe because she won't have a radio to hamper her."

Pirbright pitched in, "You'll have plenty of chances to get your revenge when the invasion comes."

My spirits lifted at hearing this.

"I'm happy to wait," I said. "After all; they say it's a dish best served cold."

The two of them looked at one another, not overly impressed with my tough talk.

I had said it more for myself than for them. I wanted to keep primed with hate so that I didn't lose my edge.

Already, the acute pain of Tom's loss was fading. Eight months had passed since his death and I was beginning to forget his face. That really bothered me, the fact that he was slowly being erased from memory – a cruel trick of the mind. I couldn't remember his voice very well either.

Stringer came over and gave me a pair of gold cufflinks.

"Tradition," he said, by way of explanation. "You probably won't see me until the mission is over. Good luck Ahab."

Chapter Sixteen

I learnt two things on the night we were flown into France.

The first was another of Richard Shaw's big secrets… The year before, when Tom and I asked about his new role at Tangmere, his enigmatic response had been, 'special duties'. As soon as I saw him waiting for us by the Lysander aircraft, I knew.

The other was that my disguise worked. Admittedly, it was dark, but despite Richard standing three yards away, he gave no glimmer of recognition. To him I was just another SOE agent, another 'Joe' as the pilots referred to us. With my altered nose and ears, facial scar and the combination of the octagonal rimmed spectacles and moustache, I was 'Docteur Xavier Bonnet'.

There was a full moon and not a breath of wind: perfect flying conditions.

Across the wide concrete runway, the control tower stood squat and pale in the moonlight. I could see the silhouettes of flight controllers in the dimly lit room at the top of the building, even make out the orange dots of their cigarette ends.

Coltrane, our SOE 'dispatcher', introduced us to Richard by our code names.

"Hello, Ahab… Stella," Richard said, shaking our hands. He was wearing tight-fitting brown leather gloves which I guessed were not standard airman's issue. Made to his exact specifications, they fitted snugly over those withered and scarified fingers.

He glanced up at the night sky.

"Ready to pluck bright honour from the pale-faced moon?"

I assumed the question was rhetorical and something he said to all the agents he flew. I didn't want to reply in case my voice gave me away, so I just gave a vague nod in his direction. Now I was Xavier Bonnet, I wanted to stay in character.

Richard walked once around the aircraft making his checks, gripping and shaking the wings as if he was making sure they were properly fastened to the fuselage. Folded maps were stuffed into the top of his left flying boot.

He came back to us and clapped his gloved hands together.

"All set?"

He still hadn't recognised me. I couldn't believe it.

"Richard," I wanted to say, "it's me... Ed!"

The urge to blow my cover had never been stronger than at this moment.

By way of reply, Stella and I gathered up our gear.

"God speed," Coltrane said, patting us both on the shoulders.

Richard was already climbing up into the cockpit of the Lysander using a ladder attached to the port side of the fuselage. We followed suit.

The canopy was a one piece unit which slid backwards on rails to allow a quick entry and exit. Behind the pilot's seat was a modified gunner's compartment – a rearward facing two-seater bench with a locker underneath, and opposite, a smaller shelf serving as another seat, facing forwards.

I sat opposite Stella on the shelf. I could see the back of Richard's head as he hunched over his instruments, his narrow neck lost in the bulk of his fur-lined leather jacket.

That afternoon, Coltrane had given us a few hours in the city of Chichester, opting to take advantage of the early summer sunshine and read the newspaper on a park bench by the car. Stella and I visited the cathedral and ate a 'last supper' in the Ship Hotel – for all we knew it might be our final meal in England. A waiter with a big mouth told us Eisenhower had been in for dinner a few weeks before and enjoyed half a pint of the local beer. To keep the waiter happy Stella and I ordered the same. With the mission on our minds, we didn't eat much. We didn't say much either, like a couple who have been married for a long time.

After the meal, we had been taken to Tangmere, Coltrane parking to one side of a small cottage and ushering us in through the back door, out of sight from the road.

The cottage served as the 'ops' centre for the 161 squadron – a place for operational flight planning – but also the last pit stop for departing agents. Maps of France and the Low Countries hung from the wall with red pins for all the drop zones and the locations of Resistance reception cells. A swathe of pins covered France with concentrated clusters over the Dordogne and the area just to the north. This cottage was the place where Tom's ghost had visited his older brother, a dusty bomb-blasted phantom wearing my shredded sports jacket. I didn't have time for further reflection as straightaway Coltrane made us empty out our pockets. This was standard procedure – just in case an English coin, receipt, or train ticket had been left inside by mistake.

My inventory was as follows:

1. Occupation notes and coins, some with holes in the centre like washers.

2. A wine cork – hollow and containing a cyanide 'L' pill. L stood for 'lethal'. If I was ever captured, I could choose to bite into it and die within seconds.

3. An olive green packet of twenty 'Gauloises Caporal' cigarettes and a French matchbox with a picture of a winged Viking helmet on the cover.

4. A bar of 'Chocolat Menier'.

Ten thousand feet below, the French coastline stood out black against the silvery surface of the English Channel.

Despite being over enemy territory at last, my thoughts were on Richard, the man sitting in the cockpit three feet away. It seemed an amazing twist of fate that he was our pilot, and behind everything, I could once again sense Tom's influence: helping direct the whole show from the control room up in the heavens – having enormous fun pushing round the pieces and making these coincidences happen.

The more I thought about it though, the more I could see it wasn't beyond the realms of possibility that Richard was the one flying us – his squadron was based at Tangmere after all, one of the main bases for flying agents into occupied territories. There couldn't have been more than a dozen pilots who did it.

Lysander operations were flown by the 161 squadron; Richard's squadron. They always flew in a 'moon period' for better visibility. Night flying was a safer duty than daytime combat and sometimes assigned to injured pilots because of the lesser use of the joystick. Poor Richard – after flying Hurricanes in the Battle of Britain, this kind of piloting must have felt like driving a London bus. So much for his desire to shoot down a German for every operation he'd endured. I suppose this was the next best thing.

I was wearing a knitted grey jersey with a crew neck and a pair of khaki canvas trousers; very 'rustic French'. I thought my shoes looked strange – black leather, but of a style I had not seen before. Nothing had been left to chance – tailors had made our clothes to a Gallic design with no give-away English sewing patterns. All English labels had been removed, even the manufacturer's mark – 'lightning' – on my trouser zip.

One of the collar studs on my shirt contained a tiny escape compass. Stella had one in a button on her jacket. Not only that, she had a silk escape map sewn into the lining of the same jacket. I had been issued with a pack of 'Escape cards' – like ordinary playing cards but with the special added feature that the back could be peeled away from the face to reveal mapped areas of France. Each card detailed a different area and together made a whole. The key to which card held which map was behind the Joker.

Stella also carried a set of forged identity papers. Mine were with the actual Xavier in France; not forged, but the real thing. I was the forgery.

Tonight on the official paperwork, Flight Officer R. Shaw was carrying two 'personnel' and two 'packages'. There was my doctor's bag and then a long duffel bag of weapons – two submachine guns and a carbine, with ammunition – a gift for our Resistance-cell hosts. Pirbright had said our contacts were a notorious group of communists who, so far, had been largely immune to any direction from the SOE. The guns were to help gain some trust straight from the off.

As well as the Resistance fighters, the SOE organiser running the entire Dordogne area would be waiting to meet us. All we knew was that his code-name was Nestor.

Through his radio-operator, Nestor had sent the map reference to London for the landing field. He would only have received confirmation the drop off was going ahead this very night, once the Met Office report had declared the weather conditions suitable. The 'go' signal would have been in the form of an open broadcast, among the personal messages of the BBC French news – a pre-arranged phrase Nestor had sent in his earlier radio message – typically, a short, quirky phrase, such as: 'the giraffe has a long neck' or 'the saxophonist is playing'.

During the flight, Richard kept checking his route map and making small adjustments to his line. The map was folded in his left hand and he held the joystick with his right. He kept turning the map over and looking out of each side of his cockpit – navigating by the landmarks below, visible in the moonlight.

The map was a composite strip of France, covering perhaps a width of hundred miles, and the fold was our plotted course; which is why he kept turning the map over, to check which landmarks were on the port side and which were on the starboard side. It meant he could do it all with one hand while flying the aeroplane with the other.

From time to time, he would shout out, as if he were a tour guide: "There's Le Mans,"… "Orleans,"… "The Loire."

He had taped a card on his instrument panel. Although I couldn't make out the writing, I deduced it was basic flight data: the latest wind speeds from the Met Office, his estimated flying times, the positions of German Flak points. Knowing that the British pilots navigated using easily identifiable landmarks, the Germans tended to place their anti-aircraft batteries there.

When Richard finished with one map, he would put it into a small compartment on the port side of his cockpit, and then pull out the next one from his flying boot. It was a neat, practical system.

Back at finishing school we had learnt the basics about the flight transfer. At some time in the last seventy two hours, Richard would have been issued with a briefing folder containing an 'Air Transport Form', including Nestor's description of the landing field, the map coordinates, the dates and times he would be ready for the drop and the planned number of passengers both ways. The folder would contain a recent aerial photograph of the proposed landing area. Richard would have studied the photograph with a magnifying glass, looking for anything which might hamper a smooth landing – trees around the edge of the field, rutted tracks, muddy patches. Every shadow and mark on the grass.

To locate the field itself, he would use larger scale maps.

The other crucial pieces of information were the 'letters of the day' – the codes Richard would need to know for the landing.

For this trip, both letters happened to be the same; I knew this because Richard had already written them on his cockpit window in in white chalk:

Recognition: V

Pilot's answer: V

In brackets underneath he had written: (dot dot dot dash).

As soon as the reception party heard our Lysander approaching, Nestor would flash the letter 'V' in Morse using a torch, and keep flashing until Richard saw the signal in the darkness. If it was the wrong letter, we would simply turn around and abort the mission. If correct, Richard would send his letter of the day – a 'V' also – using the downward identification light on the aircraft. This information would already have been sent to Nestor's radio-operator, rather than in the open BBC broadcast.

"It's a long run down tonight," Richard said over the noise of the engines. "I don't usually go this far south. Never had so many maps in my boot! It's going to be at least another hour. Get some kip if you want. I'll wake you when we're near."

I hadn't been following the time; since everything that was Xavier's was mine, everything I needed was already in France, even his wrist-watch, which I would inherit on my arrival. I had chosen to bring only my F-S dagger and not the Colt-45. It was strapped to my shin under my trouser leg. The blade was my talisman and besides, knife fighting was the specialism in which I had excelled at the silent killing course. "Pick the weapon with which you are most comfortable" the Captain had told us, "I don't really care if it's your bloody coffee cup, as long as you are prepared to kill with it." Stella had opted for no weapons at all because she was best with her bare hands.

I looked down in admiration at my doctor's bag, lying next to my feet. The boffins at 'Station IX' must have been scratching their heads for months on this.

It was a tan brown leather Gladstone bag – a 'portmanteau' – made in the classic style of those used by doctors universally. More importantly, it was a replica of the real Xavier's bag. Along with the usual medical paraphernalia – stethoscope, thermometer, blood pressure cuff and ampoules, needles and syringes – all French of course, the bag came with a false bottom, a hidden compartment holding the radio. It was a considerable improvement on the suitcase radio, weighing only two kilograms – half the weight of the standard SOE set.

The radio was Stella's area of expertise of course – I was just the mule. It had a range of a thousand miles if we set up a good aerial. I knew the basic components – the orange aerial wire on a winder, for rapid unspooling when setting up, just like the fishing tackle a child would use on holiday. There was a pair of miniature earphones and two bulkier components which made up the main weight of the apparatus – a battery and a three valve miniature transmitter-receiver, and also a place in the bag for some spare valves, nestling in my ampoule case next to the morphine, there to protect them from breaking. The most ingenious aspect of the whole contraption were the metal handles of the doctor's bag, which could be detached, and then connected up to the battery to form a hand-operated dynamo.

I drifted off into a recurring dream – a dream of pursuit, of being chased by the Gestapo across occupied France. I would run and run but in the end have to stop, unsheathe my F-S dagger and turn around to face them. That was when the dream turned into Richard's old nightmare, except in my version it wasn't the pilot Fuhrmann berating me for having cut short his life, but an anonymous German soldier, a faceless accuser, with a thin layer of skin pulled down over his features. No eyes, no nostrils, no mouth; just a blank and terrifying ghoul wearing an SS uniform, ranting at me in German: "Ich war glücklich sie wissen, und sie ruiniert…"

Richard's loud voice woke me up.

"I've just made contact on the S-phone. We'll be arriving soon."

The S-phone was an air to ground link – essentially a type of portable telephone – something Station IX had recently developed. The set and directional aerial were strapped to the operator's chest and it meant the pilot could communicate with the ground from around six miles away.

It was Stella who first spotted the Morse signal from the ground party.

"Look… over there!" she said, shouting the words.

Richard held up a hand to show he had heard her.

"It's the correct signal."

He signalled back: *dot dot dot dash*

"Now," he said, craning his neck and looking out to his left, "three of the ground reception party should switch on their torches, to form the flare-path."

Right on cue, three lights on the ground suddenly appeared in the shape of an inverted 'L'.

Richard explained the pattern, not realising we had already been taught this at finishing school.

"The long arm of the 'L' indicates the wind direction along the cleared landing strip… I'll land heading into the wind towards the short arm. The party leader always waits at the end of the long arm of the L, furthest away from the short arm. That's where the exchange of 'Joes' will take place. Don't worry, it shouldn't be a bumpy landing – the

Photographic Reconnaissance Unit over at RAF Benson has done us proud… I've checked the landing field and it looks smoother than the pitch at the Empire stadium, and twice as big."

Richard banked steeply and brought the Lysander round into the final approach, crossing the edge of the landing field at some 70 miles per hour. We flew alongside the long arm of the 'L' for another second before touching down. He hadn't been exaggerating – I hardly noticed the landing at all.

"She only needs a four hundred yard runway" he said as we rolled along on the grass.

I looked out – the receiving group had picked a good place – flat and dry.

"It's not always like this," Richard was saying. "Got bogged down in a muddy field one time and had to be pulled out by cows."

We turned around at the end of the makeshift strip and taxied back to where our reception party was waiting. Richard circled around again, so he was facing into the wind ready for take-off. He brought the Lysander to a stop, but with the propellers still turning, then turned around and gave us a thumbs-up sign.

Things happened fast – the canopy was pulled back and Stella climbed out. I handed down the doctor's bag and the duffel bag.

Richard was turning round to me and saying something. I could have sworn he said, "Good luck, Ed," though it was probably, "Duck your head." I waved and climbed out onto the ladder.

By the time I had reached the ground, Stella had already taken the weapons over to the waiting group twenty yards away. I grabbed my doctor's bag and went over to join them.

There were four men – a tall one armed with a Sten, another with the S-phone equipment strapped to his chest, like a strange exoskeleton. The third was kneeling down and examining the contents of the weapons bag. The other man was the real Xavier Bonnet and he was staring at me in disbelief. I noticed he was holding his Gladstone in his left hand, the same as mine and presumably packed with what few belongings he was taking. It was like looking into a mirror.

He was smiling and saying, "Incroyable!"

We shook hands and then he gave me his square faced watch. Before slipping it into my pocket I noted the local time as being midnight

I was acutely aware that time on the ground for the Lysander needed to be kept to a minimum. Richard had said no more than a minute for the exchange of 'Joes'. Despite having a lot of things I wanted to say to Xavier, it was he who spoke to me, in French of course.

"Look after my father."

His voice was slightly deeper than mine, and calmer sounding. I made a mental note of it.

"Like my own," I said, trying to reassure him.

"Go!' I heard the Resistance man with the Sten shout to Xavier. "Allez!"

Bag in hand, Xavier jogged over to the aircraft and climbed the ladder. No sooner was he inside the cockpit than the canopy was pulled across and Richard was accelerating across the field for take-off.

In less than a minute, the engine sound of the Lysander had grown faint and my situation came crashing down on me: I was in occupied France on a mission for the SOE.

"Christ Almighty, you mad bastard," Tom was saying in my head. "I was only joking. You didn't really need to do this. Why the hell did you listen to me?"

The man with the S-phone came and shook my hand. He was so young – younger even than me.

"My God," he said, "I hadn't thought it possible, but London have done an amazing job."

"You're Nestor?"

He laughed and so did the tall man with the Sten.

"Yes, officially I'm Nestor, but around these parts they call me Commandant Jack."

I shook his hand.

"Ahab," I said. I turned to my colleague. "And this is Stella."

"Hello, Commandant," she said.

He smiled as he shook her hand.

"Just Jack is fine. Now, let me introduce you to some people."

He pointed to the tall man with the Sten gun; black bearded with long straight black hair reaching his shoulders and well over six feet tall. "This fellow here is Limouzy."

Limouzy wasn't smiling and made no move to shake my hand.

Commandant Jack seemed to be walking a tightrope of diplomacy.

"Now we know London insist on code-names," he was saying tactfully, "and officially his name is Hercules, but—"

Limouzy/Hercules cut in, "But I don't give a shit what London say I should be called; my father named me Limouzy and Limouzy is what you'll call me."

I nodded and kept my expression serious.

"Certainly… that's not a problem with me, Limouzy."

It may have been his fearlessness which awoke the associative memories, or it may have been the sheepskin jerkin he was wearing, but he reminded me so much of someone that my mind was instantly catapulted back fourteen years.

The last time I had seen a man in a sheepskin jerkin was when my cousin Harry had visited us from New Zealand in 1930.

Harry was Uncle Freddie's son and a lot older than me, having been born before the turn of the century in New Zealand – an unanticipated but serendipitous product of Freddie's travels. During the Great War, he had fought with the NZ Third Rifle battalion and his features were a testament to the violence he had encountered – a black eye-patch and scarring as if half his forehead and scalp had been shot away. Like Richard Shaw though, the damage made for a piratical appearance, rather than a horrific one. My father said Harry was called 'Mad Dog' by his unit; and that he had charged two Maxim machine gun posts at Messines.

Being an impressionable ten year old at the time, I observed Harry closely after hearing that information – a classic case of 'hero worship'. He was with his young family and seemed a normal enough chap, and for most of the visit I saw no evidence of any mad streak. One morning though, I woke early and looked out of my bedroom window to see him sitting up in the large oak tree at the end of our garden. He was wearing his sheepskin, smoking calmly and looking eastwards. The first rays of the sunrise were clipping the top of the tree and lighting him up. Why he was in the tree was anyone's guess – to be the first for miles around to see the sun coming up over the horizon? Who knows? The shocking thing was how *high* he had climbed – not just in the lower branches, but right at the top, perhaps a hundred feet up. My bedroom was in the attic eaves – effectively on the second floor of the house – and he was at least twice that height again. No fear at all.

Swearing brought me back into the French field.

"Putain!"

It was the Resistance man rummaging around inside the weapons bag.

He pulled out one of the guns with an ugly snarl on his face.

"Limouzy," he said, "look what the fuckers sent us!"

He was holding up a Sten.

Limouzy was looking inside the bag now.

"More fucking Sten guns," he said, holding out his like it was a dirty nappy and turning angrily to Commandant Jack. "I thought I told you, these things are fucking useless!"

Commandant Jack was scratching his head like he was working out a very hard equation. Then he held his hands up.

"Okay, I'll admit it, I messed up. I asked for some Stens, but I also asked for something special for you my friend…"

Once again he was cut off mid-sentence by the Resistance man checking the bag.

"Oh, hang on a minute, look!"

He pulled out a different weapon. Straight away Limouzy gave his Sten to his colleague and took the new weapon in his hands like a new-born baby.

"Much better," he said, smiling at it.

"There, you see…" said Commandant Jack, relief sweeping across his face. "I told you I wouldn't let you down."

I recognised its distinctive thick barrel and polished wooden stock – the 'De Lisle' silenced carbine – the Rolls Royce of the weapons we had been shown in Scotland. It was virtually inaudible to anyone more than thirty feet away; in fact working the bolt for the next round was louder than the actual shot.

The De Lisle was the sort of weapon I could imagine decorating the walls of Special Forces clubhouses, long after the war was over. Ageing commandos would one day drink their pints of beer and gaze up at the old guns, remembering what they had done in the war. And perhaps a Sten would be hanging up there too, to remind them of cursing Frenchmen.

The Resistance man with the bag handed over some ammunition and Limouzy immediately loaded the De Lisle.

He put his fingers to his lips and blew a kiss at the night sky in the direction of the departing Lysander.

With the De Lisle, Limouzy was a new man, a much happier form of killing machine and, more importantly, he was now on-side.

He stared at me, looking at my scar.

"You must really hate the Germans," he said, impressed, "if you let London change your face."

It was strange the way they just referred to anything from England as 'London'.

"I do," I said, "very much indeed."

He reached out his hand and, as we shook, I could tell immediately that Limouzy was a very dangerous man. It shone off him more brightly than the light from his high beam torch. To get to be leader of a local Resistance cell you weren't going to be a shrinking violet, that was for sure, but everything I had seen so far had confirmed the fact that he was deadly. The flashes of anger. His evident muscularity barely disguised by his outer clothing. The love of weaponry. Being open about his identity. The man was fearless, just like my cousin Harry. Usually that meant you had nothing to lose. It was almost like being in the presence of a wild animal and not a human being at all. I reconsidered my impression. Was it fearlessness or just recklessness? This feral Frenchman might ruin the whole mission.

"Unbelievable," I heard him saying, staring at my face and using the same word Xavier had used.

Then he nodded in the direction of his colleague by the weapons bag, the one who had been swearing.

"That's Eric."

Eric waved at us both from his bag of booty. He was shorter and stockier than Limouzy – built like a bull – with a nose flattened onto his face; here was a man who had taken part in a hundred bar-room brawls and probably won them all.

Stella stepped forward and shook Limouzy's hand.

"Stella," she said simply.

He stared at her, this wild man, brazenly appraising her.

"Enchanted" he said – though in French it sounded more romantic. Stella blushed.

Instead of shaking her hand he lifted it up and kissed it.

It was as much as I could do not to roll my eyes.

Two other men appeared through the darkness – both with ragged beards, but younger than Limouzy and Eric. They were holding torches and I guessed that they must have been standing at the other positions of the flare-path.

"Patrick, Robert," Limouzy said to Stella and I, pointing at each of the men in turn. "They are brothers in arms… and real brothers."

Eric called out to them.

"Look at what London sent the Boss, lads!"

They gathered around Limouzy to admire his De Lisle.

"Nice," I heard one say in admiration.

"You've got Stens," Eric said, handing out the other two weapons from the bag. "Pieces of shit of course, but better than wooden clubs."

The brothers laughed at his joke but still accepted their new weapons like boys on their birthday.

Eric had inherited Limouzy's Sten, so at least they were all armed now, a considerable improvement on the situation of five minutes before.

"I must leave you," Commandant Jack said to Stella and I, leaning in so only we could hear what he was saying. "These men will show you the ropes. They're poor, they're radical, and as you've already seen, they don't take shit from anyone. But I've been doing this a while and it is my firm belief that these types make the best Resistance fighters. Think of them as wild Mustangs that will carry you wherever you want to go, if you treat them correctly…"

He turned to Limouzy, his gesture open and friendly.

"Remember, my friend, these people want to help you get rid of the Fascists."

Each of the four Resistance fighters came and slapped him on the back. "Take care Commandant, look after yourself, give our regards to our comrades in the region."

"I'll tell them you're the toughest," Commandant Jack said with a straight face, like a comedian telling a joke deadpan.

The men laughed as we all watched him move off at a steady jog across the field.

"He's alright," Limouzy said. "Not like some of those English SOE pricks with silver spoons stuck up their arses. It's only because he insisted that we let you come."

"We won't disappoint you," I said, hoping I didn't sound like a prick with a silver spoon up my arse.

Limouzy laughed as if he had heard my thought and not just my words.

"Well, you've met the whole gang, Doctor," he said, looking at me now with a sudden anxious look on face. "We'd better be getting you home… your father will be worried sick!"

The group roared again.

We walked in single-file behind Limouzy. It had become abundantly clear who was running this show and it certainly wasn't us.

Chapter Seventeen

Dordogne, 'Vichy' France
Early hours, May 9th 1944

We kept to the grassy verge of a road as we headed north, wary of the slightest movement or noise of approaching vehicles. But by that time it was nearly one in the morning and nothing came.

After half an hour's walking, the track up to the house branched east off the road, winding uphill into a forest of oak trees. Unlike their English cousins, these were small, wiry and moss-covered, more like withered elderly relatives than the mighty giants with which I was familiar. Under the spectral light of the full moon this spindly forest looked haunted, like the setting for a story by the Brothers Grimm.

Once on the comparative safety of the track, the group started a muffled conversation, punctuated by the occasional low laugh. Eric walked like a weightlifter approaching the lift, his step exuding sheer latent power. He was the one making the others laugh – from what I could hear he was talking about his wife's cooking. Limouzy remained silent and alert, scouring the forest continually for any sign of danger, and only half-listening to Eric's jokes. Once again, my instinct warned me how lethal this man was, never off duty and always ready to kill. I could tell he was itching to use the De Lisle. 'Just give me an excuse' his body language was saying.

My new friends were from the 'FTP' Resistance which stood for 'Francs-Tireurs et Partisans'. Francs-Tireurs – 'Free-shooters' – had been the *nom de guerre* of guerrilla fighters way back in the Franco-Prussian war of 1870 and now the name had been appropriated by the communists. The FTP made up roughly a third of the French Resistance, the rest being the 'Armée Secrète' – or AS for short. The AS answered to De Gaulle and generally chose to fight only when absolutely necessary. In contrast, the FTP answered to no-one except the French Communist Party and fought at every opportunity. Ardent communists, the group had only formed after Germany invaded Russia in the summer of 1941. They shunned the 'wait and see' approach of the AS, wanting to liberate France all by themselves and on their own time-table, sabotaging industrial targets, punishing collaborators and assassinating soldiers whenever the chance arose. It was fair to say the FTP were the violent, hard-core element of the Resistance.

More to the point, the FTP were *the* Resistance in the Dordogne area. There was no AS in these parts. Nestor, or Commandant Jack, had been forging SOE alliances with the local groups for months – the carrot being the provision of firearms and specialist training. It was now up to Stella and me to keep this small band on side until the invasion came.

Here was our specific mission, as read to us by Pirbright on the day we left Beaulieu:

"Recently decoded German military radio transmissions show that the 'Das Reich' 2nd SS Panzer Division has been re-mobilised from the Eastern front to the town of Montauban, south of the Dordogne. This is a strategic position from which they can be summoned to repel possible allied invasions hitting either the north or south coasts of France. Should the invasion come from the north, you are to have the Resistance ready to inflict *maximum* damage to the Das Reich as they drive up country, to prevent them from reinforcing the German defences on the coast."

While the other FTP men carried on their banter, Stella and I remained silent.

She was a hard one to read.

In the last weeks of the finishing school at Beaulieu we had spent a lot of time in each other's company; Stella was all business, always double-checking maps and re-reading her lecture notes. Sometimes, she would tap out Morse nervously on the table top – always practising.

In Scotland she had been absolutely vicious in Close Quarters Combat. At first she was paired up with the other female recruit, Nancy, but when she broke Nancy's nose, the Captain decided to put her with one of the men, and that man happened to be me. I had probably fought Stella more times than conducted civil conversations with her. In combat, she moved like a scalded cat – sharp and fast – and I had soon learned not to hold back unless I wanted to end up getting seriously hurt.

My main picture of her though, remained that of the shivering near naked woman by the loch, covered in pig's blood and asking the Captain if he was going to let the pig go to waste.

I respected Stella for her abilities as an agent. Objectively, yes, she was pretty, but my experience with Freya Nielsen stopped me from even beginning to entertain romantic thoughts. Stella was a team-mate, first and last, a radio operator whom I had to protect from capture or death, even if it meant getting killed in the process. The fact that Limouzy was already besotted seemed neither here nor there. At this early stage, I could see it was probably a bonus as it might keep him sweet for a while.

At Finishing School I had wondered about Stella's back story, what it was that drove her on so much, with such crazed single-mindedness. At first I speculated she might be an English equivalent of a Freya Nielsen, widowed, with a soldier husband who had been killed earlier in the war. As time went on though, after I had been around her for many hours, the more I became convinced that her motivation wasn't fuelled by grief. Yet she had the same slow-burn, stubborn determination as me, and hers was just as powerful, so there had to have been some kind of tragedy involved – you simply didn't get to be as tough as she was for no reason. When we had sparred in close combat she never relented. It was as though a demon was riding her back.

Then, passing her room in STS 31 one Friday evening, I happened to see her lighting a couple of candles at her desk. At the time, it didn't strike me as particularly odd, because it was dark and lots of people used candles. It was only some hours later, as is sometimes the case with unconscious reflection, that it hit me: she had been observing Shabbat – the Jewish Sabbath. I knew nothing else about agent Stella's background, but everything I needed to know about her motives was explained by the fact she was Jewish. The tragedy I had sensed in her was the knowledge of the fate befalling her entire people, and it was one which she was railing against with a fearsome intensity.

I watched her moving along the track now – her legs swinging in time with the FTP men leading us. She moved like a feline as well as fighting like one; efficiently and lithely. After the thirty mile trek at the end of the paramilitary course we had all been lying on the ground back at base and she had strolled around, fresh as you like, chatting to everyone and asking how they had found the exercise.

I was effectively her body guard – there to remove the risk of her having to carry around a radio. SOE radio-operators took a long time to train, but had a life expectancy of around six weeks once they were in the field. Not only that, but the really good ones were rare and they needed to be protected at all costs. I was fairly sure Stella could fight her way out of most situations if she had to, but by my taking on the risk of being captured with the radio, her life expectancy had improved considerably.

Perhaps more of a fall-guy than body guard: I had no illusions about that. In the eyes of the SOE I was certainly more expendable than her.

I comforted myself with the knowledge that no other agent could have become Xavier. Despite my knife skills, that was really why the SOE chiefs had thought me special. Pirbright and Stringer had known right from our first meeting. I suppose Fox or Farr-Jones must have seen a photograph of Xavier and noticed I was a dead ringer and that had been why I had been given the card and encouraged to call. My face was the main reason they had needed me – a job offer based on my looks alone! I felt quite degraded.

The winding track straightened and the steep initial climb flattened out a little.

I was starting to understand why the landing field had been a few miles away – everywhere else around here was too densely forested and hilly to land an aircraft.

Suddenly there was a crashing sound in the forest and the men drew their weapons.

Our training kicking in, Stella and I moved to the side of the track and fell to the ground.

The sounds grew closer. Something large was moving through the trees, breaking branches and approaching fast. Whatever it was, it wasn't stealthy.

I was in awe of Limouzy's sang froid as he held up his hand to reassure the others. Then we all found out why, as it burst out onto the track ahead.

"Sanglier!"

The men relaxed and re-shouldered their weapons as the wild boar barrelled off down the track in the opposite direction, its rounded bulk visible in the moonlight.

As we got back to our feet and were dusting ourselves down, Stella looked at me with a raised eyebrow.

Without thinking, I had reached down and drawn my F-S dagger.

"Feeling peckish, Ahab?"

She had been joking, but someone else wasn't.

I heard what sounded like a stick breaking and on the track up ahead the boar crashed to the ground.

Limouzy had fired a shot with his silenced De Lisle carbine, and was looking triumphant as he marched up to the fallen animal.

Eric ran to join him and hauled it up easily onto his shoulder.

"I was starting to wonder what was for dinner, boss."

The house was a few yards off the track and partly shielded from it by a high hedgerow of thorn-trees, their spindly branches reaching across the tiles of its sagging roof like Richard Shaw's withered fingers over his route maps. The place looked as though it had grown from the landscape rather than ever having been constructed by man. A wooden sign, hanging from a nail on the wall read: 'Reybenet'.

The distinctive slanted front grille of a Citroën gleamed from the driveway.

As we neared, a man with white hair opened the front door and raised his hand in greeting to our group, motioning us to enter. As we filed inside, he saw me and exclaimed in surprise, "Xavi! You changed your mind?"

My very first impression was of his eyes; blue-green, bright and alive, and not deadened by the world and all its horrors. In that brief moment I could see they belonged to a man of understanding and kindness. I expect I was looking for some sign of reassurance in his countenance, and I was relieved to find it. There was a glint of humour in his expression too; a good man, I could tell straightaway.

I laughed. "No, sir. It's me, the Englishman."

I tried to speak the way I had heard the real Xavier speak on the landing field, calmly and low.

"Really?"

He looked at me more closely. "My God!"

And then he started to laugh too – a deep rumble which then became a wheezy cacophony so that it felt as if you were hearing an inventory of every cigarette he had smoked in his life.

I knew right then I would be getting on very well with my surrogate father.

Stella and the others left soon after, but not before Limouzy had hacked a leg off the boar and handed it to Jacques.

I didn't ask where Stella would be staying – I didn't need to know. It was safer that way. Whenever she wanted to meet, all she had to do was book a doctor's appointment. That way she could come 'on a professional basis' without having to worry about looking suspicious.

Jacques led me over to a log fire which was crackling away on a large open hearth and casting a warm glow into the room.

"Sit."

I took a seat on a wicker chair and as soon as I did I realised how tired I was – it had been twenty hours since my last proper sleep.

He carried the boar's leg away to the kitchen and returned to pour me a glass of wine.

"To winning the war," he said in his husky voice.

I held up my glass.

The wine was soft on my palate, the sort of stuff you could drink by the bottle and not really notice.

Jacques pointed to some documents on the table.

"Your identity papers, Xavi."

"Thank you."

Despite all my training, this felt very strange indeed. I took another swig of the wine to try and calm down.

I reached over and slid the papers into my pocket. Xavier's watch was inside the pocket and I pulled it out and put it around my wrist.

Nervously, I took another slug of the wine as Jacques studied me.

"They even got the scar right" he said. "You've become my boy, there's no doubt about it."

A few family photographs were up on the mantelpiece and I glanced at him for permission before getting up to examine them more closely.

"Yes, it's fine," he said. "Please…"

There was one of Jacques, Xavier and a woman I presumed was Jacque's wife. I remembered her fate from the file.

"I'm sorry about what happened in Dunkirk," I said, turning to look at him.

Still in his chair, Jacques stared down at the floor.

"She was in the wrong place at the wrong time," he said, in his low voice.

It was a sentiment that applied perfectly to Tom Shaw too, or to any innocent person who had suffered a violent death.

Another photograph showed a much younger Jacques – perhaps in his late teens, standing alongside a beautiful blonde woman in the front yard of Reybenet.

She didn't look like his wife and I guessed who it was from my background reading.

"Your sister?"

He came over to me and held the photograph.

"Yes, that's Bernadette... in 1898. I was only sixteen."

"The nurse who married the American, and went to New York. The one you wrote to?"

He nodded. "Yes. Since 1901 she's been Mrs Poyntz and not Madmoiselle Bonnet. She lives in one of those tall buildings in New York – in a skyscraper as the Americans say – right next to a place they call Central Park."

Jacques put the photograph back and we both sat down again. I had only been in Reybenet for fifteen minutes, but it felt as though I had lived my life there because I knew so much already.

I raised my glass towards the pictures.

"To family," I said, draining the rest of the wine.

Jacques re-filled our glasses and we drank again in silence, each of us lost in our own thoughts.

The photographs and the mention of America had reminded me of my own family.

Pirbright had made me a deal before I left England – agreeing to send my parents regular updates on my behalf. My cover story involved being posted to America to continue the research into exercise physiology in the mountains of Colorado. SOE had supplied a dozen picture postcards of the Rockies on which I had written future-dated missives, which Pirbright promised to send on my behalf at the appropriate times. I had even used different pens with each card to make them look more authentic.

At last, old Bob Kynance's waffle at Oxford had become useful; it helped me invent all sorts of claptrap about my studies at Pike's Peak, carrying on with the work started by the renowned John – 'Jonners' – Haldane in the earlier part of the century. In the postcards I explained in boring detail how we were measuring the carbon dioxide output of athletes on the mountain using the 'Kynance bag' and how it was helping in the selection of the toughest, fittest soldiers.

As I had written this fiction Tom had been hooting with laughter in my ear, but on handing over the great stack of lies to Pirbright my amusement instantly turned to guilt. I could see my parents reading them with interest, really believing I was getting over Tom's death and that I was living safely across the Atlantic. It made me feel like a fraud.

What concerned me most was that if I was killed out here, my parents would only receive the shortest of letters asking them to collect my few possessions. Depending on the circumstances they might get a brief and highly censored explanation as to what had happened, but there would be no comforting stories from comrades or commanding officers, explaining what a nice chap I had been, and how I had faced my last moments bravely.

I didn't want them staring at a photograph of me on the piano for the rest of their lives, the way my father had been doing with that picture of his brother. I didn't want them reading and re-reading some anonymous Post Office telegram that began: *'DEEPLY REGRET TO INFORM YOU THAT YOUR SON...'*

One tragedy in a life-time was more than enough for a family to cope with. No amount of long walks in the country would be able to fix it, I knew that much. After a few minutes of this gloomy self-indulgence, I banished the thoughts from my mind, determined to re-focus on the mission.

"So what do I call you? Jacques or Papa?"

He paused for a moment with the glass of wine near his lips.

"Papa" he said, confirming his decision by drinking.

"All right then, Papa it is."

"And I'll just keep calling you Xavi, like I always do, or I'll get us into trouble."

"Xavi I will be," I said, drinking too.

"You are just like him. My God, London don't mess about, do they?"

"No they don't. I've trained hard for this too, you know, but now that I'm finally here it feels different...."

"I imagine so... but you'll get used to it."

I glanced at Xavi's watch on my wrist. It was three in the morning.

"I'm sorry, Papa, I've kept you awake half the night."

"Don't worry yourself. It was a big day. My son was so nervous he could hardly sit still."

"Apparently they've got him working as a doctor while he's there, to keep him busy."

"Well, maybe he'll find some nice English girl and give me some grandchildren before I drop off the perch. It'll do him good, this adventure of his, I'm sure of it."

I smiled in agreement, hoping things would work out for my double.

"And you, young Xavi?" he said to me. "You've got no-one special?"

"I'm not supposed to talk about my old life."

"Of course... forgive me."

He deserved the truth. I didn't care about cover stories anymore, not with a man who had swapped his own son.

"But I'll tell you anyway... A year ago I thought I had found someone – just for the briefest of moments – as stunning as your sister in that old photograph. Unfortunately, she turned out to be a spy and her actions led to the death of my best friend. And so here I am."

Jacques absorbed my words, turning to look at me seriously, to show he had understood the implicit pain in my short explanation.

"I appreciate you telling me that. It helps me understand why you're here. It makes sense to me now."

I drank the rest of my wine.

"And don't worry, Xavi" Jacques said. "I won't say anything. I'm a doctor, remember? All I do all day is hear people's innermost secrets and keep them to myself. I'm used to saying nothing."

He stood up and came over to me, taking my glass and carrying it out to the kitchen.

"Your bedroom is up the stairs, Xavi," I heard him say. "Go and get some sleep. I'll wake you in five hours."

To get up to Xavier's bedroom I had to climb a spiral iron staircase from the living room. The bedroom was a converted roof space whose walls sloped steeply on either side of the central ridge, so that it was only possible to stand fully upright in the middle of the room.

Jacques slept downstairs in a large bedroom, which led off the living room.

I lay on the bed fully clothed, listening to him moving about for a few minutes.

He mumbled a prayer and then the house fell silent.

I woke to the heady smell of fresh coffee and croissants.

Jacques had already been to the bakery in the next town to get breakfast. I had slept right through it all – not even hearing the Citroën leave or return.

"Xavi," I heard him saying from downstairs, "on mange!"

We sat outside the house to eat, at a table under some vines.

The view was of a vast wooded valley stretching all the way to the horizon. This certainly didn't feel like an occupied country... not by Germans, not by anyone. It felt like one big uninhabited forest. A morning mist hung low over the trees and at this early hour the air was still crisp and fresh. The sun was out though and steam was rising from the dewy grass.

"Bon appetit" he said.

The croissants were soft and still warm.

"Mmm... good," I said, after I had taken the first bite.

There was a pot of homemade blackberry jam on the table and we took turns in scooping out spoonfuls and dolloping them on our croissants.

"Eat up." he said, chomping away at his second croissant and taking small sips of his coffee. "We've got a morning surgery in an hour. Over there."

He pointed to a small building ten yards from the house, a place I had thought was a barn the night before. Still holding his half-eaten breakfast, he stood up.

"Come and see where you work."

I hadn't put my shoes on yet, so I could feel small twigs and stones tickling the soles of my feet as we crossed the yard. A few red berries were scattered on the ground and I didn't try and avoid them – they burst under my weight and the stains made it look as if my feet were bleeding.

Jacques unlocked the door to the surgery with a key on a string around his neck, and pushed it open to reveal a waiting room with six chairs. The air inside was cool and smelt a little of lavender.

Off this were two consultation rooms with their doors open – each had a desk, two chairs and a reclining examination couch. A few books sat atop the desks. The couches were old, the green leather cracked with age. There were glass fronted cupboards full of medicines and supplies, dressings, suturing equipment and syringes – all the things you would expect to see in a rural surgery.

"I know it looks basic," he said, "but it's what works. We've been here since my father's time. Always two of us, seeing the patients as a team. First it was me and my father, and then more recently me and Xavi."

We wandered back to the breakfast table.

As the sun rose higher I had to take off my jersey and eat the rest of my croissant wearing only my cotton shirt. May was a lot warmer here than in England.

"You eat like him, too" Jacques said, staring at me. "Even in plain daylight I can barely spot the difference. I can see why they chose you."

"I couldn't believe it either when I first saw the photograph."

"Not just in looks either, but in your character. Quiet, like my boy. I can tell you're an only child."

"I am" I said, surprised it was that obvious.

I reached up and felt my cheek.

"I was meaning to ask, Papa, how did it happen? How did I get this scar?"

Jacques smiled and sat back.

"Oh what a day… poor Xavi. When he was three years old he got into the surgery, pulled a scalpel out of the drawer and drew it down across his cheek. He didn't cry – just walked into the house with blood streaming down his face. Gave his mother one hell of a fright… God bless her soul."

Jacques reached to this chest and held up the key on the string.

"Anyway, that's when I got this key cut. Up until then we had always left the place unlocked. This is the country – there are no robberies."

A scalpel incision – no wonder it had been easy for MP to copy.

"The lads seem to like me," I said, changing the subject, "Limouzy and the others."

Jacques shrugged.

"'Like' doesn't come into it, Xavi. The only things they respect are deeds."

He had only glimpsed us all together for a minute or so, which made me doubt how he could form such an opinion on so brief an observation. It was one thing I was finding out about my new father. He seemed to be able to bore down to the truth very quickly; a useful skill for a man who had to make important diagnoses all day long.

"Don't worry," he said, perhaps sensing my uncertainty. "Limouzy is a fair man – tough, but fair."

"You've known him a long time?"

Jacques smiled.

"I was there when he was born... I was there when *all of them* were born."

I smiled with him. "That's good to know. I have to depend on them with my life."

"No, you don't have to worry about them... the ones you have to worry about are in the towns. Collaborators – people who will talk to the Germans or the Milice to make their lives easier. There are many who don't want any trouble, who just want to get through the war alive, which I suppose is understandable. But in certain situations in life, you have to be willing to step over the line, wouldn't you agree?"

He already knew my answer, because if it had been any different, then I would not be sitting out here with him in the Dordogne with my surgically altered face and a radio in my doctor's bag.

"Limouzy's men are all about violence," he said, "but without violence, there can be no Resistance... yes?"

"I completely agree," I said, sipping my coffee.

There was a small jug of milk on the table.

"I thought there was no milk in France."

Jacques pointed to a goat tethered to a chain at the far end of the garden.

"We're lucky."

I picked it up and sniffed.

"It smells like goat" I said.

Jacques laughed. "It's a few days old – Bella's not giving us much milk at the moment."

I went ahead and added it to my coffee – at least it took away the bitter taste.

Jacques said I should call him 'Papa' in front of the patients. Just as it had said in the file, he reaffirmed the fact that the real Xavier didn't say much in his consultations – preferring to give the floor to the patients for a least the first minute or so.

"His style is to ask short questions about symptoms such as: 'How long?', 'How painful?', 'Where exactly?'. When examining, he restricts his discourse to short comments also: 'shirt off please', 'hold still', 'deep breath'. In diagnosing, Xavi says it simply, in no more than a sentence: 'It's flu. You must rest,' or 'See how you are in the next day or so, and let me know if it changes'."

The other good thing was that, until recently, Xavier had been away studying in Bordeaux for his final exams.

"Most locals haven't seen him in some time," Jacques said. "And their memories of his mannerisms have faded. Besides, if they do see changes, it's because Xavi has picked them up during his time away. They won't know. Trust me."

Chapter Eighteen

At nine o'clock the surgery began.

My first patient was a slim elderly woman – Madame Derange – who talked and talked about how unwell she was. For a good ten minutes she chattered on, reciting her ailments from a list she had written down to help her remember. She certainly didn't seem too unwell.

"It hurts all over, Doctor," she said in conclusion, "and you must do something. I need a pick me up… a tonic of some kind."

"Be more specific. Where exactly is it painful?"

She pointed to her head: "Here." Then her chest: "Here." Then her abdomen: "Here… oh… and my legs… and my toes too."

"How long have you been like this?"

"Years."

Stumped, I decided to examine her – hoping it might give me a clue. I did everything I could think of: temperature, pulse, blood pressure, listened to her heart and lungs. I tested her nervous system and then her abdomen and limbs, but all to no avail. Everything was normal. She had squealed hysterically when I checked for a Babinski sign by running the blunt end of my pencil along the soles of her feet, but even so, the test was normal.

When I had finished, she sat up on the examining couch expectantly.

"Do you know what it is?"

I stroked my chin and lied through my teeth. "Yes, I think so… but will you excuse me a moment, I would like to confer with my father first."

Her face lit up.

"Of course, Doctor, of course."

I took Jacques outside into the yard and we stood on the red berry lawn.

"This Mrs Derange," I said. "I've not got a clue what's wrong with her. Maybe we should send off blood tests to Bordeaux?"

Jacques laughed.

"She came with a list?"

"Yes."

"Rule number one. If they have a list, they're not that sick. Nothing's physically wrong with her. She lost a son in the Great War and hasn't been the same since. It's in her head. Say anything, give her anything – it doesn't really matter. As long as you say it with authority, she'll believe you. It'll be many months before she returns."

I went back into my room and sat down.

Keeping a serious look on my face, I glanced down at the pencil on the desk. It gave me an idea.

"My father agrees with my diagnosis, Madame Derange… you have Staedtler's syndrome. It's rare, but there's a simple cure."

I said it with such confidence that I almost believed it too.

"Oh Doctor, that's wonderful!"

She looked better already. Some tablets would hopefully clinch it. I rifled through my doctor's bag which, in the upper compartment, contained some real medicine.

In our pre-flight briefing at Tangmere we had been given 'A' pills for airsickness and 'B' pills containing Benzedrine – a stimulant – to keep us awake. There were also 'K' pills for inducing sleep. As long as I didn't give her the cyanide 'L' pill, things would be fine. That was safely hidden away in the cork in my pocket.

I chose one B pill and one K pill, stamped an envelope with the official 'Bonnet Clinic' ink stamp and put the pills inside.

"Take half a pink pill now and half a blue pill this evening. Repeat this tomorrow and you'll feel a lot better. The condition will have resolved itself."

Essentially, she was going to have a very wakeful day followed by a very good night's sleep, and the same for the following twenty four hours.

I stood up and handed over the envelope.

"That's it?" she said.

"Yes, madam. The medicine is powerful and has only recently been developed. Two days is all you need. I guarantee it."

Her husband was waiting outside in a pony and trap.

"My darling," I heard her say, "the young doctor has cured me – all I have to do is take these pills…"

I heard his gruff voice as he picked up the reins.

"Staedtler's syndrome? I've never heard of it."

"He said it's rare and that I'm actually a special case," she said, embellishing my lies even further.

I went back inside and sat down heavily into my chair, exasperated already.

At that moment I wasn't sure which was taking more out of me – inventing new diagnoses and fooling patients, or the stress of having a doctor's bag which could get me shot if its in-built radio was ever found.

The one thing SOE final training had taught me above all else was the art of deception. If practising rural medicine involved the same techniques, at least I was well prepared. In my mind's eye, I could see Tom Shaw falling off the examining couch in laughter: 'My God Ed, I think we've found your vocation… even I bloody believed you!'

Jacques came in and I told him what I had done.

"You used the Coue method, excellent."

"The Coue Method?"

He picked a book up off the desk and brushed off the dust.

"Read this… it's helped me with a lot of my patients."

It was called *Self Mastery Through Conscious Autosuggestion* by Emile Coue.

Jacques tapped at his temple.

"The power of the mind, Xavi… there's nothing stronger."

The rest of the surgery wasn't as taxing – mostly minor viral illnesses in children, although I found their small voices and half pronunciation difficult to make out.

Then a German Feldgendarme came in to see me. His name was Kram and he was a big man, whose breath smelt of salami. Hanging around his neck was a chained shield – his badge of office. At Beaulieu we had studied all the German ranks we might encounter in the police state – the Sipo, the Kripo, the Sicherheitsdienst or SD, closely associated with the Gestapo, the Abwehr and Feldgendarmerie. There was also the French Milice, a Vichy paramilitary force designed to fight the Resistance, whose numbers equalled that of the AS and the FTP combined.

My first interaction with the enemy turned out to involve a rectal examination, which caused Kram to flinch violently and say, "Schiesse!"

He had piles. I gave him some cream to rub on and some laxatives and told him to drink plenty of water.

After Kram had gone, Jacques came into my room.

"How was the Kettenhunde?"

"What?"

"Kettenhunde – it means 'chained dog'. We call them that because of their distinctive neckwear."

I smiled.

"They didn't teach us that at our finishing school in England… He just had a simple case of haemorrhoids."

Jacques laughed his craggy rumble. "And you put your finger up his arse – I bet they didn't teach you that in spy training either."

"Well no… but at medical school, an old professor taught us that if you don't put your finger in it, you put your foot in it…"

This set Jacques off again.

"That's a good one!"

He clapped me on the back and left. Five minutes later I could still hear him chuckling away, repeating the saying over and over in his consultation room.

At the end of the session I walked out to see two young ladies sitting in the waiting room. Both were very attractive.

"Can I help?"

"We're here to see your father," one said.

"Yes, but next time, perhaps we'll choose you," said the other.

She spoke with a certain brazen confidence and they both broke out into giggles.

Jacques came out and, when he saw them, his face turned grim.

"One moment," he said, going back into his room.

He was out again in a matter of moments, a brown paper bag in his hand.

"Thank you, Doctor Bonnet," they said in unison.

He still wasn't smiling.

"You're playing a dangerous game, you two. I don't need to remind you of that, do I?"

One winked at him and then threw her hair back and laughed. Her friend was grinning too. "You worry too much. This is the modern world."

"Just be careful... and be discreet, for God's sake."

He watched them go and shook his head wearily.

"What was that all about? What did you give them?"

"I gave them prophylactics, to stop them getting pregnant."

"Is that such a big deal?"

"It is when they are conducting 'la collaboration horizontale'. It is not a good thing... you understand? If Limouzy's men found out, they would shave their heads... at best."

I understood.

"Confidentiality," Jacques said. "My doctor's oath... it's the only thing saving those girls. I told you I was good at keeping secrets."

I was cleaning up from the morning when Stella came into my room and shut the door behind her, as quiet as a ghost.

Beads of sweat had collected on the skin over her upper lip, and for a moment I thought she might be feverish.

"Are you alright?"

"I'm fine. It's warm out there."

"How was your night?"

She picked up the Staedtler pencil – probably musing on what a good improvised weapon it would make – before putting it back down and answering me.

"Fine… yours?"

"I slept well, and I'm getting on well with Jacques, but the surgery this morning was tough… worse than Morse code classes."

That made her smile.

"I'm staying with a nice woman" she said. "A widow called Madame Blanchard – my cover is that I'm her niece from down South, from a town called St. Maximin-la-Sainte-Baume, not far from Marseilles."

"That's quite a mouthful for a cover story. I wonder why London chose it?"

"Because there really is a niece from there… London have prepped me just as they've prepped you about Xavier. I can wax lyrical about the place… Apparently the basilica contains the bones of Mary Magdalen. They say she lived out her days in a cave in the mountains near there."

I frowned. "Really? That sounds a bit far-fetched."

Stella shrugged. "Think what you want – it's *your* religion."

If ever there was a conversation stopper, then that was it. I could see her biting her lip at her slip up. My observations with the candle and Shabbat had been correct.

A few seconds went by. "Be careful, Stella," I said, not wanting to sound too much as if I was telling her off.

She nodded, red-faced with embarrassment.

I picked up my doctor's bag and put it on the desk, sensing it was time to get down to business.

"I assume you want to do the first transmission."

She checked her wristwatch, a French one London had procured.

"Yes. London will be listening in one hour."

Each radio operator in the field had a strict schedule to follow, so that the Home Stations didn't get swamped with traffic. There was only a five minute window during which the home operator would be listening out. To be as safe as possible, our radio time was being kept to a minimum – with transmitting and receiving rotating on a roughly weekly basis. Only Stella knew the exact sequence, having committed it all to memory.

"Where do you want to do it?"

"Can you take the car?"

I glanced outside at the dormant Citroën.

"I think so. What's your plan?"

"You drive for five minutes, so we can transmit in a secluded place."

"What about you?"

"I'll get there on foot."

We walked through to Jacques' consultation room.

He was looking at a blood smear under a microscope.

"Can I borrow the car, Papa?"

Without looking up from the eyepiece, he felt around in his pocket and held out a key.

"Do you have a map?" I said.

"There's one of the local area in the glove compartment."

I retrieved the map and returned to my consultation room where Stella was waiting. Once I had opened it out over my desk she was quick to pick a spot.

"The high ground here," she said. "Three miles further up the track, where the road forks. We'll meet there. I came that way this morning. Don't try to hide the car, just pull over – like you're stopping for a smoke."

"Affirmative."

She didn't seem to appreciate my use of army speak, her sober expression wiping the grin off my face instantaneously. After her earlier mistake she had lost all her humour.

"Your plan is sound" I said, becoming serious too.

"Be there in forty five minutes," she said. "I want to transmit right on time."

I saw her to the door and, as she left, she briefly touched my shoulder – I suppose as a sign that we were in this together. That cheered me a little. Then she headed off towards the oak wood at the edge of the lawn, soon melting away into the trees.

With some time to kill, I went back into the surgery to talk to Jacques.
I showed him on the map where we were meeting.

He nodded.

"It's well isolated," he said, "so you shouldn't see anyone. The local German garrison all know the car by sight. If you happen to see a patrol, just slow up and roll down the window… they'll wave you past. If they ask you where you're going, say you're visiting Madame Blanchard – she lives in the farmhouse another mile on… here. She has slightly arthritic hips."

"Perfect." I folded up the map and put it away in my pocket.

"By the way" he said, "I know Stella is staying there. I was the one who arranged it."

"And Madame Blanchard really has a niece from St. Maximin?"

"Yes, who has gone into hiding. Stella's cover is as watertight as we could make it… London even arranged for photographs of Stella to be put on the mantelpiece down there."

"You've gone to a lot of trouble."

"I don't like the Germans" he said. "I want them gone."

Jacques replaced his look of bitterness by smiling at me encouragingly.

"You're doing well."

It was kind of him to say so, because I felt way out of my depth.

"You know, Papa, I sometimes wonder why Xavi didn't just become an agent himself – it would have saved a whole lot of bother."

"I wondered when you would ask that," he said.

"He wanted to?"

"Yes. The men in London wanted it that way too."

"So what happened?"

"I wouldn't allow it – I would only agree if London could find a substitute."

"Why?"

"I've already lost a wife to this damn war. I couldn't stand to lose a son too. If that makes me a weak man, then God forgive me. I'm sorry, this must sound terrible to you, as if I don't mind it if you die. Of course I would mind. It's just that… well… my son…"

"Don't feel bad. My father would do the same thing in your shoes."

As I spoke, it really hit home that Jacques wasn't my father, and if I was killed it wouldn't be his heart that would be irretrievably broken.

The feeling of guilt about my parents from the night before came back and it was still eating away at me on the drive out to the meeting point with Stella.

Part of me wanted to talk it all through with my father on one of our long walks together, but the fact was I wouldn't be able to talk to anyone about any of this. Not ever. I would be taking this episode with me all the way to my grave, even if that was in another sixty years.

"Just use the anger," I said out loud to myself. "Keep it on simmer. Controlled rage is good… it will help keep you alive."

Driving in the shadows of the sparse French oak trees, I tried to assess my situation like a SOE agent and not an insecure worrier deep in enemy territory.

Grinding through the Citroën's gears helped to distract me, and as I made my way along the lane, I focused on trying not to destroy Jacques' transmission completely. Even so, the harsh sounds of metal on metal rang out with alarming frequency.

I was glad to be in a secluded part of the Dordogne for this first drive, since it would have been clear to any casual observer that I had never driven this car before in my life. I was in dread of a suspicious 'Kettenhunde' waving me down on the track. At what stage would I resort to pulling out the F-S dagger and slitting his throat? When he started examining the doctor's bag? When he frowned at the false bottom? When he pulled out the radio itself? Would I be able to do it – to take a life? I thought of the pig's blood with its warm metallic taste and shuddered.

Arriving early at our meeting point, I left the car parked up at the side of the road as Stella had suggested. I hid my bag in the bushes and lit a Gauloise to ease my nerves. If someone drove down the track I could say I had been caught short on the way to a home visit to Madame Blanchard's and taken the opportunity to have a quick smoke.

Five minutes later, Stella stepped out from behind a tree. She had probably been there for a while, waiting to make sure I hadn't been followed.

We were efficient, acting out what we had rehearsed many times in training. I lifted out the contents of my bag until the false bottom appeared, then pulled up a thick leather flap to reveal the radio.

While Stella concentrated on the radio itself, I took apart the handles and connected up the dynamo, winding vigorously to get some life into the battery. Then I reassembled the handles into their original position. For a few moments Stella fiddled with the set before starting to transmit.

I kept a look out, the rapid rhythm of her key strokes adding to my nerves as I glanced up and down the track.

She had been one of the best in the whole SOE, with a word per minute count surpassing that of any other radio-operator. London would be recording the signal for two reasons; first, in case the message came out garbled and needed re-checking. Second, so they could compare it to their recording of Stella's Morse 'signature' from training, to be sure it was her actually sending the transmission and not some German interloper. The operator would be a young woman, listening through headphones in a large room with banks of other operators sitting by their radios, straight backed and all with the same look of calm intensity etched onto their features, pencils at the ready.

Another standard check – at our end – was the insertion of an extra random letter into the message. If Stella was ever forced to transmit under duress, she would deliberately miss out the extra letter and SOE would know she was compromised. In theory they would be able to then play along, passing on the bare minimum of information in an effort to keep her alive.

Cryptography classes at Beaulieu had given me headaches and I had drifted through on fifty percent attention levels. The instructor hadn't minded all that much, presumably aware that I already had enough to deal with in becoming another person. 'Comms' was all down to Stella – all I knew was that she was using the 'letter one-time pad' system of encryption which involved scrambled alphabets. Essentially it was a series of cipher keys screen-printed onto a piece of silk, kept hidden in her jacket lining next to the escape map. If she was ever searched, a pat-down meant less chance of discovery. 'One time' meant she had to destroy that particular key after each transmission. In the lectures, the instructor had said there were nearly twelve million ways a five letter word could be encrypted. In other words, it was basically impossible for the Germans to crack.

Still, it was a bad idea to be transmitting any longer than was necessary, since you never knew if the mobile German DF – direction finding – units were operating in the area. The message had to be done first time and without mistakes. That is why Stella's training had been intense and relentless – practise making perfect.

"Remember the enemy is listening," she had said while preparing the radio. "That's what they drummed into us. If we're on the air for more than five minutes, there's a higher chance the DF units will triangulate our signal."

In our final fortnight at finishing school we had gone on a dummy run to Bristol. The chiefs at Beaulieu had instructed us to work together as a team, the way we were doing now. We had set ourselves up in different lodgings, and then met up to transmit messages without being caught. It had been simple enough. We had even transmitted at night from the rocky outcrops near the Clifton Suspension Bridge.

I smoked another Gauloise and watched Stella work. During our training I had grown familiar with that frown of furious concentration as she tapped out the message on the Morse key, making sure there were no mistakes.

It wasn't surprising the Germans called the radio-operators 'pianists' because there was a concert-like elegance to it. For me the sound had sinister connotations, because it was exactly what I had heard on the staircase that day at East Grinstead. At least now we were attempting to nullify Nielsen's efforts and carry the fight to the enemy. I realised my war had finally begun. A strange pair of soldiers we were, fighting quietly and without drama in isolated places, our bullets being dots and dashes, and our weapon a radio.

When she was done, Stella cut off a small section from the piece of silk using scissors from my doctor's bag. This was the key she had used.

She grabbed my cigarette and burnt it, then tucked the rest of the silk away into her lining and put the apparatus back into my doctor's bag. I re-packed the upper chamber with my medical equipment and put the bag in the car. A bird somewhere in the branches overhead seemed to be singing a victory tune.

"So what did you tell them?"

She recited the message:

'STELLA AND AHAB ARRIVED SAFE TO BE ONSIDE FTP NEED BRENS NOT STENS'

Before leaving, she touched my hand in an unexpectedly tender gesture, as if to congratulate us both on our first successful outing in hostile territory. Then she stepped back into the forest with the same stealth she had shown on her arrival.

Jacques was waiting for me on a chair in the front yard. After I had locked my bag in the surgery, he cracked open a bottle of red wine and we ate fried snails with garlic, both of which he had gathered from the garden during my 'home visit' to the Blanchard farm. From the kitchen came the mouth-watering smell of a stew being slow cooked for that evening.

"What's for later, Papa?"

"What do you think, Xavi? Boar, of course…"

Chapter Nineteen

I grew mentally stronger and more confident, the uncertainty of the first few days soon fading.

A large part of that was due to Jacques – his cheerful manner and soon-familiar laugh couldn't fail to lift my spirits. I envied Xavi this life where he saw his father all the time – eating and drinking, working and talking together. It had been nine months since I had seen my parents. After a few weeks I felt I knew Jacques better than my own father. I made a mental note that if I ever made it out of this, I would see them more often.

Jacques also taught me real medicine; gems that had taken him a lifetime to pick up, things that weren't in the textbooks. He seemed to have a sixth sense about illness – more soothsayer than doctor from what I saw. Instinctively, he knew when someone was actually sick and when someone just needed platitudes and placebo, like Madame Derange on my first day.

"You can tell before they've said anything," he told me. "Just by watching the way they walk into your room, Xavi, you'll know. That's the most important part of the consultation; the rest is just filling in the gaps. What is unsaid is by far the greatest clue as to what is going on – the body language can't lie."

One evening, a week after our arrival, Stella and I met again in order to receive a message.

Like the first time, when she finished with the radio, she touched my hand in a gesture of solidarity, her face serious with the mission.

Though it meant nothing more than a standard handshake, I still found myself enjoying the brief moment of contact. I admired Stella – admired her resolve. Jewish, and yet the one to ask the Captain if we would eat the pig. She had eaten it too, sitting by the fire on the shore of the Loch. Jewish and eating pork, just so that no-one knew her background. So that she could become an agent and do some damage. Talk about commitment – nothing was going to stand in her way, not even the law of Moses. I suppose she could always borrow a line from the New Testament and say the laws were made for man, and not man for the laws.

I knew why it mattered so much to her of course, the whole world knew.

Even before the 1936 Olympics, the signs had been there. Everyone had been aware of Germany's attitude to the Jews, but everyone had still gone to the games. I remembered how the President of the American Olympic Committee had couched his anti-boycott argument: "The sportsmen of this country will not tolerate the use of clean American sport as a vehicle to transplant Old World hatreds to the United States." The way I understood this odd sentence, those speaking out against Germany – which obviously included the Jewish people – were the ones with 'Old World hatreds', and that they were the real trouble-makers, not the Nazis at all. Some of the anti-boycott Americans had even made veiled threats: "There is a great danger in this Olympic agitation… we are almost certain to have a wave of anti-Semitism among those who never before gave it a thought and may consider that five million Jews in this country are using one hundred and twenty million Americans to pull their chestnuts out of the fire."

Of course these dignitaries had been invited to Germany and been taken on stage-managed tours and shown how fair it all was. One had even attended the Nuremberg rally as Hitler's guest. There were a few short-lived protests in other European countries, including Great Britain, Sweden, France and the Netherlands, but once the American Athletic Union had voted to go, everyone fell into line. This sporting example of 'looking the other way', was an allegory for the political situation.

Ever emboldened, the Nazis had continued to apply their crazed worldview largely unchallenged. And now it was too late for the European Jews.

Horrific stories were trickling back from the East. An instructor at Beaulieu, who had been an agent in the field, told us of a conversation he had overheard in a Parisian café:

"I was sitting near a group of high-ranking German SS officers. One of them, called 'Woolf' by the others, was talking about a mass execution he'd witnessed near Minsk. He'd been with Himmler, 'the Reichsfuhrer-SS himself'. Woolf was saying how, during the shootings, Himmler had turned green and then vomited after a piece of brain had spattered onto his face. Do you know how the table reacted? They all burst out laughing as if they'd just heard the best joke of their lives. The next thing I heard Woolf say was that Himmler had urged the head of the Special Task Group to find a better method of mass extermination…so trials were conducted, dynamiting mental patients in wooden bunkers – but it was too uncontrolled and messy, with the bunkers exploding and body parts being scattered everywhere. Again, the whole table erupted. Finally, as the laughter subsided, Woolf said how the head of the Task Group had driven to an asylum at Mogilew in a truck and simply connected a hose pipe from his exhaust to a sealed room full of mental patients; all of them had died within in eight minutes – clean and efficient. At that, everyone at the table had raised their glasses and made a toast: 'to diesel fumes'."

The instructor's anecdote had been met by a few seconds of stunned silence.

"So, when you're out there…" he had said, "remember one thing; have no mercy whatsoever, because those Nazis are a lost cause – especially the SS."

Now that I recall, Stella had asked the lecturer a polite question. If I'd had my wits about me it would have been clear right then that she was Jewish:

"Excuse me sir, were you armed at the time?"

"Yes."

"Did it occur to you to just shoot them all, right there in the café?"

"For a moment it did, Agent Stella. But as much as I would like to win the war all by myself as a lone vigilante, I know this is impossible. Remember that you work as a team, not as loners. Trust your fellow agents with your lives. Only then will we win this war. Remember Thermopylae? A Spartan phalanx was an effective war machine because each soldier fought right next to his fellow on either side – their shields overlapping to form a solid wall. If one of them broke from the main unit, the whole thing disintegrated. By staying disciplined, and trusting in their fellows, a Spartan force of 300 held back a Persian Army of at least 80,000."

The reply we received was as follows, scrawled onto a piece of paper by Stella after decoding:

'YOUR NUMBER 1 RECEIVED GLAD SAFE ARRIVAL SEND MAP REF OF GROUND TO RECEIVE STORES NEXT MOON BY PARACHUTE DROP'

The next moon period was in early June. In our subsequent transmission, sent in the last week of May, Stella's message read:

'RECEPTION SAME GROUND AS LYSANDER DROP BBC MESSAGE THE WINE IS WATERED DOWN'

We chose the same field where we had first arrived because it seemed to be the only clear patch of land sufficiently remote in the entire Dordogne forest.

That transmission involved a degree of drama: I had just put the doctor's bag back into the car and was finishing my Gauloise when a motorcycle with sidecar came roaring down the road, so fast that if it had been five minutes earlier I doubt there would have been time to pack away the radio or hide it. Stella had already been gone a few minutes; at the rate she ran – she was probably half a mile away already. I was on my own.

I recognized the rider as a Feldgendarme, the neck plate glinting in the sun. Another Feldgendarme was riding in the sidecar. Christ! Two Kettenhundes! Even with my F-S dagger, I would have a tough time killing them both if it all went wrong here. I felt the blood drain from my face.

The driver brought his vehicle to a halt next to mine, but with the engine still running. He pulled up his helmet and smiled.

"Hello, Doctor Bonnet," he said, "It's me... Kram..."

He held out his hand to shake mine and I automatically shook it.

The man with piles.

"Of course! Kram. You're feeling better, I trust."

"Much better, thank you. I've changed my diet – cut down on the red meat a bit."

"That's good to hear." I looked to his companion sitting in the sidecar.

"I'm Weber," he said.

"Good to meet you."

They were both beaming at me, not in the least suspicious. Both were young, perhaps my age, with open, friendly faces, not quite fitting the image of brutal occupiers in a country that didn't want them.

Kram looked into the forest, towards the exact spot where Stella and I had been transmitting minutes before.

"What are you up to?" he said.

It was a reasonable question, and one for which I was prepared.

I smiled.

"It's a bit embarrassing to tell the truth... I got caught short on the way to visit Madame Blanchard. Had to stop the car for a leak. It's my father's strong coffee – it always acts as a diuretic."

"A diuretic?"

"Something that makes you want to piss."

Kram threw back his head and laughed, with his mouth so wide open that I could see practically every tooth in his mouth.

"How about you two?" I said. "What brings you out this way?"

Kram swelled with pride.

"We've come out for a spin, Doctor; we've been issued with a new bike you see."

"Looks fast."

"BMW R75... it can make 60 if I push it – they call it a 'Type Russia' because of all the use it has had on the Eastern Front."

"Impressive," I said, trying to look impressed. I had no interest in motor vehicles other than them getting me from A to B. "Any special reason you've been given it?"

"Weber and I have just been promoted. We're being transferred to Tulle tomorrow. It should make a change to being stuck in this backwater... oh... no offence, Doctor..."

I shrugged it off. "Not at all, Kram. I know what you mean. Anyway... I'll stop holding you up on your test run. I'd better be getting to Madame Blanchard before her old hips give out."

Kram nodded and replaced his helmet.

"So long, Doctor Bonnet."

I held up my hand. "Goodbye gentlemen."

He turned the throttle and accelerated away, the back wheel kicking up small stones and dust. It took ten minutes for my heartbeat to return to normal. They weren't so bad, I found myself thinking. What a sad state of affairs, for people to fall on either side of a divide like this. In other circumstances I could see us getting along well – they could easily have been a pair of jocular ski-guides in a Bavarian winter resort.

Just to be on the safe side, in case they turned the bike around and came back the same way, I drove on to Madame Blanchard's and poked my head in the door. Stella was already back. It was the first time I had actually been there. Madame Blanchard was perhaps in her early sixties – a similar age to Jacques. She reminded me a little of 'Madame' from finishing school, in that she was glamorous and classy and had once upon a time been very beautiful. All she did was pepper me with questions about Jacques and what he was up to. She didn't seem in the least perturbed that two British agents were in her house; in fact she was so blasé that it was as if she didn't know.

In our next reception time, a week later, London merely confirmed the plan with a laconic: *'YOUR NUMBER 2 RECEIVED AFFIRMATIVE 2 CANISTERS'*

For the first night of the moon period, Jacques and I listened to the BBC French news on Jacques' radio in Reybenet – specifically the personal messages: 'Ici Londres… écoutez maintentant les messages personelles…'

Our message wasn't read out.

Stella had been meeting the communist band regularly in the forest to give them lessons in firearms training, and in doing so, had gained their trust. They had even allowed her to see their base – a cave, deep in the wood. But now she was expressing concerns: "Limouzy and his men are becoming impatient," she told me. "They don't understand why we have to wait so long. When they found out that last night wasn't a go they cursed London openly. I'm worried Ahab, that with each empty newscast, their frustration will grow further until we can no longer control them."

This only confirmed what I had been sensing in the last week. A couple of times, the FTP band had showed up at Reybenet to collect food stores from Jacques' kitchen. I had tried to talk to them, but the conversation had been stilted and they had directed most of their comments at Jacques, their backs to me as if I were invisible. I heard myself referred to as 'L'Anglais', accompanied by a look which suggested they had stepped in something nasty. I had the distinct feeling they hated my guts. Everything about them screamed: 'Go home Englishman. We don't want you here.'

It was a lot like being at school when you have fallen out of favour with the popular crowd.

I hoped for a clear cloudless night so the drop could happen, prayed for it even, before the FTP lost all patience.

On the evening of June 5th, they happened to come to Reybenet along with Stella, all of them famished after a day of training. I watched on as Jacques fed them and it soon became clear why they had stuck with us this far.

It wasn't just the training they were receiving – Limouzy was plainly in love with Stella. It was so obvious – the soft way he spoke to her, the soppy, doe-eyed look she engendered in his otherwise hardened face.

Jacques, a reader of these things, had seen it straight off, later commenting, "I've never seen the big man so wrapped up in a girl…"

I could see Limouzy struggling with himself – to him she should have just been a 'comrade' and not someone for whom he harboured these strange feelings. His truffle-addled brain, set within its thick skull and mane of hair, was having a hell of a time coming to terms with the tornado which Agent Stella had set off in his heart. I knew what it was to fawn pathetically over a pretty girl; at East Grinstead Tom and I had become world experts in that particular pastime.

When he was near her, Limouzy had the same expression I'd seen on Tom's face whenever he had been around Nielsen – the anxious, troubled look of a lover who has no idea if his affection will ever be requited.

We all huddled around the radio set, listening intently. If the drop was delayed again I was half ready to bolt out of the door and keep running, but then came the sentence: 'THE WINE IS WATERED DOWN'.

I banged my fist on the table in relief and delight.

"That's it!"

The FTP fighters stopped scowling and broke out into smiles.

Jacques picked up his glass of wine and took a sip, frowning.

"You really think that? That my wine is watery?"

I laughed and held up my glass to his.

"Of course not," I said, lying. "Sante, Papa."

"Sante" he said back, still suspicious.

As darkness fell, we all went to wait it out in the landing field.

The drop came in at one in the morning.

Not wanting to wait, and going against protocol, Limouzy cracked open one of the cases right there in the field and pulled out an instruction leaflet headed with the words: LE FUSIL-MITRAILLEUR 'BREN'. If the word had been 'STEN' then I really do think he would have shot us on the spot. Well, me anyway. He probably loved Stella too much to do her any harm.

Unable to control himself, Limouzy came over and hugged Stella.

"Thank you, Comrade," he said with warmth, kissing her on both cheeks.

The bloody French and their constant kissing; it was worse than having to watch Boreman smarming around Nielsen, and that was saying something.

She seemed to enjoy it too, smiling and letting him hold her for a few seconds longer than seemed appropriate for a mere congratulatory hug between fellow freedom fighters.

'Comrade'. That's what he had called her.

Even Eric looked away in embarrassment.

Each parachute carried a cylindrical metal canister about five feet long. With the weight of the contents it needed three ordinary sized people to carry just one of them.

The brothers and I took one of the canisters, two on one side and one on the other, each of us taking a metal handle. Limouzy and Eric were able to carry the other on their own, simply hoisting it up onto their shoulders like circus strongmen. The parachutes themselves were shoved into large canvas rucksacks and slung onto the backs of the brothers.

Stella led the way back, watching for any patrols with the De Lisle in her firm grip. Needing both arms to manage the canister, Limouzy had given her his weapon.

The De Lisle! Christ, he may as well have offered her a marriage proposal. The carbine was his pride and joy; something I doubted he even allowed his own men to handle.

It's funny. The feelings I was having reminded me of when Boreman had moved in on Nielsen – a sense of mild outrage and frustration. And I didn't even like Stella that way.

That night was the first time I was allowed to see their hideout.

I suppose it was because they had needed my help with the donkey work, but it may also have been because I had a new standing in their eyes, a kind of reward for the Brens. In addition to the prolonged hug and kiss for my fellow agent, there had been a hearty backslap from

Limouzy for me, and on his example, the others had come over and offered their thanks for this treasure trove of a parachute drop. Suddenly I was a member of the 'in crowd'; no longer met with scowls. They even called me by my agent name, 'Ahab' again. The Brens had finally bought me some respect. Accurate to a thousand yards instead of thirty, these new weapons would ensure a proper fight and not just a 'pop-gun war' as Limouzy had been calling it.

I watched Limouzy carrying the container, his hair dark against his sheepskin jerkin. It was the first time I had ever seen him without his weapon hanging over his shoulder, not that it made him look any less intimidating. I felt puny in comparison – especially in view of the fact that I was on the canister with the two brothers and Limouzy was managing his with just Eric. I couldn't shake off the feeling that he was my 'rival' in some way.

Deep in the forested valley – about two miles from Reybenet, was a dry rocky gulley. At some stage in the past it must have been a watercourse draining into the nearby Vezere River. Wiry oaks and their roots covered any exposed areas of flat stone surface, having somehow gained a foothold over time.

We made our way along the dried-out stream bed for a few hundred yards, and then stopped. Thirty feet up was a retractable rope ladder, a hidden release rope looped around a branch above head height on the rock wall.

No-one would ever know the place was there. From the skies above, it would just seem part of the forest, and not even the most alert German spotter plane would see it. Even a patrol coming through the gulley would be none the wiser.

At the rear of our troupe, one of the brothers had been dragging a heavy branch with his free hand to rub out our footprints.

It was a large cave, set into a recess in the rock wall, the opening a long horizontal crack. You needed to duck to enter, but it soon opened up into a large chamber, where it was possible to stand at full height.

When one of the men lit a lantern I saw the interior properly; the dimensions were perhaps eight feet high, twenty feet wide and sixty feet deep.

Lining the walls were five camp cots with thin mattresses and blankets, a lot like the beds we had used during the training in Scotland – fold outs. One of the bunks was separated from the others by a makeshift curtain rail constructed out of some branches, with blankets instead of curtains. There was a large central table with an oak barrel at one end, collecting water which was falling as a continuous slow drip from the roof of the cave. The barrel had a tap and around it were all the drinking glasses of the FTP men, chipped and dirty.

The canisters were hauled up the rock face with ropes and set down on the floor. As well as the instruction leaflets, the canister Limouzy had already pried open in the field held four new greased Brens wrapped in corrugated cardboard – along with boxes containing thousands of rounds of ammunition. There were two dozen gammon grenades too. Enough to start a small war.

London had sent food in the other canister; the basics – corned beef, tobacco, cigarettes, chocolate, but luxury goods too – some jars of Russian caviar, perhaps to remind the FTP men of the motherland. It was like opening a giant Christmas hamper from Fortnum and Mason. What got the biggest cheer were the twelve bottles of 'Ricard' Pastis hidden in the straw: 'LE VRAI PASTIS DE MARSEILLES' it said on the label.

"Holy fuck," Eric said, pulling out one of the bottles. "It's been four long years since I've had a glass of this stuff…" He turned to me to explain. "The Vichy government banned it. Said it was 'contrary to their values', if you can believe that shit."

He filled the glasses with Pastis and then added water from the barrel, which turned the liquid an opaque yellow. He handed one to me.

It tasted of aniseed, and was watery, like Jacques' wine. Everything I had been drinking in France seemed to be diluted.

"Paul Ricard is a good man for the Resistance," Eric said to me, clinking my glass with his. "In the Camargue he makes petrol for the Resistance out of plums and cherries, and then he rides around on horseback shouting, 'I shit on Marshall Pétain and his government.'"

As Eric said it, he made a squatting motion and I laughed.

Our mission was finally beginning to work. Morale was good. As they drank, the FTP men were all laughing at Eric too.

When Pirbight and Stringer had read Stella's short message: 'TO BE ONSIDE FTP NEED BRENS NOT STENS' they must have got the hint and decided to really push the boat out.

The brothers continued unpacking the food and the rest of the bottles, stacking it all on the table and whistling 'Le Marseillaise' to themselves cheerfully.

I felt a tug on my shirtsleeve.

"Look," Stella was saying, her voice echoing around the cave hall with a strange resonance. "See the pictures?"

She was pointing to the cave wall.

It was only now that I noticed the fresco of animal paintings on the stone surface – woolly mammoths, bison, deer with antlers, and other creatures I didn't recognise straight away.

They had been made beautifully, in a range of ochres and blacks, all easy on the eye. The animals were merging with one another as if in movement, like stills from a movie camera.

"They're what I stare at before I fall asleep at night."

I frowned. "You've slept here?"

"A few times, after training late." She pointed over at the bunk that was curtained off from the others. "You don't have to worry about my virtue, Ahab. It's all been very civilised."

"Isn't that risky?" I said, pretending not to have been worried about her virtue. "What if the Germans happened to visit Madame Blanchard?"

Stella put her hands on her hips defiantly. "Well, what if they visited Jacques right now?"

She was right – this whole bloody mission was filled with risk. I stepped nearer to the frieze and changed the subject.

"Who made them? One of Limouzy's men?"

Stella laughed.

"No. These are incredibly old, Ahab... made by prehistoric people, maybe around fifteen thousand years ago. Limouzy found this place when he was a boy and never told a soul. His men are all sworn to secrecy. He knows he can trust them. After that Bren drop tonight, I think he finally trusts us too."

I took another swig of the Ricard and continued to stare at the images.

"Fifteen thousand years," I said.

They looked so much more recent than that, too good to be the work of dull-witted Stone Age men.

"How does he know that? How old they are, I mean…"

Stella stood closer so that her shoulder touched mine.

"This whole area is pockmarked with prehistoric caves. Back in 1940, not far from here, some children found a cave with similar murals – at a place called Lascaux – and a famous local anthropologist dated the place. He said it is from the Upper Palaeolithic era, that's around fifteen thousand years ago."

I glanced at her.

"You seem to know a lot about all this."

She punched me playfully and met my eye.

"Well, what else do you think we talk about at night?"

The pictures were made with simple bold outlines, as if the artist had done it perfectly the first time with no mistakes, a lot like the way Stella transmitted her Morse code. Perhaps the popular press had got stone-age man all wrong – these were not dull-witted brutes at all, but people in touch with their surroundings and blessed with a vivid and accurate recall of the animals they hunted.

You only had to look around at the bearded Resistance fighters to see what it would have been like thousands of years before – the cave men here in the firelight; the artist painting, another chipping away at a block of flint. Someone cooking a meal over a fire and someone else sewing furs with a bone needle.

A deep voice disturbed my imaginings.

"You like my walls?"

It was Limouzy. Warm from the walk, he had taken off the sheepskin jerkin and his long-sleeved shirt and was now in only a black woollen vest, which displayed his giant muscular upper arms to great effect. His right arm was tattooed with a five-pointed red star – the communist symbol. Like an Upper Palaeolithic man, he was chomping at a leg of meat, presumably a piece of left-over wild boar from another recent kill. He was a living throwback to the cavemen who had once lived here.

"They're amazing."

"Don't tell anyone."

I shook my head vigorously.

"Never."

"Not even Jacques."

I turned to him, sensing this was serious talk deserving of my full attention.

"I understand, Limouzy. I won't say anything."

He took a step closer and fixed me hard with his eyes for a few seconds.

"Good," he said, satisfied I had meant it.

He turned to my colleague.

"Have you shown him the beast, Stella?"

"Not yet."

Their exchanges sounded intimate, making me feel quite the outsider.

Limouzy smiled at me.

"Come," he said.

He led the way over to the cot deepest into the cave. It must have been his quarters because Stella had already put the De Lisle Carbine on the blanket.

A leaping sabre-toothed tiger appeared to be coming out from the stone surface. The animal had three sticks protruding from its torso and there were smudges of red paint around the entry points. Surrounding the stricken beast were four thin human figures – hunters – one of whom was in the action of throwing his stick. The spear was 'mid-air', on its way to sealing the fate of the prey.

It was strange how the humans who had made the drawings saw themselves as stick people, but the wildlife they hunted as full-bodied and colourful – magnificent in comparison; as if the animals were the most important things in their lives and not themselves.

"I like this one the most," Limouzy said. "Think of it, Ahab… a world where your only concern was hunting for your food, and not a world where people hunted other people."

He rested a heavy hand on my shoulder.

"That one there," he said, pointing at the spear thrower. "That's me now. Helping to kill the beast, only it's not a spear I will use but my carbine."

He pointed to the other figures.

"This one is Eric; here are the brothers."

I laughed.

He grunted with amusement and knelt down to study the pictures more closely.

"Maybe the cavemen could see into the future," he said. "Maybe they could see who would one day inhabit this place and what battles they would be fighting."

He pointed at the part where the ailing angry beast was jumping in desperation, the fanged mouth roaring in its death throes.

"See the blood? See how we will make the beast bleed?"

Still further into the cave, in its innermost recess and on the opposite wall to the sabre-toothed tiger was a painting of a wolf. At least at first I thought it was a wolf – on closer inspection it was actually a chimera; it had the head and torso of a wolf, but the limbs of a human. The creature was standing, looking straight out of the rock wall. There was something sinister about the image – it was not like the others. No colour – just black and white.

The figure was holding something in its hands – a stick-like object, but too short to be a spear.

"What about this one?"

"I don't really understand it," Limouzy said, hanging back by the image of the sabre-tooth tiger a few paces away from me. "And if you want to know the truth, it unsettles me. There's a creature in the Hall of Bulls at Lascaux which no-one quite understands – there it is called 'the Unicorn' and is similar to this… a human disguised as a beast."

I noticed Limouzy was keeping his distance and I looked at him quizzically – surely he wasn't frightened?

For the first time this tough man seemed vulnerable. He even nodded to himself knowingly, as if others had looked at him the same way when it came to this.

"I can see what you're thinking… and you would be right to think it. The figure scares me… it always has, ever since I was a boy when I first found this cave. It is always watching and waiting. It wants to kill; I feel that. Not like the hunters over there, who are killing in the heat of the moment, for self-preservation. This one is biding his time. I think it wants revenge of some kind."

"What's it holding?"

He shrugged.

"A flint knife, I think… that's all the cavemen had – spears and knives. But a wolf is a cold blooded killer, Ahab, an animal with no remorse or compunction about what it does. Killing doesn't impact on its conscience. It's part of its nature. That's not me. I am like the spear thrower – I only kill because of the situation I am in and make no mistake, I regret taking life. But it is a necessary evil, no?"

Limouzy dared himself to move a little closer to the wolf man.

"This character is a different beast altogether. This one plans. He'll kill and it won't make a dent on his soul. I think it's because he is already damaged beyond repair. His soul – or the good part of it anyway – has been destroyed."

It was three in the morning when I got back to Reybenet.

One of the brothers guided me through the forest and left me at the edge of the track leading to the house.

On the way I kept saying he could leave me and that I would find my own way home. From all my driving, I knew the whole area pretty well by now – as well as any local.

"You may know the roads," he said, "but the forests are another matter altogether. You would get lost in ten seconds if I left you now."

Jacques was still up and enjoying his watery wine when I arrived home.

Only a single candle was burning and the shadows on the walls made the place look as much a cavern as the one I had just left.

He was tactful enough not to ask where I had been after the drop. Every time I left the house I was on a mission of some kind and he knew that, but he never pried, just offered help when it was needed. That was his role, his way of avenging his wife's death. I hoped it might bring him at least a semblance of peace – that all the wrongs were being righted in a small way.

I sank into the wicker chair with my full glass of wine. I was getting a real taste for the stuff now – we must have drunk half a gallon a day between us. Never water, just coffee or wine. Our blood must have had more of this stuff than red blood corpuscles.

"You like her, don't you?" he said out of the blue.

"Like who?"

"Who do you think?"

"What? Stella?" I was immediately aware that I was blushing and sputtering. "Me and Stella? My God... No, Papa. Limouzy's the one who's in love with her. He's the one. We're just colleagues... No, no, you've got it all wrong."

He started laughing.

"You know what you are?"

"What?"

"Jealous."

Jacques continued to laugh his knowing laugh, that deep husky cigarette smoker's chuckle.

"No I'm not. Why should I care if Limouzy likes her?"

I drank my wine and tried to stay calm.

"My God, Xavi, you really don't know what's going on in your own brain, do you? Did they program that into you in training; how not to admit to yourself that you are falling for someone? That must have been some class."

Jacques had set off a chain reaction in my head and I was suddenly reappraising my entire relationship with Stella. I suppose I did like being with her, but I wasn't exactly 'in love' with her, not like the disastrous obsession with Nielsen anyway. Every time we were together with the radio, I took courage from her fearlessness and determination. It made me feel stronger. Perhaps, more to the point, it occurred to me that I missed her when our radio outings were over, that every time she touched my hand before leaving, I felt an unexpected gladness. I really looked forward to that touch.

"I'll admit I like her," I said, begrudgingly.

"Of course you do!"

I twitched and smarted.

"Tu es jaloux comme un Espagnol" Jacques said.

"… I'm as jealous as a Spaniard?"

"It's from Dumas, a trait particular to people in the Romance language-speaking countries. You remind me of a Spaniard, not an Englishman. With all your dark hair and your brooding. Maybe I should call you Don Juan…"

Ha ha ha ha!

He was rolling around laughing, really enjoying my discomfort.

"Come on – admit it, Xavi" he said, calming down. "Face the truth. You can talk to your old man."

Jacques was right. Jealousy was what I had felt earlier in the cave, when it had been 'Limouzy this' and 'Limouzy that'. It had been jealousy when she had been given his De Lisle to hold. And it had been jealousy when he had kissed her in delight at the parachute drop.

"All right," I said at last. "Perhaps I am a little jealous."

He put down his wine, clapped his hands and laughed again.

Then he pointed his finger at me. "Well listen, Xavi… I have good news for you. She likes you too. I've seen the way she sits in the waiting room at the end of the morning surgery and stares at you through your door, before you even know she's arrived."

"She stares?"

"Yes, she does. She likes you, Xavi. I know it. There are a dozen other things she does when she's around you that neither of you notice – she always tilts her head and rubs her neck, then combs her hair back with her hand. And that thing she does with her lower lip, half biting it with her upper teeth. The body language tells its own story. Just like it tells us what's wrong with the patients, it tells me she likes you. It's like reading a book. And, by the way, if it makes you feel any better, she doesn't do any of that when she's around Limouzy."

For a few minutes, we drank together in a comfortable silence. I was thinking how she had been making these subtle signals unconsciously and how I had been blind to them all.

I was very pleased to hear all this. Coming from Jacques it was almost as good as hearing the news from Stella herself.

"By the way, Papa… I saw that Madame Blanchard the other day – I think she likes you too."

Jacques nodded his head wearily and smiled.

"I know, Xavi, I know. She's already made a pass at me."

"Without meaning to be crass, it's been four years, Papa."

"I think about it, Xavi, I won't pretend I don't. Perhaps after this damn war has ended, who knows?"

"The company would be good for you."

Jacques' face was serious now.

"One day, Xavi… when all this is over, you must come back here, when you and Stella are married."

I nearly choked on my drink, but before I could say anything in reply, he was continuing, "You must come here for your holidays… with your children. I will build a bathing pool in the garden beyond the surgery with a view out over the valley. You will all be able to sit together on the terrace and watch the sunsets after dinner. Perhaps Madame Blanchard will be here. And perhaps my Xavi will have met someone too. And I will cook magnificent feasts for everyone. Wild Boar!"

"It's a tantalising thought" I said, going along with the fantasy.

"Even after I die I want you to come here for holidays. Will you do that? Stay with my son and enjoy this place."

Strangely, the scene he portrayed was easy to imagine.

"Yes, Papa, I will. I promise… if I survive the war and if she ever marries me."

"Good. I can hear the shouts and splashes from the pool already."

We both laughed at that.

He stood up, groaning a little as his old joints complained.

"I want you to learn to love this place after the war," he said quietly, "and not associate it with the occupation. It deserves better than that."

Later on in my bed, in the minutes before sleep came, I thought of the people living in this valley at the dawn of history, humans who for thousands of years had hunted these forests. The Germans had only been here four years, the tiniest blip in comparison.

Jacques was right – the place did deserve to be savoured properly, without the sour taint of recent times. A greater perspective was needed.

When I imagined Stella and the children at the poolside it made me smile again.

Then my smile faded.

My last thought was of the wolf man on the innermost wall of the cave. A being that felt nothing anymore, and who only wanted to kill.

Chapter Twenty

The next evening, on 6th June, everything changed abruptly.

We met all met at Reybenet again and listened to the radio as De Gaulle officially announced the invasion on the BBC: "*The supreme battle has begun… For the sons of France wherever they may be, whatever they may be, the simple and sacred duty is to fight the enemy by every means at their command.*"

Eric wrinkled his nose in apparent disgust.

"Now he tells everyone to fight. It's easy to talk tough from a comfortable chair at the BCRA behind the shop, with the might of the American, British and Canadian Armies backing you up… What the hell does he think we've been doing all this time?"

The team laughed – half at Eric's frustration, half at the ironic truth of his words.

The BCRA was short for the 'Bureau Central de Reseignements et d'Action' – the Gaullist Free French headquarters in London, located 'behind the shop', the main Selfridges Department Store, in Duke Street.

"Easy, my friend," Limouzy said. "We don't answer to the Great Asparagus."

More laughter resounded among the men at the mention of De Gaulle's nickname.

One of the brothers, Patrick, spoke up: "Boss – you think that De Gaulle's people will take up the fight now?"

Limouzy shrugged.

"Who cares, comrade? Around here, it's all FTP. We alone control the progress of the Panzer division. Luck is on our side… We have our weapons now, just in time for the fight."

I caught Stella's eye. In the preceding weeks, she had explained our remit to Limouzy repeatedly, priming him on the threat that the Das Reich – encamped at Montauban – posed to any invasion.

London would have had us organising the FTP – telling them what to do and how to do it, but London didn't know these characters.

This had to be done with tact.

So Stella and I remained quiet now, each of us wanting Limouzy to feel that he was in charge and that his leadership was unquestioned. It didn't matter what he did, as long as he did something effective.

"Montauban isn't that far away," he said. "The Das Reich will mobilise quickly. They'll be moving north within days… they could be here by the 9th, the 11th at the latest."

"They're tough, Boss?" said the other brother, Robert.

"Of course… they're battle hardened fanatics. For the last three years they've been on the Eastern front – Kiev, Minsk, Kharkov – places familiar with death. They make the Wehrmacht soldiers look like pussycats."

Eric grunted.

"Numbers?"

"Perhaps eighteen thousand, with a hundred tanks and more than two thousand armoured vehicles. If they get to the coast by next week, there'll be one hell of a scrap for the beach head… and if the Allied invasion fails, this war will go on for years. It's up to us to make a stand."

Limouzy pulled a tatty map from his pocket and spread it out on the table.

He pointed at the city of Brive, some fifteen miles east.

"They'll have to entrain their heavy armour here… on flat-bed freight cars. Our comrades in the city are planning to sabotage the rail lines there. But the division may also try to use the flat beds in Perigueux… and if they go to Perigueux, they'll have to come right past us. The solution is simple – we block the road at Terrasson." He poked the map with his index finger. "Here," he said.

Terrasson was just five miles away to the north east. The main Brive – Perigueux road ran straight through it, as did the Vézère River, traversed by a couple of stone bridges. It was a pretty place – the streets in the old town narrow and cobbled, and the buildings topped with the grey-blue slate roofs peculiar to the region. It was also the nearest town of any size to Reybenet. Jacques and I went to church there on Sundays, and made the occasional shopping expedition.

Usually trading in truffles and walnuts, in recent weeks Terrasson had seen the trading of retributions instead – the main focal point of Limouzy's guerrilla activity. Just the other evening they had gone in and shot three inhabitants: a local Pétainist legion chief, a glassmaker and his wife – all suspected Gestapo informers.

Two days after the Allied landings, Limouzy and his men started setting up the road blocks in preparation to meet any German forces moving to Perigueux. Since this was our official mission, Stella and I kept up a presence. Stella had openly attached herself to Limouzy's group – a dangerous choice, since it meant she was now identifiable as an FTP fighter. I monitored events more discretely, sitting at the café whose outside wall was painted with a fading blue and red 'CINZANO' advert. I drank coffee with Jacques – just a father and son taking a well-earned break from our doctoring. Though the use of vehicles by locals had been banned since the invasion, as doctors we had been given special dispensation. Oddly, since the landings, the work had dropped off and the surgeries were virtually empty. Everyone seemed to be hunkering down and staying at home, uncertain and frightened as to what the next days and weeks would bring, too preoccupied to even bother thinking about their maladies.

The townsfolk started complaining about the inevitable reprisals all of this FTP activity would involve – "Please Limouzy, not here!" I could hear them saying to him in the central square.

He had laughed in their faces. "This town has three thousand inhabitants and France forty million! What can these few people here matter?"

To their evident horror, he even proclaimed the Fourth Republic right there and then. Eric and the brothers ordered men to start felling trees for the road blocks. They led away more suspected collaborators, returning to town alone. I say 'suspected', but there was really no uncertainty about it. Everyone knew who these people were, it was just that until now, no-one had dared to do anything about it.

Rumours started about an FTP uprising in Tulle, a town as far to the east of Brive, as Terrasson was to the west. By evening, the word was that Tulle had been liberated from the local German garrison. The news bolstered Limouzy's men further; they seemed to be walking taller and with more authority than before. It was all in the body language as Jacques would have said – a new swaggering confidence.

I felt confident too. At last the tide seemed to be turning. We were beginning to make a difference, even way out here, in our little forested corner of the Dordogne.

An eerie calm came over the town as it waited for the enemy to arrive.

On the 9th – the Friday – Stella and I made a transmission:

'ARMS AND SUPPLIES GRATEFULLY RECEIVED PREPARING FOR ACTION'

Late that same evening, a band of eight exhausted FTP fighters arrived from Tulle. They drove into town in a 'Gazo', a truck rigged up to work on charcoal; 'Gazo' was short for 'Gazogene', a fuel made from burning charcoal and wood chips, contained in large barrels attached at the front to the engine. The FTP obviously weren't the types to be heeding the ban on vehicles. Besides, if you knew the back roads you could avoid bumping into any Germans, unless they happened to be taking rides on their new motorbikes.

I watched on from the café as the communists embraced each other in greeting in the town square. A few of them were wearing the chain plate necklaces of the Kettenhunde, presumably trophies from men they had killed the day before. There was a lot of posturing going on, a sort of 'who's the toughest boy in the playground' behaviour. They all had that same latent ferocity of Limouzy and his men; killers with red star badges on their berets and guns slung around their shoulders – a real rag-tag army of wild men.

They had their conference at the café which stayed open late, drinking glasses of the local wine provided by the barman on a tab that would never be settled. I eavesdropped on Tulle's fate from Duboix, the leader of the survivors. Like Limouzy, he was another bearded feral who had clearly been living in the woods for quite some time.

"Last night an SS reconnaissance battalion came in and re-took the town" he said. "Their weapons were too powerful and we scattered like rats. Today we watched from the hills outside the town and heard the announcement on loudspeakers…'Forty German soldiers were atrociously assassinated by the Maquis yesterday. Therefore one hundred and twenty Maquisards or their accomplices will be hanged. Their bodies will be thrown into the river.'"

Limouzy frowned.

"*Atrociously assassinated…* What did you do?"

Duboix made an innocent looking face, like a child who has been asked by a parent if he's done his homework.

"Well… the more enthusiastic fighters in our ranks decided to mash in the faces of some dead Feldgendarmes with their rifle butts. Some even cut off the soldiers' balls and stuffed them into their dead mouths."

Stella blinked when she heard this, but gave away no emotion.

Eric was staring at me.

I was thinking about Kram and his friend Weber, in all probability dead and mutilated, never again to drive the BMW R75. I was torn – those two had been alright.

Like Stella, I kept a poker face.

I could tell Eric wanted me to look disgusted so he could spew forth on all the shit the occupation had meant for the French people; get right in my face and explain that it was exactly what he would do when he got hold of these German soldiers. I didn't agree with what had happened to the dead Germans, and I was beyond feeling intimidated by Eric, so I held his stare.

"The reprisal began this afternoon," Duboix was saying. "We saw the whole thing from our hiding place. The hangings took place in the main street. SS officers sat on the terrace of the Tivoli café and watched the show, drinking and laughing and listening to gramophone records. One of their translators, a woman, blew cigarette smoke into the faces of the condemned. I even saw an SS soldier sketching the scene. They stopped short of one hundred and twenty when the local priest begged them to show mercy, but not by many."

I couldn't help myself from asking, "How many of the hanged were FTP?"

The FTP men in the café turned to look at me as one. Men who had just come from mashing in dead men's faces and cutting off their genitals, fixed their hard stares at me. My God, if looks could kill. It was like being stared at by twelve suspicious Gilligans in an Oxford interview, albeit with beards, berets and machine guns.

"And who the hell are you?" Duboix said.

Eric looked as though he was about to come over and break my neck.

"I'm the local doctor," I said, trying to hold my nerve, "and I'm just asking a simple question."

Limouzy leant in to his counterpart from Tulle and spoke under his breath on my behalf.

"He's one of us."

Duboix looked at me as he absorbed this good reference, and made a face of what I assumed was slight contrition.

"And so is the woman" Limouzy said, looking over at Stella.

The Tulle FTP turned their attention to Stella.

"Privet tovarishchi," she said in Russian.

They almost fell off their chairs when she said that, then raised their glasses in silence, as a gesture of respect.

"It means 'Hello comrades'." Stella said to me in French, under her breath.

Duboix rubbed his beard and caught my eye.

"You asked how many were FTP, Doctor?"

To fit in with the other hard men at the table, I tried to make that indifferent expression the French specialise in, the face which says: 'So what if I did? What's it to you?'

"Well, to answer your question, they hanged two FTP men... of what must have been around one hundred."

There was long silence in the café.

I wanted to ask them if their methods were winning much local support, but I decided it was best to stay quiet. It would only ruin the smidgeon of newfound respect Stella had just earned us by speaking in Russian.

"And so, you've come here to fight with us?" Limouzy said, placing his hand on Duboix's shoulder, as was his way.

"Yes we have, comrade."

Duboix scanned his eight fellow fighters.

"Haven't we, lads?"

They let out a collection of affirmative grunts by way of reply.

"We also came to tell you they're on their way. Some of the division are driving due north from Brive, but the rest are coming this way and they'll be here in the next day or so. Thought you boys might need a helping hand. We've got Stens and some gammon grenades."

Limouzy glanced at Eric with a satisfied look.

"We've got Brens."

I could tell Comrade Limouzy was indulging in some one-upmanship with his fellow fighters, but it appeared to have been taken at face value because a small cheer erupted from the group. Duboix addressed his men:

"You hear that, boys? Brens! We're going to have some fun this time."

He turned to Limouzy.

"You know what Das Reich have started calling this area?"

"What's that comrade?"

"Little Russia..."

Now all the communists were glowing with pride. To be compared to the Motherland was an honour indeed.

"They're going to get the shock of their lives," Limouzy said, grinning with confidence. "Those German boys won't know what's hit them."

The twelve FTP men talked late into the night about how they were going to destroy the Das Reich. Stella and I stayed because we were part of this now, whether we liked it or not. Limouzy had issued us each with a Sten gun earlier that day – passed on by the brothers who now had their Brens from the drop. He was confident that his Fourth Republic – already nearly forty eight hours old – was going to be a permanent fixture and that our cover no longer mattered. Many of the townspeople had seen this. Even though I had stashed my gun in the Citroën, they knew Xavi Bonnet was an FTP man now, and that Madame Blanchard's niece was a fighter too. There was no going back.

Fourteen people in all, against an elite armoured division of Waffen SS.

The words 'suicidal recklessness' rolled around in my head as I watched the communists banter among themselves with their glasses of 'vin rouge'. I had to hand it to them – their bravado was quite something to see; the SS appeared to hold no fear for them whatsoever. They were either very brave, very stupid, or both.

****

"Where are these bastards?"

Eric was smoking and pacing up and down, like the prospective fathers I had seen in the hospital corridors during my obstetrics attachment. Except that with Eric, it was out of pent up aggression and not nervousness.

It was pre-dawn and we were by the barricades.

On the ground was the last of the bread and cheese the brothers had brought out from the café the day before. I was hungry but the bread had turned stale and the cheese had given me a stomach ache. There had been some rough tasting wine too, but it was long gone.

I tried to focus on the card game I was playing with Limouzy, but my skittish thoughts were having none of it. They wanted to be anywhere but in the present moment.

The date was 11th June, Sunday.

Over in town the bells were tolling for Matins – the fact the Waffen SS were about to come through hadn't stopped the bell ringers. On a 'normal' Sunday, Jacques and I would be going to mass, but not today.

The Church of Saint Sour was used to war – it had been plundered by the Normans, rebuilt, then destroyed again in the Hundred Years War, only to be rebuilt once more in the fifteenth century. Now it was witnessing more strife. In a sermon a few weeks back, the priest had told this story of the past, and concluded with an unimpressed shrug, saying in an unemotional voice: "So…another century, another invader. The church will still go on once the latest little drama has finished."

A hermit called Sour had founded the church around the year 500. Before settling in the area, so the legend went, Sour had been travelling with two companions. In a farewell dinner, Sour divided up a single piece of bacon into three parts. Appalled to be eating bacon during Lent, one of the companions hid his share under his cloak, whereupon it turned into a large snake. Terrified, he begged for Sour's help – the hermit obliged, and the monster transformed back into bacon. "Eat it," Sour said to his friend, "and never forget that love is above all rules."

I had only talked to Jacques about his Catholic faith the one time: "Oh, my sister was the religious one," he had said. "She was going to be a nun once, before an American won her heart. Me? I just keep saying my prayers, Xavi."

"And you really believe someone's listening?"

"Who knows… but I can tell you this," he said, "I *hope* someone is."

"It's funny you say that… because my real papa thinks the same. You're not so different, you and he."

My father wasn't exactly a churchgoer, but he was *trying* to believe in something. He was always fighting an internal battle with himself. Sometimes he would come close and sometimes he would veer away, but he was always searching. In 1935 his old friend Reverend Rennie had come to visit, accompanied by his wife, a Maori called Materoa, and their two sons – massive strapping men in their prime with facial tattoos and war medals. While my father was with them, his whole personality had changed. Though he was sixty years old at the time, and Rennie older than that, the years fell away as they thrived off each other's energy. They were like a couple of puppies, much to the amusement of their wives and sons. And though my father didn't go to church much, he had gone with Rennie, their arms around one another's shoulders, re-telling old stories and laughing the whole time. It was easy to see why my father liked him – it's hard not to like someone who's perpetually enthusiastic, someone who takes a great interest in everything. Every night after dinner he would go and help my mother wash the dishes, and the whole time she would be telling him to go and sit down. "No, no Jennifer," he would say, "this is a great blessing!" My father had been at peace with himself the month Rennie came to visit. When the larger-than-life Reverend was around the place, it was easy to believe in a larger-than-life God.

"They're coming, comrade," I heard Limouzy say to Eric, peeling off another card from the pile and placing it down as fast as he could.

They were my cards – the ones holding my secret maps – and we had been playing 'split' on and off for the last twenty four hours, interspersed with snatched periods of sleep.

It was all part of my strategy – to keep Limouzy's mood up during the waiting, so that when the fight finally came, he would be at his best and inspire his forces.

At first I had won easily, but Limouzy was improving and had nearly caught up with me. Eric was keeping the score in a notebook. The good natured bickering had forged some kind of tentative friendship. If I had known this was all that was needed, I would have suggested a game on our first night in France.

Ever since he had stuck up for me in the café in front of the FTP men from Tulle, I had felt a bond of loyalty to Limouzy. When it came to Stella, he had switched from being a hated rival like Boreman, to a friendly rival like Tom Shaw.

She had been watching this burgeoning friendship with a curious expression, wrapped up in a blanket like a Red Indian squaw. Her gaze moved between us and I wondered if, from under that warm cover, she was pointing her finger at us in turn and trying to choose: 'eeny meeny miny moe, catch a tiger by the toe…'

"I win," he said.

"No you didn't, my card was down before yours."

"Come on, Ahab – you can't fool me. What does that make the score? Sixty seven to sixty six? I'm pulling away from you."

"No it's sixty six all."

"You're sure? Don't con me, Ahab… I know what you capitalists are like."

I laughed.

Limouzy looked up at Eric – a smouldering presence looming above us.

"What's the score?"

The question seemed to distract Eric from his bad mood for a moment – he stopped his pacing and checked the book.

"You just won, Boss?"

"I did."

Eric pulled out the short pencil from behind his ear and made a mark. We waited a few more seconds as he totted it up.

"It's sixty-six a piece," he said, tucking the pencil back behind his ear.

Limouzy slammed the rest of his cards down on the ground.

"Putain! Deal again, Ahab."

As I gathered up the cards I noticed Eric was looking out through the barricade again, more agitated than ever. He was sucking the very life out of the cigarette he was smoking. The Tulle massacre had really lit his fuse – ever since hearing about it, he had been a bomb waiting to go off.

"Just hold on, comrade," I heard Limouzy say to him.

But even Limouzy couldn't placate Eric any longer.

"Fuck it," Eric said, exhaling a great plume of smoke and throwing his cigarette onto the ground. He picked up his Bren gun, and shouldered his Sten too.

"I'm going to find out. Okay, Boss?"

Limouzy stood up and hesitated.

He could see how uptight his man was. I saw the decision made in his eyes before he said anything. Limouzy had judged that it was best for his strongest fighter to let off some steam.

"Stay hidden," he said. "Don't engage them, Eric; we want surprise. When you see them coming, you get straight back here. Understood?"

Although he nodded, I could see Eric wasn't really listening.

He just wanted blood. With his two submachine guns, he must have felt immortal.

They hugged one another and soon Eric was running at a half trot along the centre of the road towards Brive – out to face the advance elements of the Das Reich alone.

Limouzy watched him go, his hands on his hips and shaking his head.

"Stay under cover!" he said, calling out to him.

Eric raised an arm in acknowledgement and moved to the tree-line at the side of the road. Then he rounded the corner and was gone.

Though the sun was just rising out in the direction where Eric had headed, it would be a while yet before the temperature rose. I was hunched over in my jersey, which wasn't doing much to stave off the early morning chill. Xavier didn't own many warm clothes.

Limouzy took off his sheepskin jerkin and threw it into my lap.

"No," I said, holding it back out to him, "I can't take that off you."

"It's all right, Ahab. Drawing even with you has warmed my insides... you can return it later."

I put it on, and immediately felt the animal warmth from Limouzy's body. Perhaps it would give me 'Mad Dog' bravery like my cousin Harry, who had charged machine guns in the Great War and wore a sheepskin jerkin just like this one.

Limouzy came and sat cross-legged on the ground again.

"Deal," he said. "I want to get ahead now."

I started to shuffle.

That was when we heard the faint cracks of gunfire filtering through the dawn to our position at the road block.

I dropped the cards and we jumped up.

"Christ," I said, my heart thumping hard. "That was close; less than half a mile away."

"The bloody idiot has engaged them," Limouzy said in astonishment, but also unable to hide the admiration in his voice.

He turned to our assembled group: the brothers, Stella and I, and the eight other FTP fighters from Tulle.

His words came clearly and without panic.

"Get ready… he'll be making his way back now. Get to your positions and prepare to fight!"

Limouzy's call to action was cut off by a burst of sustained machine gun fire and after that, silence.

"That sounded like an MG 42," I said to Stella, recalling the weapon being demonstrated on the commando course. "More powerful than anything we've got."

She nodded back at me in resignation. Stella was ready to die, I could see that.

There were actually two road blocks thirty yards apart – each consisting of a dozen felled tree trunks and large vehicles requisitioned from the town.

Limouzy had allocated the rear defence to Duboix and the Tulle fighters, we had the foremost block. I watched as the Tulle men ran back and took up position. Some climbed the trees by their barricade; others simply went and stood on top of the barricade itself, their Stens at the ready. It worried me a little that they would be firing from behind us, at objects in front of us, and for once I was glad Stens fired high.

Within minutes we could hear the first German vehicles squeaking and rumbling along the approach to Terrasson.

The noises got louder and louder so that it felt they were on top of us.

A hundred yards further on from our position was a bend in the road. As soon as the Germans appeared, they would be meeting our ambush head on and be stopped in their tracks, pinned down by our fire. Paralysed and exposed on the road.

Right around the corner… they were right there. The creaking and grinding sounds were unbearably loud now.

My heart was thumping in my chest like an organ that didn't belong to me and was struggling to get out. I had been hoping for a scenario like this for months – ever since Tom had been killed in the bomb blast. All the waiting, all the training coming down to this moment, and the moment was coming too fast now. 'Wait' part of me was saying, 'I'm not quite ready... does it have to be now?' This was it – the most dangerous position I had been in in my entire life. Highly trained men, hundreds of them, were around that corner and they wanted to kill me. I thought of Tom again and of MP's small boy playing outside the hospital mess. I bit down on my lower lip until I could taste the blood. The images of the dead and the taste of the blood helped me cast aside that small voice pressing for a delay, and I even muttered through my teeth: "Come on then, you bastards."

An armoured personnel carrier rounded the bend and stopped.

"What the fuck is that?" Limouzy said in a whisper.

"It's a half-track," I said.

I saw it was mounted with a machine gun, an MG-42 – a metallic slayer of men.

"Not that, the thing on the front of it." He reached over to me. "Hand me your binoculars..."

They were a pair Jacques had given to me. I passed them to Limouzy.

"Jesus Christ almighty," he said, peering through the eyepieces. He hung his head and passed them back to me. "They've got Eric."

I took back the binoculars and looked.

Tied to the front of the half-track was Eric's bullet riddled body facing forwards like a ghoulish figurehead on the prow of a sailing ship.

The half-track started to advance again, moving at a steady speed towards us.

Ninety yards... eighty yards.

Other vehicles appeared behind it – more half-tracks and then a Panzer V tank.

A tank. *That's not good,* came the thought through my terror.

Limouzy gave the call, his voice filled with anger.

"Now!"

A deafening barrage of fire came from our guns, the bullets hitting the metal of the half-track and making tinkling sounds like a one note xylophone. The FTP men behind were firing from their high positions; in all thirteen fighters blasting away. It was a truly impressive example of firepower.

Then something astonishing happened, something unexpected and something we had not been taught on our battle-skills course in Scotland.

Instead of grinding to a halt, the armoured vehicles started accelerating towards us – they started *attacking*.

Any other regular force – the Wehrmacht for example – would have stopped if faced with a sudden ambush like ours, at least momentarily. They would have gone to ground, consolidated and assessed the situation before responding. With the Waffen SS though, there was no hesitation at all – they had simply attacked straight away.

Soldiers were spilling out of the half-track and running forward in the cover of the trees by the road. They were close enough for me to see their camouflaged green and brown 'peas-pattern' capes – the so called Erbsenmuster.

They were only seventy yards away now.

A withering spray of bullets from the MG-42, mounted on the armoured turret of the half-track, smacked at the wood and metal of our barrier, making us dive for cover. Our gunfire had all but petered out. In a moment the momentum had swung in favour of the SS.

Then the first shells from the Panzer started landing.

The first explosion had us rolled up into balls and crouching on the ground with our hands over our heads. The blast waves ripped at the tree branches around us, covering us in leaves and twigs and splinters of wood.

Twenty feet away from where I was, on the northern side of the barricade, both brothers were firing the Stens for all they were worth, their faces contorted in fury. Their rounds were spilling all over the place, and they were screaming and swearing as if the words were extra bullets. Then they were caught by a direct hit; one moment they were both there, the next they weren't. It was like a very loud and very bloody magic trick.

At the same time shells started hitting our rear. The FTP men from Tulle were being vaporised at their barricade too.

In the confusion I heard German shouts and commands and saw soldiers taking up positions around the half-track and the Panzer tank. They were shooting in small sustained bursts and I could hear the bullets thumping into the wood barricade near my head: *thwack, thwack!*

Limouzy took aim with his Bren and killed the man firing the MG-42 on the half-track.

A small victory.

Encouraged, I took aim through a gap, aiming low as I had been taught and letting the gun rise. Where the bullets hit the road near the SS soldiers small dust clouds jumped up, before they started finding soldiers. I saw one man do a kind of jerky dance as he was riddled. I didn't think much about killing another human being, just that we were fighting for our lives and it was necessary. Another one was hit and went down. That was two I had killed. Maybe we were getting the upper hand. Maybe we would make the tanks turn around. In my blood lust I found these irrational thoughts entering my stupid head. Another soldier took the place of the one that had fallen and I aimed again. Six hundred rounds a minute.

Much later on, I would have nightmares about the men whose lives I took that day. Before the war they had just been teenagers like me, with parents and friends and hopes for their futures, and then I had taken it all away from them. Right at that moment though, it was deeply satisfying to watch them fall. Then a replacement was firing the MG-42 and the hate came back at us with double the rounds per minute. My overheated Sten jammed and I threw it over the barricade towards the Germans in disgust. Next to me, Stella was faring better, screaming in rage like the brothers as she fired. I brought out my F-S knife in readiness. I might be able to kill one more before they overpowered me. At least I would go down fighting.

Fifty yards now…

Limouzy took out the new man on the MG-42, putting the gun to sleep again.

But then a tank shell landed and made the tree trunk in front of our barricade jump six feet into the air. The MG-42 was bad enough, but what the tank was dishing out was indomitable.

Of course, the chance of a victory here was zero, but the adrenaline pushed the futility of our efforts to the back of our minds, making anything seem possible. Besides, our aim was not to defeat the enemy, but merely to hold up the division in their rush to the real battle up north, and we had gone into it without hesitation. The delay we were causing, however, might only amount to a few measly minutes, or hours at the most. Was it worth it, for all these lives?

Only tanks could fight tanks, not Sten guns or Bren guns or any other type of hand held weapon. We were going to be dead very soon.

Behind, I saw the remaining FTP men from Tulle scrambling into their Gazo and speeding away.

Forty yards... Thirty.

Limouzy threw two gammon grenades in quick succession, and I did the same. I think they landed short but the smoke and dust from the explosions temporarily blocked out the oncoming rush of the Germans. I threw another two, and then two more.

"Get her out of here," Limouzy said to me in the short ensuing silence, knowing the day was lost.

I made to go.

"Aren't you coming?"

He aimed his Bren towards the billowing cloud and started shooting again.

Being a bolt action, his beloved De Lisle lay at his feet, redundant. When I saw this image of him – this snapshot in the heat of the battle, firing his submachine gun, with its curved magazine sticking out like a shark's fin, and his hair wild and deranged – I knew I would always remember the sight. In spite of all the fury surrounding us I still had time to make a mental note of it.

He wasn't even looking at me – he was just firing at the shadows coming through the smoke. German soldiers were falling, but others were coming. There were too many. A giant sheet of fire swept over the barricade and I felt its warmth. They were using flame throwers now.

The MG-42 started up again.

"This is a leader's fate, not yours. Get her out of here, Ahab."

I didn't need to be told a second time.

Stella and I took off towards the wooded slopes on the south side of the road. The smoke from the grenades had given us a precious few moments to escape unseen, screening us from the enemy. Then, in the shadow of the trees, I ran straight into a camouflaged soldier who had been trying to outflank us, literally bumping into him, the impact knocking both of us down to the ground and the F-S knife out of my hand. He was alone, so eager to make his flanking assault that he had become separated from the rest of his unit. Our eyes met – each of us realising instantly that one or the other was about to die. No time for hate or recognition even, just pure survival, and since he still had his weapon I assumed it was my time that had come. But he was alone and I was not. Stella gathered the blade from the ground in her stride and charged at him with such bewildering speed that it seemed as if he was frozen in time, helpless in the path of the fate that was crashing down on him so very quickly. I watched it happen, as spellbound as he was. She leapt, like a big cat, a terrible beauty in her shape and form, her body appearing to hang in mid-air as she held the seven-inch blade high above her head with both hands. No neck cut – what she delivered was a full blooded plunge straight into the heart. For a few moments, the SS soldier looked down at the hilt poking out of his chest in disbelief and then he slumped to one side, stone dead. Three seconds – just like the Captain had taught us – the perfect silent kill.

The shouts of others were only yards away now, but their forms were still shielded by smoke and they were being kept busy by Limouzy at the barricade. I yanked the knife out of the dead soldier and we ran for our lives, scrambling up the steep incline, legs pumping and arms flailing. All I could hear was the sound of my breathing – no shells, no bullets, no shouts – just the ragged, deep breaths as my lungs took in air, like a pair of heaving bellows, and pushed it out again. Behind us, I could hear the firefight reaching a crescendo as they closed in on Limouzy. The sole fighter left. The bravest of all of us.

Then things fell quiet and all I could make out were distant shouts.

After some minutes, we collapsed onto the ground, spread-eagled like a pair of runners on the track after the finish line. My mouth and throat were dry and raw. We lay there, shaken and breathless, too shocked to speak.

Stella's hair was as messy as a mad woman's from an insane asylum. It looked as though she had been dragged through the forest, like the branch the FTP had used to cover their tracks to the cave.

German shouts eventually brought us to our senses – not shouts near us in the woods, but voices carrying all the way up to us from the town below.

Taking turns looking through the binoculars, we watched on, helpless.

Having bulldozed its way through the remnants of the barricades, the first elements of the SS column had driven straight into the town and troopers were busy corralling the population into the central square at gunpoint.

I hadn't noticed during the firefight, but now I could see that the SS soldiers were all very young. So many men had been killed on the Eastern front, that the entry age had been lowered from eighteen to seventeen. Some of these boys didn't look a day older. The SS was now taking in recruits from all over Europe – Hungary, Croatia, Romania, Ukraine, even men from the French Alsace – no longer the pure-bred Aryan race they had been in the early days of the war.

Still, they were all tall.

The observation reminded me of how Tom and I had talked about the SS entry criteria, as we had walked to the caf that morning so long ago.

I kept my binoculars on the SS, as if they were a rare and dangerous kind of wild beast and I was on safari. They all had distinctive bevelled canteens strapped to their backs. Their faces were unsmiling and they held their guns at the ready, as if, at the slightest excuse, they would start shooting. I could feel the tension seeping up through the woods, like an invisible mist, to where we were concealed.

Our hiding place on the hillside was perhaps only four hundred yards from the central square, but we were well hidden by the thick forest at the southern edge of the town and had a grandstand view of everything.

Buildings were burning and the front section of the Town Hall had been damaged by shell-fire. The Germans took a flame-thrower to a house decorated with a red FTP flag, and set it alight. Limouzy had put the flag there on purpose the evening before – it was the house of the local Milice chief, Denoix.

Tanks, camouflaged with branches, and half-tracks were neatly parked around the edge of the square, in the same place Jacques and I had parked the Citroën just a few days before.

"My God," Stella said. "They're going to do what they did in Tulle."

I peered down at the town.

There must have been a few thousand gathered in the square. Apart from the odd child's cry and the German shouts, it was eerily quiet for such a large gathering.

"Shit. They have Limouzy alive…"

He was blackened and bloodied and being held up between two soldiers. It looked as though he had taken a bullet to his right shoulder. His hands were tied behind his back.

An SS man with a medic's arm-band had started addressing the crowd with a loudspeaker. I guessed he was the unit doctor, an educated man who could speak French.

He was pointing at Limouzy and looking at the crowd.

"Does anyone recognise this man?"

He repeated the question, but was met with the same frightened silence.

Receiving no response, he turned to a nearby group of officers and spoke to them in a huddle. The group had their caps off and I could make out their severe haircuts – shaved back and sides with swept comb-overs on the top. They were all smoking and smiling as they talked. The scene belonged more to a group of men in a club-house after a game of rugby, celebrating and laughing, not a group of men taking a break from mass murder.

The smiling medic turned back to the assembled population. "The commander is in a good mood today," he said. "Because it's his wedding anniversary... you're to be spared."

There was no sparing Limouzy though.

It was like a Passion scene, except instead of Romans in their body armour and cloaks, the executioners were SS soldiers in their peas-pattern uniforms: two ladders were pushed up against a balcony some ten feet high and a rope with a noose was fastened to one of the railings. And such was the relaxed manner in which the soldiers worked, you felt they could have been a couple of the bell ringers from earlier that morning, happily sorting out the noose and then tugging down on the rope in turns, to test it with their weight.

The senior group of SS officers were detached spectators, one with his arms folded across his chest, another with his right hand absentmindedly tucked into the front of his tunic, fingers wedged between the buttons. Two of the group were smoking and one of the smokers was laughing about something. The others seemed to be hanging off his every word and I assumed he was the commander, perhaps joking about the fact that if he had forgotten his anniversary the whole town would have been massacred, but worse still, he would have had to face the wrath of his wife.

The execution was swift; obviously a task which the soldiers had carried out many times before. A soldier on one of the ladders helped Limouzy mount the other, as his hands were still tied, and another soldier held the ladder steady. Limouzy completed the Golgotha scene with his appearance – bearded and bloodied and grimly facing his death. I heard him call out, "Vive La France!" as he stepped up the rungs, his voice strong and steady. There was no sound at all now; even the dogs had stopped barking. Once he was high enough, the soldier on the ladder put the noose around his neck and immediately the soldier at the foot of the ladder pulled it away roughly, leaving him hanging. Limouzy struggled for a few moments, twitching violently, and he seemed to be staring right at me, through the lenses of the binoculars.

Then the soldier on the ground grabbed hold of Limouzy's legs and yanked down hard, and there was no movement after that.

It was physically sickening to watch – I started to dry retch right there. If I had had anything left in my stomach, it would have come up, but I hadn't eaten for over ten hours.

Stella hung her head and muttered something which could have been a prayer.

After the hanging, the soldiers started waving everyone in the crowd away. It seemed the medic hadn't been joking – the CO really was going to let them all go because he happened to be in a good mood.

The townspeople looked as bewildered as I felt, that such a mundane reason as a wedding anniversary had determined their collective fate. I could see their suspicion, that it was all a joke and at any moment the SS soldiers would start firing. They kept looking back warily, expecting the worst.

"Husch! Husch!" I heard the soldiers saying, shooing them away like stray dogs.

It was so bizarre you couldn't make it up – a wedding anniversary, for God's sake – the whole town saved because some fat Hausfrau back in Cologne or Munich or Berlin had been married to this shaven-headed Teutonic bastard for the last however many years.

I was numb.

Everyone in the group was gone – the twins, Eric, Limouzy – the whole cell we had been cultivating for weeks; all dead in less than an hour.

For the rest of that day we watched Limouzy's body hanging in the square as the German armoured column rumbled through on the main road on their way to Perigueux. Neither Stella nor I said much, we just passed the binoculars back and forth, shaking our heads in disbelief.

As well as the damaged Town Hall, I counted at least eight houses destroyed. Local firemen were struggling to put out the flames.

Later that afternoon, some of the FTP men from Tulle – only two had managed to escape the assault in the Gazo – came into the square on foot and cut Limouzy down. I could hear them shouting at the locals, demanding to know what had happened. Judging from their gestures, the terrified townsfolk were urging the FTP to get out before the Germans came back and changed their minds about reprisals. In the end, they headed towards the forest just below our position and that is when Stella and I finally decided to move.

We intercepted them on a small track running out of the town, just as they were in the process of loading Limouzy's body into the back of their truck. One of them was Duboix.

He made no sign of welcome. And the fact we had survived didn't seem to cheer him in any way. Perhaps by now he had worked out that Stella and I were English agents, mere capitalists.

It made me angry, the fact I had put my life on the line for such a miserable sod, and this was how he thanked us, with no acknowledgement. I realised the only thing we had in common was our hatred for the Nazis. Otherwise we were nothing in his eyes.

"We know where he would want to be buried," I said. "We'll take him now."

He stood there for a moment, holding onto Limouzy's shoulders and staring over at me.

"As you wish, Doctor," he said, hauling the corpse out of the truck again with the help of his comrade.

Carefully, they lay him down on the ground in front of us and climbed into their Gazo.

I walked up to the driver's door, where Duboix was sitting.

"Where will you go?"

He leant out of the window and pointed west to the setting sun.

"We will take the back roads and join another group near Perigueux… help knock out some of the flat beds in the rail yard. Try and stop them moving their heavy armour north."

"Good luck," I said.

He nodded, started the engine and drove away.

I shouldered Limouzy's torso, and Stella held his legs.

He was heavy and it was slow going, but we were fit enough to manage it. Every few minutes we stopped and rested and then silently hauled him back up again and kept on. It was a morbid version of the pointless tasks we had been set at the beginning of the SOE course;

instead of moving a log around obstacles, it was a corpse through a Dordogne forest.

At the cave we used a rope to pull him up the rock face, the same way as for the canisters. Once inside, we laid him on his cot. The rope was still around his neck with the knot at the back. I cut it away with my F-S knife and then cut the rope tying his hands.

Exhausted and shocked in equal measure, we cleaned our faces and wet our hair with water from the barrel and then sat at the table and got drunk on Pastis. Stella's Sten gun was the only weapon left. One lousy gun: the sum total of our resistance cell.

That night in the cave we reverted back to speaking English.

"He didn't run," I said. "He kept shooting until they cornered him. You know the last thing he said to me?"

"What?"

"He said to get you out of there. He really cared for you."

"Yes, I know that."

I was being as magnanimous as I could be – I even told her his line about it being a leader's fate.

"There's none braver," I said in conclusion. And then I remembered Saint Sour's words from fifteen hundred years before: "It wasn't just bravery though. His feelings for you superseded everything else…love is above all rules."

We buried him at the back of the cave, by the wall painting of the sabre tooth tiger. I say 'buried', but what it amounted to was piling all the loose rocks we could gather on top of him to stop any animals getting to his corpse. Before the rocks, I covered his head and upper torso with the sheepskin jerkin he had leant me.

Stella gave the eulogy, her voice slightly slurred with the alcohol.

"It's what he would have wanted. He always loved this place and I think he would have liked the idea of his bones mixing with those of his distant ancestors. One day, it might cause a real headache for archaeologists if they ever try dating the remains."

As part of our small and spontaneous service, I recited the Lord's Prayer. As I spoke, something made me look up – and there in the lamplight was the wolf man on the far wall, staring down at me from his cold lair, half hidden in the shadows. I completely understood why Limouzy had never liked it.

Events afterwards seemed to happen in an odd staggered sequence, and I have no real memory of how it all linked together. I thanked her for saving me that day. Then we were holding hands, and then we were kissing one another. Later still, we were on her bunk and I remember thinking how very much more agreeable it was caressing her lithe body than fighting against it, as I'd had to do in close combat training.

The battle had instilled us with an intense energy. Life was so precarious. And yet somehow we had survived. It felt as if there was no tomorrow. An instinctive urge overpowered both of us, the alcohol only fuelling the fires further and making us cast aside all inhibitions. We reverted to the basics of human nature, like the proto-humans of millennia before.

Once upon a time, my fantasy had been a cabin in the mountains with Freya Nielsen. The reality turned out to be a cave in the forest with Agent Stella.

Chapter Twenty-one

Early the next morning, we made our way back to Reybenet.

For a while on the walk we held hands, shyly, like we were just getting to know one another on a first date, as if the carnality of the night before had never happened. The day before felt as though it had not even occurred in this century, but in another era altogether.

How was it that we had survived? What on earth happened last night? Had that really been us?

I was feeling terrible because of a splitting headache. The adrenaline from the battle, combined with the shocking aftermath, and then the Pastis had given me a god-awful hangover. It was all I could do to put one foot in front of the other.

Everything was different now. Stella and I had been seen with the FTP band – all it would take would be a whispered word into the ear of one of the Germans or the Milice and our number would be up. Without the threat of retribution from Limouzy's group, betrayal seemed all the more likely. I had seen the looks in the café when we had sat in on the FTP group conference that night. Even if bystanders didn't know we were British SOE agents, they knew we were aligned with the communist resistance. The fact was, we were compromised. Plus we had done the job we had come for, or at least had made a good go of it. If we had been equipped with an entire Army division we might have made more of an impact. For a group of six, plus Duboix's men, we had done what we could.

It was time to get out of France.

"When's our next transmission time?"

Stella stopped walking and checked the date on her watch.

"Not for another week."

"Damn."

She started to run.

"What is it?" I said, chasing after her.

"We have a receiving time in half an hour. I'd completely forgotten."

As we ran together in tandem, Stella started talking again, her eyes on the path in front.

"I think we need to talk about last night…" she said, her voice steady despite the running. That sounded ominous. I thought she was about to say, 'It was the Pastis, it didn't mean anything, I always preferred Limouzy… best we forget it had ever happened' – so I spoke up before she got the chance to express my worst fears.

"Let's focus on the call from London," I said. "Then we'll talk."

She glanced at me and nothing else was said for the rest of the way.

We rigged up the radio right there in the yard at Reybenet – just in time:

'YOUR NUMBER 3 RECEIVED 2 SS DIV STILL NOT ARRIVED IN NORMANDY: MISSION SUCCESSFUL'

London weren't to know that our Resistance cell were all dead and I didn't have time to dwell on it. I was paranoid about having made the call in the yard and couldn't pack the apparatus away fast enough.

Jacques was overjoyed to see us alive. I suppose if I had been killed, the real Xavi wouldn't have been able to return until after the war. And if the Germans prevailed, he would probably never have been able to come back.

I changed clothes up in my room before going down to the kitchen to clean the blood from the F-S knife. I caught sight of myself in the small mirror there – with the four day growth and my dark hair all messed up, I couldn't help thinking how like Limouzy I had become:

"L'homme des cavernes," as he would have said. Whenever I went unshaven for more than a few days, the stubble didn't grow over the scar, which made it stand out even more. Before putting the razor to my skin, I took off my spectacles and contemplated my ravaged face.

"Who *are* you?" I said out loud.

I had finished shaving and was flattening my hair with my fingers when I heard the noise of an approaching vehicle disturbing the morning calm.

From somewhere in the house – I think she'd been cleaning up in the bathroom – Stella let out a yell and I saw her sprint out across the yard towards the surgery waiting room. I followed her and we both made it inside before the vehicle appeared.

It was one of the half-tracks, with soldiers riding in its open section.

"Christ," I said, to her. "It's the SS. Someone's shopped us in already. We're dead." Then I thought of the radio link we had just finished. "My God, you think they located us with DF equipment?"

She shook her head. "Too soon."

I grabbed my auroscope from my consultation room and headed back out into the yard with Stella.

"You've got earache," I said to her.

Jacques came out of the house, relaxed and yawning, his hands around his braces as if he was holding parachute cords. He looked at me: "Calm down, Xavi. Relax."

Easy to say, I thought.

Three armed soldiers jumped out, and I almost raised my arms in the air to surrender. Then I saw them reaching up to help another man to climb down, a soldier who was in some degree of pain. I recognised him as the SS medic who had addressed the crowd in Terrasson the day before.

I realised they weren't here to arrest us.

Two of the soldiers helped him over to where we were standing.

"I am Roth, the unit doctor," he said, speaking in fluent French and grimacing. "We were told you are the best doctors around." He glanced over at Jacques. "They told us in the town that you and your son would be able to help… I have a problem with my abdomen."

Close up, Roth was like the perfect Aryan man from an SS recruitment poster – strong handsome features, fair hair and blue eyes. His armband had a swastika in the middle of the Red Cross and around it in Germanic lettering it said: 'Deutches Rotes Kreuz'.

"Who's this?" Roth said, looking at Stella.

"She's my first patient of the day… a case of earache."

I held out my auroscope torch.

"I was just examining her before you arrived."

He spoke to her.

"Do you mind if I push in, mademoiselle? I'm in a lot of pain."

"Of course," she said, touching her ear. "I can wait."

Jacques said he was going inside to make some tea, so I led Roth through to my consultation room, the two soldiers guiding him in.

"You've not been injured?" I said, trying to gather my wits.

"No. It's a chronic problem."

"When did this bout start?"

"Last night."

"Can you take your clothes off? Your top half, if that's all right."

Roth spoke in German to his men and they helped him remove his tunic, with its distinctive lightning bolts on the collar. Under that he was wearing a white vest with a large black eagle across the chest.

"The vest too, please… I need to examine you."

He was muscular. Well over six foot. No spectacles, good teeth, no scars, no acne – one of the originals.

On the inside of his upper left arm was a small black tattoo – the letters AB – his blood group. I had heard about this – all SS men had these tattoos. In case he ever needed an urgent blood transfusion and was unconscious at the time; a fool proof back-up in case his dog tag was missing.

I took his temperature and pulse – normal. Blood pressure also normal. His respiration rate was normal too.

"No sign of systemic infection," I said. "Lie down on the couch please."

I palpated his abdomen all over. There was no obvious focus to the pain. I could push deeply without much of a reaction. I frowned.

"Your abdomen is soft … I can't find anything significant here."

I listened with my stethoscope: normal bowel sounds.

Finally, I put on a glove.

"I should probably do this, I'm afraid…."

He looked at the two soldiers who were lingering at the doorway. "Warten in den Hof."

They saluted, and walked out into the yard as instructed.

Grimly, Roth nodded and rolled over.

"Normal," I said, snapping off the glove and throwing it in the bin. "Get dressed and we'll have a talk."

It was a bizarre situation, helping this Teuton back into his uniform, complete with the insignia of one of the most feared organisations in Nazi Germany. At this moment he was weak and pathetic. It occurred to me to exploit the vulnerability and break his neck right there and then, but then we would all be dead.

Once dressed, I invited him to take the chair opposite mine.

"How long has it been happening?"

"Two years," he said, holding his belly and leaning forward to help stave off the pain.

"Two years?"

"Yes… My bowel habit is all over the place and the pain comes in waves. There's no real pattern to it."

"We could do some blood tests. They might show up if you have any sign of a severe inflammatory disorder like colitis or Crohn's."

Roth shook his head.

"It's not that. I've had all the tests. They've all been normal, and I've never had any rectal bleeding."

"Been anywhere exotic? The Middle East? Africa?"

He shook his head again. "No, just the Eastern Front…"

I stood up.

"Can I confer with my father?"

He waved me off.

"Be my guest."

Jacques was in the waiting room, sitting there with Stella. I noticed he was holding a thermos flask.

"I can't find anything wrong with him – nothing serious I mean – there's a bit of generalised abdominal tenderness but nothing to write home about. All the observations are normal. He says it's been going on for a few years. Bloods have been normal."

Nodding, Jacques got up and followed me into the consultation room, bringing the thermos with him.

He sat down opposite Roth and carefully stood the thermos on the desk.

"Do you want the truth?" he said.

Roth gazed at him with his ice blue eyes.

"Go on."

"What you have is stress related. I've seen it before – usually in anxious, over-emotional young women."

In outrage, Roth tried to stand, but another spasm took hold and he doubled up instead.

"That's impossible!" he said, his voice a harsh whisper.

Jacques cocked his head to one side.

"Is it? You think you're immune to all the horrors you've witnessed close up, horrors that your unit have perpetrated… the hangings, the shootings… the death. You're a doctor, aren't you? Presumably you originally went into the profession because you care about human beings."

"I care about my brothers," Roth said defiantly, pointing at his fellow soldiers standing outside in the courtyard. "While you two look after the untermensch of this place, I treat a group of supermen; the differences between our respective sets of patients are a world apart. That's what my unit is you see – a brotherhood who will stop at nothing to save another brother."

Jacques sat back, shook his head and gave a wise and weary smile.

"That may be all well and good, but I'm afraid I know more than you do when it comes to this. What are you… twenty-five?"

Roth looked down at his boots and then screwed up his eyes as another wave of pain flowed through.

"Twenty-six" he managed to say.

"Well, I've been around a lot longer than you have. And I know people. Under all that Aryan bluster, you actually care about others too. You are suffering from a familiar set of symptoms. The release of trauma. That is what is happening to you, Doctor. It has to come out of you somehow. There's an expression you may not have heard, but it goes like this: the sorrow that has no vent in tears makes other organs weep."

The abdominal spasm apparently easing off a little, Roth raised his head and reached inside his breast pocket, pulling out a silver cigarette case. He took a cigarette and held the case out to Jacques and me.

We shook our heads in refusal.

"Suit yourselves" he said, without emotion.

He snapped it shut and put it on the desk while he fished out his lighter. The engraving on the case had a map of roads in Germany with the word: 'REICHSAUTOBAHNEN'; a trinket celebrating the Nazi Motorway programme of the mid-1930s.

"I sense I'm being judged. Is this a court?"

"No," Jacques said.

Roth had lit up now and was taking a deep drag on the cigarette. He blew out the smoke in a long trail, almost like a sigh.

"I'll admit I've seen some things... my God, I've seen some horrors. We hanged more than 100,000 at Kiev and Kharkov. What we've done here, doctor... at Tulle and yesterday... in our circle, it was *nothing*."

The consultation room was quiet.

'In our circle it was *nothing*.' That sentence would stay with me for years, I knew it right then.

"I've heard there are chambers where people are gassed with diesel fumes" I said, remembering what the hollow-eyed agent had told us back in Beaulieu. "Is it true?"

Roth nodded.

"Sonderbehandlung," he said, lapsing into his native German.

"What does that mean?"

"It means 'special treatment'."

He said it in almost a weary and monotone way, as if he were discussing very boring figures from the annual accounts.

"You've seen it for yourself?"

He looked at me and took another drag on his cigarette, holding it in his fist almost, with the tip poking out from between his index and middle fingers. Despite his attempts at being nonchalant, a veil of guilt or regret had come down over his features.

"Yes" he said. "I've seen the whole process. In a killing facility called Belzec in Poland. As an observer, you understand… for part of my education. Two years ago. It was August. Warm. There were a lot of flies… millions of them. And there was this smell. My God, it was terrible. Anyhow, the trains arrived, carrying thousands. Many were dead on arrival, in fact more than a thousand. The rest were whipped out of the wagons and ordered to undress. Their shoes were bound together and thrown onto a large pile. A pile for spectacles, another pile for artificial limbs. There was a place for valuables to be handed over. No receipt or voucher given in return. Then in the next room the women and girls went to the barber. Approximately one hundred chairs. Their hair was removed in a few snips and put into potato sacks to be used later."

"Used later?" I said. "What on earth for?"

"For submarines – insulation, sealing gaps and the like."

There was a short silence.

"After that, they were led outside naked, along an alley lined with barbed wire. Signs there read: 'To the inhalation – and the bath rooms'."

"And they just walked in?"

"Some did, yes. An SS officer at the entrance told them to take deep breaths as they went in, because the gas would help prevent the spread of diseases. But most weren't so stupid, they knew what was coming. They could smell it. Still, on the whole, they went in silently, accepting of their fate. I heard one Jewess call down vengeance on the head of the murderers for the blood which was to be shed there. My host – an SS Captain – whipped her across the face before she disappeared into the chamber. People were praying. The chambers filled up – "Pack well," the captain ordered – and the SS squeezed them together tightly, perhaps seven hundred and fifty into each chamber, of which there were four. It was standing room only."

Roth shook his head, as if seeing for the first time just how barbaric the scene had been. Jacques and I sat there, rooted to the spot, hearing out the confession.

"The doors were pushed closed. For the first time I noticed another sign: *'Hackenholt Stiftung'.*"

"What does that mean?" I said.

"Hackenholt Foundation – he was the driver of the diesel engine. It was a joke by the SS men who work there, their nickname for the facility."

"It's not funny," I said, not being able to help myself from saying it.

"No? Well, perhaps not. Even less amusing was that the day I was there, the diesel didn't work. Embarrassed because I was observing, the captain hit the Ukrainian assistant, slapping him a dozen times across his face. There was a long delay. Inside the chamber I could hear crying and sobbing. It went through three different phases – first it built to a crescendo, like screaming on a fair ground ride, as the Jews realised it wasn't for disinfection at all. Mass hysteria you could say. Then the crying died down to a low grade whimpering. In the end all the crying stopped, and I could hear a few groups praying and singing together. Finally, after three hours, the diesel started up. The screaming started again. It took half an hour for it to fall totally silent."

I looked at Roth in horror, scarcely able to take in his description. Jacques was shaking his head slowly.

"...The wooden doors on the other side of the chambers were opened and work parties of the strongest Jews removed the dead. Everyone inside was still standing, since there was no space to fall down or even bend forward. Families still holding hands. They had to be pried apart. The corpses were dragged out in a hurry to make room for the next batch – children's corpses tossed into piles. All the while, the work parties were being encouraged with the whip. Elsewhere dentists were opening mouths and looking for gold: corpses with gold to the left, corpses without, to the right. Other dentists were breaking gold teeth and crowns out of mouths with chisels and hammers. Some workers searched the genitals and anuses of the dead for gold, diamonds and other valuables. The captain gave me a heavy can full of gold teeth to hold: 'Lift this' he said, 'Just from the last two days.'"

"What happened to the bodies?"

"They were thrown into large pits, and covered with sand, though in a few places I could still see heads and arms sticking through."

Roth ground out his cigarette on the sole of his boot, folding his arms across his chest, as if to say: 'Well, that's what I saw, but I obviously had nothing to do with any of it.'

"My God," I said.

"Some facilities use crystalline hydrogen cyanide pellets, simply pouring them down air shafts into the chambers. It's the way forward – cleaner and more efficient than exhaust fumes."

I took a deep breath and looked around, at anywhere in the room except for this man in front of me. Hearing about the cyanide made me want to make the bastard bite down hard on the 'L' pill hidden in my cork. I would tell him it was medicine for his bowel complaint. I even felt around in my pockets for the cork, before realising it was in my other trousers, draped across my bedroom chair.

The door to the consultation room was ajar – Stella must have heard everything. It was hard to imagine what must be going through her head.

Another spasm hit and Roth bent forward again.

It felt good to see him in agony now, having heard his account. I think it was the first time I had ever actually enjoyed seeing another human in pain.

Jacques pointed at the flask on the desk.

"If you want something to help with your belly ache, I have found that peppermint tea can be useful. I started brewing some when you arrived. It's in that thermos."

Through his discomfort, Roth looked stunned.

"What? You knew then?"

"I knew it when your men helped you out of the vehicle. Call it experience. Your complexion and countenance is too robust for anything to be seriously wrong. Now do you want the tea, or not?"

"Alright," he said, finally relenting and reaching out for the drink. We watched in silence as he sipped the tea.

I could see Roth was tormented, that there was still a good part within him that knew exactly what evil he had been a party to. I tried to guess the exact moment he had crossed the line – when his soul had been irretrievably corrupted. Had it been as soon as he had joined the Waffen SS? Or in training perhaps, becoming seduced by a particularly erudite and mesmeric lecture on the Nazi worldview? Or had it been at some event out on the Eastern Front, witnessing a massacre so heinous that it made the killing here seem like 'nothing'?

Could he ever be forgiven? Did he *want* to be forgiven?

The grimace on his face had gone and he was smiling and shaking his head.

"Peppermint tea… well what do you know?"

On the way out, he passed Stella in the waiting room.

"Ah… your earache, Mademoiselle. I'm sorry to have kept you waiting."

She didn't reply, and didn't smile. Still in shock from his story, I imagined. I wondered if she was going to break his neck in a violent series of moves. She could have done it, of that I had no doubt.

As she stood up, he did a double take and looked at her closely, like he was examining her, almost smelling her.

Seeing Roth standing there with his eyes locked onto Stella was the most frightening thing I had seen in the whole war.

"Are you a Jew? I know about this. I studied the facial characteristics in my training."

"That would be difficult," she said, not missing a beat, "since both my parents are Catholics from St. Maximin, in the south." As she said it, she pulled down her top slightly to reveal a silver crucifix necklace.

"Oh," he said, bowing slightly and clicking his heels together, "my mistake. Please forgive me."

Just then there was a loud shout from outside.

Roth hurried out into the yard and we followed. When I saw what the commotion was about the blood drained from my face. One of the soldiers was looking through the kitchen window and was gesticulating to his fellows.

Christ! My F-S dagger!

After cleaning the knife, I had put it on the window sill while I shaved. And when the half-track had pulled up, I had completely bloody forgotten about it. Even Jacques hadn't noticed when he'd made the tea.

Rather than go into the house to get it, the soldier smashed the window with his rifle butt and simply reached inside. He gave it to Roth who took it in his hands. The appearance of the weapon seemed to hypnotise the gathering.

Roth turned to me.

"Where did you get this?"

"I found it…" I said, pointing into the trees. "Yesterday in the forest."

"Dies ist ein Britisches Messer," Roth said to his colleagues, "von ein Kommando…"

The soldiers came in closer to get a look.

"Wasn't Siegfried stabbed yesterday during the assault?" one of them said.

Slowly, they all turned their attention to me.

"In the forest," I said, trying to look as offhand as possible. "I found it…"

They switched their attention back to the knife.

Perhaps some of them were coveting the weapon, wishing they had been issued with something like this rather than their clunky, ceremonial effort, the so-called SS 'Ehrendolch', or 'honour dagger'. You only had to look at the two knives to know who was going to win the war; the F-S blade was all business and no show.

A few minutes ago I had been treating their unit doctor, and now they had discovered a British commando knife in my kitchen. Their brains had collectively short-circuited. These people didn't seem to be able to think laterally, only in direct lines forward, attacking and trampling over everything in the process. Never stopping to think or reflect. It worked well in battle, but not so much in detective work. I don't think it occurred to them that I could be a British agent: it was too big a mental leap to make. But something wasn't right, they knew that much.

Roth brought out a piece of paper from his pocket, unfolded it and looked directly at me.

"This is our 'Order of the Day' from two days ago… I'll translate from the German for your benefit: *In the course of its advance, the division has already dealt with other Resistance groups. The armoured regiment has succeeded, thanks to a neatly executed surprise attack, in carrying out the knife stroke – a 'coup de filet' – against a band organised in company strength. The division is now proceeding to a rapid and lasting clean-up of these bands from the region, with a view to becoming speedily available to reinforce the fighting men and join the line at the invasion front.*"

He folded the piece of paper in triumph and put it away.

"I'm sorry… but what does that have to do with me?"

"Number one," Roth said, holding up a finger, "you must be Resistance… a British Commando must have given you that knife."

"I'm not… I'm just a doctor, like you."

"And number two," he said, ignoring my protests and holding up a second finger, "I just wanted you to know that the Das Reich isn't finished yet, not by a long way."

He turned to his men: "Wihr nehmen ihn die Milice."

Jacques stepped forward and was about to say something but was cut short by Roth. "Halt die klappe!"

It was as if we had watched a man metamorphose in minutes, from one personality to another: one almost contrite about what he had done in the war, someone with a degree of insight into his wrongdoing, to a man filled with a zealous hatred, another human altogether: inhuman in fact. That Jacques had cured Roth's ailment now made no difference whatsoever. Here was the man who could laugh at a large crowd, thinking they were about to be massacred, and then tell them they were all very lucky because it happened to be the commander's wedding anniversary that day.

The SS soldiers were both clever and stupid: though they had caught me, Stella was completely overlooked – they really did think she was a patient whom I had been examining. They never checked anything else in the consultation room either; specifically they never found the radio in my bag, which would have really given the game away.

As I was driven off in the half-track, Stella simply stood there next to Jacques and watched me go.

They drove the fifteen miles to Brive and handed me over to men in blue uniforms who spoke perfect French – the 'Milice', the Vichy police force. They had strange badges on their berets – a Greek gamma symbol in a circle. I wondered why they had chosen such a letter – in our school reports; a gamma was the worst mark possible.

"Well, who do we have here?" one of the miliciens said.

"The doctor from Terrasson... he just happened to have this knife in his surgery."

Roth handed over the exhibit.

"This is British Commando issue... says he found it in the woods... I think he's from the Resistance. I want you to take him to Schmerz in Tulle. He'll get to the truth."

The milicien smiled, gently testing the sharpness of the point of the F-S knife on his finger.

"You're right. This sort of thing is right down Schmerz's alley. Are you sure you don't want to question him further?"

"No," Roth said, turning to leave. "We've got more important things to do... like getting to Normandy. The task of eliminating the FTP danger must be transferred to the local divisions. Panzer divisions in the fifth year of the war are too good for this."

I was thrown into a room and left alone for the night.

The next morning I was woken with a bucket of cold water thrown over my face, and then taken out to a car. As I was driven from the city, the thought occurred to me that my father had been right when he had warned me how a war could muck everything up – *"as a medic you'll end up in it, just as I did. And I can guarantee you'll have no control over what happens"*.

Chapter Twenty-two

Dishevelled and handcuffed in the back of a large Daimler Benz, I studied the brilliantined heads of my captors in the front seats. Their neatly combed dark hair, perfumed and shiny, gave them an almost effeminate air. It was hard to equate these two with men like Limouzy and Eric, even though they all stemmed from these same forested hills. Studying these miliciens set me wondering how many Englishmen might have gone down the same path had the Germans successfully invaded in 1940.

The only conversation during the drive occurred as we were leaving the city limits.

"Where are we going?" I said.

"*You're* going to paradise," came the reply of the man in the passenger seat, who spoke without turning round.

The road ran east, upwards into the hills, with steep cliffs and forest on both sides.

After half an hour, we drove into a town, pulled up outside a factory of some kind, and were waved through the main gate into a large courtyard. 'Manufacture d'Armes de Tulle' it said in large letters on the side of the building.

A door slammed somewhere and soon the sound of footsteps could be heard coming down the long parquet corridor. The miliciens turned me to face the approaching figure. He was perhaps in his mid-thirties, with one of those severe haircuts - shaved down to the skull on the sides, but with the top longer and swept back – just like the SS officers who had watched Limouzy's hanging. *Did these bastards all go to the same barber?*

He was holding a cigarette – set in a long, ivory holder – in a curiously effete pose with his elbow at ninety degrees and his hand cocked outwards at an angle too. His face was plump, slightly bloated even, and he was smiling at me knowingly, as if we were both in on the same joke. Though he was smiling, his eyes were black and blank, like a shark's.

Then I noticed something that filled me with utter dread – his plain grey jacket, innocuous at a first glance, had a dark diamond-shaped badge at the bottom of his left sleeve, and within the badge two silver capital letters: SD.

I started regretting not having my cyanide pill to hand.

Christ, I *was* going to paradise.

SD stood for Sicherheitsdienst, the SS security service with close links to the Gestapo. Heydrich himself had once called the SD 'the cream of the cream of the Nazis'. In the finishing school, we had learnt the SD were the group behind the 'enhanced interrogation' techniques – the 'Verscharfte Vernehmung'.

Somewhat incongruously, he was holding a small young dog in the crook of his other arm – a German shepherd puppy. The dog was clearly the only thing he really loved in this world, apart from himself and the Nazi cause.

One of the miliciens held out a brown paper bag containing my knife.

Seemingly only vaguely interested, the man stroked the dog and peered into the paper bag being held open for him.

He repeated Roth's words from the previous day, saying: "Das ist ein Britisches Messer," to no-one in particular.

My other captor was holding a file. The SD man motioned with his head for the milicien to open it to the first page and, just as he had done with the knife, he leant forward slightly to take a peek. After reading for a few moments he straightened up and looked at me with a thin smile. He addressed me in French.

"Doctor Bonnet?"

"Yes, sir."

"I'm Lieutenant Schmerz."

He said it like we were meeting at a cocktail party. His voice was normal enough, with soft tones. If it hadn't come from a Nazi torturer and murderer, the voice could easily have belonged to a congenial friend, sharing in-jokes and bantering away about the quirks of life.

"We need to have a chat, if that's alright with you – there are some things we need to *iron out*, I'm afraid."

He said it quite languidly, with an air of fatigue, as if what was about to follow was all going to be fairly boring and bureaucratic.

"Certainly, Lieutenant, I should be happy to clear all this up. It is one big misunderstanding."

"Yes," he said, deadpan.

He held up the dog and addressed it lovingly, talking to the animal and not me at all.

"Yes… I am sure it is all one big misunderstanding. I am glad the man is happy to try and clear all this up. Shall we help him clear up the misunderstanding? Shall we, my darling? Yes, we shall!"

He let the puppy lick his face for a few moments and then glanced at the two men on either side of me, each in turn, his expression cold once again.

"Take him to the laboratory."

I was at peace with myself, ready for what was about to come – after all, I had practised for this in the 'conference room' back at Beaulieu. This was going to be my big test in this war – not the shoot-out at the road block. That hadn't tested me much at all, except my ability to curl into a ball and then run away fast. No, my test was going to be taking everything Schmerz had to dish out and not give anything away.

I went through the scenarios in my head: there would probably be a bath – 'The Paris technique'. In fact I *wanted* there to be a bath, that way I could go into my 'salt bath mode' and get through it in a degree of imaginary comfort.

I was confident I was going to beat this monster.

If I could do it, then in my eyes I would have avenged Tom Shaw's death. And not just Tom's, but all the FTP men who had died in Terrasson. Limouzy had been brave when it counted and now it was my turn. This was going to be for all of them. I would not be giving away any secrets – and they would never know about Stella.

Others came to mind now. I wanted Pirbright and Stringer to know I was unbreakable. I wanted Fox and Farr-Jones and the Captain to know it too.

This is how I would get back at Freya Nielsen.

Perhaps I wanted to do it for MP most of all, for that small boy of his, one of the innocents who had been caught up in this great evil.

This was a fight for all of them.

I felt like a boxer being led into the ring, inwardly snarling in my eagerness to lock horns with my opponent.

At first Schmerz was a hair puller, yanking my hair hard like a girl in a playground fight.

As he did it, he smiled his dead smile and said, "This file says you fought with the communist Maquis."

"That can't be," I said, hoping he was bluffing.

The SS soldiers had spouted their theories as they handed me over to the Milice. But these were just their clumsy clod-footed assumptions. I hoped to God no-one in Terrasson had given me up, that no witness was about to walk in and point at me and say: "That's him – I saw him in the bar with the FTP!"

Schmerz slapped me across the face – again, a very feminine action. I had been expecting solid punches to the face with fists. So far this had been the only surprise.

"It's not true," I said, pretending to be more shocked than I felt. "I'm just the village doctor."

Schmerz called out and the two miliciens came into the room – my escort. Their jackets were off and their sleeves were rolled up.

Shit, I thought. *Here we go.*

"Take off his shirt."

Instead of unbuttoning it, they just tore it off so that the buttons flew around the room and punched me in the stomach for good measure. My heart almost stopped, not because of the violence of my undressing, but because one of those buttons – a collar stud – contained the miniature compass. I saw it by my right foot, contorted myself in fake pain and at the same time ground my foot down onto it, crushing the piece of evidence into dust. No-one noticed. It was all I could do not to smile at this small victory.

Schmerz was at a table now, pulling back a brown cloth to reveal an array of instruments which would have impressed even the Captain.

It was obvious the slaps and hair-pulling were just the starter. Now he was going on to the main course.

Bon appetit, you bastard…

He came back over with a rubber truncheon and the two miliciens held me firm. Schmerz took a practised swing, striking me in the midriff over the ribs. I heard the snap and a searing pain radiated across my torso and made me wince: real pain for the first time.

I registered it, put it into a filing cabinet in my head, and slammed the cabinet drawer shut.

"You're a doctor, aren't you?" Schmerz said without emotion. "So you know what I've just done. That was your seventh rib breaking, if I'm not mistaken… possibly both your seventh and eighth together."

"Please, this is madness. I am innocent!"

Through the pain, I continued playing the part of an outraged, innocent and frightened village doctor.

He came close to my face. His aftershave smelt strong, as if he had to cover up a stinking body odour with large doses of the stuff.

"Now, are you going to start telling the truth, or am I going to have to hit you again?"

"I'm telling you the truth, sir, I promise. My father and I run the clinic together. All we do is help sick people. That's it. I even treated an SS doctor yesterday, for God's sake!"

He tossed the rubber truncheon from side to side.

"I don't believe you."

Another swing and another impact – a dull thud. I was aware it was the weapon on my skin again, but it felt more distant this time, and I didn't hear a break. It was because he had chosen the same spot as before. After a tiny time delay of a second or so, the pain came, so strong it made me almost faint.

I wanted to try and file away the new pain, but the filing cabinet in my head had toppled over with a loud crash.

Jesus. This was already a lot worse than the forty eight hours of my simulated torture and we were only ten minutes in.

I started sweating profusely and was struggling to fight off the wave of nausea. The world was beginning to fade into the background.

Fear clamped down hard on me now and I had to fight the impulse to scream out everything about who I was. I could do it if I concentrated. A voice inside me said: 'You're not talking – so find a way to absorb the punishment.'

I retched rather than vomited – because I still hadn't eaten anything since the road block, two days before.

Another impact.

The space in my head had been totally ransacked now, along with the toppled pain cabinet. Pictures of loyal friends and family were hanging off the walls, a desk was upturned and papers were lying everywhere.

"I'm just the village doctor," I said, my face contorted. The room was spinning.

"You're Maquis… You're in the Red Resistance aren't you?"

"No… No… No…"

He brought his face close to mine and started a long soliloquy in a quiet voice.

"I was the only SD survivor from your uprising in this place, you know. I had to watch my colleague shoot himself in the head rather than be captured by the FTP. But I stayed alive… I hid all night in a burning building until my brothers from the Das Reich came to the rescue. If it had been up to me, I would have had the entire town massacred in reprisal."

He looked around the room and let out a small laugh.

"General Lammerding was merciful... only 120 chosen... to serve as an example to the whole of France. I chose the condemned myself you know, just out in the courtyard where you arrived. Any man who had not shaved, whose hair was untidy, whose clothes were un-brushed or soiled, whose shoes were not polished – well, I picked out that man from the crowd, because that man was a Maquis in my eyes. Later that day I sat at a table at the Tivoli café with some friends. We listened to music and laughed and smoked as we watched the hangings. Ninety nine, until we ran out of rope. I was so pissed off with the Partisans, I wanted to do it with my shoelaces. You know what they did to our dead guys? They sexually mutilated them."

"I wouldn't know about that... I'm not Maquis!"

Another hit to the midriff.

I couldn't say anything now. I could hardly breathe.

Schmerz was straight in with the pain. He knew how to hurt, that was for sure. Made the lads at Beaulieu seem like a pair of choirboys.

My safe inner space had completely collapsed now, along with the building it was in – the whole edifice a pile of rubble in my mind. So much for the 'filing away of pain into separate compartments' theory of torture resistance: Schmerz had taken a wrecking ball to it.

I heard the sound of something being unwrapped. He was removing my F-S dagger from the paper bag.

"So you're an agent for the British then?" he said, coming close and pushing the point of the knife onto my cheek. "You were issued with this."

"No, sir. I found it in the forest... Yesterday... I found it and brought it back home as a souvenir. Why would I not have hidden it? An agent would have hidden it, not had it out in plain view with a squad of SS present..."

"That's a good point...unless you are a *stupid* agent."

He was right. I was a stupid one.

Schmerz had become interested in my facial scar.

"How did you get this?"

He was jabbing at it with the point of the knife.

"When I was a boy, sir – I don't remember doing it, I was only small, but I did it to myself with a scalpel in my father's surgery."

Frowning, he went over to check the file.

While I had been locked up in Brive overnight, the Milice had obviously gone back to Reybenet and interviewed Jacques thoroughly. I hoped they hadn't done anything to the kind old man.

Schmerz came back to me.

"You know, I think you French are all weasels – a country of small rat-like weasels."

The miliciens looked at one another and then at Schmerz, and then back at me. They didn't seem to mind too much about being lumped into the 'weasel' category.

"Sir, Papa and I, we're just doctors… it's what we do."

"Weasels," he said again, drawing the dagger slowly down my torso so that it made a fine superficial wound.

As he cut me he talked, like a chef teaching his trainee chefs how to debone a joint.

"When did the British come to you? How did they approach you?"

"Please, sir… I don't know what you're saying. I know no British people. I'm just the doctor…"

My ire made Schmerz smile in surprise.

"You can tell me. It's all right."

He had spoken in English. Damn clever.

In my traumatised state I nearly replied in English too; almost said, 'I won't tell you a fucking thing.' The sentence had formed in my brain and was on its way down to my mouth when I managed to put a brake on it. Instead I looked at him in confusion and spoke in French.

"What are you saying?"

He drew the knife down my skin again, on the same place as before. Schmerz was one for repeating pain; it seemed to be his special method. The wound felt cold now – it was like someone was holding a long icicle against my chest and abdomen. Then it started to smart and I could feel the blood running down towards my waist. I wondered if my guts were about to spill out onto the floor with a great sloppy splash.

I started to fantasise about all the ways I could kill him with the F-S dagger, then stove in his dead face with the handle, then cut off his balls and stuff them into his mouth. I was starting to understand the hate of the FTP now.

"You're a spying weasel, aren't you? You report to London."

I shook my head.

"Sir, you're wrong. I'm no spy. That knife – I found it. I swear on my mother's soul."

This made Schmerz laugh. He went back over to the file.

"Ah yes, your mother… She died in the assault of Dunkirk in 1940, didn't she?"

"Yes… a tragedy."

Schmerz turned around and made a pretend sad face.

"A tragedy indeed…" He came close again, almost whispering. "Is that why you decided to fight for the British… because of what happened to her?"

The man was no idiot. He was honing in on some kind of truth here and I had to fight off any thoughts that might give it away. I was aware that if my expression changed, he would sniff it out of me in a second.

"No, sir. She was unlucky. In life people can just be unlucky. I see it as a doctor every day – how fate can suddenly step in and change everything. I don't think it was anyone's fault in particular. I hold no grudges.'

"My God," he said, turning to his henchmen, "there's a philosopher in our midst."

They laughed cruelly at Schmerz's witticism.

"I'm an honest man, sir. My parents brought me up well. Not to lie. That knife was found, I swear it. I am just a doctor. A humble doctor in a quiet French village… and I have been unlucky, hauled in by soldiers on a mere suspicion. It's a short story, but it's the truth.'

Schmerz was looking at me with a dark intensity now, trying to fathom whether I really might be telling the truth.

He had no evidence other than the knife. That was all he had to go on – a single blade. Then the doubt was gone again and the monster returned.

"Where did they train you? Scotland? I hear they train the commandos up there."

"I don't know what you're talking about."

I met his eye and tried to really think that I didn't know what he was talking about. I had to really convince myself of the untruth, like a bad politician who tells the same lie so often that in the end he starts believing it.

The two miliciens held me down on the floor while Schmerz proceeded to pour the contents of a beaker onto my wound. It was acid.

"I studied to be a pharmacist before the war, you know," he said as he poured slowly, eking out the agony.

The pain amplified itself as the chemical played havoc with my nerve endings – it crossed boundaries which I had never even imagined existed.

"Just a doctor… just a doctor," I said in a whimper.

Schmerz spoke to his colleagues without looking away from my face.

"This is getting tiresome. I think it's time we ran him a bath at the hotel."

I was half hauled, half led, back out to the car and driven the short distance to the centre of town, to a building called 'Hotel St Martin'.

Up on the first floor, we entered into a large tiled room, with a great white enamel bath tub set down right in the middle.

Ah, at last, I thought – *the 'Paris technique'*. At least now I was in vaguely familiar territory.

As they ran the cold tap and stripped me completely naked I tried to console myself that I really had practised for this: granted, not in a bath, but with plenty of cold water. The SOE had trained me well. There was, however, the uncomfortable knowledge that Schmerz would go a lot further than the men at Beaulieu had done.

He approached me before I was immersed.

"I admire you, Doctor," he said. "I really do… but in the end everybody talks. Even the innocent."

My legs were tied to a bar resting across the top of the tub. A chain was attached to the centre of the bar. With my hands handcuffed in front of me, I was completely helpless; when Schmerz yanked the chain up, I would slip under the water.

I was shivering, the same way I had done in the simulated torture. Memories came back to me, like images from an old holiday. Memories of my 'salt-bath mode'. I had been here before.

The questions began again – a similar pattern – following the same themes. Repetition to which I gave my stock set of answers. This was okay with me, this was the game. It was better than ribs being broken.

I began to switch off – nearly drowning, then gasping for air, then giving my replies before the next dunking. This went on for a long time... maybe even hours. He stopped at one point to pull out one of my fingernails with a pair of pliers, but to be honest it didn't make much of a difference – I was so cold I could hardly feel it, so I won't try and pretend that I was being particularly hardy.

When I had gone another round of holding out, he would lean down and remove the next fingernail, and so on. In the end I felt myself slip permanently into a zone between two worlds – not quite in this one, but not all the way into the other one, that of death, either.

I became aware that someone else had come into the room and taken up a position behind me and to my right, at the head end of the bath – the opposite end to my torturers. Although I couldn't see who it was I knew it was Tom Shaw.

"You're doing well, Ed," he said, his voice perfectly clear in my head, "in holding out against this bastard, I mean."

I tried to jerk around to see him, but with the bar holding my legs it was hard and I couldn't make him out.

"Tom?" I said in surprise, thinking it and not saying it, because instinctively I was aware that was how he was talking to me. Only I could hear him, not Schmerz, nor the others.

"Yes it's me. Tom. Who else would it bloody well be? Looks like you're in a real fucking fix... Smoke?"

I could smell the cigarette.

It was just like being back at East Grinstead. We were back in our old routine. There was always a lot of swearing when we worked together in the bath room.

"Thanks, Tom. That would be good right at this minute."

He held the cigarette to my wet blue lips and I took a long drag.

The imaginary nicotine helped me relax.

"So," he said, "I saw what was happening and decided to come and help you. He's not going to let you off for a while yet. You've probably worked out he's a complete sadist. He's never been outfoxed yet, but there's always a first time, eh old pal? Now there's two of us, we stand more of a chance."

"I hope so, Tom. Give me another puff of that cigarette, will you?"

He was so real that I kept straining my head to try and see him. His presence felt solid in that part of the room.

"Why don't I put some hot water in too? You look frozen stiff."

"Good idea."

"There you go. I was always a better hose-man than you... How's that feeling?"

It was odd, but I did feel warmer. My shivering stopped, although my breathing remained fast and shallow..

"Better," I said.

"I'm pretty sure that's the same temperature as East Grinstead... a positively tropical 105 degrees Fahrenheit. You're warming up, old boy..."

As Schmerz continued to pull me under the water by my foot bar, I carried on talking with Tom. I would deal with his having come back from the dead another time, right now I just had to go with it or I was going to die myself.

He gave me another drag of the cigarette.

"You remember that night we gave the Czech pilot the bath?" he said.

"Yes, I do."

"What was his name?"

I remembered straight away. "Siska."

"Yes, Siska – that's it! What did he call the surgeon who had used the tannic acid?"

"A man who fucks horses."

Tom roared with laughter.

I smiled but had to turn it into a grimace so Schmerz wouldn't become suspicious.

He was still going through his list of questions and I was replying automatically: "I'm just a doctor; I swear to God… please… I just found the knife in the forest…"

But the conversation which really held my attention was the one with Tom – the one in English.

"You know, I think this bastard fucks his puppy dog," he was saying. "There's a word for that isn't there?"

"Bestiality," I said.

The puppy was sitting in the corner of the room, staring right over in the direction of Tom. Schmerz had brought the animal with him to watch me have the bath.

"Ed," he said in a whisper, "I think that Nazi pup can bloody well see me."

As if on cue, the dog padded over, taking up a new position on the floor and continuing its staring routine.

The place where Schmerz had cut me was stinging – even through the cold insulation of the water I could feel the acid blood line made by the F-S knife, screaming in torment. The bathwater had turned pink from the wound. The pulps where my fingernails had been were throbbing.

"Come on, Ed. Stop thinking about it. Concentrate on me…"

"What do you think of my fellow agent?" I said, apropos of nothing.

"Ah… she's very pretty," Tom said, sounding impressed. "Very pretty indeed, and the toughest bird I've ever laid eyes upon. Her real name's Naomi by the way…"

"Naomi… that's lovely."

"Yes well, don't start getting all soft on me. Oh, speaking of beautiful women, I heard you saw our old friend Freya again."

For a moment I didn't know what he was referring to, but then remembered my interview and my attempt to shoot her.

"It wasn't for long, Tom; they wanted to know if I had what it took to kill."

"And did you?"

"I did then – it was the same day as your funeral and I was full of hate. Luckily for her, the gun wasn't loaded."

"Think you could kill this Nazi fucker here?"

"Right now I could. I killed the other day Tom, at the barricades, saw SS soldiers go down. But that was in the heat of battle. This would be one-on-one, personal and cold-blooded. I have a feeling that if I ever killed a man in that way – even a bad man – it would stay with me for the rest of my life. I wouldn't want this bastard standing on one of the Devil's Jumps and shouting at me every time I fell asleep."

"Ha! You know what Ed? That butcher Schmerz has a point – you *have* become a philosopher in your old age."

"Maybe I should've been one," I said, "and not a doctor at all. Then I wouldn't have had to sit there in the parks and watch you prodding that bloody lung with a stick."

Tom laughed again, and gave me another smoke of the cigarette.

"You heard about your brother and Nielsen?" I said.

"Yes, Flyboy gave her the time… I'm happy for him. He wasn't to know."

"I think they're going to hang her."

Tom was quiet for a moment. I felt he wanted to tell me something, but was holding back. I could tell he was sitting there with a frown on his face, smoking the cigarette himself.

"Hey there," I said, "are going to share any more of that? I'm the poor fucker being tortured here!"

Schmerz was really going to town on me, leaning over and smacking me around the face when I came up from the water, shouting the same questions – calling me a spy and asking about the knife. He was winding things up into a crescendo. I kept giving him my pleading innocence, almost relishing how frustrated it was making him.

Without saying anything, Tom reached over and put the cigarette on my lips once more.

Ironically, considering my current predicament, I felt the need to cheer Tom up.

"You want to know something funny?" I said.

"What's that?"

"I really do think this bastard fucks his dog!"

As if on cue, the dog started to howl – a little puppy dog cry – clearly aware that something strange was going on in that part of the room. It seemed to know Tom was there, just as I did.

Tom and I kept on laughing together as I was dunked for a last time – longer than all the previous submergings, so long I started seeing dots and wavy lines and zig zags in my vision.

"I've seen these somewhere before, Tom – these strange geometric patterns."

"In the cave," he said.

"You're right."

That's where they had been, scattered around the large animal portraits. I hadn't thought much of them at the time, such was the splendour of the main frieze.

"They're what see when you hallucinate," he said. "The retina, the visual cortex – they're playing tricks on you. Those cavemen were in a trance when they made those patterns, drugged up to their eyeballs with something… in altered states of consciousness, anyway. I'm afraid this torture is messing about with your neural architecture, Ed – because you're hyperventilating."

The zig zags danced in my vision in a pleasant way.

Then something occurred to me.

"Is that why I'm talking to you, because I'm hallucinating?"

"Might be" he said, as if he held all the trump cards and wasn't going to let me see them. "Might not be. All I can tell you is that you are way down deep in the cave."

"Hey… You can't just keep it all a secret. Is this all coming from my head or are you really there? I bloody well got you into medical school…you owe me!"

"Well, consider this little coaching session as some payback… Oh, what do you know? I see at last that Schmerz doubts himself. He really thinks you are Xavier Bonnet, an innocent country doctor who happened to come across a commando knife. You know what's changing his mind? The fact that the puppy dog he fucks is crying. Isn't that funny? He thinks the pup believes you're innocent! *Hahahaha!* Time for me to take my leave, my friend, my job here is done."

He made a pretend howl right in the face of the puppy, which only served to make the creature whine even louder.

"No, Tom, wait. Don't go!"

A huge surge of disappointment came over me as he departed.

I felt myself being pulled up out of the water. My vacant bleeding nail-beds throbbed like fury in the open air. By Christ I was hurting now.

"Undo his legs," I heard Schmerz say. "Gentlemen, I think this clown really is who he says he is... No-one could stand what we've just done. It's impossible. Clean him up, give him some food and bring him to my office tomorrow."

He went over to his whimpering dog and scooped the creature up.

"There, there...it's okay, girl... yes it is, yes it is... You didn't like the bath Daddy was giving that man, did you? You think the French weasel is who he says he is, don't you? Well... you know what, my little darling? Daddy thinks so too."

Schmerz anthropomorphising the puppy would have been a repulsive sight at the best of times, but after Tom's conjectures it was almost comical.

My ghostly friend had scared the poor creature witless.

The miliciens led me through to another room where a German medical attendant dressed my wounds and helped me into some clean clothes. He gave me a couple of painkilling tablets and I fell asleep on a mattress in the corner.

Later, someone brought in a plate of Andouillette sausage with some potatoes and placed them on the floor.

I was still sad because Tom had left. I missed my friend and wondered if I would ever encounter him again in this lifetime. Did I have to almost die every time?

I drifted off again.

****

I was taken downstairs to a bright office bathed in sunlight.

Schmerz was there with his dog sitting in his lap.

When I walked in, he pushed it off gently and stood up.

"Herr Doktor," he said, by way of a greeting.

"What day is it?"

"Thursday the fifteenth," he said. "You were out for more than a day… I must apologise. It seems we misjudged the situation. I have done further checks. Your story appears to be quite genuine. We have had word that British agents have indeed been in the area – one was captured some days back; a female, feisty little thing too by all accounts. Even put up a bit of a fight with a Sten gun. She'll be thoroughly interrogated of course and then sent somewhere secure. Anyway, it became apparent to me during your interview that my suspicions were entirely misguided, as I am one hundred percent confident that you would have told me if it was anything otherwise."

He held out my F-S dagger.

"I have had it cleaned and oiled. Please take it… after all, you found it. For what I have done to you, I will allow you to keep your little souvenir. I've even had papers drawn up to explain the situation, to confirm that all is in order if anyone else becomes suspicious. These men will take you back to your surgery so that you can continue your work."

Very suddenly he raised his right arm out straight.

"Heil Hitler!"

I nodded back at him and folded my arms across my chest.

Inside I was in total turmoil.

Was Schmerz talking about Stella? She could certainly be described as feisty. She carried a Sten. Jesus. It must have been her. After all I had done in holding out, she had been captured anyway. I felt myself burning with rage and sorrow.

"You'll forgive me if I don't salute back," I said. "All my shoulder muscles seem to have been torn during our earlier… interview."

No matter what, I thought, *there's no way I'm saluting this fucker.*

"Not at all, Doctor," he said. "I completely understand."

I had got to the door when I heard him call out to his dog.

"Here girl, come to Papa."

I turned to see Schmertz sat back at his desk and the puppy leaping up onto his lap again. He stroked the underside of its chin.

"Who's a good girl, eh? Who's a good girl?"

He even kissed it with puckered lips right on it's wet, shiny nose.

Maybe Tom had been right, and the sadistic bastard really was into bestiality.

Schmerz seemed to be oblivious to the fact that a few hundred miles north, a battle was being waged that would decide his, and Europe's, future. I sincerely hoped his dog would desert him on the day of his capture – the way a flighty girlfriend might run off with someone else – and choose the lap of an Allied soldier instead. That would be the only thing to ever upset the man.

Chapter Twenty-three

The 'Caf', Oxford, Early Summer 1946

I looked at the empty seat in front of me, and let out a long sigh. I was missing Tom Shaw. If he'd been here we would have been arguing about something together; no longer his nagging about anatomy, or my complaining about having to poke through sheep's lungs, but it would be definitely be *something*, and I felt the absence acutely.

Maybe it hadn't been a good idea to come in here again.

I sipped my mug of tea half-heartedly, allowing my mind to wander.

He was in my thoughts of course, but only in the form of 'normal' memories now; not as the entity who had come to me during my interview with Schmerz. I was convinced that the voice had been Tom's, not just my mind playing tricks with me. I had talked to my father about it, knowing he had experienced something very similar with his dead brother many years before. My father wasn't stupid – he'd seen my facial scar and my recovering fingernails and realised I had been involved in a serious incident of some kind. At least by then MP had reversed the changes to my ears and nose; that would have been harder to explain. I had to adjust my story, of course – to the one the SOE had decreed I use – of my being trapped on Pike's Peak one night during a fierce storm, and falling onto a sharp rock and sustaining the facial injury. And of coming down off the mountain the next day with frostbitten fingers. But aside from that I told my father the essential truth; that I really *felt* Tom had been there, that I had talked with him, and that he had helped me survive my ordeal. My account moved him deeply and his eyes had reddened with tears. "For forty five years, I've been trying to reconcile what happened to me," he had said. "At first I believed he had been there, though the more time that passed, the more I thought it a figment of my imagination. Knowing the same thing happened to you, Ed, so powerfully, and in dire straits like mine... well, it convinces me all over again that it *was* real, and that I shouldn't have doubted. Their spirits have lived on, in some incomprehensible way... and when we needed their help the most, they came and saved us. You and I have brushed up against the next world, Ed. Not many people get to have that experience."

I came back to the present and looked around.

The caf hadn't changed. I didn't think it ever would; only the people inside it would come and go, and in time turn old and grey. They might even change the seating and spruce the place up, but it would still be the same. The grease was part of the fabric of the building by now, infused into the walls.

This was the first time I had been back to Oxford since Tom's funeral. I was here for another – Gilligan's. I wondered if all my future visits to the caf would be because some old Oxford acquaintance had died.

If appearances were anything to go by, Kynance wasn't long for this world either. The night before, at the college dinner celebrating Gilligan's life, he kept nodding off at the table, upright but with eyes closed. Tom and I were lucky to have been taught by them in their last good years. It was sobering to see his intellect dulled and his spirit ebbing away. God forbid I ever ended up like that, existing but not really living. There was something to be said for avoiding that kind of end. It was one outcome that people like Tom, Limouzy and the other FTP men had at least managed to avoid.

Flashes came back to me from the war.

The miliciens dumping me back at Reybenet after my torture, and of Jacques running out of the house and hugging me, with tears flowing down his cheeks. "You're alive, Xavi!" His cavernous laugh, followed by the words: "My son… my beautiful, strong son…"

Then the biggest surprise of all – and the biggest relief I had ever known – Stella appearing from the forest and stepping inside. It hadn't been her after all, but another British Agent – codename 'Louise' – who had been captured by the Das Reich in a field near Limoges. Her real name was Violette Szabo, and they executed her at Ravensbrück in January 1945.

Despite my delight at seeing Stella alive, at first she wasn't quite so pleased to see me, assuming I must have cut a deal to save my own skin. The exchange was still vivid in my mind:

As she came into the house she was pointing her Sten at my stomach.
"For God's sake, Stella" I said. "Look at my fingernails."
"You've shopped us in."
"No! They would be here by now… Do you see anyone here?"
She frowned.
"How could you resist? I heard they took you to the SD."
"I convinced them of my innocence."
"How?"
"You wouldn't believe me if I told you."
"Talk to the Sten – it's listening. You'd better come up with something good."
"A dead friend talked me through it. Like a ghost. He made it bearable."
She laughed.
"A ghost! If you think that's going to get you off the hook, you can think again."
"I swear it, Stella."
"Oh? And what did this ghostly friend tell you?"
Something Tom had said came back to me. I knew why he'd done it now.
"We talked about you. He told me your real name."
"Impossible," she said, with an incredulous sneer. "Go on, tell me… is it Rumpelstiltskin?"

My voice went very quiet, hoping to God Tom had got his facts right. "No, it's Naomi."

Stella turned pale when I said that, and lowered the weapon. Nothing much fazed her, but that did. "My God," she said, "either I talk in my sleep or you really did speak to a ghost."

Memories of Reybenet made me smile. As I prepared to drink more of my steaming mug of tea, I sniffed at it suspiciously – even though it was made with normal cow's milk, I still couldn't convince myself that it didn't contain just the faintest trace of goat.

Satisfied with my ghost story, Stella had recounted what she had done after the SS had taken me away; immediately burying my doctor's bag in the forest. Good tradecraft. Just as I had thought, the Milice had gone to Reybenet to carry out a more thorough search that same evening – while I was still in Brive. They had interviewed Jacques and put together the background file which Schmerz had used during my interrogation. Although the Milice had turned the place upside down, they had not found the cyanide hidden in the wine cork, nor had they suspected Jacques of any wrong-doing. A life-long student of human psychology, Jacques would have given a convincing impression of being a trustworthy and innocent old man, the father of an equally innocent son.

A few days after my return to Reybenet, Stella and I exhumed the radio and called for a Lysander pick-up at our allocated transmission time:

'GLAD SUCCESSFUL BUT FTP CELL DEAD REQUEST PICK UP NEXT MOON SAME GROUND BBC MESSAGE THE CAVEMAN IS EXTINCT'

In late June, we received a brief but reassuring response - *'YOUR NUMBER 4 RECEIVED AFFIRMATIVE RECOGNITION LETTER T, PILOT ANSWER H'* – and on 7th July, the BBC message was broadcast, telling us the collection was a 'go'. All that training for just four transmits and four receives – eight radio messages in all, and four dead men. The Das Reich stalled for perhaps a few hours at most. Had it been really been worth it?

I stared at my mug of tea and thought about my F-S dagger.

I had left it with Jacques, along with the typed sheets attesting to its provenance signed by Schmerz. No German would be able to touch the real Xavi now, not with that documentation. Jacques said he would explain to Commandant Jack what had happened. The Commandant could make things right with any FTP men who still had any suspicions about Xavi Bonnet and the torture he had endured.

On leaving Reybenet for the last time, I had noticed a new photograph on the mantelpiece; one of Jacques and I standing outside the surgery with our arms around each other's shoulders. The local photographer had taken the picture as a favour after we had treated his young son. In the hurried circumstances of that night – with all the practicalities of the pick-up – there was no time for sentimentality and I had only registered the briefest of impressions on seeing the framed picture next to the others. It had been one of gladness, that my French father really had let me into his heart.

With Jacques, Stella and I, there were just enough of us to make the flare-path in the landing field – one person holding up a torch at each point of the 'L'. Stella had flashed up a T and the reply had come back: H.

At the pick up everything happened quickly again. The real Xavi came down the ladder and went straight over to hug his father. I just had enough time to shake Xavi's hand and give Jacques a last backslap, before running over to follow Stella up into the Lysander. In total I had known Xavi Bonnet for approximately one minute.

In the rush, I had forgotten to give him back his wristwatch and it had become my one memento from France. Although the doctor's bag with the radio came back too, Station IX had requested its return.

The pilot – not Richard this time – had made a detour around Normandy. There was a battle, he said, being fought around Caen, so instead he flew home over the lights of Dieppe further up the French coast. As we did, I remember thinking that somewhere down there to the west, the blood group tattoos of the SS soldiers would be getting due usage, and also that if he was still alive, Roth's bowel problem would be playing up again.

Living in the Dordogne had felt like forever, though it hadn't even been two months. The rest of the war, on the other hand, flew past in a blurred sequence of events, as if time had decided to accelerate.

Stella taught radio skills and Morse at the finishing school, and I was made a 'special advisor' on the torture simulations, helping prospective agents to cope with whatever might come their way.

It was hard to teach people to ignore pain. I couldn't exactly talk about ghosts coming to their aid, but I did tell the recruits to try and think themselves into another place, somewhere they could imagine so clearly that it could push everything else to one side. As a regular visitor to the 'conference room', I saw how some had the knack and some didn't. Either way, none of them would ever have the help I had been blessed with, and I very much doubted any of them would withstand a session with Schmerz or a Schmerz-like interrogator. You couldn't really prepare for that.

For the cock-sure ones who thought they knew it all, I would pull up my shirt and show them the long scar trailing down my front. It had healed messily because of the acid and looked quite dramatic. The recruits would shut up and listen after that. The scar sometimes made the skin on my chest dance with a strange neuralgia, but it tickled rather than hurt.

In the end, my fingernails grew back so well you wouldn't have known what had happened to them, but it did take six months.

As time went by, fewer and fewer agents came through the system. In early 1946, the SOE was disbanded and I returned to medicine. General practice, not surgery, was the path I wanted to follow, although when asked in job interviews why I had chosen that specialty, the discussion became awkward. I would tell them: "I'm afraid it's classified," and they would look at one another briefly, eyebrows raised, before continuing. Many said no, but in the end someone took me on; a team of country doctors down south, not a million miles from Beaulieu, as it happened. Although I couldn't tell them what had taken place between July 1943 and January 1946, which included my short-term stint in French rural medicine, they seemed to like me well enough, and in time came to appreciate some of the skills I had picked up from BD and Jacques during that intense apprenticeship.

The door to the caf rattled and a man came in, calling over to the cook for a coffee.

It was Pirbright, as smooth as ever, hair swept back in a distinguished manner, though greying at the temples slightly. There was no smile of greeting, much like the first time I had seen him in the parks with Tom, his saturnine mood revisited.

I knew it wasn't a coincidence – things never were with him. He had deliberately sought me out.

"Hello, Professor," I said.

He sat down opposite me in the booth, not in the least surprised that I wasn't surprised. Nothing much fazed me anymore, not after what had happened in Tulle, and Pirbright would have been savvy to that.

"You look well, Hunston. How's married life treating you?"

"She's a different person when she's not fighting a war on behalf of her people," I said. "Not quite so angry."

This made him smile.

"We knew she was a dangerous tool."

"The best, I imagine."

"Yes. I would agree with that."

The cook called out that the coffee was ready and Pirbright went to get it.

While he did, I thought about my wife.

After returning from France I had still been uncertain where things stood between Stella and I, and we were so busy at the finishing school that our issues remained unresolved for some months. It was only in the

October of 1944 that we finally had the chance to take a walk together – out to the shingle beach on the Solent, across the water from the Royal Victoria Military Hospital. The Americans had been given the run of the place and you could see their jeeps driving around the grounds. There were rumours they even drove them down the long hospital corridors instead of walking between the wards.

I wanted to tell her stories about my father having been there in previous wars, and how my uncle was buried in the hospital cemetery – but I couldn't because I thought I was just 'Ahab' to her, the agent with whom she had enjoyed a wild drunken fling that night in the cave.

We sat down on a fallen tree-trunk and out of the blue, she leant against me, put her hands to her face and started weeping. She wouldn't stop – just kept crying. I stroked her hair and waited for her to tell me what was wrong. Something happened then, as I sat there waiting. Seeing her like that – vulnerable, I suppose – made me fall in love with her. It happened in a single second. Jacques had been very accurate in his diagnosis about my liking her a lot, but this was different. The feeling suddenly took over my whole being, swooping down like a giant bird of prey – gripping my heart with its talons and almost stopping it in the process. I wanted to look after her forever.

"Roth," she eventually said, "… what he said about those chambers… the way he looked at me. The *way* he asked if I was a Jew, as if I was from a different species… he haunts me. Those scenes he described in the chambers at Belzec haunt me too."

The first time I had ever seen her defenseless and exposed had been on the side of the Loch in late 1943. And now here she was again, almost a year later, this time on the shingle of a deserted English shoreline, fully clothed and yet even more defenseless and exposed than before. I held her tight in the cold wind.

"A brainwashed fool… They're beaten now, Naomi; they are no more. And you're still here."

It was true, the Das Reich had been erased from the face of the planet, though it had been a ferocious demise, first in Normandy, and then later in the Ardennes. They had finally capitulated somewhere in the east – little more than a rag-tag group of survivors.

I thought of Roth and the order he had read out to us. He hadn't lied – the Das Reich wasn't finished with its 'clean-up' on the drive up to Normandy, not by a long way. Eighty miles north of Reybenet they wiped out an entire village at Oradour-Sur-Glane, in retaliation for the kidnapping of an SS officer by the FTP. They locked the townspeople in the church and surrounding barns, and then machine gunned and torched the buildings until everyone inside was dead. More than six hundred – six times worse than the massacre at Tulle. For one man.

I was still mulling on all these horrors when she turned her tear-stained face to look up at me: beautiful, and now not quite so sad. We both fell back under the spell which had been cast on us in the cave, kissing one another for several minutes right there on the shoreline.

"Through all of our training, I loved you," she said, her lips whispering the words into my ear. "But I had to stay disciplined, the way we had been taught. The morning after we were together in the cave, I wanted to tell you my true feelings, but when you shut the conversation down I assumed you didn't want to hear."

"I was worried you preferred Limouzy to me."

Stella pulled back her head, laughing and rolling her eyes. "Oh, Ahab, I liked him, but not in *that* way. He was like an oaf of a big brother. It was always you. You know why I fell for you? It was your intensity – how driven you were in training – how you were going to let nothing break you." Then she started laughing again: "My God… and they all thought *I* was the intense one!"

I suppose I had Tom Shaw to thank for that; losing him had turned me into a mad, angry, screaming Ahab, and now the hate was being transmuted into love, as if a powerful alchemist was at work on my soul. Something positive had come from my friend's death.

Naomi and I were married soon afterwards, and our son, Tom Limouzy Hunston, was born in July 1945.

It was hard to imagine living with anyone who had not been through the Special Operations Executive, because it would be a life of too many secrets. We might have to keep our secrets from others, but at least we could share them between ourselves. The tricky part was when people asked, "How did you two meet?" We came up with a story about working together during my altitude research in America. I said she had been a 'specialist technician', responsible for operating the equipment, so in a way there was some truth in it.

Despite her real name being Naomi, I would occasionally slip and call her Stella. She was perhaps the only wife in England who forgave me calling her by another woman's name. Whenever I did it she would retaliate and call me Ahab. In time, they became our intimate names for one another, the way people call each other 'sweetheart' or 'darling'.

Pirbirght was back with his coffee and appraising his surroundings. "It's a bit of a dive, isn't it?"

"This is where I spent a lot of time as a student," I said by way of explanation. "I have some good memories of being in here."

He made a face, as if anyone who had good memories of this greasy spoon must be crazy.

Sipping his coffee, he looked at me but didn't say anything. In his computational mind, he was analysing my comment – deducing that I was probably referring to my old friend, and allowing a respectful few moments of silence to pass.

Eventually, he put his cup back down on the saucer.

"I thought you would be back for the funeral," he said.

"You knew Gilligan?"

"Yes, a little," Pirbirght said, his voice low. "He and Kynance were part of your cover story, remember? With the Pike's Peak research…"

We fell silent again, as I often was these days when the war was mentioned. To hear my secret mission being referred to so clearly in a public place felt dangerous, even now.

"I presume you have something to say, rather than just pleasantries, Professor."

"Well, yes," he said, brushing off some invisible crumb from his jacket sleeve, "I did come to tell you something, actually… I thought you would want to know."

"I'm all ears."

Pirbright leant forward with his elbows on the table, the same way Tom used to do when he was about to say something important.

"It's about Freya Nielsen."

To hear the name again brought back a swathe of mixed feelings – her undeniable beauty, all the time that Tom and I had wasted obsessing about her, and then the kiss she had given me in the tower; a Judas kiss of betrayal.

I hoped Pirbright wouldn't see how disturbed I felt at the mere mention of her name.

"I suppose they hanged her for being a spy" I said.

He sighed.

"No, actually… they didn't. She was sent back to Denmark at the end of the war."

I sat back. It felt like Pirbright had just punched me from across the table.

"What?"

"You're right, Hunston, spies who didn't turn were hanged. But this was… well… a delicate matter."

"Delicate in what way?"

"She was pregnant," he said, with characteristic bluntness. "It only became obvious at around six months. In February of 1944 – while in prison – she had a son. Once the war was over, the decision was taken to send her home. It transpired the father was Richard Shaw, you see – further questioning of both parties revealed a brief liaison in the early summer of 1943."

She *had* seemed different on the day of my SOE interview. I remember thinking something about her had changed. I should have guessed. Jacques would have known – his sixth sense would have picked that up in a second.

Another thought hit me. In Schmerz's torture room, Tom – or his ghost, or my imagined figment of him, or whatever you wanted to call it – had known. He had bloody well known and hadn't told me. That's why he had gone quiet when I had mentioned her. Maybe he hadn't said anything out of kindness – I suppose one more shock that day would have made my heart stop.

"And Richard knows about the child?"

Pirbright's face was grim.

"Yes, he was quite torn up when we told him. In the end he decided it was best he stayed away. He couldn't ever see her again, not after what had happened to his brother. He did ask, however, that she be granted an amnesty so the child – his son – wouldn't grow up without a mother. After all, the boy was going to be without a father."

"And the authorities agreed to that?"

"We're not monsters, Hunston."

Of course, I thought, Stringer and Pirbright practically ran the whole show.

"So let me get this straight… there's a two year old boy out there… my God… what's he called?"

"Sebastian."

I thought back to the memorial in the South Downs commemorating Freya Nielsen's dead husband, shot down on Eagle day by Richard Shaw. Sebastian Fuhrmann, the pilot calling out to Richard in his nightmares.

My tea was cold now but I drank it anyway. My mind was reeling so much I hardly noticed.

Pirbright glanced down at the dirty stained table.

"I've told others involved with the case," he said. "A few weeks ago I went to East Grinstead to tell MP personally. He served the SOE with distinction and deserved to hear the truth. After all, his son was killed by that bomb."

"How did he take it?"

Pirbright frowned. "Hard to tell. I was a spymaster and I must say, he's the most inscrutable man I've ever met."

"Poor bastard."

"Quite," Pirbright said. "Something in him is irretrievably damaged, I fear."

To distract myself from thinking about MP's torment, I looked over Pirbright's shoulder; the caf was still empty except for the galley cook, the same man Tom and I had known as students. He hadn't aged a day

– his skin perfectly preserved by the cooking fat saturating the air around him.

I thought it best to change the subject.

"Tell me, did they ever catch Schmerz?"

On my two day debrief after returning from France, Stringer and Pirbright had been very impressed that I had withstood the torture session. "As far as I know, Ahab," Stringer had said, "No other agent has managed to convince his captors under duress that his cover story was in fact the reality."

It was the nicest thing he had ever said to me.

"They did as a matter of fact," Pirbright said, brightening up. "We heard from Nestor that he was captured soon afterwards and shot by the Resistance. He'd been nicknamed by the Tulle locals as 'le chacal' – the jackal. The hotel he took you to was notorious in the region for SD bath torture. Nestor reported that his last words were 'Ich hatte Befehl' – which means: 'I was ordered to do it', a sentiment a lot the Nazi war criminals have been using in their defence."

So, they got him in the end – a sadist called the jackal. Never taking responsibility for any of it. I wondered what had happened to his pet dog.

I was quiet, my mind treading around the edges of the memories.

Pirbright shuffled his way out of the booth and stood up to leave.

"Your country owes you a debt, Hunston. You were a tiny cog but your actions at Terrasson made a difference. Holding back the Das Reich for the few hours you did may have been all that was needed to tip the balance. They didn't get to the Perigueux railhead until 12th June and didn't leave until 15th June. By the time they arrived in Normandy it was too late. Eisenhower himself praised the actions of the French Resistance."

"I heard that too. Sounds like politics."

My cynicism made him smile.

"Alright," he said, "let me put it another way. There's an old African proverb which goes something like this: 'If you think you're too small to have an impact, try going to bed with a mosquito in your tent'."

I laughed and we shook hands.

"Try to enjoy your life, Hunston," he said, before walking out of the door.

After he had gone, I lingered in the caf for a while, staring into space and mulling on his last words: *try to enjoy your life.* It was almost as if he'd given me another mission.

Twenty minutes later, I was wandering down the street, feeling in no particular hurry to be anywhere or to be doing anything. The stonework of the old college buildings was glowing like amber in the warmth of the early morning sun, and without really meaning to, I stopped walking, closed my eyes and turned my face to the light.

Epilogue

July 1946

When I read the headline from *The International Herald Tribune*, my blood ran cold.

 'KISSING BENCH' MURDER LEAVES DANISH POLICE BAFFLED.

 9th July; a young woman was found murdered in Copenhagen's Rundetaarn, her throat slit.

 The name of the deceased is believed to be Freya Fuhrmann, a local photographer, whose husband died in the war while serving with the Luftwaffe. Her body was discovered alone on the so-called 'Kysseboenken' – or kissing bench – a traditional meeting place for romantic couples. The Round tower, as the name translates, dates back to 1642, and is renowned for its unique spiral ramp, 230 yards long and twisting seven and a half times around a hollow core.

 The murder is thought to have occurred sometime between five and six pm, the gruesome discovery made by a caretaker when making his checks before locking up for the night.

 Police say the woman's young son was found, alive and well, in the observatory room at the top of the tower. His name has been withheld.

 Of the murder itself, the lead investigator commented: 'Only the smallest nick was made on the neck of the deceased – exactly over the internal carotid artery and less than an inch in length. Our analysis suggests the incision was made by an extremely sharp knife, possibly a surgical scalpel, although so far no weapon has been found. The precision of the cut suggests the perpetrator had an excellent knowledge of anatomy and physiology; the victim would have bled to death in less than thirty seconds, becoming unconscious in half that time. The intent seems to have been to inflict a quick and painless death.'

The motive is unknown and there were no witnesses. Police are appealing for anybody who might have information to help them with their enquiries. The child has been taken into the care of the authorities.

My first thought was for young Sebastian. I felt sure Richard would want to claim him and that the Danish authorities would be happy to release the boy into the care of his natural father. Perhaps he was already on his way to England where he would become Sebastian Shaw. For a second or so, I had wondered if Richard had been the one… but I dismissed the thought just as quickly. He had hated her, but he wouldn't have killed the mother of his son.

It was soon clear to me.

July 9th was the third anniversary of the East Grinstead bombing. No fluke.

Unexpectedly, the image that came to mind was the Wolf figure in the cave: always watching, always planning, ready to kill without remorse.

For a long time I had likened the lone wolf-man to the ruthless SS soldiers I had encountered. Even the insignia of the Das Reich was a 'Wolfsangel' – or Wolf's hook. That day at the Terrasson barricades I had seen it painted onto the side of the half-track; a back to front 'N' with a vertical line down the middle. But the SS weren't the wolf-men I had thought them to be. For a start they were not solitary like the lone wolf. They relied on their ethos of a brotherhood; all for one, and one for all – a group of psychotic musketeers. And besides, the Wolfsangel was actually an ancient runic symbol thought to *ward off* wolves.

When I saw the newspaper report, I had to adjust my thinking. The wolf man was a logical, determined killer, with an awareness of right and wrong. Unlike the SS, he also had a sense of proportion – an eye for an eye, and not six hundred eyes for an eye. Most of all, he was a loner. There was no brotherhood.

This type of killer would never deviate from his set course; not by superstition, nor the law, nor even his own conscience. Though the rationale for his kill was entirely understandable, that still didn't make it right. It was a dark act – all the more sinister for the amount of waiting and silent rage which had preceded it – and it spoke of a tortured mind, a person not at peace. Pure violence, distilled down into the quick flick of a scalpel blade. One second.

There was one superstition I couldn't shake off – that of Sussex folklore, which said if you walked seven times around the Devil's Humps, the beast would be summoned. I wondered if, as she climbed the seven turns of the Round Tower's spiral path, this is what Freya Nielsen had done. And he had come.

I had last seen MP in Beaulieu in September 1944, when he had surgically reversed some of the changes to my face. He was just as taciturn, his grief just as palpable. I could see the loss was eating him up; a rage against God, for having allowed such a terrible thing to happen. "You've still got a wife and son left, MP," I wanted to say, but of course I didn't dare.

Our limited conversation made a lot more sense now.

He had mentioned the large photograph in Nielsen's tower room at East Grinstead – the one of the inside of the Rundetaarn, and how, the day after the bombing, he had taken it and put it up on his wall at home. "For some strange reason it gives me a feeling of hope," he had said. "I stare at it a lot."

I told him about the kissing bench in the tower and how Nielsen had once said she liked to go there, that it was her favourite place in the world. As soon as I said it I felt an odd sense of betrayal, even though I owed her no loyalty at all.

As I recall, he hadn't paid me much attention after that, and I wondered if he had even heard what I was saying. He had been gazing out of the window, just staring, but not really at the view. It was as if the window was a mirror and he was staring back into his own soul.

When Pirbright had gone to him and said that Nielsen had been released, I could see how the plan would have come together in his mind:

A ticket to Denmark...

A stakeout of the Round Tower until she turned up...

Vengeance...

I wished I could somehow go back in time and talk MP out of it. I would tell him things he already knew, but I would tell him anyway.

I would say that revenge wouldn't make any difference to his pain. Not even a little bit. Loss is loss and pain is pain, and nothing on earth will ever make it completely go away. All you can do in the end is learn to live with it and get on with your life the best you can. And hope that one day the anger and the hurt become something better.

Author's Notes

A wide range of sources were used for this book, the full listing of which appears on the author website. However, some notes are set out below:

John Hunston's previous experiences are from *The Sudden Metropolis* and *The Long White Cloud* (GWL publishing, 2017 and 2018 respectively). The proverb he quotes: 'when fate arrives...' is from: Peter McDonald, *Oxford Dictionary of Medical quotations* (OUP, 2004).

In 1911, two Oxford physiologists, John Scott Haldane (1860 – 1936), fellow of New College, and Claude Douglas (1882 – 1963) fellow of St. John's College, conducted a high altitude research expedition at Pike's Peak, Colorado. In this story, 'Jonners' is loosely based on JS Haldane and Kynance on Douglas. The 'Kynance bag' refers to the 'Douglas Bag', used for collecting gas samples in respiratory physiology. The 'two brothers and eight cousins' remark is attributed to the evolutionary biologist JBS Haldane (1892 – 1964), son of JS Haldane. Legend has it that he sketched this out on the back of an envelope (in: Stephen Jay Gould, *Ever since Darwin* First published, 1978). Ed Hunston saying that sacrificing himself would be 'the right thing to do' is based on ideas discussed in C.S. Lewis's *Mere Christianity* (First published, 1952).

One pilot did indeed shoot down 15 bandits, one for each of his wartime operations – Pilot Officer Geoffrey Page (1920 - 2000), who recounts his story in: *Shot down in flames* (Grub Street, 1999). Richard

Shaw's description of being shot down is based on Page's account, including the choice words addressed to his rescuers: "you stupid pair of fucking bastards, pull me out!". Shaw's elite sporting background is modelled on that of Roger Bushell (1910 – 1944), who won the Oxford-Cambridge ski race in 1931. Bushell was later an RAF pilot in the 'Millionaire's mob'. Shot down on 23/5/40, he escaped from Stalag Luft III POW camp in 1944 only to be re-captured and executed by Gestapo (in: Paul Brickhill's *The Great Escape*, Faber and Faber, 1951). John Gillies, the son of the famous surgeon Harold Gillies (1881 -1960), was shot down on the same day as Bushell and was a POW until the war's end. Harold Gillies rowed in the Cambridge Boat Race crew of 1904. The NZ plastic surgeon Archibald McIndoe (1900 – 1960), was indeed Gillies' cousin.

Richard Shaw's exploits on 'Eagle day' (13/8/40) are based on those of Pilot Officer Mayers (1910-1942) of the 601 squadron (http:// www.bbm.org.uk/airmen/Mayers.htm). In the morning, Mayers shot down a Junkers 88, piloted by Capt. Joseph Oestermann. The website http://www.battleofbritain1940.net/0025.html details the dogfight and Pat Burgess and Andy Saunders' *Battle over Sussex 1940* (Middleton Press, 1990) describes Oestermann's downed Ju-88 at Treyford. The site is now marked by a memorial on the South Downs Way. The wreckage Hunston finds is based on an oil gear remnant of a crashed Ju-88 (shot down in May 1943, recovered in 1972) displayed in the Tangmere Military Aviation Museum. Like Richard Shaw, Mayers was downed himself that afternoon over Portland (he survived, but died later in the war). The Perseids are an annual meteor shower peaking on August 12th. Records of it date back 2000 years (in: Jacqueline Mitton's *Cambridge Illustrated Dictionary of Astronomy*, Cambridge University Press, 2007).

Jacqueline Simpson's *Folklore of Sussex* (originally published by B.T.Bastford 1973, The History Press 2009) provided the tales local to the area.

Murray C. Meikle's *Reconstructing Faces: The art and wartime surgery of Gillies, Pickerill, McIndoe and Mowlem* (Otago University Press, 2013) and

Emily Mayhew's *The Reconstruction of Warriors* (Greenhill Books 2004) superbly detail airmans' burn injuries in WW2 and the work at East Grinstead. Personal communication with Professor of Plastic Surgery (retired), M.D. Poole - the author's father - helped with understanding the tubed pedicle and other surgical details. The East Grinstead Museum exhibits the Russell Davies forceps. The saline bath scene was inspired by a photograph from the museum and a quote from Stout and Duncan's *War, Surgery and Medicine* (Historical Publications Branch, 1954, Wellington): *'An assistant was actually removing, under an anaesthetic, an extensive coagulum from both legs of a burnt patient. Most of it was floating on a bath of foul smelling pus.'* The Tobruk evidence on the unsuitability of tanning was also from Stout and Duncan. Further information on *tannafax* came from the Hunterian Museum, Royal College of Surgeons (London). Kevin Brown's, *Fighting Fit: Health, Medicine and War in the twentieth century* (The History Press Ltd, 2008) was also helpful. Richard Shaw's 'spindle shaped appendages' are based on the hands of Geoffrey Page (photographed in Miekle). McIndoe's presentation to the Royal Society was published in the Lancet (Nov 16, 1940, 621-22).

Burges is loosely based on the surgeon, William Ogilvie (1887 – 1971) who disagreed with McIndoe about tanning and the correspondence is authentic (in: Mayhew). Both Richard Hillary (*The Last Enemy*, Macmillan & Co 1942) and Geoffrey Page experienced tanning at the Royal Masonic Hospital.

Josef Siska is based on Josef Capka and Alois Siska, French Foreign Legionnaires who joined the RAF's all-Czech 311 squadron after France fell. Both were treated at East Grinstead (in: Miekle). McIndoe's comment: 'you've had your bark knocked off' is in Sebastian Faulks' *The Fatal Englishman* (Vintage 1996).

Freya Nielsen's role as photographer is based on that of a 'Miss Lehmann' who was on McIndoe's team in 1940 (in: Miekle). Her spy persona was inspired by the Abwehr spy, Vera Eriksen (aka. Vera Schalburg). On 29/9/40, Eriksen and two male spies were landed by seaplane off the Scottish coast, rowing ashore in a rubber dinghy. They were all soon arrested because of basic errors; a stationmaster noticed their soaking shoes and one of the men's wallets was crammed with far too many banknotes (£327). An examination of their luggage revealed a Mauser pistol with 19 rounds of ammunition, a flick knife, wireless equipment, a list of RAF bases, batteries and a torch marked 'Made in Bohemia'. The men were later executed, whereas Erikson was released from custody at the war's end. Why she was spared is unknown. It was rumoured that while spying in London in 1938, she had had an affair and a son with a prominent member of British society. One theory suggests she was a double agent, and that the British gave her a new identity after the war, allowing her to settle on the Isle of Wight with her young son.

On 9th July 1943 the Whitehall Cinema in East Grinstead was hit by a lone German bomber. A double feature was being shown – a Hopalong Cassidy cowboy film first, hence the high number of children present, to be followed by a Veronica Lake film ('I married a witch'). At 5.17pm two bombs smashed through the roof of the cinema, landing in the front seats. In the six seconds before they exploded some managed to escape. Other bombs landed in the town. 108 were killed and a further 235 injured. 53 of the injured were treated at the Queen Victoria Hospital, including two of the hospital staff. One nurse lost her life. Many were buried in a communal grave the following week (source: East Grinstead Museum).

Details on the Levallois technique of flint knapping were from a Neanderthal display at Manchester Museum (The University of Manchester).

Patton's army entered Palermo on 22/7/43, hence the paper boy's call during Ed's drive into London.

Although the SOE was based at 64 Baker Street, they conducted their interviews in Room 321 of the Northumberland Hotel (in: Terry Crowdy's *SOE Agent: Churchill's secret warriors*, Osprey Publishing 2008).

The head of F section was Maurice Buckmaster and the F section interviewer's name was Selwyn Jepson. Stringer and Pirbright are loosely based on these two men. Elizabeth Vigurs' DPhil thesis *The women agents of the Special Operations Executive F section – wartime realities and post war representations* (The University of Leeds, September 2011) details SOE recruitment and training. The typed quote Hunston sees outside

Room 321 is from a speech Winston Churchill gave to schoolboys at Harrow in1941. The Nazi poster of the disabled patient Pirbright describes in the interview is displayed in the 'The Topography of Terror' museum in Berlin.

'The Captain' is loosely based on Capt. W.E Fairbairn (1885 – 1960) and Capt. E.A. Sykes (1883 – 1945), close combat trainers to SOE operatives and co-designers of the F-S Commando Knife (example on display at the Tangmere Military Aviation Museum). Fairbairn's *All in Fighting* (Originally published by Faber and Faber Ltd 1942) describes SOE training including bleed-out times from stab wounds. The Captain's speech: 'some of you bourgeois liberals…' is based on the Introduction: *'Some readers may be appalled at the suggestion that it should be necessary for human beings of the twentieth century to revert to the grim brutality of the Stone Age in order to live. But it must be realised that, in dealing with an utterly ruthless enemy who has clearly expressed his intention of wiping this nation out of existence, there is no room for any scruple or compunction about the methods to be employed in preventing him.'* For the firearms training, Fairbairn and Sykes' manual: *Shooting to live with the one-hand gun* (originally printed Oliver and Boyd, London 1942) is excellent. Details on the Bren and the Sten are in: Hastings (Appendix B), and Paddy Ashdown's *The Cruel Victory: The French Resistance, D-Day and the Battle for the Vercours 1944* (William Collins, 2014): *'The Sten was a truly dreadful weapon, often as lethal to its owner as it was to the enemy…its habit of going off and unleashing a whole magazine when dropped also caused the accidental death of a good number of Maquisards…'*

A De Lisle rifle was seen by author on the wall of the Artists' rifles Clubhouse, Bisley Camp, Surrey.

Ahab sensing Shaw next to him on the march is based on a phenomenon experienced by people in acute danger or exhaustion (in: John Geiger's *The Third Man factor: surviving the impossible* (Cannongate Books, 2009). Richard Shaw seeing Tom's ghost comes from an SAS soldier who 'saw' a comrade in England even though he had just died in the Falklands (in Frank Collins's *Baptism of fire*, Doubleday 1997).

The film: 'Now it can be told' (1944) features SOE training and deployment, using agent Jacqueline Nearne in the filming (https://www.youtube.com/watch?v=dlZ15_KoKQc). Some operatives were surgically altered: http://wwwbbc.co.uk/history/worldwars/wwtwo/soe_training_01.shtml

Details on the Lysander flight, including the route maps and how pilots stuffed them into their flying boots, are from: Hugh Verity. *We Landed by Moonlight* (Crecy Publishing Ltd, 1978). Max Hastings' *Das Reich: The march of the 2nd SS Panzer Division through France, June 1944* (first published 1981 by Michael Joseph Ltd, Pan Books 1983) provides great detail of the SOE and the SS in that part of France.

The quotes from those opposing an Olympic boycott are from: Daniel James Brown's *The Boys in the Boat* (Pan 2014). Himmler vomiting after observing a massacre near Minsk is based on the testimony of his adjutant Karl Wolff (in: Adrian Weale, *The SS A new history* (Abacus 2010)).

The cave hideout is inspired by the other caves in that area, the most famous being Lascaux which was discovered in 1940. Details on the paintings are from Richard Leakey's *Human Origins* (Phoenix, 1996), including the finding that different animal images occupy certain parts of caves, with carnivores usually deepest in the cave system. Later in the story, during Ahab's torture, the strange geometric patterns he sees are based on the first stage of hallucination – where so called 'entoptic' images are seen. Leakey comments on these patterns in pre-historic cave art, as well as human/animal chimeras which occur in the third stage of hallucination.

The Saint Sour legend is in: Sabine Baring-Gould's *Castles and Cave dwellings of Europe* (published 1911).

Eric's fate is based on that of Maurice Vergne, a resistance fighter who was draped across the bonnet of one of the Das Reich half-tracks (in: Hastings). Details on Waffen SS battle tactics and entry requirements are from an excellent lecture by novelist Paul Watkins (given to the New Jersey WW2 book club in 2011, and available at:

https://www.youtube.com/watch?v=owgrCWmjyOE), as well as from Weale's book.

An FTP man was indeed hanged at Terrasson, now commemorated by a plaque under the balcony (translated here): *'Here on 10 June 1944 the Germans hung Limouzy Fernand, Resistance fighter, Picked up wounded from the field of battle'*. In this story I have merged the FTP commander for the area – 'Hercules' – with Limouzy Fernand. The sparing of Terrasson's population because it was the CO's wedding anniversary is true, as is the fact that the unit doctor addressed the assembled crowd (in: Hastings).

Roth's harrowing description of the gassing at Belzec is based on testimony from an SS-medic called Gerstein who had witnessed the events (in; Weale). Roth's ailment is Irritable Bowel Syndrome; although it was yet to be so named. Peppermint is a well-known treatment. His words: 'in our circle, it was *nothing...*' were said by an SS veteran at Oradour (in: Hastings), as well as an SS Major at Tulle (in: Douglas Boyd's *Blood in the Snow, Blood on the grass: treachery, torture, murder and massacre – France 1944* (The History Press, 2012)). General Lammerding, CO of the Das Reich, who ordered the Tulle and Oradour massacres, was sentenced to death in absentia by a 1953 War Crimes tribunal in Bordeaux. However, he was not extradited and lived out his life in Dusseldorf, dying in 1971 (in: Hastings).

After the departure of the Das Reich on 11th and 12th June, the laboratory of the Arms factory at Tulle was used as a torture chamber by the SD and miliciens to help identify FTP members. Methods included beating with coshes, and using acid. Lt Schmerz is based on Lt Walter Schmald, a translator for the SD. He was executed by the resistance in Augsust 1944. An SD team operated at the Hotel St Martin in Tulle, notorious for the torture sessions carried out in its baths (in: Hastings).

Ahab experiences the typical torture tactics carried out on SOE agents: in 1944 Wing Commander Yeo-Thomas ('The White Rabbit') endured over 2 months of torture in Paris by the Gestapo, including immersions in ice-cold water, head down with arms and legs chained. He refused to disclose any information and subsequently managed to survive Buchenwald, eventually dying in Paris in 1962. Odette Sansom ('Lise') was captured in 1943 and tortured at Fresnes prison near Paris, having all her fingernails pulled out. As with Yeo-Thomas, she gave nothing away and survived the war, dying in 1995. The captured female SOE agent in the story refers to Violette Szabo ('Louise') who joined the SOE after her husband was killed in action at El Alamein. Parachuting into the Limoges area for D-day she was captured by the Das Reich and later executed at Ravensbruck. The release of Ahab by the SD is not without foundation. In 1944, an agent called Anthony Brooks (1922 – 2007) - 'Alphonse' - helped hinder the progress of the Das Reich in the area of Montauban. He was arrested near Lyon and interrogated at Montluc prison. Despite having 72,000 francs on his person, his cover story stood up so well that he received an apology from his German interrogator, the two even exchanging a 'Heil Hitler' when Brooks was released. After the war he worked for British Intelligence (SOE display, Tangmere Aviation Museum)

Professor Foot, in his official history of the SOE French section, wrote of the Das Reich episode: 'The extra fortnight's delay imposed on what should have been a three day journey may well have been of decisive importance for the successful securing of the Normandy bridgehead...' (From the foreword in: Hastings).

Abbreviations:

AF	Atrial fibrillation
Afu (radio)	Agenten funk
AS	Armée Secrète
BCRA	Bureau Central de Rescignements et d'Action
Bf (110)	Bayerische Flugzeugwerke (Messerschmitt)
Div	Division
DF	Direction Finding
FTP	Francs Tireurs et Partisans
Gazo	Gazogene
GP	General Practitioner
HMS	His Majesty's Ship
HQ	Headquarters
Ju (88)	Junkers
KC	King's Counsel
KG (54)	Kampfgeschwader
Kripo	Kriminalpolizei
MC	Military Cross
MG (42)	Machine-gun
NZMC	New Zealand Medical Corps
POW	Prisoner of war
RADAR	Radio detection and ranging
RAF	Royal Air Force
RAMC	Royal Army Medical Corps
SD	Sicherheitsdienst
Sipo	Sicherheitspolizei
SOE	Special Operations Executive
SS	Schutzstaffel
STAB (1)	Stabschwarm
STS	Special Training School

Made in the USA
Columbia, SC
05 April 2018